D1233526

THE
EMPRESS
OF
TIME

Books by Kylie Lee Baker
available from Inkyard Press

The Keeper of Night
The Empress of Time

THE
EMPRESS
OF
TIME

KYLIE LEE BAKER

inkyard
PRESS

ISBN-13: 978-1-335-91585-6

The Empress of Time

For questions and comments about the quality of this book, please contact us at CustomerService@Harlequin.com.

Inkyard Press
22 Adelaide St. West, 41st Floor
Toronto, Ontario M5H 4E3, Canada
www.InkyardPress.com

Printed in U.S.A.

Recycling programs
for this product may
not exist in your area.

To Sarah, who hates sequels

CHAPTER 01

EARLY 1900S
TOKYO, JAPAN

In the last nights of the nineteenth century, the humans began to whisper about a new demon, hungrier and crueler than all the rest.

The Yōkai hunted where shadows grew deep, in the thin breath of twilight that bridges night and day. It crawled from the spindly shadows of chair legs on hardwood floors, the crooked shade that lamps cast on wallpaper, even your own silhouette—the one shadow you could never escape.

But none of those things were really shadows at all.

They were holes carved into the human world, peering into a void that echoed down and down through an endless night. Its darkness could peel away your skin like you were a soft summer peach, crawl deep in your bone marrow and rot you from the inside out, soak the soil with your blood. The night stole the parts of you that no one wanted—all your lies and broken promises and disappointments.

From these holes, the Yōkai clawed its way up and up into the stark light of a new world. Then all of the terrors that night's veil normally concealed—the things you were never meant to see—were laid bare. The Yōkai's jaw swung open like an unlatched gate and it began to feast.

The police always arrived too late, long after the echoes of screams had faded away and the blood had run dry, leaving dark stains across the floor. They would find no clues at all, no broken doors or windows, no fingerprints or stray hairs, as if the monster had never even existed. The only pattern between the deaths was the state of the bodies: rib cages opened up like books, organs spilled across the floor, and hearts mysteriously absent.

So the humans prayed to gods who couldn't intervene even if they'd wanted to, made shrines to benevolent Yōkai, and lit one thousand lights to banish the shadows. But none of it made any difference, because it wasn't a Yōkai at all.

It was me.

I came to Tokyo on a night of gray rain, carrying one knife and a list of one hundred names, my lips cracked and dry from all the blood I'd scrubbed off them. I hated rainy days because the clouds dispersed the sunlight and weakened the shadows, leaving me to travel most of the way by foot.

Today, a man whose name I couldn't remember was going to die. All I knew was that he rowed boats full of opium smuggled from Formosa up and down the canals of Ginza, a crime that even humans would punish by death.

Chiyo, my servant who managed the records of both the

living and dead, had handpicked him and ninety-nine others for execution today, as she did every day. Every morning, she handed me a list of names, and every evening I returned with all of them crossed out, their souls in my stomach and their blood splashed across my kimono.

This was not, strictly speaking, something a Death Goddess was supposed to do.

Though I hadn't exactly received a Death Deity Handbook the moment I'd stabbed my fiancé, Hiro, in the heart and inherited his kingdom, I was fairly certain that I wasn't meant to collect souls long before their Death Days just to make myself more powerful. My Shinigami were supposed to be the ones who wandered among the living, dragging souls down to the banks of Yomi and devouring their hearts in my stead, each soul another drop in the dark sea of my power.

That was what Izanami, my predecessor, had done for thousands of years. That was what my fiancé had intended to do. That was what any honorable god would have done.

But there was no honor in sitting on a stolen throne.

My Shinigami always whispered that I wasn't really their goddess anyway, so what did it matter if I made my own rules? The deep darkness demanded payment, and ten years of souls hadn't been enough. If my Shinigami wouldn't bring me more, I would do it myself.

At least all the humans on my list were men who had strangled their wives or women who had poisoned their children, abusers and molesters and criminals who were too smart to get caught by the police. Chiyo kept careful files and judged them impartially, presenting me a list of her selections, carefully spread across Japan so that the humans could never find any pattern. Generally, I trusted Chiyo to know what I wanted, but that was one order I had given explicitly: that none of the humans on her list were innocent.

It wasn't because I was kindhearted, or thought I had a divine right to pass judgment on Earth's sinners, or anything so noble as that.

It was because one day, I would eat enough souls that I would be strong enough to bring my brother back from the deep darkness, and I would have to look him in the eye and explain exactly how I'd done it. If I told him his life had been bought with the blood of innocents, he'd probably walk straight back into the void and let the monsters devour him rather than live with that debt on his soul.

I would carry the debt for him, so he would never have to know how heavy it was.

I melted into the shadow of a passing streetcar, letting it carry me closer to Ginza, the smell of wet pavement and oil sharp beneath the wheels. It wasn't the rainy season, but my presence often darkened the sky wherever I went, wringing hot mist from the clouds.

As I passed through the streets, the humans stiffened and looked around, wondering why their skin suddenly prickled with goose bumps, why their hearts beat faster, why the crowds around them had become faceless and the sounds of the city had faded into a thorny static. Humans could sense when Death was coming, but for most of them, it would be no more than a fleeting sensation. Fewer humans stayed out at this hour, especially in the heavy late-summer heat, and more of them began to disperse as I passed them.

In the ten years since I'd come to Japan, the cities had started to fill up with echoes of London—streetcars with hand-crank engines that sputtered down the roads, railroad officers in Western suits and flat-topped straw hats with black ribbons, women carrying alligator leather handbags. My old life was following me, crossing the ocean piece by piece.

I saw the changes more in the crowded streets of Tokyo than in the farming villages, which was one reason I avoided urban areas as much as I could. That, and everything in the city felt just slightly off balance, like the sheer number of humans had tilted the Earth off its axis. Everything in the market leaned precariously away from the buildings—all the bright canopies over storefronts, the lantern garlands, the bright painted posters over the theaters—making the crowded streets even smaller by narrowing the sky overhead into a thin strip of white. Even the lotuses in the city's central park seemed to tilt to the left, ignoring the pull of the sun.

The humans here must have sensed who I was, but none of them would look me in the eye. The hot days of summer cast a humid haze over the distance, blurring the far ends of the streets so that everything in the distance was a dizzy secret. Children bounced balls in street puddles of gray water too murky to show their reflections. Men rushed around pulling jinrikisha with crates that might have contained rice or pottery or contraband. It was a city of mysteries and possibilities, not all of them good.

I jumped off the streetcar and grabbed onto the shadows below a stone bridge that stretched over the canal, stepping waist-deep into tepid brown water. Men paddled up and down the still stream, boats piled high with mysteries beneath black tarps, bobbing unhurriedly away. No one sat on the docks that lined the canals, driven away by the choking humidity wafting off the waters.

At 8:34, according to the silver-and-gold clock chained to

my clothes, a man with a gray face and green gloves rowed his boat under my stone bridge.

He would never make it to the other side.

I clenched a fist around my clock, and the whole street held its breath.

The gentle lapping of the canal against its stone barriers went silent, the waters turning to glass. The distant hum of mosquitoes and faraway calls of street vendors disappeared.

I looped my clock's chain around my hand a few times to bind it to my palm, then hauled myself onto the boat, my skirts heavy with the foul water.

The man had become a statue in the time freeze, his skin the color of unbaked clay under the shadows of the bridge, his eyes red and pupils as thin as pinpricks. With the touch of my hand around his throat, he awoke.

He thrashed against my grip, rocking the boat dangerously to the side. But the shadows tore themselves from the waters and strapped the boat down with their long arms, holding us steady.

"It's faster if you stay still," I said, pulling a knife from my left sleeve. I always offered humans this advice, but they rarely listened. This man was no exception.

He moved to grab my sleeves as if to throw me from the boat, but before he could, more shadows came unstuck from the mossy walls of the stone bridge and dragged him down until he was sprawled atop his smuggled opium. Now that I ruled over the Realm of Perpetual Darkness, all the shadows in the world obeyed me. They knew what I wanted, and they did not hesitate.

"Who are you?" the man said, choking out each word as he fought the shadows wrapped around his throat.

I said nothing, because I didn't know what answer he wanted. I was the monster that humans whispered about at night. I was a Shinigami and a Reaper and a murderer. I was a goddess who he would never worship because he didn't even know I existed. And I was Ren, but I didn't want a human to call me that. No one had called me that in a decade. No one dared to. These days, it was just "Your Highness."

The human thrashed against my shadows, but they held him tight.

"What do you want?" he said.

Ah, now that was a better question.

"Your soul," I said.

His eyes went wide, his jaw clenched tight. "Well, you can't have it!"

"I wasn't asking your permission," I said, drawing my knife.

Once the glow of the setting sun reflected off my blade, the human began to fight in earnest. I had all the darkness of the underworld at my disposal, but it was a simple mortal weapon that scared him the most. How amusing.

"Why?" he said. "Why me?"

I kicked aside a corner of his tarp, gesturing to the many black boxes beneath it. We both knew what was inside.

"Why do you care?" he said. "Why do I deserve to die for this?"

"It's not about what you deserve," I said, frowning. "It's about what I need."

Then I sliced a line down his chest, splitting his shirt in half so it wouldn't get in my way.

His eyes went flat, his opium-shrunken pupils somehow eating all the color from his irises, his whole body vibrating with fear.

I was used to fear in humans' eyes at the end of their days, for I'd spent hundreds of years collecting souls as a Reaper. But this was different, and the humans must have sensed it too, because they always fought harder and longer. Today wasn't this man's Death Day, and his body knew it, sensed the wrongness of it, and fought back like creatures of the deep sea dragged up to land.

But who was going to stop me?

Now that Hiro was dead, there was no higher power in Yomi anymore. My only adversary was the invisible wall a thousand miles high that barred me from the deep darkness.

While my servants could venture past it unimpeded, Death could not. When Izanami had ruled Yomi, her husband, Izanagi—the father of Japan and ruler of the living—had built the wall to stop her from entering the deep darkness. Those who destroyed Death inherited her kingdom, and if the monsters beyond the wall devoured Izanami, they would take her throne and all the souls in Japan. Now I was the new Izanami, and the wall would not yield for me either. At least, not yet.

For over a decade, I'd sent my guards beyond the wall to search for Neven in the darkness, but every day they returned empty-handed. I'd decided that no matter what rules Izanagi had laid down thousands of years ago, I needed to grow strong enough to break them. I couldn't rely on anyone else to save Neven.

Maybe it would take a thousand more souls, or a million more, or all the souls in Japan to make me strong enough. Whatever the cost, I would pay it. If I kept taking and taking, then one day, I would throw my fists against that great invisible barrier, and the wall would crumble into a thousand pieces. I would finally cross into that land of drowning darkness and bring my brother home.

As I held the knife high, the man let out a whimpering cry and I made the mistake of looking into his eyes again. Long ago, human tears hadn't mattered to me. No matter their age or gender or hometown, they all had the same look of wild desperation when they knew they were going to die: pupils wide, eyes glassy with tears but also alight, like they could see clearly for the first time in their lives. But now, when I looked at them, I only saw my brother's eyes.

I pictured his face for only a moment, and that second alone made the darkness thrash in my chest, threatening to shatter my ribs and break free, turning the whole world to night. It was always the same—the memory of the last time I'd seen him as Hiro's guards dragged him away, his pale hand reaching out, my name the last thing I'd ever heard him say, maybe the last word he'd said at all. I could no longer remember his face in any moment but that final one. I couldn't recall the look in his eyes when we'd stayed out late throwing stale crumbs to pigeons in the clock tower, or when we'd shared Mary Shelley's new novel because neither of us could wait for another copy, or anytime when he'd looked at me like he loved me, even if I hadn't known what love was at the time.

I wanted to ruin this human for making me remember him, and what had happened after. For when I had seen that look in my brother's eyes, I had done nothing at all.

I split the human's sternum with my knife and opened his rib cage like cellar doors, reaching in and pulling out his pulsing heart, then crushing it between my teeth. Scalding hot blood tasting of salt and iron dripped down my neck. My teeth weren't sharp enough to tear through the muscle, maybe because I was only half Shinigami or maybe because I was taking souls too early, but I chewed and chewed and swallowed it down even when it felt like I was choking. He screamed—a sad song of agony that no one but me would ever hear—until his blood filled the bottom of his boat and his skin went white.

The blood burned away the skin of my hands until I was crushing his heart in fingers that were nothing but bones wrapped in rivers of veins. These were the hands of something long dead, flesh peeled away by time, just like the Death Goddess before me. But as trails of blood seared down my neck, her voice echoed across the damp walls of the tunnel, for she was everywhere, always.

Well done, she whispered.

Finally, the soul scraped its way down my throat. This one felt like firecrackers sizzling through my veins, everything prickling and stinging but so painfully alive. My shadows devoured the new energy, suddenly darker in the murky waters, tighter around the human's limbs. Then all the sticky blood and the ghosts of the human's screams raking my eardrums and the nauseous sensation of flesh caught in my throat didn't matter at all. It was fine, I was fine, because it brought me one step closer to Neven.

I leaned over the side of the boat and thought for a moment that I was going to be sick. It didn't matter if I was, because the soul was already in my bloodstream, but I tried to swallow it down anyway. I panted and stared back at my reflection in the dark waters, face and neck painted red, eyes wild and burning black. I didn't look like the Goddess of Death, but a girl who couldn't remember sunlight. A wicked creature who lived under bridges like a troll, ugly and alone.

I spit blood at my reflection and wiped my face on my sleeve, fighting through nausea. Then I stumbled off the boat and fell to my knees in the water, tucking my clock away once more.

At 8:35, the man's boat emerged from the other side of the bridge, his opium spilled into the dirty canal waters, his body ripped open, and his heart in the belly of a beast.

My shadows returned to me like a retreating tide, revealing mossy stones and murky waters as they crawled back into my cold heart. I stood, once again, alone under the dark bridge.

My right hand drifted to the chain around my neck that looped through a wedding ring made of silver and gold. Sometimes, when I felt like just another shadow that harsh daylight would scrub away, I held the ring so hard that I was sure it would break. Sometimes I wanted it to, but it never did. I knew that keeping the ring made me a terrible person, but it was hard to feel too bad about a piece of jewelry when I was eating one hundred hearts a day.

I walked back through Tokyo in the shadows, hiding from the humans so I wouldn't alarm them with my bloody clothes. I was a monster more dangerous than their legends could ever imagine—too terrifying to even show my face in public.

As I walked alone through the still evening, I remembered that this was what I had traded Neven for—the power to do anything except for things that mattered, a dark festering anger that had no end, and shackles of darkness around my feet. Everywhere I went, I dragged the weight of the entire night sky behind me, and I carried it alone.

When I finally reached the wet soil of a park just beyond the city's edge, the darkness grabbed me by the ankles and pulled me down, dragging me through layers of mud and buried bones, the pale starlight above me extinguished as I sank deeper and deeper.

When I opened my eyes and saw nothing at all, I knew I'd arrived.

The footsteps of one of my guards echoed across the courtyard, coming to a stop a careful distance away.

"Your Highness," he said, "welcome home."

CHAPTER 02

Deep down below the land of the living, in a place where light could not reach, I lived in a castle of shadows.

It sat on a high platform of stone, its towers spiraling into Yomi's endless sky with rooftops sloped like claws and edges that blurred away in the night, as if a black fog had wrapped its arms around the castle and choked its breath away. Most people would never have the displeasure of seeing the monstrosity of my home in the total darkness of Yomi, but Shinigami, like me, could sense it clearly.

I knelt in an empty courtyard marked by smooth tiles just beyond the lotus lake, every breath echoing forever into the darkness. At times, the night was so still and vacant that I felt like it was listening to me, waiting for me, and if I only said the right words, the whole world would unfold and light would break in from above.

One of my shadow guards hovered beside me, his shape ebbing and flowing, pulsing like a heart as he waited for my instructions. My guards were people of the shadows—inhuman creatures born from the lost dreams of the dead, spirits with no body to call home, formless and ephemeral. My palace was filled with too many of them and an absurd number of handmaids—women bound forever to the palace from deals they'd made with Izanami. Most of them had bargained for more time with the living, either for themselves or their families. I didn't know if their quiet subservience was out of fear, or if Izanami had bound them with some sort of curse.

"Have Chiyo send someone to clean the courtyard," I said, glancing at the muddy marks I'd left on the stones. The mess didn't bother me, but it would surely bother Chiyo, and I wanted the guard to leave me alone.

"Yes, Your Highness," the guard said, evaporating into the darkness.

Before going inside, I turned to the west wing of the courtyard, where the darkness grew thick like treacle, clinging to my sandals as I walked. After a few steps, I could no longer see my hands in front of me, even with my Shinigami vision. The world was nothing but my own slow heartbeat and the cold sweat on my skin, the weight of a thousand worlds crushing down on my shoulders as the darkness grew heavier and heavier.

I fell to my knees at the border of deep darkness and reached a hand out in front of me. My palm pressed into a cold wall, unyielding but invisible. Beyond it, the darkness was so dense that it seemed like the world had simply ceased to exist.

I pressed harder against the wall, feeling my bones creak and joints protest. Even before I'd become a goddess, I'd been strong enough to crush bricks to dust and bend steel like dough. As a goddess, my anger could make mountains tremble and my touch could shatter diamonds. Yet the wall that barred me from the deep darkness would not yield. It had grown weaker over the years—I could hear the tinkle of hairline cracks forming on the other side—but still, it remained standing.

At first, I would sit outside for hours pushing against the wall until my fingers broke and my wrists snapped, but now I knew that if I wasn't strong enough, no amount of time spent pushing would change that. Only more souls in my stomach could weaken the barrier. So instead of trying anymore, I fell forward onto my hands and glared across the darkness, whispering a secret prayer and hoping that somewhere in that dark infinity, Neven could hear me.

When humans grew desperate, they offered me anything at all to spare them and their loved ones from suffering. But there were no gods left for me to pray to. I had become my own god, and now I knew the cruel truth: gods were just as helpless as humans when it came to things that mattered.

I rose to my feet and trudged back to the palace doors, where two more shadow guards stood at attention. They bowed as I approached, then raised the great metal bars that sealed the palace and let me inside.

Chiyo stood waiting just beyond the door, her arms crossed. Out of all the handmaids Izanami had left behind, I'd chosen her to attend and advise me. Despite the way Death often blurred one's features, Chiyo's eyes had a sharpness to them, like she was ready for a sudden attack. She was the only servant who seemed like she'd retained even a piece of her soul after having her heart eaten by Shinigami. The others had vacant stares and cowered in fear, but Chiyo always had a sour look on her face when I frequently displeased her, which I much preferred. My guess was she'd died somewhere in her thirties, though the sternness in her face made her look older.

"That took longer than scheduled," Chiyo said, frowning at the trail of mud behind me. "The Goddess of Death can't even kill efficiently?"

"I felt like making you wait," I said, stepping through the doorway. Chiyo did little to conceal her disapproval for my extra soul collections, but she helped me because I was her goddess and I'd asked her to, and she had to trust that a goddess knew what was best, even if we both knew that was a lie.

I lit the ceremonial candles in the hallway with a wave of my hand, casting the palace in dim light. Chiyo flinched like I'd set off fireworks, but I ignored her and trailed muddy footprints down the hallway.

One of the many changes I'd made from Izanami's reign of total darkness was that I required at least dim light in the palace at all times. Even though my Shinigami senses could make out the furniture and wall paintings in the darkness, I'd also started to see faces that shouldn't have been there. In the formless swirl of darkness, they came together piece by piece, hazy nightmares that dispersed whenever I blinked and then reappeared when I turned around.

Chiyo bowed and opened the door to the bathroom. She tried, as she did every day, to help me undress, but I shooed her away with a wave of my hand while other servants filled a tub with scalding hot water. I cast off my soiled human clothes and dropped them in a wet pile on the floor.

"Burn them," I said to Chiyo, stepping into the tub. My clothes reeked of blood and wouldn't have been salvageable even if I'd wanted them.

"Most deities don't waste quite so many kimonos," she said, gathering the dirty fabric.

"Most deities don't do anything," I said, scrubbing the blood from under my fingernails. "They just bask in humans' prayers and have their underlings do their chores. But I have tasks that only I can do correctly."

Chiyo made a noncommittal humming sound that she always made when her thoughts weren't polite enough to say to a goddess, but she didn't deny my words. The Shinto gods all had great adventures and conquests and tragedies when the world was first beginning, but since the modern era, none of them seemed particularly active.

While I hadn't expected any of them to welcome me with open arms, none had deigned to even speak to me. Chiyo mentioned their doings in passing—when typhoons tore through Japan, that was likely the doing of Fūjin, the god of wind. And when the population increased, that was the doing of Inari, goddess of fertility. But none of them ever drained the seas or turned the sky purple or performed any sort of godlike miracle, anything that couldn't be explained by nature or luck. I imagined that they merely sat in their palaces and watched the changing winds.

"Has anything of importance happened in my absence?" I asked. Chiyo knew well that *important* meant any situation I had to deal with immediately or risk total chaos and peril. Anything else, she could handle on her own.

"Yomi is quiet, Your Highness," she said. "It is Obon, so the dead are on Earth."

Just like every year, I had forgotten about the Obon festival until it was upon us, marking the waning days of summer, one more year of nothing changing at all. It was now a Buddhist holiday, but I observed it even as a Shinto goddess, for the two religions had long ago become intertwined in the lives of humans in Japan. Every year, the souls of the dead traveled back to their hometowns on Earth, summoned by fire. After three days of festivals and dancing, fire bid the spirits goodbye, and they returned to Yomi. Usually, that meant that no one bothered me for three days.

"However, there are Shinigami waiting upstairs," Chiyo said.

"Why?" I frowned, combing my fingers through my wet hair. The water clouded with blood.

"I believe they are hoping for a transfer."

I sighed, nodding as I scrubbed the blood from my forehead. It was my fault for daring to hope that Obon would mean a few days of peace and quiet in Yomi. What right did I have to peace?

"I don't suppose you could tell them to come back tomorrow?"

Chiyo's thin smile twitched, her eyes glinting like sharpened knives as she turned toward the light as if considering my request. Chiyo had to be patient with me, but I knew her patience was not infinite.

"Fine," I said, sinking deeper into the water, "but I'm not going to meet them sopping wet, so they'll just have to wait a bit longer."

"Of course," Chiyo said, bowing in a way that somehow felt sarcastic, even if I couldn't prove it. "I will take care of your clothes and have the floors cleaned," she said, turning to leave.

"Chiyo."

She stopped in the doorway. "Yes, Your Highness?"

I could not look at her face when I asked my next question because I would know the answer from her eyes alone. Instead, I stared at my reflection in the muddy water, dirty and distorted like me.

"Have the guards found anything in the deep darkness?" I asked.

Every day, right before she answered, there was a moment of breathless silence when I allowed myself to hope. Sometimes I would stop time and cling to the moment just a bit longer, allowing myself to think that maybe today was the day.

"No, Your Highness," Chiyo said. The only time her voice was gentle was when she answered this question. "Perhaps tomorrow."

"Yes," I said, shifting in the tub so that my reflection rippled and broke, "perhaps."

She bowed again, then hurried out of the room. I glanced at my ring on the counter, then sank under the water.

I closed my eyes as a wave of fresh souls rushed over me, a warmth spinning through my blood, burning from my heart to my fingertips. I could always feel when my Shinigami brought me fresh souls. A thousand names flashed behind my closed eyes, streaks of bloodred kanji burned into my vision. The ache in my bones abated slightly, heat returning to my core. With every soul, I felt a little less like I'd been dragged through wet earth with a sick stomach full of hearts and more like someone who might be a goddess one day.

I stepped out of the tub and into my room, where servants were already waiting with clothing.

When I'd first taken the throne, they'd tried to dress me in twelve layers of fabric, so heavy that I could hardly stand up.

"The royal junihitoe is the proper clothing for a goddess," Chiyo had said.

But I hadn't felt like a goddess then, and I still didn't now. I was just a pathetic girl whose anger had killed her brother and then her betrothed, and my prize was an eternity of lonely darkness. I didn't deserve the throne, nor did I want it. But this was the only way to stay in Yomi and wait at the edge of the deep darkness, either until my guards brought Neven back or I finally grew strong enough to break through the wall and find him myself. So, for the time being, I would have to play the part.

"I want a simple black kimono," I'd said to Chiyo. "I don't want to look pretty. I want to be able to move."

"Your Highness," Chiyo had said, the first traces of impatience starting to curdle her expression, "for a goddess, black clothing looks rather mournful."

"Yes, and?" I said, casting the last of the purple fabric to the ground and standing only in my slip. "My brother is gone, my mother is dead, and I stabbed a ceremonial knife into my fiancé's heart. I will mourn if I want to."

To that, Chiyo said nothing, bowing deeply to hide her expression. The next day, she'd brought me a closet full of kimonos as dark as Yomi's endless sky, and that was what I'd worn ever since.

The servants dressed me, tying my kimono tightly behind me. Even now, it reminded me of the first time someone had helped me into a kimono with hands that glowed like moon-beams and skin that smelled like brine.

A servant bowed and offered me my clock, which I clipped to my clothes and tucked into my obi. Finding a new clock of pure silver and gold had been difficult in Yomi, but it turned out that Death Goddesses got almost anything they wanted. I had never found Neven's clock that I'd dropped on the floor of the throne room all those years ago, despite having my servants turn over every mat and empty every drawer in the entire palace. I suspected Hiro had destroyed it.

Chiyo tried to tie my hair up, but I stepped away from her and brushed it myself. I'd spent too long hiding the color of my hair from Reapers to simply tie it up and hide it again for the sake of proper styling. Nothing about me was traditional or proper, so what difference did a hairstyle make? I slipped my ring necklace over my head and rose to my feet, pushing the doors to my room open before the servants could do it for me. They threw themselves to the ground in apology, but I ignored them, charging down the hallways past the murals of Japan's history—Izanagi and Izanami stirring the sky with a spear, the birth of their first child, Hiro, and their final children, the gods of the sun, moon and storms.

At first, I'd thought someone had painted the murals so the history wouldn't be lost. But the palace had a mind of its own—mere days after my ascension, I'd walked past a new painting. It showed an angry girl cast in shadows, holding a candle in one hand and a clock in the other, standing at an outdoor shrine that dripped with blood, the body of a man at her feet.

I'd ordered the servants to paint over it and watched un-blinking until it was done, but the next day, the picture appeared again. It seemed no matter what I did, I couldn't erase it. I no longer visited that wing of the palace.

The guards at the entrance to the throne room bowed and opened the doors as I strode past them.

Inside, two Shinigami knelt on cushions on the floor, one man and one woman. They wore crimson red robes embroidered with gold dragons that captured the pale candlelight. How unfair it was that they could wear the uniform of Shinigami when I never had the chance, their lives so simple and whole.

I stepped up onto the platform and sat on my throne. The ceremonial candles lit the platform around me like a stage, Izanami's katana mounted on the wall above me.

This was the room where I'd first met Izanami, back when I'd truly believed that she could help me. Once, the distance between the sliding doors and the great platform of Izanami's throne had felt like a thousand miles, the pale reed mats an endless desert that pulled nervous sweat from my palms as I crawled across them. Now it was just a room of echoes and darkness, a chair that was expensive and uncomfortable, and a murder weapon mounted above my head because I didn't know where else to put it. What had made the room magnificent was the fear that Izanami inspired, and now she was gone.

I sat down on the throne and crossed my arms as they bowed to me, then closed my eyes. The names of the Shinigami appeared in the darkness of my mind.

"Yoshitsune and Kanako of Naoshima," I said, opening my eyes. "Speak."

"Your Highness," the man, Yoshitsune, said, "we've come to ask for your permission to transfer to Tottori."

I sighed. What a waste of time. This had hardly been worth getting dressed for.

"No," I said. "Was that all?"

"But…" Kanako frowned, rising up from her reverent bow, "why not?"

"'Your Highness,'" I reminded her, scowling. In truth, I hated the title, but letting them speak informally to me was a quick path to being called *Ren* and then *Reaper.*

"Why not, Your Highness?" Kanako said, though the title sounded more like an insult than any sign of respect.

"You know why," I said. "Do not waste my time with this."

"Her father lives in Tottori, and he's growing old," Yoshitsune said, frowning as if I was singularly responsible for this. How quickly they had gone from pressing their noses to the floor to glaring at me. This was how it always went—they were willing to pretend I was their goddess until I didn't give them what they wanted.

Most Shinigami didn't even keep in touch with their parents enough to justify such a request. Just like Reapers, Shinigami families were only useful for alliances and protection. Once children married, there was no practical need for them to see their parents anymore. One of the many reasons my father had renounced me was probably that he'd never expected me to marry, so he wouldn't have had a convenient excuse to disappear from my life. I doubted that the Shinigami before me truly wanted to relocate for noble reasons.

"I don't need more Shinigami in Tottori," I said. "The population there is hardly growing. You may transfer to Tokyo or Osaka, but Tottori is already bursting with Shinigami who are bored to death. My answer is no."

"Izanami allowed us to stay with our families," Yoshitsune said, glaring at me through the darkness.

Lies, a voice whispered, the words scratching down my ear like my head was full of spiders. I had figured as much, but comparing myself to Izanami rarely ended well. As much as I wanted to grant their wish and shut them up, the only thing worse than angry Shinigami was uncollected souls floating in the ether because there weren't enough Shinigami to reap them. Then, instead of thinking me heartless, the other Shinigami would think me incompetent, which was much worse.

They had no innate respect for me, a foreign girl who had abruptly replaced the creator of their world. Reapers had impeccable hearing, so I knew all the things they whispered about me before I summoned them to my meetings—that I had seduced Hiro just to steal his throne, that I had taken Japan as an English colony to enslave, that I had no right to sit on Izanami's throne and give orders. I couldn't bring myself to disagree with the last one.

So, if they wouldn't respect me, they had to fear me.

My shadows reached out and wrapped around their arms and legs, tearing the couple to opposite sides of the room. They screamed as the shadows pinned them to the walls, long tendrils of darkness crawling around their throats, lifting up their eyelids to examine the soft flesh below, tickling up their noses to peer at their brains.

Tears pooled in Yoshitsune's eyes as the shadows dived down his throat, but Kanako bit down on the dark coils before they could choke her, spitting inky blackness back at me.

"Which one of you would like to die first?" I said in Death. The language was useful for intimidation, for even if my words

were inelegant, Death curled them into a sinister lilt that made the Shinigami break out in goose bumps.

"You can't kill us and you know it!" Kanako said. "The population is growing too quickly and you need all the Shinigami you can get."

Unfortunately, she was right. Though the death of any Shinigami would result in the birth of another, I couldn't exactly wait the hundred years it would take for them to grow up and complete their training. More Shinigami were already being born to meet the needs of the growing population, but all of them were still too young to reap.

"There are things worse than Death," I said. This, I knew all too well.

I snapped both of their legs and dropped them to the floor.

They groaned as they fell limp against the mats, my shadows retreating back to me. They would heal in a few hours.

"Chiyo," I said.

The door slid open instantly, as if she'd been waiting with an ear pressed against it. Her eyes were wide and alarmed, and for a moment I hesitated—she was used to my outbursts when dealing with Shinigami, so surely a few broken shins wouldn't have unsettled her. Something else must have happened.

But whatever it was, she could find a way to resolve it herself. I didn't have the patience for another catastrophe right now.

"Have them taken outside," I said. "They can crawl home."

"Yes, Your Highness," Chiyo said. "If I may––"

I strode past the Shinigami, but one of them grabbed my ankle, stopping me in my tracks. I turned to Kanako, her face twisted in pain but her grip iron strong around my leg.

"Have you no respect?" I said, my jaw tense. "I could have killed you. I can spare one Shinigami, I promise you that."

Kanako shook her head, nails biting into my skin.

"I don't worship foreign gods," she said.

I sighed, then yanked my ankle away and stomped firmly on her hand. It crackled with a sound like stale bread.

"Take them out now," I said to Chiyo, storming past her.

Foreign gods, I thought, stomping toward my study. That was always the problem. Years ago, I'd given up fighting the word *foreigner*, knowing it was futile. Gods weren't supposed to care what lower beings thought of them. All my power was supposed to extinguish that sort of weak, mortal doubt. Because if it didn't, then why had I sacrificed everything for it?

Somehow, despite all my power, I was still trapped. It didn't matter if *foreigner* stung less now than it had ten years ago, because the result was the same—no one respected me. No amount of introspection or confidence could change the fact that I had no say in who I was. Even as the most powerful being in all of Yomi, I felt like none of it truly belonged to me—my palace was a dollhouse, my riches trinkets, and all of it was a sham, because someone like me was not allowed to be a goddess.

"Your Highness!" Chiyo called, hurrying behind me.

"I'm going to my study," I said.

"But Your Highness, there's someone here in the lobby—"

"I don't care if Izanami herself has risen from the grave and come over for tea. I am not seeing any other guests today."

Chiyo clamped her mouth shut, but at the mention of Izanami, her eyes went wide.

"Chiyo," I said, slowing to a stop. "Is Izanami—"

"No, no, Your Highness," Chiyo said, shaking her head. "But there is someone I think you'll want to speak to."

I sighed, my jaw locked with annoyance. "Who is it?"

Chiyo looked at her feet. "He didn't exactly say, but his face…"

She trailed off, but it was enough to make me hesitate. Chiyo knew better than to waste my time, so if she was stopping me for this visitor, he must have been of some importance.

I turned back down the hallway and headed toward the main entrance, Chiyo following close behind. I entered the main lobby, bristling past the shadow guards into the golden entranceway, its ceiling painted with a thousand flowers and its walls mapped with more of the castle's murals cast in a backdrop of gold.

A man stood by the door, arms crossed as he examined the painted walls. He wore a kimono in ethereal white that glowed so brightly it seemed to emanate a pale mist of light. He turned around, as beautiful and terrifying as an endless sea, skin of moonbeams and eyes of exquisite coal. Someone I never thought I'd see again.

"Hiro?"

CHAPTER
03

I pulled my knife from my sleeve. The shadow guards formed a wall between me and Hiro, as if they could protect me, but I charged through it as easily as smoke. I had to see if he was real, or if he would vanish into the hungry shadows like all the other faces that haunted me in the dark.

But this Hiro didn't seem like an illusion. So many creatures in the infinite darkness of Yomi looked like they only halfway belonged to this world—blurred at the edges, almost translucent in the darkness, more like feelings than true images. But this Hiro had cold, hard edges and a brightness that rivaled starlight. Looking at him, I felt that I'd been dreaming my whole life and had only just opened my eyes.

He was the same exquisite nightmare I remembered, his presence dripping with Death in the ghostly white of his kimono, the whispering darkness of his shadows, the haunted sheen in his black eyes that spoke of distant pain. His face was all glass-sharp lines and moonbeam skin and the kind of perfection that wasn't supposed to exist.

This was the Shinigami who had sent my brother to the deep darkness.

I charged forward and pressed my knife to his throat, but his hand closed around mine, holding the blade a breath away. His skin burned sun-hot, keeping me back without so much as trembling, even though my strength could crush mountains.

I looked into his eyes, and for one terrible moment, all the questions of how and why he had returned dissolved. I imagined that this was the Hiro from before, the one who had held my hand on the shores of Takaoka and tried to warm my frozen skin as we read Hakutaku's book together by moonlight. The Hiro who'd only existed in that tiny sliver of time when I'd still believed in happy endings. Whenever I thought of that Hiro, grief carved me open and hollowed me out until there was nothing left inside of me but echoes and empty rooms.

My bones felt like paper and my knees shook and I swallowed down something bitter in the back of my throat. My knife clattered to the floor, my muscles suddenly weak. I yanked my hand away and he released me instantly. It wasn't until I took a step back and truly looked at him that I knew something was wrong.

He stared back at me with uncharacteristic coldness. Even when he was furious with me, Hiro's eyes had never looked so deadened and faraway. He stood taller than the Hiro I'd known, his face longer, like a shadow stretched out by the afternoon sun. His black pupils glowed with a moon in each eye, surrounded by tiny pinpricks of faraway starlight. I took another step back, looking at his feet that stood straight and uninjured.

"You're not Hiro," I said, a hollowness unfolding in my chest. I should have been relieved that Izanami's rightful heir hadn't returned for revenge, but somehow I felt like Hiro was dying all over again. *He's never coming back*, I thought, and I hated myself for the flash of disappointment that wrenched through me.

"I'm not," he said.

I closed my eyes and turned away as he spoke. His voice was almost identical to Hiro's—his words hummed through my bones like organ music and lingered long after they had faded. Ten years ago, I'd thought I would never hear that voice again. Five years ago, I'd started to forget what he sounded like, time scraping away everything I had left of him. What kind of cruel joke was this?

I clenched my fists, the shadows spreading thick across the floor, like spilled blood. They wrapped around the man's feet, shackling him to the floor.

"If this is some sort of joke," I said, "I will kill you."

Not-Hiro frowned at the sticky darkness trapping his feet. Even his facial expressions were so unlike Hiro. Where Hiro had been filled with more life and light than any creature of Death had a right to be, this person was more like a marble statue come to life—perfect but rigid, his expression carefully controlled.

"I am not joking," he said, raising an eyebrow. "I've barely said two words to you. That's hardly enough for a joke."

"It's not your words, it's your face," I said, enough feeling returning to my fingers to grab a knife from my other sleeve.

Not-Hiro tilted his head to the side as if contemplating this.

"I'm sorry if my appearance displeases you," he said after a moment, "but I cannot change it."

I exhaled through clenched teeth as the dark shackles around his ankles tightened. I wouldn't stand here playing games with a shadow of my dead fiancé. Whoever had come to torment me this way would pay.

"Then who are you?" I said, the shadows circling his throat, not yet touching but the threat clear. He glanced down at them then back at me, lips parted in mild surprise but eyes not giving away any distress.

"I am Tsukuyomi," he said at last, "the god of the moon."

The crescent moons in his eyes glittered as he spoke, hundreds of tiny stars twinkling in his pupils. I realized with cold terror that I was threatening an ancient god and my grip on my knife weakened. *But I am a god too*, I thought, *and he's in my palace.*

"I believe you were acquainted with my brother, Hiruko," he said.

My hand clenched around the knife, the wooden handle splintering. I took another step back, some inexplicable part of me wanting to run far and fast.

"Brother?" I said.

He nodded. "Hiruko was the firstborn child of Izanagi and Izanami," he said. "I am the second youngest, born when my father washed his right eye after escaping from Yomi."

I swallowed, unable to move. Had he come to avenge his brother by killing me? But he carried no weapons and surely could have killed me the moment I entered the room—he was older and undoubtedly stronger than me. There were a thousand things I could have said to him: *Why have you only come here now, ten years after his death? Why did Hiro never men-*

tion you? What do you want with me? But in the end my mouth filled up with ash and I could only say one thing:

"His name was Hiro," I whispered, the words barely a murmur. Some powerful goddess I was.

"Pardon me?" he said. "I don't believe I heard—"

"I said his name was Hiro, not Hiruko!" The darkness spiraled into a furious wind that rippled the man's robes and tore his hair back, the floorboards wailing at the onslaught. Hiro had done terrible things, but Hiruko meant leech boy, the cruel name that Izanami bestowed on him in her lofty disappointment, and that was never who he was. "I worried that you'd come to avenge him," I said over the chaos of the wind, "but you don't even know his name."

Tsukuyomi said nothing, waiting with icy composure, like how human parents waited for their unruly children to exhaust themselves. I wanted to keep the darkness spiraling just to spite him, but something about his calm and distant expression made my anger burn itself out into cold ashes. He looked like his soul had been cast out somewhere far away, a kite that the sky had stolen, leaving him holding on to nothing but a thin string.

As the wind died down, he combed a hand through his hair to settle it.

"I'm not here to 'avenge' anyone," he said, grimacing as if the word tasted sour in his mouth. "When gods take things that don't belong to them, disaster always follows. We all have our place, and mine is among the stars, not down here in Yomi. That is what my brother did not understand. That is why he failed."

"How brave of you to come here and pass judgment on him now that he's dead," I said, no longer shouting but still wound tight, itching to hurl one of my knives at his head. "That's all you other gods do. Nothing but look down from the stars and judge while the world suffers."

My words were supposed to anger him, but his expression didn't change.

"That depends on the god," he said, shrugging. "The god of war has certainly been idle lately, but perhaps that's in everyone's best interest. If anything, the goddess of fertility has become too dedicated to her work these days. In fifty years or so, I'm sure you'll see a corresponding increase in your death rate."

I took a steadying breath. "Why are you here?"

"Ah, yes," he said, standing up straighter. "We have important things to discuss. Perhaps we could go somewhere more private?"

"You wear the clothing of commoners," Tsukuyomi said as I led him through the halls of my palace.

He'd graduated from frowning at every candle that we passed to frowning at me instead, like he wanted to translate me into a language he understood. Chiyo and a few other servants trailed behind us, trading wide-eyed looks of panic. I had never before invited anyone into the palace, and after our exchange in the lobby, they didn't know whether to bow to Tsukuyomi or be ready to slit his throat if I gave the signal.

"Do all the gods have such astute observation skills?" I said.

"The royal junihitoe is tradition."

"I don't see *you* wearing a twelve-layered dress," I said. "Until you've tried walking in that, don't talk to me about tradition."

He seemed to ponder this for all of two seconds before launching into further observations.

"I suppose it wouldn't matter so much if no one could see you, but so much light is unusual for Yomi."

It took far too much effort not to grind my teeth down to the bone. This was definitely not Hiro.

"I am aware," I said, "but unlike Izanami, I don't need the darkness to hide my decaying body."

"You misunderstand," he said. "That was not the purpose of the darkness."

"And you misunderstand my level of interest in this conversation."

This, at last, silenced Tsukuyomi, though he looked almost physically pained at the effort it took to refrain from commenting further.

I led us down the rest of the hallway, stopping in front of a sliding door that my handmaids hurried to open for us. The small room had only a low table, some cushions and old scrolls with paper too cracked to unfurl.

My palace had many rooms that would have been more appropriate for hosting a fellow god—a council chamber with silk floor cushions and empress wood tables, a great dining hall where servants would present us with elaborate feasts that neither of us would eat, a study filled with Yomi's oldest scrolls and a crystal chandelier—but something about Tsukuyomi's chilling propriety made me want to unbalance him. I wanted him to feel thoroughly unspecial, welcomed into my home and then relegated to a storage room.

"Leave us," I said to the handmaids, taking Chiyo's candle and stepping over the threshold.

"Your Highness," Chiyo said, shooting Tsukuyomi a pointed glance, "are you sure that—"

"*Go.*"

Chiyo hesitated for only a moment, glaring at the back of Tsukuyomi's head, then bowed and left with the other handmaid.

Disappointingly, Tsukuyomi made no comment on the room I'd chosen, as if he conversed in storage closets every day. He sat at the table, taking the seat facing the window that looked out over the colorless night. I set down the candle in the center of the table and waved my hand over it, the flame warming the room. It cast a pale glow over Tsukuyomi's face, his shadow looming behind him like a great monster. How could this man look so similar to Hiro but feel so completely different?

I didn't think he intended to hurt me, at least not in that moment, but his presence screamed of danger and power and Death. He carried it in the moon-white cast of his skin, the rigidity of his jaw that never seemed to unclench, the sharpness of his eyes. The longer I looked at him, the more Hiro seemed like an echo of Tsukuyomi and not the other way around. My memory of Hiro was a watercolor painting compared to the vivid statue that was Tsukuyomi, carved from cold moonstone.

"I came here to warn you," he said. He spoke with such elegant confidence that I had the strange sensation that he wasn't speaking *to* me but narrating the Legend of Ren with practiced poise. Every word was pronounced in such clear, enunciated Japanese that surely he had rehearsed it a thousand times.

"About what?" I asked.

Suddenly, he leaned across the table. I wanted to back away, but I couldn't show him weakness. With his face only inches from mine, I saw the entire universe in the blackness of his eyes, tiny spinning planets and blinking stars and a swirl of cosmic colors. I held my breath, forcing myself to look only at his eyes and not let my gaze drift down the harsh marble edges of his cheeks to his lips. *Not Hiro, not Hiro, not Hiro*, I thought.

"Do you see the moon phase?" he said.

I blinked, focusing on the bright moons at the front of his pupils, the whiteness shaped like fat almonds lit up on the left side.

"It's a waning gibbous," Tsukuyomi said, leaning back, "the same as in the sky."

I wanted to let out a breath when he finally retreated, but I held it tight in my chest.

"I watch the Earth from the moon, though its clarity waxes and wanes," he said. "When the moon is full, my powers are at their peak. On those nights, I can see everything in Japan, no matter the clouds or trees or rooftops in my way. The moonlight can pierce through anything."

I stared back, careful not to change my expression, but inside my heart was beating faster because I knew where this was going. He must have seen something terrible. Something that involved me. Had he seen me stealing souls? Was he going to report me to Izanagi?

"On the night of the full moon yesterday," he said, "I saw an incident in Izumo concerning your Shinigami."

I froze. Normally I wouldn't recall which Shinigami I'd sent to a particular place—I had thousands of Shinigami, after all—but the names of three of them had come to me in a dream recently.

Somewhere in the land between nightmares and reality, a sharp pain had lanced through my head and their names had flashed across my closed eyelids as if branded:

Saburou of Yasugi.

Masao of Unnan.

Fumiko of Hamada.

It was similar to the way names came to me when I breathed in human souls, but I had never before experienced such a thing with Shinigami. I'd gotten out of bed to find the Shinigami register, squinting through a headache that felt like my skull was being crushed, and found only one thing in common between the three: I had placed them all in Izumo. By morning, I'd sent a messenger out to investigate, as I'd been too busy hunting down souls in secret to deal with it myself. I hadn't realized until now that the messenger never returned.

"What sort of incident?" I asked.

Tsukuyomi folded his hands in his lap. "While escorting the dead from their homes, they ran into two foreigners with white blond hair and silver cloaks."

Coldness clamped around my heart, like some creature of the night had sunk its teeth into me. I wanted to be sick, but I sat unmoving, unblinking as Tsukuyomi spoke.

"It's strange though," he said, leaning back and crossing his arms. "They only spoke for a few moments. They asked the Shinigami how to get to Yomi, but the Shinigami wouldn't tell them. Then, no more than a second could have passed, but suddenly the Shinigami were dead, and the foreigners were gone."

I shoved away from the table and stood up. Tsukuyomi

blinked at me in surprise while I stared down at him, my whole chest feeling full of rocks. I turned away and gripped the windowsill, staring into the nothingness beyond.

"No," I said, shaking my head. "They wouldn't come for me now. It's been over a decade. *Why would they come now?*"

"Who?"

I closed my eyes, my grip on the wood so hard that it started creaking under my fingers, the shadows rushing across the floor, swallowing all the candlelight.

I was no longer a goddess of night but a lonely little Reaper girl kneeling in the snow while the other Reapers laughed at me and stepped on my fingers and tossed my clock into the gutter. I had crossed oceans and killed people and lost everything that mattered just so I wouldn't have to be Wren of London anymore, but now London had followed me here. What more could I possibly give to make them leave me alone?

The windowsill cracked into jagged chunks in my hands, my shadows writhing like a boiling soup, the stone foundations of the palace rumbling.

"Ren?" Tsukuyomi said, rising to his feet.

But all I could think about was Ivy and her eyes like northern lights, her boot on my face, her hand grabbing my hair and pulling and pulling, her scissors suspended above my eye. How dare the Reapers follow me after driving me away? My blood burned and curdled, the whites of my eyes washed away by a plague of Death, the skin of my hands peeling away to yellowed bones.

My shadows crashed through the window in a burst of glass and bled out to the courtyard below and the sky above, the lotuses wilting in the garden, the koi bobbing dead to the surface. The darkness latched its claws into the ground and shook hard, the floor trembling and floorboards splitting. The candles rolled over and pooled hot wax and white fire on the floor.

I would show them what happened to foreigners who charged into my land and took what was mine. I would welcome them to Japan with Izanami's katana shoved down their throats. I would slice their souls to ribbons and crush their bodies to dust and eat them like I ate the hearts of humans. They had come here expecting to find a runaway orphan, but I would show them a goddess.

"Ren!"

Hands closed around my wrists, forcing me away from the window. My skin burned like hot iron against their grip, but still they held on tight.

"Ren, you're causing chaos," Tsukuyomi said. I could hardly even see him anymore, for my shadows had snuffed out the candles and let the deep darkness bleed into the room like poison gas. Then Tsukuyomi released one of my wrists and pressed a hand over my eyes.

All of the darkness disappeared.

Behind my closed eyelids I saw the silent landscape of the moon, pearly white and peaceful and still against a backdrop of stars. In every direction there was nothing but the glowing white sea, tranquil in its infinite sameness. Somewhere far below, the Earth was small and round and blue, spinning under a cotton canopy of clouds. Was this truly the moon where Tsukuyomi came from? Was everything here so clean and quiet?

It had been so long since I had felt anything but chaos and darkness. Even in my dreams, I saw the names and faces of the dead. Even when the servants left me alone, the darkness of Yomi screamed to me as if in agony, all the pain of the dead in my kingdom gathering overhead like storm clouds that only I could see. But for the first time in so long, I could breathe without feeling like I was drowning.

When I opened my eyes, the room had fallen silent, and Hiro stood in front of me.

No, not Hiro, I reminded myself. It was Tsukuyomi's cool hands on my shoulders, the crescent moons in his eyes glowing white against the darkness of the room, now that all the candles had gone out.

"Are you all right?" Tsukuyomi said.

I looked away from him, out the shattered window where the cool night breeze wafted inward. Of course nothing was all right.

"Yes," I whispered.

Tsukuyomi nodded and took a polite step back. The space between us felt cold once more.

"Ren," he said, "what are they?"

"Reapers," I said. A word I hadn't spoken aloud in a long, long time. I said it in English so he would know I didn't mean my Shinigami, but he nodded as if he understood.

"British Reapers?"

I nodded, still looking away.

"Why would they come here?"

"For me," I said. "Because I'm one of them." I held up my clock to show him.

"How interesting," Tsukuyomi said, tilting his head like I was some rare species of endangered bird. "The other gods whisper about you, you know. 'The Half Blood Shinigami who killed Izanami's Heir.' They never said what the other half was."

"I have bigger problems than gossip," I said, turning away. "I don't give a damn what you and your friends 'whisper' about me," I lied.

Tsukuyomi shook his head. "They're not my—"

"I have to go," I said, waving a hand to shut him up. "Are the Reapers still in Izumo?"

"I don't know," Tsukuyomi said. "That's where they were last night, but—"

"Then I need to talk to them."

I had a feeling it would be anything but a pleasant conversation, but one way or another, I needed them gone.

I turned to Tsukuyomi but couldn't find the words to dismiss him. Part of me wanted him to stay here, a perfect image of someone I thought I'd never see again. But a bigger part of me wanted him to leave and never come back, to let me pretend that I'd never seen him at all. It was easier that way.

"The guards will show you out," I said at last. "Thank you for the warning," I added quickly, only because it felt like something a goddess was supposed to say.

But Tsukuyomi made no move to leave.

"I'm afraid it's not quite that simple."

I froze in the doorway, my hand tense on the frame. "Why not?"

"My father asked me to watch over you, should you ever need protection. As I'm sure you know, whoever kills you will inherit your kingdom."

"So I've heard," I said, resisting the urge to roll my eyes. It was no secret that Izanagi thought me incapable. "I don't need a guardian. I promise I'm not going to hand the keys to my kingdom over to the Reapers. There, now you can go."

"My father's requests are not exactly optional," Tsukuyomi

said, grimacing. "If anything…unfortunate happened to you, I would be punished severely."

"When I die, it will not be at the hands of Reapers," I said. If I was sure of anything, it was this. I would do anything to stop the Reapers who had driven me to a land of darkness that had eaten my brother whole. The people who had ruined me, made me cruel and cold.

"My father doesn't want to take unnecessary risks," Tsukuyomi said.

I clenched my teeth. I didn't have time to waste arguing. The Reapers were here for me. If Tsukuyomi wanted to find out how it felt to be time tortured by High Reapers, he was welcome to come. Maybe it would scare him off.

"If you come with me," I said, "I'm not responsible for whatever the Reapers do to you."

"That won't be a problem," he said, wiping some melted wax off his immaculate white kimono.

"You've never met a Reaper before."

"Well, now I've met one," he said, nodding to me. "And I can promise you, Ren, I've seen creatures far more fearsome than you."

CHAPTER 04

Izumo was a city of gods, which was exactly why I hated going there.

It was home to one of the oldest shrines in all of Japan and the first door to Yomi, hiding in the guardian shadow of Mount Yakumoyama. The highest point in the city was the gold-embossed shrine, its sloped roof reaching up to the clear sky like a bridge from the Earth to the heavens. Izumo was long stretches of unbroken shoreline and lush breathing forests and a river so clean it sparkled, and I was absolutely not invited there.

Six years ago, I'd learned that all the gods gathered here on the tenth month of the lunar calendar each year, welcomed by a great festival. All of them except for me.

When I'd pointed this out to Chiyo, she'd merely shaken

her head and said that if I hadn't been explicitly invited, it wasn't a good idea to go and upset every single god in the Shinto pantheon at once.

I narrowed my eyes at Tsukuyomi and wondered if he might tell me what went on at those meetings, but I didn't know how to ask without sounding like a bitter child.

We walked down the dirt roads, the late-summer sun burning so intensely that I wondered if even the sun goddess hated me, wanting to scorch me until I crawled back to the darkness like a cockroach. I realized from the sun's low perch on the horizon that morning had already come once more. There was so little distinction between day and night in Yomi that it was easy for days to melt into each other like hot pools of wax. My eyes stung with dryness from the lack of sleep, but this trip couldn't wait.

We passed by soft grass that bulged with tombs, rounded half spheres that broke the clean lines of the fields. Below us, I sensed bones from the oldest days of Japan, death that the humans had yet to uncover. We crossed over a canal that sliced through the city like a fresh wound, bleeding gray water from the Hiikawa River. On the rocks far above us, a white lighthouse loomed over the city, its blinking light the pulse of a slow-beating heart.

The humans gave us a wide berth as we approached the town. Maybe they sensed the cloud of Death around me. Maybe it was because samurai had been abolished several decades ago and it was highly unusual for a woman to walk around with a katana. Or maybe they just thought I was a foreigner.

I spent so little time walking openly among humans that their opinions of me hadn't been an issue for much of the last decade. The Shinigami and the dead of Yomi had to at least pretend to respect me until I displeased them, but there was nothing special about me in the eyes of the living. Nothing would ever be enough for them, not even the decade of Chiyo's stern teachings that I'd suffered through.

Chiyo had nearly fainted the first time she'd seen me write in Japanese—my handwriting back then was a lopsided scrawl with haphazard stroke order that even I couldn't decipher. After that, she'd taken it upon herself to ensure that the Goddess of Yomi would, at the very least, not embarrass herself by being too British. She insisted on a curriculum of Japanese classics, calligraphy, tea ceremonies, even games of shogi. With no one who spoke English around me, my Japanese had improved immensely over the years. But there were no words in Japanese, or English, or any of the languages I spoke that would convince the Japanese people to see my face as anything but foreign.

I spent hours in front of my mirror trying to see what they saw. There was no single facial feature that was patently English, no single thing I could point to and wish it were different. Everything was just slightly not enough, too reminiscent of the sternness in my father's face, his cold conceit and perpetual disappointment.

Once, the judgment of humans had made me want to gouge their eyes out and bleed them dry. Now their words and stares were more like the sun that singed my pale skin. I would never be enough for them, and my anger was supposed to end once I could swallow that truth. I was a goddess, and I was supposed to stop caring what humans, or anyone, thought of me. It wasn't supposed to matter that I had no home in any land on Earth. I was Ren of Yakushima, the Goddess of Death, the girl who was supposed to die but had somehow stolen an entire kingdom instead, and that was supposed to be enough.

I stared back defiantly at a human woman, reminding myself that one day she would die and become one of my subjects, and that made me feel slightly better. I put one hand on my katana, hoping it would scare off more of the humans, and walked ahead of Tsukuyomi.

I'd expected him to look washed-out and ghostly in the sunlight, but if anything he looked even more infuriatingly regal, the sun stretching out his dark shadow like a cape. It was too easy to imagine that it was me and Hiro traveling through Japan again, not me and Tsukuyomi trying to stop the worst thing that could possibly happen. We crossed a wooden bridge over a river so flat it could have been a sheet of glass, heading closer to the gray mountain shade.

"I don't see anyone with blond hair outside at the moment," Tsukuyomi said, walking a polite distance beside me. He seemed more preoccupied by the sunlight than me, shielding his face with his hand and casting wary glances to the sky. "However, my vision improves at night. Perhaps they're hiding?"

I shook my head. "I doubt they're expecting me so soon," I said. "They don't know I have an all-seeing moon god relaying messages to me."

"I'm hardly all-seeing," Tsukuyomi said. "You must have been someone of great importance for them to go to all this trouble to find you."

I paused before I reached the end of the bridge, my shadow warped over the uneven ground, looking more like the crooked monster I was inside.

"I wasn't," I said. "I was no one." In fact, I was worse than no one. *No one* wouldn't have taken up space in classrooms or brought shame to the Scarborough family or blinded two High Reapers, sending the catacombs into an uproar.

"You weren't from a noble family?" Tsukuyomi said, raising an eyebrow.

I scoffed. "No," I said, even though that wasn't technically true. My father, Ambrose, was on the High Council. I could have inherited his seat if he hadn't signed away all my rights, leaving me an orphan on paper. I thought of him on occasion, hoping that he was finally starting to wrinkle and wither. Or that he'd been blamed for my disappearance and finally been ejected from the High Council, the only thing that mattered to him.

"Then why would they come here for you?"

I thought of me and Neven crawling through the vents above the Council's chambers as they planned how to drag me back for execution.

"We'll find her," High Councilor Cromwell had said. *"She's too dangerous to let live any longer."*

"Because they swore they would punish me," I said, "and when Reapers promise something in Death, they have to do it, no matter what."

That was the only reason I could think of, but it didn't explain why they'd only come for me now, ten years after I'd left. Had it really been so hard to track me down? They might have promised to end me, but they hadn't specified *when*, so surely they would have been content just to have me gone. Something must have changed.

But Tsukuyomi nodded, as if that made perfect sense. "No society can function without integrity."

"That's not really the point," I said, glaring at him. "And there's hardly any integrity in killing my Shinigami."

"This is also true," Tsukuyomi said. "What a strange contradiction. I wonder if they're aware of it."

"You can ask them when they're breaking your spine," I said.

Tsukuyomi nodded, as if actually considering it. His face was such a mask of poise that it was impossible to discern his thoughts. His gaze dropped to my necklace.

"Why do you wear a ring around your neck and not on your finger?" he said.

I tucked the ring into my clothes, looking away. Damn Tsukuyomi and his endless questions.

"It's silver and gold," I said, staring at the ground. "Good for time turning."

"But I've read about Reapers," Tsukuyomi said. "Is that not what your clock is for?"

"I didn't realize you were an authority on jewelry," I said. "You have an awful lot of opinions on my appearance for someone who wears the same color kimono as a corpse."

Tsukuyomi nodded. "My brother gave the ring to you, then."

I frowned. "How—"

"You seem to get quite volatile when he's brought up."

I took a steadying breath before I spoke again, just so I wouldn't prove him right. "You haven't seen me get 'volatile' yet," I said.

"I only find it interesting that..." He trailed off, his gaze focused somewhere behind me.

"No, please finish that sentence," I said, preemptively

clenching my fists. What a shame it would be if he got blood all over his white kimono.

He shook his head, squinting past me. "There's someone with blond hair behind you."

Without a word, I grabbed him by the sleeve and pulled us under a nearby tree, dragging shadows down over us.

"Don't say my name," I said. "Don't say anything in English. They can hear everything."

Tsukuyomi nodded stiffly, eyes wide. I realized belatedly that I had slammed him up against the tree's trunk by his wrists. I released him, my face suddenly warm, and took a step back to peer around the tree. I only caught a glimpse of blond hair before the person turned a corner down another street.

"Come on," I said, rushing out into the throng of humans, not bothering to check if Tsukuyomi was following me. We wove in and out of the crowd, ducking into doorways and under canopies as we tracked the two Reapers deeper into the city. Even if they hadn't had white blond hair, they would have been easy to spot from their sloppily knotted obi and English boots.

The longer we followed them, the more hesitant their steps became. They must have sensed Death drawing closer the way birds sensed impending storms. But they didn't know Tsukuyomi's face, and it was easy enough for me to turn around when they looked over their shoulders, showing them nothing but a curtain of long black hair, like every other woman in the street.

"I think someone's following us," one of them whispered. It was easy enough to parse those few English words from the sea of Japanese around us.

We had to get them *now*. When Reapers felt threatened,

their first instinct was to grab their clocks and time jump somewhere else, leaving their pursuers alone on the natural timeline.

I saw my chance when they crossed in front of an alley, shrouded in shade from the tall buildings.

My shadows reached out and grabbed the Reapers by the wrists, hauling them into the alley and stuffing their mouths with darkness to muffle their cries.

I pulled Tsukuyomi into the alleyway after them, yanking down a curtain of darkness to separate us from the humans.

My shadows had crushed the Reapers against the wall, their hands bound above their heads as they thrashed, eyes bulging wide. Before anything else, I pulled my knife from my sleeve and cut out the clips binding the Reapers' clocks to their clothes. Tsukuyomi watched with fascination as I finally yanked my shadows from their mouths.

Two young male Reapers stood bound before us, their eyes molten blue as they glared at me. They couldn't have been more than three hundred years old.

"Why are you here?" I said, the English words strange on my lips. It had been so long since I'd spoken to anyone in English. "Speak. Now."

But instead of speaking, one of the Reapers spit at my feet.

I sighed, then stepped forward and pried his jaw open with one hand, reaching in and yanking his tongue with the other. Once it was pinched firmly between my fingers, I held up my knife.

"Have you ever had to regrow your tongue?" I said. "It's not pleasant. It's not as bad as regrowing teeth or fingers, but we'll have time for those later."

The Reaper tried to squirm away, but my shadows only held him tighter, cutting off circulation to his hands and feet.

"Who the hell are you?" the other Reaper said, his words fierce but eyes starting to spin nauseous colors that gave away his fear.

"Ah, so you can talk," I said. "You answer my question first. Why are you here?"

The Reaper whimpered as I pinched his tongue harder, my fingernails digging in. The other Reaper glanced from his friend's tongue to my face.

"We were sent after a Shinigami named Scarborough," he said.

I'd figured as much. "Why would the Council sanction that?" I asked. "Why send so many Reapers abroad to bring back one person?"

The Reaper frowned. "How do you know about the Council?"

"Answer me!" I said, the Reaper in my grasp crying out as I yanked his tongue.

"I—I don't know," the Reaper said. "Ever since the Cromwells took over for Ankou—"

"What?" My grip went slack enough for the Reaper to snatch his tongue back inside his mouth and try to bite me. I elbowed him in the stomach, not looking away from the first Reaper. Ivy's family had taken over? As the heirs of Ankou, they were expected to take his place eventually, but no one thought a change of power would happen so soon.

"The Cromwells overthrew Ankou," the Reaper said. "Next in line was the High Councilor, but he turned up dead the day before ascension. Ivy Cromwell is the Ankou now, and she's changed a lot of rules."

I couldn't move, couldn't feel anything but my sweaty grip on the knife as I stared back at the young Reaper. Of course, Ivy would do anything for power, even kill her own father. That was the way of High Reapers—they culled the weak from the flock, no matter who it was. Love meant weakness, and weakness meant death.

"She sent you after me?" I whispered.

"You?" the Reaper farther from me said, reeling back, his face twisted with anger. "I knew it! You're Ren Scarborough, aren't you?"

I cursed under my breath, raising my knife to the first Reaper's throat. His eyes turned to a stormy amethyst as he cowered back against the wall.

"You're the reason we had to spend ten months at sea and scout out this rancid town?" the other Reaper said.

"Shut up," said the Reaper beneath my knife, glaring at his companion. "You heard what she did. She'll peel our faces off."

"What, exactly, did I do?" I said, narrowing my eyes. I was far from merciful, but I didn't revel in torture like some Reapers, and peeling faces off sounded more like Ivy than me.

"Ivy said you gouged out the eyes of three High Reapers," the second one said as he thrashed against the shadow chains.

I rolled my eyes. "That was an accident. And their eyes weren't gouged out. They were seared."

Tsukuyomi made a startled noise behind me, but I ignored it.

"She said the only reason you were even allowed to reap is because you seduced High Councilor Cromwell."

"What? That's absurd!" I glanced behind me at Tsukuyomi, but his face didn't show his thoughts. I wanted to deny it more fervently before Tsukuyomi got any disgusting ideas about me, but I didn't want to show the Reapers that their words mattered.

"She said that Shinigami eat their own children, but since you don't have any, you kidnapped your brother to roast him on a spit."

I slammed my fist into the wall behind the first Reaper's head, wood splintering, the whole building quaking.

"You can tell her that she's wasting her time," I said, the noxious words of Death rolling off my tongue. "Only Shinigami can reach my home in Yomi. She can tell all the lies she wants, but she can't find me unless I want to be found."

The Reaper let out a sharp laugh, the first shooting him a pained look.

"We already killed three Shinigami," he said. "Just what do you think Ivy will do if you hide underground like a turnip? Do you think she'll just shrug and go back to England? There's plenty of humans here that I'm sure she'd love to reap until you can be convinced to come talk to her."

Without meaning to, I dug my blade harder into first Reaper's neck, cold blood trickling down to his collarbone.

"Where is she?" I said. *"Tell me."*

The Reaper beneath me wilted, dazed from the potency of our language breathed in his face.

"She's not here yet," he said, each of his eyes a different color as he blinked away the dizziness.

"Yet?" I said, pressing the blade down harder. The Reaper flinched, trying not to swallow lest I slice his throat open.

"We're mapping the land for her," he said, words croaked and dry. "Her ship left a week after ours."

Only a week? I thought, making sure to steady my hand.

For once, I was glad not to have eyes that changed color like a Reaper. They would have seen my anxiety in the color of my irises. "And how long have you been here?"

"Liam," the other Reaper said, shooting his companion a warning glare. But all I had to do was dig my blade in a little harder and the Reaper trembled. I was far scarier than a High Reaper.

"Three days," he said.

I held my breath. That only left me four days until Ivy arrived—hardly enough time to prepare, even if I'd known how.

The other Reaper heaved out a sigh, then turned his glare to me. "Don't worry, half-breed," he said. "She's coming for you soon enough."

My whole body tensed up. "What did you call me?" I whispered.

The shadows tightened around both Reapers' wrists, snapping them like twigs. They cried out, but I could hardly hear them anymore. How long had it been since anyone had called me that? Ivy was probably the last person to do so.

But instead of the burning rage that I'd expected, instead of Death whispering to me about how easy it would be to snap their spines and crack their rib cages open and feast on their hearts, I felt like I'd swallowed an ocean of ice.

My hands trembled, my throat closing up. Shinigami didn't need to breathe but I *couldn't*, and my chest screamed for air. My bones felt brittle and frozen, like any sudden movement would fracture me into shards.

Ten years ago, Ivy had ripped my hood away and scoffed down at me. *Half-breed*, she'd said, *as if anything could hide what you are.*

And now she wasn't even here, but she was somehow stripping away my palace and servants and gilded katana, whispering those cruel words in my ear. If Ivy and I were both goddesses now, on even ground, then who was more powerful? I'd imagined tearing the old Ankou apart bone-by-bone if I'd had to, but Ivy had never seemed like someone who could bleed.

"Aw, look, I think I hurt her feelings," the second Reaper said, smirking down at my trembling hand, knife no longer against his companion's throat.

"This is supposed to be the heir of a High Reaper?" he said. "No wonder she was renounced."

My hand tightened around my knife. Before the Reapers could say anything else, I stabbed my knife between the second one's ribs.

He gasped, red blooming against his white shirt. I yanked the blade away in a spray of blood and moved toward the other Reaper, but a hand held me back.

"Ren," Tsukuyomi said.

I whipped around. I'd nearly forgotten that Tsukuyomi was here.

"Ren, I believe it may panic the humans to leave bodies here," he said. "We can complete this interrogation elsewhere."

"No," I said, tugging my arm back. But Tsukuyomi's grip didn't even waver, like he'd turned to marble.

"Ren, I understand that they've been unkind to you, but—"

"You understand *nothing!*" I said, grabbing my blade with the hand that Tsukuyomi hadn't restrained. I hurled the knife behind me and pinned the other Reaper to the wall through his stomach. He cried out, blood filling his mouth. Long ago, my knives might not have done much damage to a High Reaper, for Reapers only fell to more powerful creatures. But I was a god now. My blade meant death for any Reaper, regardless of their status.

Tsukuyomi released me, his eyes wide.

"You know nothing about me, or them," I said, taking a step closer. "Do not ever get in my way again."

"Ren," Tsukuyomi said, his voice far too patient, like I was a feral beast he was trying to soothe. My shadows dropped the limp and bleeding Reapers to the ground. "I only mean that strategically, it may have been wiser to—"

"When have you ever had to strategize?" I said, darkness lifting up around me like a fallen angel's wings, a thousand sharp talons ready to attack. "Don't tell me how to handle my own people! They know who I am, Tsukuyomi. They'll run back to Ivy and tell her they saw me."

Tsukuyomi said nothing, but somehow his unchanging facial expression only enraged me more.

"You think you know everything, but you were born into greatness," I said. "You were handed everything at birth, but I've fought for my right to stand among gods. So don't lecture me about the right way to get what I want."

For a split second—a moment that I could only see because I was a Reaper and could break time down into a million moments—the carefully sculpted perfection fell away from Tsukuyomi's face.

His lips parted, eyes flashing with hurt as the stars in his eyes dimmed. In that moment, when he was unguarded, he looked almost exactly like Hiro. All the anger drained from me, washed away by a cold wave of regret.

"That's...that's not true, Ren," he said at last, the words so quiet that I could hardly make them out. His voice sounded so much like Hiro's, the same raw honesty that could scrape me apart from the inside out. Then he blinked and the moment ended, his face falling back into indifference as he stood up straight. He looked to the Reapers behind me and sighed.

"I suppose there's nothing left to be done here," he said, turning and heading out of the alley. I took my knives back, sparing only a glance at the dead Reapers in the bloodstained alley. Maybe other Reapers would come by to collect their souls, or maybe they would stay suspended in the ether forever. Either way, it wasn't my concern.

The humans must have read the murderous expression on my face, for none of them dared say a word about the dirty knives clutched in my hands, or the trail of bloody footprints left behind me, growing fainter and fainter until they disappeared into the soft soil at the edge of town.

CHAPTER 05

My Shinigami always came when I called for them. They didn't have a choice.

Chiyo brought me a clean sheet of mulberry paper, a horse-hair brush, and an inkwell. She bowed and set the materials on the table as I pulled my knife from my sleeves and dismissed her.

I ran the blade across my palm and a bright red line appeared, cold scarlet dripping down my wrist. I squeezed my fist above the inkwell before my body could heal the cut, letting my blood fill up the shallow bowl. I had just enough before the cut finally closed, leaving my palm stained red.

I picked up the brush and dipped it into the inkwell, then began to paint their names across the empty sheet of paper.

KIYO OF TOKUSHIMA

AMA OF NAGANO

MEGO OF SAITAMA

One by one, I wrote the names of all of my head Shinigami, one for each of Japan's forty-seven prefectures. Blood was thicker than ink and had a tendency to clot, so my strokes came out unbalanced, but the prettiness of my writing was of no concern in this case. When the name of a Shinigami appeared in the blood of their goddess, the name tattooed on their spine would light up and begin to burn, awaiting the message. This time, beneath all of their names, I wrote a single word:

RETURN.

Under normal circumstances, I only summoned my Shinigami for an annual meeting after the new year. My message was sure to confuse them, but this couldn't wait until spring. The Reapers were already here.

"Chiyo," I said, opening the door to my room. "Prepare the—"

But Chiyo and the handmaids had already set out the royal junihitoe on my bed. I sighed and stepped forward, untying my black kimono and dropping it to the ground so the servants could dress me.

The presence of my head Shinigami was the only reason I would willingly wear the royal junihitoe. I couldn't stand before Japan's oldest and most powerful Shinigami in commoner's clothing, for they could see me clearly even in total darkness and judge me accordingly. Though my blood ran cold as death, I still found myself sweating under all the lay-

ers of fabric. The skirts might as well have been made of lead
for how much they weighed me down.

The outermost layer was a regal purple silk, textured in a
honeycomb pattern and embroidered with white suns, signify-
ing the Shinigami's dominion over light. My sleeves—so wide
that they fell to my knees—revealed the other layers of fabric,
pale lilac and royal gold and mossy green and funeral white.
The fabric had no seams, held together with only rice glue.

The servants brushed a white powder over my face and a
safflower pigment on my lips and cheeks. I always refused
to let them shave my eyebrows or blacken my teeth, arguing
that even the humans were starting to shun those traditions.
Chiyo never fought me on this, but always powdered my face
a bit more aggressively than necessary.

When I was finally ready, I stepped out into the hallway
and pressed my hands to the walls, picturing each and every
candle in all the various hallways and rooms. In a single
breath, I extinguished them all. The palace fell once again into
quiet darkness, as it had been when it belonged to Izanami at
the beginning of the world.

This was the masquerade I had to put on for the head Shinigami. I didn't know if together they were strong enough to
unseat me, but I couldn't take that chance. For them, I would
pretend to be a true goddess.

In the haze of darkness, my dormant Shinigami senses
fizzed back to life, the silk veil of night lifting until I could
sense the detailed murals and polished floorboards despite
the total, crypt-like darkness. The world fogged and shifted
like a restless reflection in a lake, my Shinigami eyes weak
from disuse.

"I see that you'll wear the royal junihitoe for your Shinigami, but not a fellow god," a voice said at the end of the hallway.

I sighed as Tsukuyomi stepped closer. As Izanagi's child, he was technically a Shinigami and could see in the darkness even if he didn't live in Yomi. His image became more vivid as he drew closer, like he was stepping out of a dream. The moons in his eyes glowed pure white, casting a glow around his face.

"It suits you," he said, like it was a fact and not an opinion.

"I'll let you wear it after the meeting, since you like it so much," I said, biting back harsher words.

His eyes widened, the moons inside them expanding as if rushing forward to meet the Earth. "That was not what I meant! I only—"

"I know," I said, waving a hand to make him stop talking. "Why haven't you gone home yet? I told you I had to make preparations."

"My instructions were to protect you until the threat was eliminated," he said. "The Reapers are still at large. You may have killed two, but others are coming."

I closed my eyes. My irritation was making me overheat, and I couldn't afford to show up and greet all my Shinigami while openly sweating. They would sense it like sharks smelled blood across an ocean.

"Your Highness," Chiyo said.

I turned—excruciatingly slowly with all my skirts—to where Chiyo was bowing.

"Your Shinigami have arrived."

"Good," I said, adjusting my collar. "Let's get this over with."

Before I could walk away dragging the weight of one

thousand skirts, Chiyo sighed and pulled out a handkerchief. "There's lipstick on your teeth and your eyebrows are dripping."

I scowled and scrubbed my teeth with Chiyo's handkerchief while she pulled out a brush and repainted my face. Tsukuyomi observed the scene like he'd never seen a makeup brush before in his life. Surely he would have taken notes had he had any paper on hand.

"The only goddess they can compare me to was a decaying corpse," I said to Chiyo, handing her back her handkerchief. "Surely my makeup looks fine in comparison."

"That 'decaying corpse' created Japan," Chiyo said, taking a step back to check her work. "She was allowed to be... less presentable."

"She had maggots in her eyes."

Chiyo pinched her lips together and made a noncommittal hum that must have translated to: "I can't reprimand you the way you deserve because I know you can kill me."

At last, she bowed and led me down the hallway, Tsukuyomi hurrying after me.

"You're not invited," I said.

"Your plan to defeat the Reapers is relevant to me."

"It isn't. And I won't have the head Shinigami thinking I need your help."

"Ah," Tsukuyomi said, nodding, "so that is your concern. I can tell them I'm here on scholarly business."

"This is my home, not a library."

"Then simply tell them I'm your guest."

"I don't have 'guests,'" I said, "and you wear the face of my dead fiancé. They're going to make assumptions."

"I can tell them—"

"*You* will tell them nothing," I said. We were drawing too close to the throne room, and we were sure to be heard arguing if we came any closer to the thin paper doors. I stopped and yanked Tsukuyomi back before he could turn the next corner, my hands twisted into fists in the white fabric of his sleeves. My Shinigami were waiting for me, so I couldn't waste more time. Apparently, arguing him away wouldn't work.

"If you go into that room, you will not speak over me," I said. "You will not address my Shinigami. *You will not ruin this for me.*"

"Ruin it?" he said, frowning, "Why would I—"

"They don't need a reason to challenge me," I said. "If you give them one, I'll kill you."

I didn't wait for his response, storming away toward my throne room. I had a job to do, one far more difficult than reaping souls.

My Shinigami bowed as I entered the room. They knelt on cushions placed on the floor, evenly spaced in rows facing my throne. Their red robes blurred into the darkness like a stormy sea of blood.

I did not give them permission to lift their heads until I sat down on my throne on a platform looking down at them, my skirts spread out in a great red and yellow train that spilled like water down the stairs. Tsukuyomi stood at the back by the door, watching me with no expression, small and faraway across the ocean of darkness between us. So many powerful creatures waited in suspense for my next words. The feeling would have thrilled me once, but now I only felt vaguely ill.

"Rise," I said. At once, all the head Shinigami sat up, so many dark eyes suddenly staring at me. I'd long learned that there was no point in giving flowery speeches. That only gave them more chances to find errors in my pronunciation. It was best to just tell them what I wanted and finish our business sooner, before their patience wore too thin.

"Japan has been invaded," I said.

Murmurs rippled through the group, but in the darkness I couldn't see who had dared to interrupt me.

"British Reapers are somewhere in Japan. They have already killed three Shinigami, and I doubt they'll stop there."

Something about my accent must have been off, because quiet laughter rippled through the room. I clenched my jaw, my shadows stirring, lashing back and forth like seagrass at the back of the room. Tsukuyomi frowned, though I didn't know if it was directed at me or my Shinigami.

"They carry silver-and-gold clocks to control time," I said. "If you take them away, the Reapers will be powerless..." But already their attention had been lost, and the Shinigami were talking among themselves.

"Why have they come here?" Naka of Hiroshima said from the front row. Though her words were polite enough, her eyes burned and her eyebrows arched downward in a harsh line. She had a long, narrow face and hair that was even longer, the ends dusting the floor.

"Ask them that question after you bring them to me," I said, looking away before her gaze could sear holes into my skin.

"Do you not know them?" another said. "Are they not your comrades?"

"Of course not!" I said, slamming a fist into the arm of my

throne. But the crowd swallowed my words and more began to voice their objections.

"How can we stop creatures that control time?"

"Why have you brought them here?"

"How can we collect souls and fight off these foreigners at the same time?"

The barrage of questions pinned me down, my face hot and my lips unable to form words. This was how it always went with the head Shinigami. A single wrong word or mispronunciation and I was no longer their goddess but a foreign girl playing dress-up. I could demand respect from humans and Yōkai with violence, but that wouldn't work with Shinigami. The loss of even one of them meant a net loss in collected souls, not to mention the risk of rebellion. They were hundreds of years older than me, so who knew what they could achieve if they banded together in anger?

I ground my teeth, eyes closed and fists clenched. I ached to grab my wedding ring pendant because it was the one thing I could crush but not break. But I couldn't show the Shinigami my weakness. Instead, I slipped my hand into my sleeve and closed my fingers around my clock.

"Shut up, all of you!" I said.

The words echoed across the room in the sharp silence that followed. But of course no one heard me. I had already stopped time.

All the Shinigami stood frozen, their eyes like coal fire, somehow even more piercing now that they were still and silent, even if they saw nothing in this moment between moments. I stepped forward until their gazes were no longer locked on me but where I had been, letting out a breath once I was no longer the singular subject of their anger. In the back of the room, Tsukuyomi had crossed his arms, eyes narrowed in what might have been confusion or concern. Surely he thought me pathetic now. What kind of goddess couldn't hold her subjects' attention for two minutes?

He doesn't matter right now, I thought. Nothing mattered but convincing them to take me seriously. If Ivy was coming, I couldn't drive her out on my own.

I took a deep breath, then grabbed Naka under the arms.

I could hardly move with my long skirts catching under my feet and Naka's limbs rigid with time freeze, but I managed to drag her over to the wall and spread her arms and legs out like an X without brushing her skin with mine and releasing her from the time freeze.

I took her sword and stabbed it into the wall through her sleeve. Then I took the swords of the other Shinigami who dared to stand up and stabbed her other sleeve and her skirts, pinning her like a moth.

Finally, I took Izanami's sword down from its stand and held it at Naka's throat. How easy it would have been to press just a bit harder. The katana had sawed Izanami's spine like soft fruit. It would be no problem at all to plunge it into Naka's throat and drown her in blood, extinguishing her disobedience forever.

But that wouldn't help me kill the Reapers.

With one hand, I tightened my grip on the katana. With the other, I let go of time.

All the yelling and complaining rushed back at once like a tidal wave slamming into me, a stark difference from the pure silence of stopped time. But the sounds died almost instantly when the Shinigami realized I had vanished from my throne. One of them gasped when they saw Naka pinned against the wall, standing at my mercy. As the Shinigami turned to us, Naka thrashed against the swords but couldn't break free without slicing her throat open.

"How did you—"

"This is what the Reapers will do to you!" I said, this time shouting in Death, a language I spoke without an accent. Stunned silence fell over the room.

"Or rather," I said, "this is what a kind Reaper will do to you. An inhospitable Reaper will spend one hundred years peeling off your skin, or a thousand years carving out your eyes."

I waited for their anger to rise again, but this time no one spoke, their eyes wide and fixed on me.

"These are the creatures that have come to Japan, and *you fools won't listen to me when I tell you how to stop them*?"

The Shinigami flinched at my reprimand. Behind them, my shadows had painted the paper doors black, as if we were all standing out in the expanse of deep darkness. One by one, my Shinigami knelt back down and bent forward in deep bows.

I withdrew my blade from Naka's throat but didn't sheathe it, my heart thundering through my chest as I looked over my Shinigami, their faces pressed to the floor,

"What do you want us to do, Your Highness?" said one of the Shinigami in the back of the room, his voice quavering.

"You will detain anyone with white blond hair, color-changing eyes, and clocks," I said. "Their clocks will be on chains tethered to their clothes. Remove the clocks and bring the Reapers to me. I will dispose of them."

Behind me, Naka scoffed. The other Shinigami looked up at the sound.

"If they can do this," she said, nodding toward her pinned sleeves, "then the moment they see us, we're dead. How do you expect us to overpower creatures that control time?"

"Don't pretend that you're powerless," I said. "I've defeated Reapers with only light before."

"Because you're one of them!" Naka said, thrashing against the swords. The other Shinigami murmured in agreement.

"If I see one of those *things*, I'm running straight back to Yomi," said a Shinigami in the front. "I haven't lived for thousands of years just to die at the hands of foreigners."

The rest began to rise, nodding their agreement.

This was quickly spiraling out of control. I'd tried to scare them and it had worked too well. Shinigami only answered to those they respected or feared—earning their respect was a lost cause, and they feared the Reapers far more than they feared me.

My Shinigami rose to their feet, yelling at me for my incompetence, how I was sacrificing them, how Izanami never would have done such a thing. And the worst part was that they were right.

"Sit down," I said under my breath. But of course none of them could hear me over their own protests. My hands trembled, my shadows simmering just beneath my skin. Even being a goddess wasn't enough for them. What more could I possibly give to this country to satisfy them? I'd been born here, and the insatiable soil had swallowed up the blood of my mother, my fiancé, and maybe even my brother. I'd lost absolutely everything to stand before them in Izanami's place, so what more did they want?

"I said sit down!"

As if I'd kicked open the floodgates, all of my shadows poured out of me.

Darkness crashed down from the ceiling like the night sky had suddenly collapsed, slamming the Shinigami into the floor with a simultaneous crack of shattered noses and ribs and teeth.

"Who do you think you're talking to?" I shouted in Death. *"Do you think I don't like the taste of Shinigami hearts?"* The words spilled out of me even though I didn't mean them, like I was only a vessel for rage and darkness to pour from. *Izanami's words*, I realized, though they felt dangerously like my own. My skin peeled away from my fingertips, and I remembered Izanami's skeletal hands reaching out in this same throne room as she'd hurled vitriol at Hiro.

Naka peeled her face from the floor, her mouth filled with blood, her teeth in pieces on the floor.

"You need us," she said, her words slurred as blood oozed between the gaps in her teeth. "You know you do, especially if Reapers are here. So don't bore us with empty threats."

I stood rigid at the front of the room. It didn't matter how many layers of elaborate dresses I wore, or how perfect my makeup was, or if I sat on Izanami's throne. All they would ever see was a foreign little girl.

"Get out," I said. I dragged my skirts through the pools of blood on the floor, leaving a red trail as I stormed down the hallway. Tsukuyomi stepped out of my way to let me through the door, but followed me as I tried to get away as fast as I could with the absurd amount of skirts I wore.

"Ren—"

"You can get out too," I said, trying to move faster so Tsukuyomi wouldn't see me cry. I scrubbed away my makeup with one of my floor-length sleeves, ruining the fabric and smearing lipstick across my face. But what did it matter? None of it had helped. The Reapers would come here together as an army and I would have to face them all alone.

"Ren—" Tsukuyomi said again.

"I don't want to hear it!" I said, whirling around to glare at him, but I tripped over my skirts and toppled backward. Tsukuyomi grabbed my arm and held me steady, his face inches from mine, moon eyes so wide and so damn sincere. My heart flipped in my chest, and then I was thinking about Hiro again, my gaze dropping down to his lips. I shoved away from him before my thoughts could spiral any further, catching myself on the wall.

"I thought *I* was the foreigner, but apparently you're the one who doesn't speak Japanese. I said *go!*"

I ripped away the outer layer of the junihitoe, hurling it against the wall. The sound of fabric ripping was too satisfying, so I tore away another layer as I hurried toward my study.

"Ren, you are a goddess. You can't undress in the middle of the hallway."

"I'm wearing twelve dresses!" I said, hurling the next layer at his head. "I'm going to leave one of them on!"

Tsukuyomi caught the next layer of fabric, gathering up all the ones that I'd tossed away until he held an unwieldy bundle of fabric in his arms.

"Are your Shinigami always so combative?" he asked.

I said nothing, letting down my hair and hurling a handful of pins at him.

"I should remind you that it's my duty to help you," Tsukuyomi said, dodging the pins, "so if your Shinigami are unhelpful, perhaps I can be of some use."

"What can you even do?" I said. "You're just a voyeur who watches people from the sky."

"Moonlight is powerful," he said. "It can bind people."

"And if the Reapers don't come at night?"

Tsukuyomi had no response, bending down to gather more of my dress. I had only two layers left, and the rage had begun to fade, my shadows slowly slithering back to me across the floor, tickling Tsukuyomi's ankles. When they finally crawled back under my skin, I felt a thousand years old and impossibly heavy. I fell to my knees in the hallway, my hands scraping across the mural before me.

Tsukuyomi came to a stop behind me. For a long moment he said nothing, and I thought he was waiting for me to speak.

"You have a painting of me?" he said at last.

I frowned, looking up at the mural in front of me. I hardly ever passed through this part of the palace, so I wasn't very familiar with its murals. This one had a god dressed in white, a crescent moon in his hands.

Just like Tsukuyomi, his face was cold and stern. His eyes, full of the universe, looked at some place faraway. The next panel showed him sitting on the crescent moon like a swing, his moonlight shining down on Japan. People below him danced and held hands and lifted their children on their shoulders, while Tsukuyomi sat up in the sky, all of the Earth's light reflected in his eyes.

"There are murals of all the gods," I said finally, my gaze tracing the rest of Tsukuyomi's story.

In the panels before his, there was an image of Izanagi's purification, only the silhouette of his shoulders visible as he stepped into the Tachibana River, his clothes abandoned on the shore.

In the next panel, Izanagi washed his left eye in the river's purifying waters, and a great beam of sunlight appeared. This was Amaterasu, the goddess of the sun. When he washed his right eye, a full moon rose high in the sky, looking down over a dark and empty world. This was Tsukuyomi. And lastly, he washed his nose, and ocean waves rose up to meet the birth of Susano'o, the god of storms and seas.

In his panels, Susano'o was only a shadowed figure, face hidden in the lightless depths of the water. I crawled closer, feeling the textured paint of the ocean waves that thrashed in the churning storm, the ships shattered on the shores from Susano'o's wrath.

Perhaps having Tsukuyomi around could be helpful after all.

Reapers could do anything with time, but they could not come to Japan any way but by sea.

"Tsukuyomi," I said.

He stepped closer, scanning the mural of his birth with unease.

"Do you still insist on helping me?" I said, turning to him.

"It is my responsibility," he said without hesitation.

"Then take me to Susano'o."

He froze, eyes locked on the painting of Susano'o before him.

"My brother has no interest in the dealings of Yomi," he said after a long moment. Though his words always sounded rehearsed, these sounded far too pale, like he feared his voice would betray his thoughts.

"But more Reapers are coming," I said. I could still picture the promise written above the catacombs back in London: *When Ankou comes, he will not go away empty.* Ivy would not leave before she got what she wanted. "If he controls the seas, he can stop Ivy from reaching our shores."

Tsukuyomi shook his head slowly, still staring at the mural as if seeing beyond it. "There are many things he *can* do, but that doesn't mean he will. There are reasons that our father asked *me* to help you, rather than Susano'o or Amaterasu."

"Such as?"

Tsukuyomi finally tore his gaze from the wall. The glow of moonlight around him had grown dimmer, as had the stars in his eyes.

"They are not very…philanthropic," he said.

I raised an eyebrow. "Is that why you're helping me?" I said flatly. "Philanthropy?"

He shook his head. "It's my duty."

"But not theirs?"

"They're not…" Tsukuyomi shook his head. "I don't think Susano'o will be as helpful as you think."

He glanced uneasily to the right, and I followed his gaze to another painting of Susano'o, this time in a dark and empty world, grinning over the mangled corpse of a horse ripped in two while the sun goddess cowered in a cave in the background. Fields of golden wheat were replaced by an ominous expanse of prickly gray stalks in the next panel, all the world's crops dead from darkness and cold. Chiyo had told me that once, Susano'o had terrified the sun into hiding her face, dooming the world to eternal night.

"But what else can I do?" I said, sinking back to the ground. "I have to do something. Ivy will arrive in four days."

Tsukuyomi's gaze fell to the floor. His eyes shifted back and forth, as if considering a great many things to say. "I can bring you to him," he said at last, "but I can make no promises about what he will say."

I nodded, rising to my feet. "He is a part of this country just like we are. If he intends to hand Japan over to Reapers, then let him say it to my face."

CHAPTER 06

We returned to the shores of Izumo, but this time, we did not venture into the town. Tsukuyomi led us to a secluded area of the beach, where we kicked off our shoes into the white sand and let the cold water lap over our feet.

The city, as a center for the gods to meet, was the ideal place to breach the human sea and enter the realm of gods, where Susano'o hid beneath the darkest waters. Yet, nothing about the shores of Izumo suggested the presence of a god. The waters were still and flat, disappearing into a haze of fog on the horizon. The wet sands had no footprints but ours, all echoes of life washed away by the tide.

"Like you, my brother lives in darkness," Tsukuyomi said. "We have to swim to the deepest parts of the ocean."

He pulled a thin length of hemp rope with small tassels from his sleeve and tied one end around his wrist.

"What is that?" I said.

"It's shimenawa," Tsukuyomi said. "It marks a sacred place and wards off evil. Anyone who means us harm will not be able to break it, so we won't be separated by the ocean's pull."

"You think Susano'o will try to harm us?"

Tsukuyomi avoided my gaze, gesturing for me to hold out my arm. He tied the rope around my wrist in silence, tightening the knot until it chafed against my skin. I looked down at the dark, ominously still water and began to wonder if meeting Susano'o was a bad idea.

"Ren," Tsukuyomi said, eyes still fixed on the shimenawa, "do you remember that I told you I was born from my father's eye when he purified himself after escaping Yomi?"

"Yes, I've read the Kojiki," I said.

"When Susano'o was born, our father made a mistake," he said.

I stilled. "What kind of mistake?"

"The Death from your kingdom clung to him," he said, still staring at the rope. "My father's eyes were clean when he emerged from Yomi, so my sister and I were unscathed, but Susano'o was born covered in Yomi's darkness."

I blinked, waiting for more, but Tsukuyomi watched me as if expecting me to yell or cry or cause another earthquake.

"Is that all?" I said. "*I* am drenched in Yomi's darkness. That hardly scares me."

Tsukuyomi pressed his lips together in a fine line, looking past me as if carefully arranging his next words. "Susano'o does not behave as gods are meant to," he said at last.

"Then it sounds like we'll get along well."

Tsukuyomi sighed. "I'm only asking you to be careful with your words," he said. "He can be rather unpredictable, and I don't want him to hurt you."

The strange sincerity in his words made heat rush to my face. I toyed with the frayed edge of the knot around my wrist rather than look at him.

"What difference does it make to your father if I get hurt?" I said, my words coming out sharper than I'd intended. "As long as I don't die at the hands of foreigners, it doesn't matter, does it?"

Tsukuyomi neither confirmed nor denied this, merely tugging on the rope and stepping into the sea.

"Come," he said.

Then he turned and walked into the frigid waters, pulling me after him.

I stepped into the sea, the same freezing temperature as my blood. It slipped through my fingers and felt more like I was floating through space than swimming. Tsukuyomi sank beneath the water's dark surface, and I had no choice but to follow.

No fish swam around us, no seaweed swayed in the current, no crabs scurried across the sand. The sea was as dark and barren as Yomi, a flat plane of sand that sloped suddenly downward into an unseen abyss.

Tsukuyomi swam deeper, tugging me along as I gazed around the vast emptiness. I could hardly even see the sunlight above us. It was as if the ocean had dragged us much farther down than we'd swum, shutting a door behind us and locking it tight.

The water pressure announced itself as a dull ache behind my eyes. All at once, the ocean grew even colder, the last of the distant sunlight swallowed up in the black sea. But here, at last, the ocean came to life.

Fish the same color as the black sea swam around us, only their white eyes visible as they hovered like a constellation of disembodied eyeballs. The seaweed was dead and gray, swaying stiffly with the waves, ready to shatter to pieces. Coral the color of ashes formed a spidery forest all around us, fossilized trees in a dark and silent wood.

The moment we set foot on the ocean floor, sand wrapped around our feet, anchoring us in place. I tried to pull my ankles free, but the sand wouldn't release its hold, the grains scraping against my skin.

"He's coming," Tsukuyomi said, his voice distant but still clear through the water.

Then a voice came from everywhere all at once—the brittle seaweed, the thousands of eyes orbiting us, the flickering glimmers of sunlight from someplace far above us like a distant dream.

"Why have you come here?" it said.

The words rumbled in the sand below us, vibrating up through my bones. I looked behind me, desperate to put a face to such a powerful voice.

"Brother, it's me," Tsukuyomi said.

"I have many brothers," the voice said, *"and not all of them are welcome here."*

"Then come out and see me for yourself," Tsukuyomi said, crossing his arms.

For a moment, no one answered. The seaweed stopped its rigid swaying. The gentle tug of waves stilled. Then a tall figure stepped out from behind the coral.

Like Tsukuyomi, Susano'o was also a shadow of Hiro, but much, much colder.

His eyes carried all the darkness of Yomi, not in their color but in their endlessness—staring into his eyes felt like falling down and down into an abyss. His face was thin and shadowed, with gray under his eyes and in his cheeks and a lifeless purple in his lips. He loomed taller than either of his brothers, too thin under his white kimono that breathed with the heartbeat of the ocean, the heavy fabric of his sleeves pulsing like a pair of wings trying to take flight.

His gaze met mine, and coldness crept up my bones.

"Susano'o," Tsukuyomi said, "This is Ren, the Goddess of—"

"I know who she is," Susano'o said, his eyes fixed on me. "Have you replaced Hiruko already? I'll admit that Tsukuyomi is an improvement, but not by much."

My hands curled into fists. I tried to tug my ankles free, but the sand held them tight.

"His name was Hiro," I said.

"But that's not why we're here," Tsukuyomi said, glaring at me.

"Then tell me what you want," Susano'o said. "This is the second time I've asked. There won't be a third."

"You've let Reapers into Japan," I said. I hadn't intended to start with an accusation, but something about his sharpness made me want to be even sharper, to show him that he couldn't make demands of a goddess. Tsukuyomi shot me a withering look of disappointment.

"I let a ship with foreigners arrive in our waters, yes," Susano'o said, raising an eyebrow. "Japan is not a closed kingdom anymore, so I must allow for trade. Have you spent so much time sitting underground like a potato that you know nothing of our country's politics?"

"Reapers are not part of Japan's politics!" I said.

Tsukuyomi looked between the two of us like he expected a bomb to go off at any moment. The potency of Death around us had already darkened the sea, made it taste bitter on my lips and needle sharp on my skin.

"The god of Reapers is coming for me," I said. "I need you to stop her from setting foot in Japan."

Susano'o scoffed. He leaned back against a bed of coral, crossing his arms. "This is your problem, not mine," he said. "You brought the Reapers here, so you can handle them on your own."

My fingers itched to scratch the smug look from his face.

"Brother," Tsukuyomi said, "the Reapers aren't coming just for Ren. They'll harm both Shinigami and humans."

Susano'o whirled toward Tsukuyomi, a rush of water blasting in his direction. Tsukuyomi flinched at the onslaught of brine, salt crystals scraping tiny cuts across his forearms as he shielded his face.

"I was banned from the mortal plane!" Susano'o said, his voice startling away a school of fish and raking up a tempest of gray sand. "Do you think I care about Izanagi's kingdom anymore?"

Banned from the mortal plane? I looked to Tsukuyomi for explanation, but he wouldn't meet my gaze.

"If Ankou kills me, she'll take my place," I said to Susano'o. "Do you really want Reapers in control of Yomi?"

Susano'o turned to me. Clouds of sand fell like gray snow around us, and the floating eyes suddenly looked only at me.

"There is already a Reaper in control of Yomi."

His words knifed through my chest, already painfully tight from the pressure of the deepest sea. This was how he saw me, how all the Shinigami saw me. I thought of how I'd once hoped being a goddess would exempt me from these identity politics, and I almost laughed at how foolish I'd been.

"Susano'o," Tsukuyomi said, the way one might warn a dog not to bite.

But Susano'o ignored him and came closer, the temperature of the salt water plummeting. "I know my place," he said. "It's time you learned yours. And if that means the Reapers must cut you down and pry Izanami's katana from your dead hands, then so be it. If they can do it, then they deserve it more than you."

I swallowed, my shadows pulsing in the ocean water, long swaying strands of darkness that caged us in. "You'll let your bitterness stop you from helping a fellow god, even if it means the downfall of your country?"

Susano'o said nothing for a moment, then he laughed—a cold, wicked sound that scraped through my ears and cracked the delicate coral trees around us.

"Gods of Japan are not born in British sewers," he said. "You can smite your people with Izanami's katana and sit on her throne and command her darkness, but you will never, ever be a goddess."

He shot me one last cursory glance, then turned his back to me and walked toward the coral canopy.

Something twisted sharply in my chest as he walked away, like my lungs were demanding air even though I didn't need to breathe. It wasn't his words that stung the most. It was the look in his eyes as he turned away, like I was a stain to be washed out. Back when I was nothing and no one in London, the Reapers had looked at me the same way.

And maybe he was right. Maybe I would never wield the same power as Izanami, who had created all the islands of Japan, every stretch of endless sky and deep black sea. But I was the one who had won her sword and somehow, against all odds, I was still standing.

I tore my ankles out of the stony grip of the sand, even as the sharp grains raked the skin from my feet. The ocean tried with all its might to drag me back, but I took another step forward.

"Don't walk away from me!" I said, the words of Death forming in black clouds around me that spun through the water. My shadows fought through the crushing pressure of the sea and grabbed Susano'o's ankles, dragging him along the ocean floor. A swarm of fish rushed toward me, but I sent them spinning away with a wave of my hand, my shadows slicing them to pieces, filling the ocean with blood.

"It wasn't a request," I said, standing over Susano'o. He glared up at me, grabbing fistfuls of sand as if he could claw himself upright. "I've killed a god before, Susano'o. I can do it again."

His eyes narrowed as if he'd very much like to dismember me, chest heaving and teeth clenched tight together.

"Ren," Tsukuyomi said delicately, taking a small step toward me, "I think—"

"Shut up," I said, holding up a hand to stop him. "I'm not leaving here empty-handed."

Tsukuyomi barely managed to conceal the disapproval on his face, his expression mostly neutral save for the irritated twitch near his left eye.

Susano'o took one look at his brother, then tipped his head back and laughed.

"All right," he said. "You may be a foreigner, but at least you're not a dog eating out of Izanagi's hand like that one over there." He nodded toward Tsukuyomi, who frowned and crossed his arms. "Perhaps it will be fun to watch you ruin him too. Let me up."

I didn't move at first, looking to Tsukuyomi. He sighed as if exhausted, waving a hand for me to obey.

"He's capricious," Tsukuyomi said. "He does this sometimes."

"I'm done talking to you," Susano'o said, waving his hand and sending a spray of sand in Tsukuyomi's face, making him cough and sputter.

I pulled back my shadows and Susano'o rose to his feet, looming over me.

"I think we can form an alliance," he said, smiling with pearl white teeth that looked just slightly too sharp.

I blinked. "I'm not marrying you."

Susano'o rolled his eyes as Tsukuyomi choked behind us. "Yes, we all know how well your last marriage went," he said. "That is not the only way gods make alliances. I'll give you something you want if you give me something I want."

"And what do you want?"

Susano'o waved at a coral formation that split and crackled into a new shape at his command. The white coral formed a sword, not curved like Izanami's but a rigid line with a sharpened point and serrated edges like the curves of ocean waves.

"I seek a sword called Kusanagi No Tsurugi, which looks like this," he said. "I found it in the body of a great serpent and gave it as a gift to my sister, Amaterasu, many years ago as a sort of…misguided apology, if you will."

"Misguided?" Tsukuyomi said, raising an eyebrow. "You cut a hole in her ceiling and dropped a dead horse through it."

"I said *I'm not talking to you*," Susano'o said, spraying more sand in Tsukuyomi's face. He turned back to me. "Amaterasu gave it to the first emperor of Japan—don't ask me why she bothered with human affairs—and for years, it was safely enshrined on Earth. But your predecessor did a wonderful job of upsetting the nearby Yōkai."

"You mean exterminating them?" I said. Izanami grumbled her disapproval in my ear, but I clenched my jaw and ignored her.

"I couldn't care less, but that's certainly how they saw it," Susano'o said. "Many of them raided shrines out of disdain for the gods. They took my sword many years ago, but it is rightfully mine, and I want it back."

"Are you asking me to interrogate every Yōkai in Japan to find your sword?" I said. "I'm in a bit of a hurry."

Susano'o waved his hand and the sword replica sank back into the coral formation. "Don't bother with the Yōkai," he said, his lips curling down. "If I were you, I would start by asking Amaterasu."

"Sister?" Tsukuyomi said, frowning. "What use would she have for your sword now?"

Susano'o rolled his eyes. "It's a curse, being the smartest sibling. You make too many assumptions, Tsukuyomi. I never said she had it."

"Smartest sibling?" Tsukuyomi echoed, jaw clenched.

"Would you please stay focused?" I said, kicking sand in

his direction. I turned back to Susano'o. "Why should I ask Amaterasu about it?"

"Because as the sun, she's all-seeing in daylight," Tsuku-yomi said, before Susano'o could speak. "Her vision is even more powerful than mine, so she's likely to know where something so important has gone. Isn't that what you mean, Susano'o?"

Susano'o applauded melodramatically. "Congratulations, you've figured out how the sun works! It only took you several thousand years. Imagine what wonders you'll discover in the next millennium."

"Can't you just ask her about this yourself?" I asked, before Tsukuyomi could think of an angry retort.

"I am banished from her palace," Susano'o said, his expression gray.

I raised an eyebrow. "And you think she'll just help me on your behalf?"

"What you are asking of me is not easy or simple either," he said. "I would need to inspect every ship coming into every harbor. You expect me to do that at no cost?"

I looked to Tsukuyomi for advice, but his expression was strangely distressed. Some great help he turned out to be.

"All right," I said. "I will find your sword if you keep the Reapers out of Japan."

Susano'o nodded. "It's a deal." He held out his hand to shake but withdrew it before I could reach. "Just to be clear," he said, "this is a business exchange. Do not think of me as your ally, and certainly not your friend."

I resisted the temptation to roll my eyes. "Don't worry, I despise you as well."

"Excellent," he said, finally shaking my hand. His skin

scratched like jagged coral against my palm. He turned to Tsukuyomi. "Be careful with her, brother," he said, grinning. "Don't end up like Hiruko."

Then he turned and walked back into the dark waters, where his shape quickly grew hazy. The sands rose and swallowed him whole, spinning up a surge of bubbles and swirling waters. Before I could speak another word, the ocean wrapped its hands around me and pulled.

I flew back in a great wave, crashing into a bed of coral that shattered under me. The rope around my wrist chafed as Tsukuyomi was yanked after me.

The current tossed us around like toys. It wasn't the lack of air that bothered me, but not knowing which way was up or down, whether I was swimming toward sunlight or tumbling deeper into the darkness.

I grabbed my clock and time slammed to a halt, leaving me nauseous and suspended upside down. The water had thickened into a salty syrup with the time freeze. I managed to turn myself around and swim toward what little sunlight I could see, Tsukuyomi dragging behind me as the rope pulled taut.

I held tight on to the time freeze until we reached the shore and Tsukuyomi's weight grew too heavy to pull any farther. I let go of time and the ocean crashed over us. Tsukuyomi sputtered, arms flailing as if trying to swim, but only scraping up handfuls of sand. He blinked, eyes wide and hair hanging in wet clumps over his face.

He wiped the water from his eyes. "How did we—"

"'Thank you' would suffice," I said, untying my end of the rope.

He spit out salt water and untied his own end, tucking it back in his kimono. "That went better than expected."

I frowned. "What did you expect?"

"To have my lungs filled with sand," he said. "All things considered, it could have been worse."

I couldn't help but agree. I had seen what gods were capable of when they were truly angry. "I suppose our next stop is the sun palace?" I said.

Tsukuyomi sighed, turning to look at the sun, low on the horizon. "It's almost sunset," he said. "We'll have to wait until tomorrow. There's no way to enter her palace at night."

I sighed. I had no time to waste before Ivy's arrival in four days, but even if I could run to the sun goddess now, showing up at her palace soaking wet was probably not the best way to win her favor. I hugged my knees close and stared at the town in the distance beyond the rocks.

"What did Susano'o mean about being banished?" I asked.

Tsukuyomi grimaced. "Our father, Izanagi, renounced Susano'o and banished him from the kingdom of the living," he said. "I'm not surprised that he won't help Izanagi's people."

"Why was he renounced?" I said, my mind already running through a thousand horrible things Susano'o might have done. He didn't seem the type to use his godly powers for good.

Tsukuyomi sat still, watching the ocean lap back and forth across his feet. To a human, he might have looked indifferent, but I could sense the sudden stillness in his form, how he had stopped breathing entirely.

"I do not remember very much," he said after a long moment. "We were children when it happened. Our sister told me that Susano'o missed our mother so much that he cried for hundreds of years, draining all the rivers and seas. Izanagi came down to Earth and demanded to know why he was crying instead of ruling the ocean. When Susano'o told him, our father was so disgusted by his weakness that he expelled him, sending him to the bottom of the sea."

"All because he cried for his mother?" I asked. That hardly seemed fair. Though if Izanagi was anything like Izanami, he probably didn't understand what fairness meant.

Tsukuyomi turned to me, his expression blank. "Gods are not supposed to cry, even when they are children," he said. The words sounded vacant, like something he'd memorized and recited, not something he truly believed.

I huffed out a breath, leaning back in the sand. "Just how many children have your parents thrown away for ridiculous reasons?"

I'd meant it as more of a criticism than a true question, but Tsukuyomi's rigid silence told me more than words ever could.

I turned toward him, sliding closer. "Are there more than just Hiro and Susano'o?"

Tsukuyomi's shoulders tensed, his hands gripping his knees and pulling the fabric of his kimono taut.

"Hey," I said, shoving his shoulder, "I can still see you if you don't move, you know."

He let out a breath, still not looking at me.

"Tsukuyomi," I said. "How many?"

"Five," he whispered, wincing like he regretted the word as soon as he'd spoken it.

Five? The first two must have been Hiro and Awashima, the children born before Izanami and Izanagi's proper marriage ritual. I'd also read of Kagutsuchi, the fire spirit that had burned Izanami when she gave birth to him, who Izanagi had beheaded in his rage. Now there was Susano'o, who apparently had been poisoned by Yomi's darkness since birth. But that was only four.

"Who is the fifth?" I said.

Tsukuyomi said nothing, staring resolutely at the sand, and that was the only confirmation I needed.

"It's you, isn't it?"

Tsukuyomi frowned, the bright stars in his eyes suddenly eclipsed by darkness, the crescent moons dimming from white to ghostly gray. He leaned closer, and though he wasn't that much taller than me, his looming presence inhaled the last breaths of light on the horizon. His eyes held an insatiable darkness, too much like Hiro on the night he'd tried to kill Tamamo No Mae.

"Don't," he said, his jaw clenched, his hateful eyes daring me to recoil.

But I wouldn't make the same mistake twice. I had let Hiro feed me half-truths, let him soften me and tie my soul to his, and by the time I'd known who he really was, it was far too late for me to be objective. It would not happen again. I would know exactly who I was traveling with and what he wanted, or I would go alone.

"You don't scare me," I said, glaring back at him. He might have thought he could intimidate me with dark looks, but I was the queen of darkness. "Tell me why you were renounced."

Tsukuyomi made no move to answer, his hands clenched into fists.

"What did you do?" I said, rising to my feet. "I have a right to know before I go one step farther with you."

Tsukuyomi let out a dry laugh, looking up to the sun. Finally, he leveled his gaze with mine.

"I killed my sister."

CHAPTER 07

For a moment, Tsukuyomi's words slid off me like rain sloughed off an umbrella. But when they echoed back in my mind, a stinging coldness began to curl its way through me, a vine of ivy wrapping around my heart and into my veins, crawling through every part of me. Ever since Tsukuyomi had come to my palace, I'd found him strange and unsettling, but I'd never considered something like this.

I leaned away from him. "You killed Amaterasu?" I whispered.

"Not her!" Tsukuyomi said, a scowl striking through his careful mask. "I would never hurt her! Have you not read the Kojiki? I have many sisters."

"Then who?" I said, my words wafer-thin.

Tsukuyomi watched me for a long moment, until he finally straightened his shoulders and his face assumed the same moon-white cast, devoid of any expression.

"Her name was Ukemochi," he said, his words stiff and detached. "The goddess of food."

The waves around us crept closer, soaking our feet as the moon guided the tide onto land, the voice of the sea speaking in the tense silence between us.

If I had been a good person with a clear conscience, I might have turned around and left Tsukuyomi on the shore. Maybe he had his reasons, even very good ones, but there was little difference between killing good people and bad people, for everyone had shades of day and night inside of them. Tsukuyomi was capable of betraying his own family, so he was capable of betraying me too.

But I had sent my own brother to his death and spilled enough human blood to fill the East Sea. I knew too well that even people with good intentions were capable of unspeakable cruelty if they stood to gain something from it.

"Why?" I said.

"Because Amaterasu…" He trailed off, shaking his head and slumping farther into the sand, elegant posture forgotten. "You must understand, Amaterasu is not just the goddess of the sun, but of the heavens and all the universe," he said. "All of my brightness comes from her, for the moon has no light of its own. Without her, I am a cold rock dressed in shadows. She knows it, and our parents know it too. That is why she wears the crown of the whole universe while I only have the night sky."

He paused, glancing at the setting sun and wincing at its piercing light. "In our entire lives, she only asked me for one favor—go down to Earth and visit our sister Ukemochi on her behalf. I thought it was a simple task, so I agreed, hoping that if I did well, maybe she would…" He sighed, closing his eyes. In the dying light, his expression grew sickly.

"Ukemochi was supposed to greet me with a great feast. I had never met her before, so I didn't know what to expect. But when I entered her home, she locked the doors…"

"Come in and eat," she said to me.

I looked across the long, empty table. It had enough seats for a hundred men, but not a single grain of rice lay on top of it. "How can I, when there is no food?" I asked.

Ukemochi shook her head at me and smiled. "Soon, there will be," she said.

I had never before seen or tasted food, so I thought that maybe I was being naive. Maybe food appeared only when you sat at a table, or could only be seen by human eyes. *If I ask too many questions, Ukemochi will tell Amaterasu what a fool I am*, I thought.

So I sat down and waited.

Ukemochi sat at the far end of the table, what felt like a thousand miles from me. Still, there was no food. I placed my hands on the table's surface and felt nothing but smooth cedar. I checked underneath the table and saw nothing but the polished wooden floor. I even peered out the windows, in case food was like a summer breeze that blew in from the outside world. But across the table, Ukemochi said nothing at all, still staring at me with a waxen grin.

"Sister, forgive me," I said at last, "but where will the food come from?"

She stood up, and somehow her grin had grown wider, her teeth sharper than swords.

"From me, of course," she said. "I am the food."

Then she tipped her head back and plunged her hand deep into her throat.

She yanked hard, and out came a thousand fish, gushing across the table and sliding toward me, sizzling from the acids of her stomach. She bent over the table and retched, and mountains of rice caked in foaming saliva poured from her mouth and piled on top of the fish, dripping from her nose and then bursting from behind her eyes. Stalks of wheat grew from her ears like crooked golden hairs. Her pores yawned open wide, letting silkworms crawl out and squirm across the table.

The feast oozed closer and closer to me across the long table, but I felt like my whole body had turned to stone and couldn't move.

"Eat, brother," she said. "I made it just for you."

I stood up, throwing my chair back and turning to leave, but she crawled across the table like a spider and grabbed my ankles, dragging me closer. She pried my jaw open, then grabbed a handful of bitter rice and shoved it past my lips. It tasted of dirt and ashes, but she kept shoveling handfuls of food into me, even when I cried and scratched her arms and yanked her hair, anything to make her stop.

"What kind of god cries over rice?" she said. "This is why big sister won't share her sky with you. This is why mother and father know you don't deserve it.'"

She laughed and laughed until her voice no longer sounded like a voice at all, but shards of glass scraping across tile. She forced silkworms between my teeth until I was sick, and even then her laughter cleaved me open, grabbing me by the veins and unthreading me piece by piece. Her laughter didn't stop until I grabbed a knife from the table and stabbed her in the heart.

★ ★ ★

Tsukuyomi's fingers dug deep into the sand, his arms shaking. "You were not born a god, so I don't expect you to understand," he said. "You don't know how it feels, Ren, to watch as another god strips your power away. Us gods are only born because we serve a purpose. We use our strength to hold the universe together. Without that strength, we are nothing. Less than humans, because at least humans still exist without their jobs. We are nothing but our assignments and our power, and in the face of Ukemochi, I had lost both."

He relaxed his fingers, staring at the water that had now formed a shallow bath around us.

"I thought that Amaterasu would be proud of my strength. I thought that it was a test, and that I'd proven myself to be strong. But she was furious. She threw me down to Earth and said she would never speak to me again. That is why day and night are separate, why the sun and moon seldom cross each other in the sky. I haven't spoken to her since."

He pressed his hands to his eyes, as if he could rub the memories away. I sat rigidly beside him, his awful words falling over me like sharp hail.

"My father is ashamed of me for killing one of his children, and for being so weak," he said. "That is why I am his puppet. Because unlike Susano'o, I care about having my status restored. He sent me to you because he doesn't care if I die."

He hugged his legs against his chest, the most ungodlike position I'd ever seen him in. I sat still and gripped the ends of my sleeves, unsure of what to say.

If his words were true, then I could hardly fault him for killing his sister. I had turned my knife on people for far less than what Ukemochi had done, even on people that I loved. But who was to say that any of his story was true?

"Am I meant to believe this so easily?" I asked.

His face twitched. "Why would I make up such a terrible story about myself?"

"Because I would have found out about Ukemochi eventually. But who's to say you didn't kill her for other reasons?"

He sighed. "Read the Kojiki if you don't believe me."

"The Kojiki is a single version of events compiled by humans," I said. Legends were rarely so straightforward.

"Ren, what are you asking of me?" he said, fingers sinking into the sand again. "I have no proof to offer you."

I bit my lip, turning to the sea. There was no way for me to know if his words were true. I would have to decide for myself. I thought back to Hiro, and how easy it had been to pour all of my faith into him even when Neven sensed his bad intentions from the start.

But I was no longer a lost little girl who needed someone to guide her across Japan. Hiro had been able to enchant me because I had washed up wide-eyed on the shore with no one else to turn to but a handsome stranger with a sweet voice, but Tsukuyomi was knocking on the door of a goddess. The only things in the world that could tempt me to lose sight of my mission were things he couldn't possibly give me.

"Are there any other secrets you've neglected to tell me?" I asked.

Tsukuyomi kept staring at the horizon, as if my words barely reached him. For a moment, I imagined how it would feel if Neven refused to talk to me for millennia the way Tsukuyomi's sister had.

"I've had a very long life," he said after a moment, "but I can think of nothing else that would upset you."

I shook my head. "Don't play word games with me. Do you have any secrets or not?"

"I'm only saying that I can't predict how you would feel about every—"

"Look, Tsukuyomi," I said, holding up a hand to silence him, "I've kept bad company in the past and I won't be made a fool of again. If you do anything to so much as make me suspect you've lied to me, I will end you. I killed my fiancé. I have no qualms about killing someone I've just met. So if there's anything else you need to tell me, this is the last time I will listen."

He shook his head, eyes steely. "There's nothing else," he said. "And I don't lie."

"Then there won't be a problem."

Tsukuyomi nodded, relaxing his shoulders. "Thank you," he said, the words softer than the shifting sands beneath the waves.

I turned toward the ocean because his eyes looked so unnaturally sincere. "There is nothing to thank me for," I said. "For now, we'll plan to go to the sun palace in the morning."

Tsukuyomi paled, but nodded. He opened his mouth to speak, but quickly closed it, shaking his head.

"No, stop doing that," I said.

He raised an eyebrow. "What—"

"You don't hide information from me," I said. "Tell me what you were going to say."

Tsukuyomi sighed. "I just don't expect that Amaterasu will have the answers you seek," he said. "Susano'o wouldn't have given you such an easy task."

He was probably right, but what else could I do but go to Amaterasu and find out? I stared at the sinking sun in the distance as if it would give me the answers I craved, but mockingly it dipped below the horizon, the last of its pink light shivering away.

"I need to go back to Yomi," I said. "And you…" I trailed off, glancing at the sky. "Will you go back to the moon tonight?"

He looked to the sky. "The moon is at the apogee of its orbit," he said. "Tonight, it would take me several hours to return. If you wouldn't mind…"

I nodded, waving for him to follow me as I headed toward the town.

We walked until we found wet soil in the shadows of Izumo. Once more, I pulled us down from the clear night air into the thick darkness of Yomi, the hard tiles of the courtyard slamming against our knees.

But instantly, I knew that something was wrong.

Chiyo was running toward me, tripping over her skirts. Chiyo never ran.

"Your Highness!"

I flinched at her harsh tone.

"Where have you been?" she said. As she finally reached me, she collapsed onto the stone courtyard, falling onto her hands and knees.

"What is the meaning of this?" I asked. "I've hardly been gone a few hours."

Chiyo shook her head, gasping for breath.

"Your Highness," she said, "your brother has returned."

CHAPTER 08

"They came just after you left," Chiyo said, the three of us running toward the palace.

I shoved open the main gates, charging through the shadow guards, who evaporated at my touch. I knew from the footsteps behind me that Tsukuyomi was hurrying after me, but I didn't have time for him anymore.

"Where are they?" I said, spinning around in the lobby when Neven didn't immediately appear. *Tell me!*

Chiyo flinched, bowing at a ninety-degree angle. "The throne room," she said. "We tried to keep them in the west wing, but they're rather—"

I took off running.

I couldn't feel my legs as I sped down the hallways, my whole body filled with a strange numbness, save for my heart thundering in my chest, so painfully loud that I was sure the whole palace could hear it. I tripped over my sandals and kicked them off as I crashed around a corner, yanking up handfuls of my skirt so it wouldn't get in my way. My servants pressed themselves against the walls to let me past as I tore through the labyrinth of hallways.

Neven is here, I thought. *Only a few doors stand between us now.*

I felt light, like I'd been buried alive for the last ten years and only now had clawed my way back to the surface. Finally, this nightmare would end. I could finally give Neven the safe and quiet place I'd wanted for him since we first set foot in Japan. I could stop stealing human hearts and try to be a goddess instead of a monster.

The sound of shouting drew me to the throne room. Without hesitation, I slammed the doors open.

My shadow guards were restraining a man and woman in the middle of the room, their clothes and skin dripping with darkness like black paint, a pool of it on the floor around them, bleeding toward the open doorway. The man elbowed the guard and spat out a curse in a voice that wasn't Neven's. I would know his voice anywhere, but this one was low and cracked and bitter and not my brother's at all.

It's not them, I thought.

My brother was a teenager and his Yōkai was a child. My guards knew this, and yet they'd dragged two adults into my palace. All of the hope I'd felt moments ago evaporated, leaving behind a hollowness so vast and hungry that it swallowed up everything around it—the words from my lips, the tears from my eyes, even my racing heartbeat, which was now so slow that I wondered if it was beating at all. How stupid I'd been to think that Neven would just waltz out of the darkness without my help.

I closed my eyes so I wouldn't have to see the strangers anymore. The last of the adrenaline faded away and I felt like the ruins of an ancient city crumbling to dust. I gripped the edges of the doorway so I wouldn't fall to my knees, my hands trembling against the wood frame. I turned around just as Chiyo and Tsukuyomi finally caught up to me, pausing a careful distance away when they saw my face.

"How dare you," I whispered.

Chiyo shrank back at my voice. "Your Highness?"

"How dare you!" I said, grabbing Chiyo by the shoulders. The language of Death slithered past my tongue, my shadows winding their way around Chiyo's throat. "You know what my brother looks like, Chiyo! You've seen him! Is this a joke to you?"

"Your Highness, please!" Chiyo said, pulling a muddy, circular object from her sleeve. "He was carrying this, so I thought—"

I snatched the object and dropped Chiyo to the floor. She coughed and gasped as I scrubbed away the tar of deep darkness from the object's surface.

It was a silver-and-gold pocket watch.

There were teeth marks on the outside, and though the glass inside was shattered, the hands still turned. *This is Neven's clock*, I realized, cold shuddering up my spine. I thought Hiro had thrown it away ten years ago. How could these strangers have found this?

"Ren!"

I turned around just as the man sank his teeth into one of

the shadow guards, tearing out a piece of darkness and spitting it at my feet.

"Ren, tell them to stop!" the man said.

He's speaking English, I realized. A language no one had spoken to me in a decade. And how did he know my name?

I held up a hand and the guards tightened their grips on both the man and woman, forcing them to still where they knelt on the ground. The woman stared at me with wide eyes, while the man panted and scowled, spitting out more inky darkness onto the floor.

I sank to my knees in front of him, the bitter cold of the deep darkness bleeding through my skirts. Though his eyes were bloodshot from the sting of night dripping into them, they glowed a distant blue, then flashed green like the changing hues of a rushing river. I reached out a trembling hand and combed the slick darkness from his hair. It splashed to the floor, revealing streaks of white blond hair.

"Release them," I said, my voice trembling.

The guards evaporated, freeing both the man and woman. The man stared at me, and even through all the dirt and darkness, the signs of age that didn't make sense, I knew.

"Neven?" I said, the word so quiet that no one but another Reaper could have heard it. I was so afraid to speak his name out loud, afraid that he would say "no" and all the weight of Yomi's darkness would crush me. There was so much that I didn't understand, but even without his glasses, he had those same eyes that I'd known for over a century.

I reached out to wipe more of the sludge from his face. I had to see more, had to be sure.

He slapped my hand away.

The sound shattered the delicate silence of the room. Chiyo

gasped and the guards forced his hands behind his back, but I could only look at him as he stared back at me with so much sun-hot anger.

"Don't touch me," he said, each word grated out through clenched teeth.

I blinked, unable to speak. He looked so much like Neven, but his gentleness was gone. I turned to the woman, who lay still beside him. Her features were unfamiliar, but I could still remember the same moon-bright eyes of the Yōkai who had ruined my plans ten years ago. This had to be Neven and Tamamo No Mae.

"What happened?" I asked. "Why are you older? You look my age."

He pressed his lips together, glancing around the room as if looking for a way to escape. He squinted, probably trying to make out shapes without his glasses. For a moment I thought he would refuse to speak to me.

"How long has it been?" he finally said.

"Ten years," I said, my voice cracking.

He scoffed. "Only ten?" he said. "I used up more time than I thought."

His clock felt cold and heavy in my hand. Had Neven and the Yōkai hidden out in stopped time for a reprieve from whatever chased them in the deep darkness? All this time, I'd thought that Hiro had destroyed the clock, but Neven must have managed to grab it before he was thrown into the darkness, and it had likely saved his life. But at what cost? For him to look my age, at least a century had to have passed.

I wanted so badly to hug him, but if he wouldn't even let me touch his face, surely he'd push me back. After ten years of waiting for this moment, he was still so far away.

"Let him go," I said to the guard. He released Neven, who winced and rolled his shoulders.

There was so much I wanted to say to him, but where could I even begin? My poor, sweet brother who had given everything for me, who I thought I'd killed, had finally come back to me. No words could express all the things I had to tell him. *I love you more than the universe, more than I could show you in a thousand lifetimes.*

"I'm sorry," I said, tears caught in my throat. "Neven, I'm so sorry."

He stared back at me like I'd slapped him, his features sliding into a deep frown.

"Do you think your words mean anything to me now?"

His eyes burned brighter and brighter blue, like the hottest molten iron, and my breath caught in my throat. I deserved Neven's wrath, but I hadn't expected it. The Neven I knew was kind and forgiving.

"Do you truly think that's enough?" he said, his voice rising. "I spent centuries in darkness after you promised me…" His voice trailed off, tears streaking through the sticky tar on his face. "The other Reapers used to tell me to ignore you. They said that standing by you would ruin my life, and they were right."

My heart, already slow beating and cold, stopped entirely. My lips went numb, unable to form words.

"I left my home for you," Neven said, "I would have died for you, Ren. But I'm glad I didn't, because you wouldn't have done the same for me."

"Neven," I whispered, every part of me petrified where I knelt in the pool of darkness. This was wrong. All of this was wrong. I was supposed to hug Neven and never let him go again. The nightmare was supposed to be over. I could finally keep him safe, and we could live together in Yomi like we'd planned a decade ago.

"And where is he now?" Neven said. "Your fiancé, who was so much more important to you than me."

I shook my head. "Gone," I whispered, the only word I could manage. "Neven—"

"Good," Neven said. "I hope you sat alone in your darkness every day since I left."

I closed my eyes and prayed that I would wake up, that all of this was some horrible dream and I was back in London, where I would be reaped for my crimes. That would have been easier than this. I had imagined a world where I was alone forever, suffering for my mistakes. I had imagined a world where the shadow guards brought back Neven's body, and I drowned all of Yomi in darkness to feed my endless grief. But I had never imagined a world where Neven didn't love me anymore.

My sweet, kind, and gentle Neven was gone. Finally, he understood how it felt to carry so much anger inside of you that you wanted to drown the whole world in night. I had always wanted him to be more like me so I wouldn't have to apologize for my sharp edges or feel so monstrous when juxtaposed against his kindness. Finally, my wish had come true.

He stood up and walked past me. For a moment, I thought he was leaving me and I whirled around to grab onto the hem of his kimono or his ankles or his shoes—anything to keep him from walking away. But he didn't head for the door. Instead, he grabbed Izanami's katana from its hook above my throne, moving with more speed and grace than I'd ever seen before as he tore it down from the wall, the display hooks clattering to the floor. The guards swarmed him, but halted the moment he brought the blade to the back of my neck.

"Stay back!" he said to the guards. The Yōkai was the only one who didn't back away at once, her eyes flickering between me and Neven.

I should have been scared that Neven wanted to hurt me, but all I felt was the hot sting of blood where the blade scored my skin and a cavernous expanse of darkness unfolding inside of me, swallowing all the world's cold black oceans and starless nights and colorless mornings.

"You promised me," Neven said again, but this time his words were wet with tears, his hands shaking with the weight of a god's sword, scraping lines into my neck as it trembled against my skin. "You promised not to leave me in the dark."

Tsukuyomi took a step forward from the doorway, like he was about to interfere.

I turned just enough to look up at Neven, his face still streaked with darkness.

"Do it," I said.

Neven tensed, the blade stilling. Tsukuyomi froze.

"What?" Neven whispered.

"Do it, Neven," I said again, closing my eyes. "If it's what you want, then do it. Please."

I didn't want to die. I didn't want to find out where the damned souls of Reapers and Shinigami went after Death. But if I had truly hurt Neven this much, then I deserved whatever punishment he saw fit.

"Your Highness!" Chiyo said.

"Do not interfere!" I said, making all the servants cower. "That's an order!"

Chiyo looked between me and Neven, paralyzed by my

command. I closed my eyes again, tears dripping hot onto my hands. I remembered when Neven had first been born, when I'd realized I didn't have to be alone anymore, when he'd stood up for me against the other Reapers, when he'd followed me across the sea. He'd given me all the love in the world, and I'd thrown it away. Of all the horrible things I'd done, betraying Neven had been the worst. I deserved a fate worse than his, worse than Hiro's.

The longer he waited, the more that fear started to curl its cold fingers around my heart. I would never go to heaven, if such a thing existed. Maybe I would burn in eternal fire, or maybe I would be nothing at all, unmoving and unbreathing, frozen in nothingness for eternity. I started to shake, feeling like Neven had stopped time and was keeping me locked in this moment before death for all of eternity, wondering when the blade would fall, when my whole world would go dark and never light up again.

The blade clattered to the floor beside me. I looked up as Neven took a few halting steps backward, looking at me like I was more horrible and fearsome than any Yōkai. He wiped tears from his eyes, then grabbed Tamamo No Mae's hand and hauled her to her feet, storming toward the door.

I held out a hand, my shadows rushing across the floor and slamming the door shut.

He spun around. "I let you live, so you keep me trapped down here?" he said, slamming a fist against the door.

"Neven," I said, my whole body still shivering, "there are Reapers aboveground looking for me. They could capture you and use you as bait."

"So we're going to be your prisoners?" he said, his face red, veins standing out in his neck. The Yōkai winced at the tight grip on her hand but said nothing.

"Neven, they'll kill you!" I said, the sudden volume in my voice startling him back against the wall. For a single moment, the anger left his face. I turned away before it could come back.

"We've been in the darkness for centuries," Neven said, his voice softer now. "I won't stay here any longer."

I turned to the Yōkai, who still hadn't said a word. She didn't look angry like Neven, yet her round eyes focused vacantly on me, like I was a motion picture and she wasn't actually in the same room, just watching me from another world.

"I'll take you to sunlight," I said, tearing my gaze from the Yōkai. "I'll be there in case any Reapers appear. But it's night in the human world right now. So please, Neven, stay here. Just for tonight."

We watched each other from across the room like strangers trying to make sense of each other. Neven finally nodded.

"Chiyo," I said, looking to her because it was easier than looking at Neven. Instantly, she stood at my side. "Show them to the guest rooms. Take care of them and give them whatever they ask for."

Chiyo bowed, first to me, then to Neven and the Yōkai. "This way," she said.

I did not watch them leave. I could only listen to their footsteps growing quieter down the hallways, the servants filing out.

Tsukuyomi approached me, but I only stared at the floor.

"Please leave," I said. I didn't have the energy to explain anything to him right now or hear his unsolicited thoughts.

But instead of speaking, he picked up Izanami's katana,

wiped it clean on the immaculate white sleeves of his kimono until they were stained black, then set it back on its hooks. He picked up another object, wiping it off as well, and knelt before me, offering it to me in the palm of his hand.

It was Neven's clock, now shining silver once more.

I reached out and took it from him, his fingers startlingly warm as they brushed mine. I cradled the clock close to my chest.

Tsukuyomi rose to his feet, offering me a hand. "Goddesses do not kneel in puddles of deep darkness," he said. But unlike when he'd first come to my palace and his words reeked of condescension, now his voice was gentle.

"Goddesses do not do many of the things I have done."

"You might be surprised," he said. "But kneeling here is beneath your dignity."

I wasn't sure if that was true, but I let him pull me to my feet anyway. Was this how Tsukuyomi had felt when his sister threw him down to Earth? It was all too easy to imagine being ripped from the sky and tossed down like a shooting star, all my flesh scorched off in the atmosphere, all my bones turned to dust on impact.

"What did you do?" I asked.

Tsukuyomi paused, but the look on his face told me he knew exactly what I meant.

"There was nothing to be done," he said. "I went back to the moon, because that is who I am, and that is what the world requires of me." His words were perfectly even, so impassive that I knew they couldn't be real.

But he was right. The world required many things of me as well.

I left Tsukuyomi and headed to my room, where I could

finish my mourning in private, feeling as though the world had broken into one thousand sharp pieces.

One hour later, I knocked on Neven's door. How strange it was to knock on doors in my own palace, when in the past I'd simply burst into any room and demand that its occupants leave.

It wasn't Neven who answered, but Tamamo No Mae.

I could see my own silhouette reflected back in her round, black eyes, like two pools of ink. When I'd last seen her, she'd been a child, but now she could be my age. She looked less like the duckweeds she'd been named after and more like the chrysanthemums that grew around the palace lake, regal and exquisite, perfect in their symmetry. She had a face that could start wars and bring great kingdoms to their knees.

"Thank you for letting us stay here," she said. Her words were like poetry. Surely no one had ever spoken Japanese as sweetly.

"Where is my brother?" I said, ignoring her comment.

"In the bath," she said, nodding to the room behind her. "He let me go first."

"Didn't Chiyo give you separate rooms?" I said, gritting my teeth.

"Yes," the Yōkai said, "but Neven said you might kill me if he left me alone for too long."

I sighed, pressing a hand to my forehead. "I'm not going to kill you, Yōkai." Neven already hated me, and hurting his only companion wouldn't help my case. Besides, if she meant him any harm, it would have been easy enough for her to kill him in the century of deep darkness and blame it on a monster.

"I know," she said, shrugging. "But boys aren't always very smart."

She wasn't wrong. My thoughts drifted to Tsukuyomi, still hovering somewhere in the palace.

"I also wanted to thank you for taking me from my village," she said.

My skin went cold. "What?"

"When I was a child," she said, "I remember that I was going to be sold to the yakuza, but it was your idea to take me away."

"You remember that?" I said, wincing at the thought of Hiro spearing her grandmother with a katana. "Why are you thanking me instead of being angry that I sent you to the deep darkness?"

"Because I know you didn't mean for us to go there," she said, her voice light, as if centuries in darkness had truly not mattered that much to her at all. "Besides, Yōkai can see what's inside people's hearts. I know what's in yours, Ren."

I forced myself to stand still, to not recoil. How could a Yōkai know what was in my heart when I didn't know myself?

"You don't fool me," I said at last. "I know what you are, and what you've done."

I expected her to get angry at me, for fox ears to tear from her scalp and fangs to descend as she ripped a bite out of my throat. But instead, her lips pressed into a crooked line, her posture drooping like a sunless flower.

"In all of my past lives, I was raised as a prize, or a whore, or a weapon," she said. "No one ever cared for me. I could see it in their cruel hearts. But, for the first time in thousands of years, I met someone who wants nothing from me."

She paused, glancing over her shoulder toward the bathroom, then lowered her voice.

"I cannot change what I've done," she said, "but in this lifetime, I am not the same. There is no place for that kind of hatred to take root. Neven has shown me nothing but kindness."

I narrowed my eyes, but the Yōkai just stood there like a wounded puppy, her eyes too round and sad. It could all be an enchantment, of course, but if there was anyone whose love could soften even the cruelest person, it was Neven.

Before I could answer, Neven stepped out from the bathroom, dressed in a white kimono like what Tamamo No Mae wore, his hair wet. I was amazed again at how much taller he was than before, but still far too thin, like time had stretched him upward but not outward. His white blond hair had grown too long, falling over his eyes. He could pass for my older brother now. But even though his features were the same, the look in his eyes, the earnestness and innocence, was gone.

"Mikuzume?" he said, squinting at the scene in front of him. That was the name Tamamo No Mae's grandmother had called her, the one Neven had always insisted on, probably because that name didn't carry the weight of all the kingdoms she'd destroyed. "What's going on?"

"I'm going for a walk," the Yōkai said. "I want to see the murals." Then she slipped past me without a word, skipping barefoot down the hallway.

Neven blinked at her sudden departure, gaze sliding over to me. His eyes were probably narrowed because he couldn't see well, but I still hated being the focus of his glare. I would have to tell Chiyo to get him new glasses.

"I can feel you judging me even if I can't see your face well," he said, turning away and grabbing a towel. "She's still a child to me, Ren, even if she doesn't look like one anymore. She's like my sister."

You already have a sister, I thought. But I said nothing, stepping inside and sliding the door shut behind me. I took Neven's clock from my kimono and set it on the table by the door.

"Your clock," I said quietly, unsure how much he could see without his glasses. He hummed in acknowledgment but didn't turn around.

"I came to tell you about the Reapers," I said. It was easier to pretend this was a strategy meeting or a business transaction, because to Neven I was only a host and not his sister. "Some of them are in Japan, killing my Shinigami. I've enlisted the help of the god of storms and seas, but I need to do a task for him first."

"Okay," Neven said, still facing away from me as he ran a towel through his hair.

I started to step forward into the room, but thought better of it.

"I probably won't have time to come back here every night," I said.

"All right," Neven said.

"I need to know what you want."

Neven froze, finally turning around. "What?"

"I need you to be safe," I said. "You can stay here in Yomi with my guards, or you can come with me and Tsukuyomi, where we can watch and protect you." Selfishly, I prayed he'd choose the latter. I didn't trust my shadow guards who had already thrown him to the deep darkness once. The only one who could watch over him, who would lay their life down for him, was me. And more than that, I didn't want him to leave again, even if it meant both of us would be in danger. Just like before, I was selfish. I wanted Neven with me at all costs. The idea of him slipping away while I was gone was unbearable.

"I went without your protection for years," Neven said, his words bitter but his face merely exhausted. "I learned to slay monsters with my bare hands even in total darkness. I don't need you."

"You know how dangerous High Reapers are, Neven," I said, ignoring his words so I wouldn't start crying in front of him. That was something to think about later, when I was alone.

Neven sighed and nodded. He was the one person in Japan who didn't need to be convinced of the true danger of Reapers. While he'd likely survived for so long in the darkness because of his clock, he had no advantage over a High Reaper who could turn time more skillfully than him.

"I don't want to keep you trapped here, Neven," I said, "but you can't just walk around Japan when the Reapers will use you to get to me. Unless…" I trailed off, and for a moment all I saw was a horrifying image of Neven on a ship sailing away. "Unless you wanted to go back with them?"

Neven hesitated, and I wished that I was standing on soft soil so the shadows could drag me down and I wouldn't have to hear his answer. But this floor was firm and unyielding and I had no choice but to stand and wait.

"You've seen Reapers here," he said at last. "Was Father among them?"

My mouth felt too dry, my throat full of sharp rocks. It shouldn't have surprised me that Neven still wondered about Ambrose, even after he'd called him a coward in front of the

High Council. While I thought of Ambrose as a dark stain on my life that grew fainter over the years, to Neven he would always be his father.

"No," I said, the word coming out harsher than I'd meant it to.

Neven nodded like he'd expected that answer, staring at the wall. After a moment of silent thought, his shoulders fell. "Even if I wanted to go back with them, I don't think they'd let me bring Mikuzume."

"You would bring her back to England?" I asked, unable to stop myself.

"She has no home, after what you and Hiro did to her village."

I winced. I'd been referring to her history of enchanting emperors and overthrowing governments, not her lack of family. What would she do to the poor queen if set loose in England?

"She's not a danger," Neven said, like he could read my thoughts. "I spent centuries with her, Ren, I would know. Even as a child, she protected me."

I shuddered, imagining what she would have protected him from.

"What happened?" I said quietly. "What was the deep darkness like?"

Neven went very still. He was no longer breathing, his eyes a dull blue-gray that shifted slowly, like ice melting.

"I don't want to talk about it," he said, closing his eyes. When he whispered, his voice sounded just as young as I'd remembered.

I hesitated before my next question. I shouldn't ask, but if Neven and the Yōkai had survived the deep darkness, perhaps they weren't the only ones. My mother had been cast into the darkness as well.

"Did you see anyone else there?" I said. "Any Shinigami?"

He shook his head. "No one."

The disappointment was sharper than I'd expected. I learned of my mother's death a decade ago. It wasn't supposed to matter anymore.

"So what do you want, Neven?" I asked. "Do you want to stay here or come with me?"

He turned toward me, looking vaguely in the direction of my face.

"I spent centuries in darkness," Neven said. "I won't stay there any longer."

"Okay," I said, a warmth filling my chest. Neven was finally back with me again. And though he was angry with me now, he had a soft heart. Over time he would come to love me again, and we'd have the peace we'd been chasing for so long.

"But once the Reapers are gone, I'm leaving."

My stomach dropped. I scrambled for excuses but found none. Once the Reapers left, there was no reason to keep Neven here. Other than the fact that I wanted him here, but what I wanted didn't matter to Neven anymore.

"Oh," I said, unable to even pretend it was okay, that any of this was okay.

I stood there, just in front of the doorway, with so much I wished I could tell him. That I was prepared to eat every human heart in Japan if it meant he'd come home safely, that I'd spent years becoming a monster because I loved him and how could that not matter to him at all? Neven had come home, but my brother hadn't.

I watched his back as he resolutely looked away from me,

and for the second time that day, bitter tears stung my eyes. *Gods don't cry*, Tsukuyomi had said.

"Is that all?" he said.

I swallowed, afraid my next words would come out teary and weak. "I'll have Chiyo find someone to make you new glasses," I said.

"Thank you," he said, the words so formal and distant that I wanted to scream.

I turned toward the door, even though walking away from Neven again felt like saying goodbye forever, as if I'd wake up in the morning and he'd be gone.

"Who is he?" Neven said before I could leave. "The man who was with you."

I paused, silently grateful not to have to leave yet. "You mean Tsukuyomi?" I said. "He's the moon god, Hiro's brother."

Neven shot me a deeply unimpressed look, somehow more condemning now that he was older.

"It's not like that," I said. "He was sent here to help me stop the Reapers, and his father won't allow him to leave."

"If you really wanted him gone, he wouldn't be here."

I opened my mouth to argue, but no words came because Neven was right. But he didn't understand that it wasn't Tsukuyomi I wanted here with me.

"I don't understand," Neven said, "why, after everything that happened with Hiro, you're so willing to trust his brother."

"He's here because he's useful to me," I said. "That's all."

Neven frowned, turning away from me and lying on his side.

"You can make the same mistake a thousand times, Ren," he said. "But this time, I won't take your punishment for you."

CHAPTER
09

At dawn, I stood once more in my throne room after a night of shallow sleep. Izanami's katana hung above my throne, its jeweled scabbard reflecting the weak light of my candle, the blade curved like a faint but wicked smile. I set my candle down and pulled the sword from its display hooks, unsheathing it. The light shimmered off its clean surface, wiped free of blood, thanks to Tsukuyomi. I held the blade to my finger to test its sharpness and it instantly bit through my skin, blood coating my palm and rushing down my sleeve.

"Wow," a small voice said from the hall.

I turned to find Tamamo No Mae hovering in the doorway with wide eyes, gaze fixed on the blade. As she stepped inside, I wiped the blood on my black kimono, sheathing the blade once more.

"Can I touch it?" the Yōkai asked, already touching it as she knelt on the ground before me, running her fingers across the gold detailing in the scabbard, the jewels woven into the handle. I indulged her for a moment before tucking the sword into my obi.

"You're going to use that when we meet Amaterasu?" she said.

"I don't intend to," I said, "but we need godly weapons when dealing with gods." I thought back to my encounter with Susano'o, how unprepared I'd been in the face of his power. The knives in my sleeves were fine for slitting Reapers' throats or threatening Yōkai, but I doubted they'd scare the sun goddess. Even if I didn't need the sword, I wanted her to know that I had it. That I had won it.

"And that could actually hurt her?"

I frowned. "It's the sharpest sword on Earth," I said. "It could destroy anything it touches. It could slice through your skull down to your toes like cutting through cream."

I'd hoped my bluntness would discourage the Yōkai from talking to me, but instead she clapped and bounced on her heels.

"Could it cut Matsuzaka-gyū?"

I stared back at her. "This sword has beheaded people. You want me to use it to cut beef?"

The Yōkai pouted. "It's so difficult to cut thin strips."

"I'm leaving," I said, heading outside rather than listen to her anymore, though she trailed behind me all the same.

We arrived in the courtyard just in time to see Neven throwing Tsukuyomi into the lotus pond.

The Yōkai gasped, rushing forward. "Neven, don't!"

As Tsukuyomi peeled the lily pads from his eyes, Neven

landed a solid punch on Tsukuyomi's jaw, connecting with a crunch that made me wince. Tsukuyomi blinked in disbelief, cradling his jaw, then swiped his leg under Neven, sending him spilling onto his back in the water. The Yōkai stood flapping her arms at the edge of the pond as if she could distract Neven, but I was far less concerned. If Neven meant any serious harm, he would have used his clock.

"Why are you two mauling each other in my pond?" I said, crossing my arms.

Tsukuyomi froze at the sound of my voice, but Neven took the opportunity to lunge at him, sending them both into the shallow water with a splash that gushed over my toes. I sighed, looking to the Yōkai, who stood wide-eyed at the edge of the pond.

"Would you please?"

She nodded, managing to grab Neven's arms and force them behind his back while I hauled Tsukuyomi out of the water. He rose to his feet, smoothed his wet hair out of his eyes, and put on an expression that might have been dignified if he didn't look so much like a half-drowned dog. Neven panted, jerking away from the Yōkai but making no move to attack again.

"What is going on?" I said, making no effort to hide the exasperation in my voice. We were supposed to be fighting Reapers and visiting gods, not quarreling among ourselves like children.

"Self-defense, clearly," Tsukuyomi said, his words a bit slurred. He held his jaw in both hands and popped it back into place with a sharp motion, wincing.

I turned to Neven, waiting for an explanation. I wasn't exactly shocked that he was distrustful of someone who looked so much like Hiro, regardless of whether Tsukuyomi actually meant him harm. But if he told me Tsukuyomi had hurt him, I would have fed the moon god to the deep darkness myself, and surely Neven knew that.

"Nothing," Neven said, looking away from me. He moved to the edge of the pond and swiped a pair of glasses off the ground, settling the round frames on his face. I had no doubt the glasses were Chiyo's doing—she could probably drain the seas and rearrange the stars with ease, but only if she felt inclined to do so.

I turned to Tsukuyomi, who merely shrugged. I pressed a weary hand over my eyes and pointed back at the palace. "Just go change quickly. And try not to kill each other."

When they finally returned in dry clothes, we set off for Mount Tate just before sunrise in the human realm, when most of the world would still be dark. I could only bring such a large group through shadows that were deep and wide, not thinned out by afternoon sun, and even then, traveling through them often felt like clawing my way out of my own grave. Carrying three people with me would make the task even harder. I wouldn't try to squeeze us through narrow strips of half darkness, lest I accidentally leave one of us stranded in the Earth's core or some equally terrible in-between world. Plus, in the early morning, there were fewer humans to see us and interfere.

When I held out my hands to pull the other three up through the shadows, Neven switched sides with Tamamo No Mae, forcing me to take the Yōkai's hand instead of his. I took Tsukuyomi's hand in my left and the Yōkai's in my right and extinguished my lantern so that Neven couldn't see the look on my face, couldn't know exactly how much it stung. Then I dragged us up to Earth a bit more violently than usual, tearing through darkness that slapped against our faces and tugged at our clothes and shattered like glass as we crashed through it.

We emerged in the shade of a rocky mountain, a flatland of puddles in hellish shades of red spread out below us, the echoes of volcanic chaos. Above us, Mount Tate sloped upward until it disappeared in a veil of clouds and snow, and below us the world rolled forever downward off the edge of the plateau. I could only bring us this far, for higher up the mountain was nothing but steep stony paths and loose rocks, no soft soil that I could pull us through. Tsukuyomi had said this was the closest of Japan's three Holy Mountains, tall enough that it could carry us to Ama No Ukihashi, the Floating Bridge of Heaven that would take us to the sun palace.

The pale sunlight, softened by the whisper of clouds, felt like an omen of death as it broke over the horizon—a mocking reminder that an entire day had passed since the Reapers had warned me of Ivy's arrival, and yet I was still completely unprepared. If it took me so long just to make a plan, how was I supposed to actually find and return a long-lost sword in only three days? The clouds shifted below us, revealing the gray coast in the distance, and I imagined Ivy's ships arriving on the shore, their anchors biting into the sand, Reapers sparkling across the city in time flashes, the ocean swirling with red as they bled humans into the brine. Then the clouds covered the town once more, leaving me feeling far too cold, my stomach tight with dread.

Neven fell to his knees in the red dirt.

I stepped forward, but Tamamo No Mae reached him first, kneeling beside him and setting a hand on his shoulder. He turned his face up to the sun, still pale on the horizon, but he drank up the light on his bare face anyway, eyes closed, arms spread out wide. Guilt curled in my stomach. Neven had lived for so long in the dark. But he didn't want my comfort anymore.

I turned away, facing the mountain sloping upward into the sky, imagining where the sun palace might appear. Tsukuyomi had said that the task wouldn't be as simple as it seemed. Maybe Amaterasu would only share her knowledge in exchange for something valuable. Maybe she would ask for all my dead servants, or the power of a thousand souls, or Izanami's katana. I would hand over any of those things without hesitation.

"We should start walking," Tsukuyomi said. I looked over my shoulder, but he was speaking to Neven and the Yōkai, not me. "Humans may arrive soon, and if any of them are in sight, the bridge won't appear. We've already been delayed by our...swim."

"I haven't seen sunlight in centuries," Neven said, glaring at Tsukuyomi over his shoulder. "Surely, you can spare a few minutes."

"We are going to the sun palace," Tsukuyomi said, glancing at me as if I could decode Neven's anger. "I assure you, there is sunlight there as well." Coming from anyone else, the words might have been biting, but Tsukuyomi seemed to genuinely not understand Neven's hesitation.

Neven huffed out a breath, then stood and shoved past Tsukuyomi, heading up the mountain. The Yōkai frowned as she watched him walk off, shooting Tsukuyomi a bitter look, then hurried after Neven. From the back, now that the Yōkai's hair was long like mine, it was easy to pretend I was watching myself walking side by side with Neven. A brief flash of anger, as quick and sharp as a snakebite, rushed through me, ripping back the skin of my hands and exposing raw bones.

Get rid of the Yōkai, Izanami's voice whispered in my ear.

"Shut up," I said under my breath, crossing my arms to hide my hands. "That won't make Neven forgive me."

Tsukuyomi gave me an odd look, but I pretended not to notice as the ground grew steeper.

The four of us climbed the mountain, loose rocks rolling away under our feet, the air growing thinner, the mountain below us slowly swallowed up in a haze of mist, like it had all been a dream. Ahead of us, Neven laughed at something the Yōkai said, and my blood burned despite the chill of mountain air around us.

"You're angry."

I looked to Tsukuyomi, consciously unclenching my fists. I chanced a glance at my hands and let out a breath when I saw they looked normal again. "You're brilliant," I said, shooting him a glare.

"I am," he said, shrugging, "but anyone could have made that deduction."

"You don't need to say all your thoughts out loud, you know."

"If my thoughts never interface with the outside world, then what use are they?"

"Get a journal."

Tsukuyomi said nothing, and for a moment I thought I'd actually silenced him.

"Your brother is not a god," he said.

I sighed. "He's also not a raccoon. See? I can make deductions too."

Tsukuyomi shook his head. "What I mean is that gods are very good at holding grudges. Our hearts are cold. They have to be, in order to witness so much death and suffering among the humans."

Tsukuyomi's gaze bored into me with an unusual intensity as he spoke, like he was trying fervently to win a one-sided debate. "But lower creatures have softer hearts," he said. "They can't hold on to their anger for quite as long."

I shook my head, glancing at Neven and Tamamo No Mae, who were kicking rocks down the mountainside and watching the fog inhale them. "I don't think my brother's heart is soft anymore," I said. "Not for me, anyway."

"If it wasn't, he would have beheaded you when you gave him the chance. Your severed head would be on the floor of your palace and we wouldn't be having this conversation right now. Since you would be headless."

I looked up at Tsukuyomi, but he was staring straight ahead, apparently satisfied that he'd made his point. "Are you attempting to console me?"

He frowned. "I am reminding you of facts. If that consoles you, I have no objection to it."

I couldn't hold back a laugh. Tsukuyomi raised an eyebrow, but I offered no explanation.

"What can I expect from Amaterasu?" I asked, rather than elaborate. "What is she like when she's not…" *throwing you down from the sky?* "…upset?"

Tsukuyomi frowned, staring up at the clouds. After a moment, his expression softened. "When we were children, she was always interested in stars," he said. "I think it's because there's no one else like her but other stars, no one who has the same kind of raw power. It's as if her true family is many universes away. I think she always felt lonely."

His words grew quieter as he finished speaking, his gaze dropping to the path. He walked beside me but seemed very faraway.

"I wasn't really asking about topics for small talk with her," I said, my words flat because I didn't know what else to say to his sudden sentimentality.

Tsukuyomi turned as if he'd forgotten I was there. "Of course," he said. "I'm sorry, I was just thinking out loud."

"When are you not?" I said, rolling my eyes. "What I meant is, how dangerous is she? Is she going to slay me on sight?"

He shook his head. "She wouldn't do that. I told you of her anger, but she never laid a hand on me until I…" He trailed off, face gray.

I narrowed my eyes. "She sent you to eat vomit."

"She didn't know about that," he said, his words far too soft as he mumbled them to the pebbles beneath our feet. "I don't think she even knows now."

"You never told her?" I said. I stopped walking, but Tsukuyomi glanced nervously at Neven and the Yōkai, tugging my elbow to keep me moving. Clearly, he didn't want their attention on us.

"How could I, when she threw me from the sky?" he whispered.

"But that was thousands of years ago!" I said. "You never—"

"Ren." The coldness in his voice halted my words. "Our paths only cross briefly during solar eclipses. That's not enough time to explain, and there are no words that will bring our sister back to life."

"But I can—"

"She's not going to believe you," Tsukuyomi said, his voice quiet. "She'll just think I lied to you and become even angrier."

I wanted to argue, but for once, Tsukuyomi's face pinched in as if he was genuinely distressed and not just disapproving. I closed my mouth and we ascended the path in silence.

As we walked higher around the mountainside and the air grew thinner, the path beneath us began to rumble as if waking from a long sleep. Small rocks began to spill down the mountain, clouds of dust rising around our feet.

"Is it an earthquake?" Neven asked.

The Yōkai sniffed the air, edging closer to the mountain, away from the path. "I don't think so."

"You can sense earthquakes now?" I said. It was a genuine question, but the look Neven shot me said that I'd sounded more cross than I'd intended.

"There's anecdotal evidence of animals acting erratically before natural disasters," Tsukuyomi said. "Yōkai, do you feel a sudden urge to flee? Or burrow into the ground?"

"She's not an animal," Neven said through clenched teeth.

"Well, technically I am," she said, shrugging. "But no, nothing like that."

I looked to Tsukuyomi, flinching when I saw how close to me he'd moved, as if he could somehow shield me from an avalanche with a body that looked as sturdy as a string bean. I took a deliberate step away from him.

"Do you feel that?" the Yōkai said, cocking her head to the side.

We all fell silent. The rumbling beneath us had crescendoed to a hungry gurgle, leaves on the trees shuddering as the ground trembled.

She took a step closer to the mountain.

"It almost sounds like—"

The mountain burst open, a spray of dirt and rocks raining over us in a bruising hail. The first thing I saw were eyes—ten feet tall and searing gold with a thousand interlocking prisms in a honeycomb pattern—then two sweeping antennae slicing through the air like whips, crashing into the nearby trees and tipping them over as easily as teacups.

The beast unhinged its jaw, revealing three rows of needle-like teeth and hooked fangs, breathing out a gush of burning hot air that smelled of deep earth and bones. It let out a sound like old machinery croaking back to life, and lunged forward.

I grabbed Neven's arm and yanked him toward me, sending both of us spilling down an incline, crashing into an uprooted tree. Tsukuyomi dived in the same direction, rolling easily back to his feet.

But the Yōkai hadn't moved at all.

The beast surged forward and swallowed Tamamo No Mae whole.

CHAPTER ❀ 10 ❀

I stopped time the moment Neven began screaming. His voice cut out, leaving me alone on the still mountain, staring down the beast that had burst from the earth.

It was the color of soil found deep below the ground, the wet black-brown layers of earth where bodies were buried. Its shell was polished like marble, a thousand tiny legs arcing in different directions beneath it.

A centipede, I realized. Mountains were often occupied by Yōkai called ōmukade—giant centipedes that thirsted for blood. While the humanlike Yōkai respected me far more than Izanami for the simple fact that I left them alone, it was impossible to explain a change in leadership to animal or insect Yōkai.

I touched Neven and Tsukuyomi on the backs of their necks, jolting them both into the time freeze.

Tsukuyomi looked around wide-eyed at the frozen scene. Arriving in stopped time felt like leaving the mortal plane and being dropped into a glass museum, where nothing truly existed but you. To someone used to staying on the natural timeline, the feeling must have been disorienting.

Neven shot to his feet, rushing toward the beast and calling the Yōkai's name. I lunged forward and grabbed him by the back of his collar before he could reach it.

"Don't touch it!" I said. "You'll pull it into the time freeze!"

He yanked away from me but thankfully stood still, his expression pinched. Any one of us, having stepped off the natural timeline, could awaken others by touch, so it wasn't quite as simple as slaying the centipede and pulling out the Yōkai from its mouth.

"Mikuzume—"

"She's fine," I said. "She's lived for thousands of years. An insect isn't going to kill her." I didn't know if that was true, but I didn't want Neven to get upset.

"Besides, she's Buddhist," Tsukuyomi said. "If she's suffered puncture wounds from the teeth or been dissolved from digestive acids to the point of death, she'll just be reincarnated somewhere else in Japan."

I grabbed Neven just before he lunged at Tsukuyomi.

"You're not helping," I said to Tsukuyomi.

"I thought it would be reassuring," he said, shrugging.

Neven finally pushed away from me. "I could have helped her!" he said. "You pulled me away!"

"You are not as strong as a Yōkai," I said, crossing my arms. I'd probably saved his life, or at least saved him the trouble of regrowing a limb, but I couldn't expect gratitude for something he hadn't asked me to do. If I didn't get Tamamo No Mae back, there was no way he would ever forgive me.

He let out a frustrated scream, kicking a fallen tree that splintered apart. "Now what?" he said. "If we can't touch it without waking it up, how are we supposed to get her back?"

I stepped around Neven, pausing a few feet from the Yōkai's flank. I drew my katana, giving an experimental strike against the shell. Cracks raced across the surface, a steaming black liquid gushing out, scorching the grass. I backed up, raising my sleeve to shield my face as the scent stung my eyes. This didn't seem like the easiest way to get Tamamo No Mae back, unless I wanted my flesh scorched from my bones. I conjured my shadows, but they fluttered around me like silk ribbons, gently caressing the ōmukade's face—this high on the mountain, nearing the sun palace, there was little shade or darkness that I could control.

"I think that the Yōkai would still be close to the mouth," Tsukuyomi said at last. "Perhaps we can cut her out from there, rather than trying to kill the creature?"

Neven rushed toward the ōmukade's mouth at Tsukuyomi's suggestion. I tried desperately to keep my expression neutral as I came face-to-face with the giant insect, its prismatic eyes casting my own reflection back at me in gold a thousand times. Its mouth was wider than the double doors to my palace, and its face was coated in fine black hairs.

Insects are not the most fearsome creatures you've seen, even if they're big, I told myself, my hands uncomfortably tight around the katana. I drove the blade into its mouth, splitting the flesh above its lip easily, but the blade clinked against a hard surface and would go no further.

"Probably the teeth," Tsukuyomi said, kneeling closer to examine the Yōkai, as if he saw these every day and they were no more notable than ants or squirrels.

"Would touching teeth pull it out of a time freeze?" Neven said. I looked over to where he knelt in the dirt, his expression queasy. "Maybe we can wrench its jaw open."

I shuddered at the thought of going inside the Yōkai's wet, cavernous mouth. "I suppose," I said. "We were always told it was skin that connects us across a time change. Hair doesn't wake people up, so teeth might be the same."

"This creature doesn't have skin," Tsukuyomi said. "What were you taught about exoskeletons?"

"Nothing, because there are no giant insects in England," Neven said, shooting Tsukuyomi a harrowing look and rising to his feet. He held out a hand to me, and for a moment I thought he wanted to help me to my feet.

"Give me your knife," he said instead, his expression stern.

I drew one of my knives from my sleeve and placed it in his hand.

Without so much as flinching, he bent down before the mouth of the Yōkai and plunged my knife into its lip with a wet squelch, dragging the blade to the side. I thought back to the young Neven who had shuddered away from spiders the size of his fingernail.

"I suppose we're dissecting it now," Tsukuyomi said, holding out his hand. "I would like to participate."

I sighed and placed my other knife in his hand. "Don't touch the ōmukade with your bare skin," I said.

"I gathered that," he said, plunging the knife to the left of the creature's mouth with unnerving stoicism. Between the three of us, the Yōkai's flesh quickly began to fall away, leaving its yellowed teeth exposed as if it were grimacing at us. I knelt before it, reaching a tentative hand out.

"And what is your plan if it wakes up?" Tsukuyomi said, my hand hovering inches from the teeth. "If touching its teeth does actually awaken it and you get swallowed as well?"

"We stop time again," Neven said, crossing his arms.

"And then we'd have two people stuck inside of it instead of one, and then what? Touch its teeth and wake it again?"

I sighed, examining the creature's face for any weak points. I knew most of my Yōkai well, but I hadn't taken the time to memorize how to kill each and every one of them.

"Then you stab its eyes," I said at last. That seemed like a safe bet. Most creatures, human or beast, weren't very effective at attacking with daggers in their eyes. "I'll cut my way out from the inside with Izanami's katana."

"*You* will?" Neven said, rising to his feet. His voice might have been intimidating if I didn't know that he used to cry over dead squirrels.

"Yes, *me*," I said. "The one with Izanami's katana."

Neven narrowed his eyes. "Mikuzume is my friend, not yours."

And you're my brother, I thought, but didn't want to say out loud in case Neven responded with something terrible like *not anymore*.

"Aren't you here to see sunlight, not the inside of a centipede?" I said.

"I'm not going to sit here and let her die!"

"Neither am I," I said. "Be reasonable, Neven. I've eaten thousands of souls this week. I can handle a centipede."

Neven's expression withered. Even in his anger, he must have known that I was right. His grip on the dagger loosened.

"Just be ready to help me, okay?" I said. Back when he still wanted to be my brother, that request had always centered him.

He swallowed, finally nodding and stepping aside. Tsukuyomi was already in position near the Yōkai's left eye, my dagger in both hands.

I crouched down before the Yōkai's mouth, held my breath, and reached forward.

Its tooth was cool to the touch, like marble. I let out a breath when the creature didn't instantly burst to life and devour me. I ran my hands across the grooves of its crooked teeth, feeling around for a surface to grab that wouldn't slice my hand open.

The teeth on either side of its fangs had a wide enough base that I managed to slip my hand under them and yank upward. The beast was stiff from time freeze, but he was still just a Yōkai, and I was strong enough to crush skulls like grapes. I jammed a foot between the creature's upper and lower teeth, gripped his top teeth with both hands, and wrenched his jaw open.

The stench nearly forced me to my knees. I clung onto the creature's teeth but couldn't hold back a retch as the smell of half-digested flesh came over me in waves.

"Breath through your mouth!" Tsukuyomi shouted.

"Can you see her?" Neven asked.

My eyes watered, but through the cavernous darkness I saw Tamamo No Mae's white kimono and long hair. She lay on her side on the bed of the creature's ribbed tongue, facing away from me. Despite the disgusting circumstances, she looked peaceful in her sleep. I thought back to when I'd broken into her house so many years ago and found her sleeping beside her grandmother. She was the same now, so soft and unguarded. Not like Reapers, who slept with one eye open and a dagger under our pillows.

"She's here!" I called over my shoulder.

Neven sighed in relief behind me.

"Has she dissolved in venom?" Tsukuyomi said.

"I'm going to murder you," Neven said, followed by sounds of scuffling behind me that I didn't care to address.

"She's in one piece," I said. "I just have to..." I hesitated, my gaze trailing around the inside of the creature's mouth, wet with spores, lumpy from the tongue's many textures. I would have to go inside without touching anything with my skin, or the creature would wake and I would end up in its stomach.

Tentatively, I released my hands from the teeth, and the time freeze thankfully held the gaping jaw in place. I stepped onto the tongue, grimacing as my sandals squished, saliva bleeding over my socks.

I tried desperately not to think about what awaited down the back of the creature's throat ahead of me, where the darkness converged into a tunnel. I didn't think about how one rolled ankle or careless stumble would send both me and Tamamo No Mae plummeting into a vat of stomach acid, where a time freeze wouldn't help us. And I didn't think about how much I absolutely hated insects.

The shadowed depths of the ōmukade's throat provided just enough darkness for my shadows to wrap around Tamamo No Mae's arms and drag her toward me, but the closer to the sunlight they came, the weaker they grew. Toward the front of the mouth, they struggled to move her at all.

"Hand her to me," Neven said when she reached the teeth. But that was easier said than done. My shadows were too weak to lift her, and I didn't want them to drag her across three rows of needle-sharp teeth.

I grabbed her under the arms, careful not to touch her bare skin, then tried to wrap a hand under her knees, but her limbs were stiff from the time freeze and wouldn't bend. Her outstretched hand bumped against my neck, and she jerked awake with a gasp.

She thrashed away, probably not realizing that the danger had paused. I tried to keep her in my arms, but the texture of the ground was too uneven and I stumbled forward. She fell onto her hands and knees, sinking into the tongue.

All at once, the beast roared to life, letting out a harrowing wail when it realized it had been maimed. The sound blew us back against the teeth with a blast of sickening hot air. The creature's whole body shook as it tried to swallow us down, tilting its head back so we began to slip down its throat.

I grabbed onto one of its fangs and snatched Tamamo No Mae's wrist before she could tumble down, holding on even as saliva and the creature's black blood wet my hand. In the distance, I could hear Neven and Tsukuyomi shouting, but it was hard to make out any words over the creature's wails. The Yōkai was whimpering below me, so I swung her up until she could grab the teeth as well.

When the creature screamed once more, I began to wonder if I would ever be able to hear again. That is, if I got out of this alive. The sound was like a thousand church bells hammering away at once. The world lurched and righted itself, slamming us into the tongue. Then the violent shaking stopped, the beast now only trembling and lurching nauseously from side to side.

"Ren!" Neven called, his voice muffled behind the rows of teeth. "We pinned its head down! You have to get out now!"

Pinned its head down? I couldn't pause to consider how they'd managed that. Instead, I jammed my feet between the teeth and began wrenching its jaw open once more.

This time, it fought back.

I could barely raise its jaw an inch before it nearly severed my fingers, the sharp teeth knifing into tendons before I adjusted my grip. It felt like I was trying to force the Earth off its axis. Beside me, the Yōkai screamed, clinging onto the teeth as the creature tilted to the side.

I pushed back with all the strength I had, my shadows stripping the thin darkness from the cave of the creature's mouth and congealing into arms that fought to pry its jaw open. I held its teeth apart even when they gnawed past the flesh of my palms and bit down on bone, even when my arms trembled so hard that any moment they could shatter. The gray sky came into view, as did Neven's and Tsukuyomi's frantic faces. They'd managed to stab my knives through the beast's antennae, holding its head close to the ground.

"Go!" I said to Tamamo No Mae. "Get out, now!"

Her tearstained face turned to me. "Ren, how will you—"

"Just go!" I shouted in Death, the words laced with more malice than I'd ever spoken before, but it did the trick. The Yōkai scurried across the rows of teeth and tumbled onto the ground.

Blood rushed down my wrists, my sandals starting to splinter.

Then Tsukuyomi was in front of me. At first I thought he wanted to catch me, but he reached for my obi, pulling out Izanami's katana. With one quick stroke, he sliced through a muscle on the side of the ōmukade's mouth and its jaw went slack. With the sudden lack of resistance, I fell forward into the dirt, rocks and soil stinging my lacerated palms. The creature let out a sorrowful wail as it shuffled backward into the tunnel from which it had emerged, leaving a giant cavern behind it like a gaping mouth.

Something crushed me back into the ground. The world was still spinning with adrenaline and I nearly drew my sword, but it wasn't there anymore. After a moment, I registered that it was only Tamamo No Mae, her arms around my neck and her face pressed into my collarbone.

"What's wrong?" I asked, trying to get a look at her face. Had the ōmukade's teeth cut her open? Had its acidic saliva seared her palms? But I saw no blood or burns on her face, just moon eyes wet with tears. "Why are you crying?"

"Because you saved me!" she said, pressing her face to my chest and rubbing tears and snot into my clothes.

"That's hardly worth crying over," I said, but I let her cling to me anyway as my palms stitched themselves back together. "Obviously I wouldn't feed you to an ōmukade." As irritating as I found her, that didn't mean I wanted her eaten. Something about the Yōkai was just so frustratingly pure, despite her past. In a world of death and blood and agony, it was so easy to sink deeper and deeper into my role and forget that the rest of the world was different. Tamamo No Mae made it hard to forget.

"Thank you," Neven said, kneeling beside us, his eyes fixed on the ground. For the first time since he'd returned, Neven's voice sounded as soft as I'd remembered it. But I didn't want him to start thinking I was a good person. He would only end up disappointed.

Tsukuyomi gently took my wrist and examined my palm, a line of fresh pink skin slashed across the center.

"If everyone is all right, I suggest we keep going," he said. "There are no centipedes in the sun palace."

Neven managed to separate me from the Yōkai, who sniffled and wiped her face on her sleeves. The four of us rose to our feet and climbed higher and higher into the sky, eager to get off the mountain. Tsukuyomi hovered closer to me than before, sneaking not-so-subtle glances at my healing palms. It might have been endearing to someone less cynical than me, but I couldn't help feeling like a prized cow that Tsukuyomi had to bring home healthy in order to get his day's wages.

We weren't far from the mountain's peak—a small platform of rock floating in a sea of clouds, the air so thin that it was hard to think without dizziness spinning my thoughts off-kilter.

"Now what?" Neven asked, clinging to the Yōkai's sleeve as he peered over the edge.

"Now we cross the bridge," Tsukuyomi said, offering me his hand. I looked down at it, then back at his face.

"The bridge..." I echoed, trying to make sense of his offered hand.

"The bridge will unfold for gods," he said, as if that answered my question.

I raised an eyebrow. "Are we not gods if we're not holding hands?"

"Our combined powers should be enough to unfold it," he said. "You're a new god, and my sister is not fond of me, as you know, so our powers might not have much weight here. I think this is our best chance of not falling all the way down the mountain."

"There's a chance of that?" Neven said, taking a step back from the edge.

Tsukuyomi shrugged. "There's a chance of almost anything. But our odds would improve immensely if..." He trailed off, extending his hand once more.

I sighed, glancing back at Neven, who did little to hide the disapproval on his face. But I didn't particularly want to tumble down the mountain either. I placed my hand in Tsukuyomi's.

Warmth pulsed from his hand into mine, spreading from my palm, down my arm and through my chest. Without meaning to, I thought of Hiro holding my hand on the beach, his grip tight enough to drag me to the ends of the Earth with him. Tsukuyomi squeezed my hand, then stepped off into the sky.

For a moment, the clouds rushed away and the gray sky yawned open wide beneath his feet, ready to swallow him. I ground to a halt before I could follow him into the open sky, my grip on his hand bone crushing.

But the breath before he would have crashed down, a great ribbon of clouds unfurled before us, as if an invisible brush had drawn a single white stroke across the sky. The bridge of clouds spanned endlessly forward, disappearing at an unseen point in the distance. Tsukuyomi's foot sank into it with little resistance, as if it were new snow. I took a tentative step behind him, one foot still grounded on the mountain. The clouds held my weight, their strange warmth wrapping around my ankles. Tsukuyomi tugged my hand and I stepped fully onto the bridge, dizzy at the thought that I was now standing on the sky.

I looked back at Neven and Tamamo No Mae, who stood frozen and wide-eyed on the mountaintop.

"Come on, you won't fall," I said, reaching out a hand.

I'd expected Neven to flinch away, but he grabbed onto me without thinking, squeezing my fingers as if I alone was keeping him tethered. He looked up at me and jolted when he seemed to realize what he'd done, but he didn't let go.

I gave him a gentle pull and he stepped up onto the clouds beside me.

Tamamo No Mae watched us with wide eyes, then leaped forward onto the bridge, a swirl of clouds spraying up around her.

"Mikuzume!" Neven said, releasing my hand and grabbing hers.

"It's fine," she said, grinning and batting the spinning mist from her face. "It's like a pillow."

Neven sighed, his shoulders finally relaxing. I turned to Tsukuyomi and realized I was still holding his hand, then pulled mine away with as much politeness as I could muster.

We crossed the bridge that arced across the entire afternoon sky, mist swirling all around us. Sunlight chased away the chill of the clouds, the bridge growing brighter the farther we went. Every now and then, the clouds parted with the passing wind, and we caught a glimpse of the world below, green fields and blue oceans and silver cities too far away to be real.

"It's harder to get to the sun palace than the underworld," I said, growing wary as the end of the bridge never seemed any closer.

"Amaterasu is reclusive," Tsukuyomi said. "She wasn't always. When we were children, we would sit among the clouds while she cast her rays down on Susano'o's sea, as bright as she possibly could." A soft smile crossed his face. "The light bounced off the waves and looked like the whole sea was made of liquid diamonds, a thousand colors all at once."

"Would she do that for us?" the Yōkai asked, latching on to Tsukuyomi's sleeve.

He jolted away from her touch. "There are too many humans to do something like that now," he said. "People would notice."

The Yōkai pouted and released Tsukuyomi, who inched farther away from her.

Soon, the sky grew warmer, no longer soft and comforting but a crushing heat that rippled across the horizon in shimmering ribbons. Tsukuyomi stopped walking.

"This is as far as I can go," he said.

The three of us turned to him. "What do you mean?" I asked.

"The sun and moon can only cross paths during an eclipse," he said, staring past us into the haze of heat waves. "That is my sister's rule. I'll wait for you here."

I nodded, unsure what else I could do. As strange as Tsukuyomi was, and as much as his resemblance to Hiro unnerved me, the idea of being alone with Neven and Tamamo No Mae was far more uncomfortable.

"You're quite close to the palace now," Tsukuyomi said. "Tell my sister..." He trailed off, shaking his head. "Don't tell her anything, actually. But be careful. The sun may be beautiful, but she can still burn you." He waved us off, swallowed up by the heat waves as the Yōkai pulled us farther down the path.

She walked next to me, forcing a reluctant Neven to also stand beside her, the three of us walking in a line. Any silence between me and Neven used to be easy, but now it made my palms sweat and fingers twitch like when humans spoke to me, like my skin was too tight against my bones.

Tamamo No Mae took hold of my arm. I frowned, glancing over at her, but she only looked straight ahead at the ever-brightening light before us, her other arm looped around Neven as well.

"Gods don't often concern themselves with Yōkai, you know," she said, looking up at me. "Now I will have met two goddesses in two days. Not many Yōkai have that honor."

Maybe it was the glow of the approaching sun palace, but her smile beamed uncomfortably bright, more warmth and kindness than I was used to seeing directed at me. I looked away, squinting at the vague shape of a palace in the distance.

"You've grown up in darkness," I said. "What do you even know about other gods and Yōkai?"

"She knows more than you do," Neven snapped.

I shot him a glare, but the Yōkai shook her head. "No, no I don't know more than Ren. I just have some hazy memories of past lives." She turned to me. "Neven told me how much you studied back in England. He said you speak five languages."

Neven had talked about me in the deep darkness? I looked at him, but he had turned away, staring out across the clouds so I couldn't read his expression.

Before I could consider it further, the Yōkai gasped.

"Look!" she said, bursting into a run and dragging both me and Neven forward with surprising strength.

Perhaps she'd sensed it with her Yōkai abilities, or maybe it was a testament to the poor eyesight of most Reapers, but somehow Tamamo No Mae had spotted the sun palace before us, a tiny twinkle of light among the haze of clouds.

The Yōkai was like a shooting star dragging us across the sky, refusing to slow down even when Neven stumbled or my skirts caught under my feet. Every now and then she looked over her shoulder, grinning.

"Hurry up!" she said. "I want to see what a palace outside of Yomi looks like!"

As we drew closer, the mist of clouds lifted, revealing a building of blazing light.

The complete opposite of my castle in Yomi, the sun palace was built from glittering white light, radiating a welcoming glow across the courtyard of clouds. It had the familiar tiers and sloped roofs of the other palaces I'd seen across Japan, but while other castles were fortresses meant to keep out intruders, this palace seemed to draw us closer, the warmth massaging the tension from my shoulders, pulling me by the hand as if beckoning me home.

We came to a stop before the palace's great white doors, towering ten stories high, smooth like polished sunbeams.

"Should we knock?" Tamamo No Mae said, already beating her fist against the door, the sound echoing across the sky. "I want to see the inside."

"What if she's dangerous?" Neven said, gently pulling the Yōkai away. "Should we really just show up on her doorstep?" But it was too late to consider that. Footsteps were already echoing from beyond the doors.

We stepped back as the doors opened outward, revealing an enormous hall paved in golden tiles and massive windows that bathed the palace in warm sunlight. A servant in a yellow kimono stepped into the doorway, his eyes a glowing amber. He scanned the three of us, his gaze finally settling on me.

"Welcome, Goddess Ren," he said, dropping to the floor in a deep bow. "Goddess Amaterasu has been expecting you."

CHAPTER 11

I swallowed even though my throat felt full of glass, praying my voice came out at least a little goddess-like. Neven and the Yōkai turned to me, waiting for my response while the servant remained bowed at my feet. I wasn't used to this kind of reverence outside of Yomi. My guards certainly weren't this formal when greeting guests at my palace. On more than one occasion, I'd overheard Chiyo throwing open the front doors and screaming *What do you want?* at visitors. Tsukuyomi's criticism of how I ran my palace made a little more sense now.

"How did she know I was coming?" I said at last.

"She saw you approaching from Mount Tate," the servant said, still facedown on the ground. "I am under strict instructions to welcome in everyone but her brother."

"He's not here," I said. "And you can stand up."

The servant rose to his feet. "In that case, please follow me." He took a step back against the doors, holding one of them open for me and bowing at the waist.

"Your Highness—" he began, but Tamamo No Mae rushed inside first.

"Come in and see this!" she called. Neven hurried in after her, and I followed them both inside as the servant closed the door with an expression I recognized well from Chiyo as barely concealed disdain.

The golden tiles of the foyer warmed my feet, the gentle heat wafting up to my knees. The glass windows in the main hall seemed to magnify the sunlight, casting glittering prisms across my vision. I had to shield my eyes and lower my gaze to the floor, too used to the darkness of Yomi. Even Neven, who had craved the sunlight, looked pained by the display.

The Yōkai flopped down on the floor, pressing her cheek to the tiles. "It's so warm," she said, closing her eyes.

The servant hovered over her, hands twitching like he wanted to grab something. "Miss, we have chairs if you'd like to take a rest. The floor is rather…"

"Undignified?" I said. "Get up, Mikuzume." I didn't exactly want to call her by her Yōkai name in front of Amaterasu's servant. Flaunting the fact that I was dragging an ancient evil Yōkai around with me wasn't likely to win me any favors.

The Yōkai pouted but rose to her feet. The servant led us out of the foyer into a smaller hallway where the lighting mercifully lessened, revealing an endless length of paper doors and murals just like in my palace, but these ones were backlit with white light instead of shadows. I slowed down as I realized that these paintings were different from my own, not just the style but the stories they told.

My palace's murals only showed Tsukuyomi as a man sitting on a crescent moon after he was born from Izanagi's tears. But on this mural, Tsukuyomi had his feet planted firmly on Earth, wrapped up in a kimono of stars and moons, his teeth as sharp as a wolf's, eyes empty and searing white. The Tsukuyomi in this mural tore apart another goddess with his bare teeth—Ukemochi, I assumed from the banquet surrounding them—bathing the room in blood, strands of intestines dangling from his mouth. In the next panel, Amaterasu descended from the sky and pulled the remaining crops from Ukemochi's body, planting fields of rice on Earth. Tsukuyomi vanished from the following panels, like he'd ceased to exist.

"Your Highness?" the servant said.

I turned to find everyone else halfway down the hallway, waiting for me to follow. I shook my head and hurried after them. It made sense that Amaterasu's version of events would be different from mine, casting her in a more positive light. But I couldn't scrub the image of Tsukuyomi with hollow white eyes from my mind.

"Hmm," the Yōkai said, crossing her arms as she looked around. "I think your palace is prettier, Ren."

The servant's face twitched, but he wisely ignored the Yōkai. We reached another large set of doors, these ones glowing bright white from under the seams.

"Your Highness," the servant said, knocking on the doors. "The Goddess Ren and her companions are here."

Without waiting for an answer, he slid the doors open and stepped aside to let us through, bowing once more.

We entered a room of gold-flecked marble that either had no ceiling at all or one of perfectly cleaned glass, letting the pure rays of sunlight glow over us.

Amaterasu sat on her throne at the top of a tiered platform, shrouded in a dress all the colors of fire, rippling gently like a breathing flame. Her skin glowed pale gold, her black hair lightened to amber in the sun. She smiled down at us, and all the coldness of the mountain mist bled from my body, as if I was standing in a warm bath of light. She was like late afternoons in autumn, when the sun reflected off the changing leaves and all the world was blazing gold. She looked like she could create the whole universe with a single smile and end it with a touch of her finger. I wanted to fall to my knees, for that felt like the only proper thing to do in the face of such majesty.

Neven and Tamamo No Mae could not resist the pull, falling to the ground and bowing deeply. Though my knees shook, I forced myself to stand up straight. *You are her equal*, I told myself, even though it didn't feel true.

I knew from Izanami, Hiro, and Tsukuyomi that gods were supposed to command power and majesty, radiating perfection that had nothing to do with physical beauty—it was the way that the whole world seemed to hold its breath as they spoke. Real gods walked through the Earth knowing it belonged to them, knowing they could crush it in their bare hands and start the universe all over again if they felt so inclined.

But out of all the gods I'd seen, Amaterasu radiated the most power, the most strength. It was hard to even piece together a sentence in front of her. Surely my words were so pale and insignificant that the sunlight would scorch them away the moment they left my lips. I looked down at my black kimono, covered in red mud and centipede saliva. Tsukuyomi had called it commoner's clothing. My shoes trailed dirt in behind me and the mist of clouds had left my hair frizzy and tangled. My skin felt pale and raw from my time underground, itching from the concentrated sunlight. I was a soiled rag doll standing before the sun goddess.

Worst of all, her intense sunlight drank up my shadows as if parched, the bright light tearing through the cloak of darkness trailing behind me. I tried to stretch the darkness out once more, but my shadows didn't answer, chased away by the sun. Dread hummed through my bones like the low tone of a church organ.

"A creature of Death has never before climbed all the way up to my palace," Amaterasu said. Though she sat high up on a platform, her voice sounded as if she had whispered it in my ear. "What brings you here, Ren of Yomi?"

Ren of Yomi, I thought. No one had ever called me that before. For once, I was not Ren of London or Ren of Yakushima, but defined by the one place that had been my choice to find, the place I had taken for myself. I straightened my back, looking up directly at Amaterasu, even as the sunlight seared shapes onto my vision.

"I'm looking for Kusanagi No Tsurugi," I said. My voice echoed across the marble floors, thready and young compared to Amaterasu's, but at least there was no fear in my inflection. "I was told that you know where to find it."

Amaterasu tipped her head back and laughed. I had barely even spoken, yet I was already a joke to her?

"You already carry my mother's sword," she said, nodding to the katana by my side. "Now you want my brother's as well? Those swords were not designed for two-handed combat."

"It's not for me," I said. "Susano'o wants it back."

"Ah," Amaterasu said, rolling her eyes. "He's sent you on

his errands, has he? Men are so predictable. Tsukuyomi runs around doing cartwheels if father asks him to, while Susano'o goes to such impressive lengths to avoid doing anything at all. You shouldn't trust my brother so easily, you know."

"I..." I paused, the sunlight sapping all the moisture from my mouth, making it hard to form words. "Which one?"

"Either of them," she said, leaning back in her throne. "They are disgraced for good reasons."

I thought back to the mural of Tsukuyomi sinking his teeth into Ukemochi's stomach. But that was just how Amaterasu saw him, wasn't it? And I already knew Susano'o's dark story. At least, according to Tsukuyomi.

"I saw you ascend the mountain with Tsukuyomi, and now he's not here," Amaterasu said, resting her chin on her hand. "Have you left him sulking outside in the clouds?"

You know exactly why he can't come any closer, I thought. "He is respecting your wishes," I said instead, since that seemed more diplomatic, and I still needed Amaterasu's cooperation.

She sighed. "Hardly. My wish is for him to stop existing. But at least now I only have to see him every solar eclipse. It's unfortunate, but can't be helped."

I thought of the look in Tsukuyomi's eyes when he'd told me of his sister turning the sea to diamonds, the soft smile on his face that for once hadn't felt forced. How could she speak of him so flippantly? She was lucky I couldn't call my shadows.

"It doesn't matter to me what you think about your brothers," I said, because I didn't want to talk about Tsukuyomi anymore. "I need Susano'o's help, so I need the sword."

"My useless, banished brother refuses to help you, so now I must?"

I grimaced. "I'm not asking for charity," I said, praying the conversation wouldn't go downhill quite as fast as my bargain with Susano'o. "Tell me what you want in return."

Amaterasu smiled. "You think there's anything you could offer me that I don't already have? You, a newborn god? How cute."

"You must want something," I said. "Everyone wants something. Even a goddess."

Amaterasu hummed, drumming her fingers on the arm of her throne. Then she rose to her feet, all the light in the room shifting with her, as if the sun had arced higher in the sky. She glided down the tiers of her platform, the long train of her dress spilling behind her like liquid gold. As she drew closer, the warmth of the room increased, waves of heat wafting over me. She was painfully bright to look at, but I couldn't tear my gaze away.

She came to a stop right before me, at least a foot taller than me. I felt like I was trapped in a kiln, the air around me flaying my skin, making my eyes sting and water. I reached for my shadows reflexively, but still they couldn't break through the sunlight. I was all of Yomi's darkness and she was all of Earth's light, and now that we were face-to-face, it was clear who was stronger.

Neven and the Yōkai had already taken a few steps back, repelled by the heat, but I forced myself to stand firm, not to show weakness.

"And what would you know about being a goddess?" she said. She reached out and touched my cheek, her hands like a brand on my face. I couldn't help but wince as her sunlight spread into my blood, like it was ripping open my veins.

"Everything has a cost," I said, my words stiff, trying not to show pain at her scalding touch. "Believe me, I know that."

"Do you?" she said, tilting her head, eyes flaring gold.

I swallowed, wanting to pull away but not wanting to cower. This wasn't going how I'd hoped. There had to be some way to gain the upper hand. I tried to block out the sting of her touch and focus on what I knew about Amaterasu. What would make her listen?

There's no one else like her but other stars, Tsukuyomi had said. *I think she always felt lonely.*

Amaterasu didn't seem particularly lonely. But I could begrudgingly admit that Tsukuyomi was pretty smart, or at the very least knew more about Amaterasu than I did. I took a steadying breath. "I can bring the stars to you," I said.

The searing hand on my face suddenly turned freezing cold, the contrast so sharp that I couldn't help but flinch away. Amaterasu's hand fell to her side.

"What?" she said, the word ominously quiet.

"Four of my Yōkai are constellations," I said, my teeth chattering from the cold, the words sticky in my mouth. "I could tell them to come to you."

I couldn't decipher Amaterasu's blank expression, and her silence wrung nervous words from my mouth. "Tsukuyomi told me that as a child, you wanted to meet the other stars so you would feel less alone. I thought—"

"Tsukuyomi said that?" Amaterasu said, her voice low.

I nodded, somehow feeling that this wasn't the answer she wanted.

Amaterasu shook her head slowly. "My brother should know better than to act as if he knows me," she said, the words strangely frail.

"I think he only meant—"

"It is far too late for Tsukuyomi to start caring about what

I want," Amaterasu said. Tears pooled at the corners of her eyes, the liquid trapping the sunlight, like melted gold was running down her face.

I glanced back at Neven for help, but he could only gape wide-eyed at Amaterasu. I could handle angry gods, but *sad* ones? I cleared my throat, searching for the right words. "I think he has always cared," I said slowly. "If you listened to him, you would see that."

But that was the wrong thing to say.

Amaterasu's eyes narrowed, a single tear rushing down her face. When it hit the ground, the world went dark.

Night slammed down on all sides. A coldness gripped me, squeezing my bones until they felt like they'd shatter apart. I tasted blood as dryness cracked my lips, my hands suddenly numb and unresponsive.

"Neven?" I said, turning around.

"I'm here," he said, reaching out and gripping my arm. Even through my sleeve, his touch burned with coldness, and he shivered so violently it was like he was shaking me back and forth. The Yōkai whimpered somewhere in the darkness.

At the sound of shattering ice, I turned back toward where Amaterasu had once stood. She knelt on the ground, the floor slowly cracking beneath her palms like the fractured surface of a pond, threatening to drop us into open sky. Her amber hair looked starkly black, her gown no longer glimmering but drowning her in pools of pale silk.

"Amaterasu?" I said, taking a careful step forward.

She looked up, her eyes hollow black, inky tears bleeding down her chin. Her breath came out in shuddering clouds, her whole body racked with shivers, like her bones were alive, trying to tear free from her skin.

I remembered the mural in my palace where Amaterasu had fled deep inside a cave, abandoning the world to perpetual night. Even though darkness reigned in Yomi, the land of the living needed sunlight to survive. What would happen to the humans if the sun hid her face again? The chilling coldness creeping through my bones was enough of an answer—everything would end.

"Do you know what it's like to visit your sister and see her gouged to pieces?" Amaterasu said, her words echoing as if we were trapped in an endless cave. *"Do you know what it's like to carry the universe on your shoulders while your brothers burn down your fields and slaughter your family? Do you, Ren of Yomi?"*

I couldn't answer, my teeth chattering so hard that I couldn't form words. The floor shuddered and cracked, wind howling through the gaps beneath my feet, misty clouds rising to my ankles. I tried to back away from the fragile ground, but the cracks followed me, the floor yawning wider as it opened up to the screaming sky below. My shadows spun around the room, greedily drinking up the darkness, but they couldn't help here. The palace needed sunlight to hold it together, not more shadows. If the floor cracked wide-open, would it drop us from the heavens all the way down to Earth?

"Do not insert yourself in matters of the original gods," Amaterasu said, slamming a palm into the ground, more cracks shooting across the floor. *"Whatever horrors you think my brothers are capable of are nothing but a raindrop in the sea of their depravity. You have no idea what they can destroy."*

"I'm sorry!" I said, the words choked out of me, the cold pulling the air from my lungs. "I understand!"

Amaterasu took a deep, trembling breath. Then slowly, light spread from her palms across the floor, the cold thawing as brightness pooled beneath us, mending the cracks and spreading up to the ceiling. Neven and the Yōkai sagged against me, but I somehow managed to keep myself standing, even as my knees shook.

Amaterasu remained kneeling on the floor, her hair once again a warm amber.

"This world was entrusted to me," she whispered. "I cannot trust men who try to destroy it, even if they are my family. I cannot afford to make mistakes while holding the world in my hands. It is far too fragile."

She looked up, her eyes still murky, but with thin whispers of gold flickering through them like koi fish in a pond. "I do not want to meet your Yōkai, Ren," she said. "It would be an uneven exchange, because I don't know where the sword is."

I clenched my jaw, fighting the urge to break something. I hadn't expected Amaterasu to have the sword lying around in a coat closet, but I'd expected her to at least have an idea where to send me. "I thought you were all-seeing," I said, as politely as I could manage through clenched teeth.

Amaterasu's eyes narrowed. "I have seen many things, Ren, such as everything you've done in the human realm the past ten years. You're not exactly a traditional Death Goddess, are you?"

"What?" Neven whispered behind me. I tensed, praying that Amaterasu didn't choose that moment to casually mention the several thousand souls I'd eaten on Neven's behalf.

"You told me not to interfere in your business, so you stay out of mine," I said with all the firmness I could muster while staring directly into the sun. Harsher words burned on my lips, but I didn't want to send her spiraling into darkness again.

She doesn't respect you, Izanami said, *so she has no reason to help you.*

I gritted my teeth, hating that Izanami had a point. None of the gods respected me, and I was letting them push me around too easily. Surely, between the goddess of the sun and the god of storms and seas, the Reapers wouldn't stand a chance, yet neither of them would help me.

Teach her the true meaning of fear, Izanami said. *If she cries at what her brothers have done, she will crumble when she sees what Death can do.*

I swallowed, thinking of Amaterasu's inky black tears, the sight of her cowering on her knees, her perfect palace shaking apart. All it had taken was a few careless words, and Japan's most beloved goddess had fallen before me. I bit down on my tongue, the pain grounding me as I tried to shove down Izanami's thoughts, ashamed of feeling tempted. Izanami's answer to everything was chaos and death, and that wouldn't find the sword for me.

"I am sorry I cannot help you more, Ren," Amaterasu said. "I do not know where the sword is now, but I know where it *was.*"

I looked up, Izanami's voice suddenly snuffed out. "Where?"

Amaterasu turned and gestured out her broad windows at the world below the clouds. "Thousands of years ago, there was a human named Ikki, who lived in Kagoshima. He befriended many Yōkai, who eventually gave him the sword for safekeeping. But I don't know what he did with it."

I sighed. "A lot can happen to a sword over thousands of years, and Kagoshima is not exactly a small place to search."

"Perhaps not," Amaterasu said, "but it depends on what the sword wants."

I frowned. "How can a sword want anything?"

"It is a godly possession, and a character in a great legend," Amaterasu said, raising an eyebrow at my sour tone. "Objects of great importance are either meant to be lost forever or are waiting to be found. Either way, things touched by gods do not tend to have quiet lives. I suspect that you'll find an answer, one way or another."

I briefly considered smashing my forehead open on her delicate marble floor. I needed a location, not a riddle. I almost preferred Susano'o's bluntness to Amaterasu's lyrical speech. "I'll keep that in mind," I said, which was by far the politest response I could muster. "Is there anything else?"

Amaterasu shook her head. "I'm sorry I've disappointed you, Ren, but I have many other things to do besides keeping watch over my errant brother's toys."

I sighed. "In that case, I think we're done here," I said, hoping Amaterasu wasn't expecting anything in exchange for such an unhelpful answer. I grabbed the Yōkai's wrist, since that would make Neven follow too.

"Wait."

A hand closed around my other arm. At first I thought it was Neven, for the touch was strangely cool, but I turned around to Amaterasu.

"Did Tsukuyomi… Did he have anything to say to me?" she said, unable to meet my eyes.

I hesitated. What did she care, after insulting him so easily?

"No," I said. "Now let me go."

She looked up, and for a moment, her eyes were not glowing gold but earthy brown, almost as if she was human. Then she blinked and the gold returned, although dimmer than before. She turned away, and I didn't wait around for her blessing to leave.

I slammed through the front doors, all but tossing the Yōkai out onto the bridge.

"Damn her," I said, gripping my hair.

"What was she talking about?" Neven said. "What did you do in the human realm?"

I turned away to hide my expression. "I was working. She just doesn't understand people who deal in death," I lied.

"At least she told us something useful, right?" Tamamo No Mae said, and for once I could have hugged her for changing the subject.

"Hardly," I said. "In case you haven't noticed, we don't have a lot of time to kill hunting down humans."

I stormed back across the bridge, eager to escape the damned sun palace and the Yōkai's grating optimism and Neven's dangerous questions.

It wasn't long before Tsukuyomi came into view, staring off the edge of the bridge at the world below. As soon as I saw him, I thought of the clean surface of the moon, and a fraction of my rage fell away from me. He frowned when he saw my expression, stepping closer as I told him what his sister had said.

"Then we need to go to Kagoshima," he said.

I shook my head. "Ikki was human, and he lived there thousands of years ago. He's long dead now, probably on the outskirts of Yomi."

"Yes, exactly. He's dead," Tsukuyomi said, glancing between the three of us. "Do you know what day it is?"

I blinked. The calendar had meant little to me as a soul collector and meant even less now as a deity.

"It's the last day of Obon," he said.

"Obon?" Neven asked, looking to Tamamo No Mae.

"It's a festival of the dead," she said, eyes widening. "Ancestors will return to Earth."

"Not just Earth," Tsukuyomi said. "To their *homes* on Earth. And Amaterasu just told you exactly where Ikki's home was."

"So today, we know exactly where Ikki will be," I said. "At least, until sunset."

If today was the last day of the festival, then at sunset the humans' bonfires would bid the spirits goodbye, sending them off once again to Yomi. It could take years to comb through the outskirts of the darkness in search of someone long dead. We needed to find him tonight.

"Kagoshima is in the southernmost part of Japan," Tamamo No Mae said, looking up at me. "Can you take us there before the festival ends tonight?"

It was a fair question. I'd never carried four people such a distance through shadows. I thought of Amaterasu and her majestic elegance, how she probably wouldn't so much as bat an eye if asked to rearrange the stars. I didn't know if there was a way to gain that kind of power without leaving a trail of corpses behind me, but I would have to try. For Japan, and for Neven.

"Don't be absurd," I said, turning toward the horizon where the late-morning sun was violently bright, burning away the shadows on the mountaintop.

"I can get us there before lunch."

CHAPTER 12

Down in Yomi, the Obon festival meant little more than a few days of empty streets and blissful silence when the spirits of the dead went to visit their families. It had never even occurred to me to see what all the festivities among the living entailed. After all, the idea of an entire festival to honor the dead seemed rather frivolous to me—the dead did not care about pretty lights or dances or food they couldn't eat.

But for Kagoshima, apparently Obon meant all the colors in the world.

In the streets below our perch on the mountainside, paper lanterns striped with red and white and pale green hung in zigzags across the streets, unlit under the afternoon sun. The humans carried bouquets of chrysanthemums to the cemeteries—shades of buttery yellow and burning orange and pale magenta. Even the humans' summer yukata were different shades of cool lavender and blue, unlike the stark white clothes of the dead in Yomi. The air smelled of ashes that fell like scorched rain over the city from the volcano across the water, like a bizarre gray confetti for their celebration.

Though Japan's mountains and forests had become part of the fabric of my soul and were mapped out in my mind, I had never traveled this far south, so close to Yakushima, where my mother had lived. Before I'd known she was dead, I'd wanted so badly to go there and see the wet green forests and blue fires over the water. Now I wanted to stay as far away as possible. Yakushima was just another place that could have been mine if I'd been dealt a different hand.

I'd brought us through the shadows to a mountain just a breath outside the city, where our appearance wouldn't be too conspicuous. Judging by the position of the sun overhead, late morning had bled into afternoon, narrowing our window of time to find Ikki. As much as I wanted to charge into the town, my bones felt like they'd all been crushed and then puzzled back together after dragging the four of us across the country. I held on to the railing and pretended to take in the scenery while I waited for my legs to stop shaking, lest I trip and roll down the mountain or something equally ungoddesslike.

Neven and the Yōkai were already distracted, leaning over the railings and peering in wonder at the city beneath us. I couldn't help but do the same, taking in the sharp scent of Death wafting off the rooftops, a milky white haze hovering above them from the spirits crossing back and forth across the sky. Far in the distance, at the city center, a large pile of wood awaited the departure fires at nightfall.

Tsukuyomi, seemingly indifferent to the wonder of Obon, was scowling up at the sun, sweat dripping down his face.

"I take it you don't spend much time in the south," I said, leaning back against the railing.

He wiped his face with his sleeve, shaking his head. "It's the sunlight," he said. "My sister likes to remind me how strong she is. That's easier to do in the south, where it's already hot."

I raised an eyebrow. It was certainly warmer in the south, but I didn't feel like I was melting the way Tsukuyomi seemed to. "If she were scorching you right now, wouldn't the rest of us feel it too?"

Tsukuyomi glared at me, the intensity buffered by sweat dripping into his eye, making him wince. "I live on the moon. The total opposite of the sun. I am unaccustomed to sunlight."

"And I live in Yomi, in total darkness."

"You make frequent trips to the human realm."

"Yes, but…" I paused, my grip tightening around the railing. "How do you know that?"

"As I told you, the moon sees everything," he said, shrugging. "I watched you collecting souls."

I tensed, the sudden urge to flee rippling up my spine. No one but Chiyo was supposed to know about me breaking the rules, gagging down souls, crying and weak.

"I was just…" I struggled for the words to explain myself. It shouldn't have mattered if Tsukuyomi thought I murdered for sport, but the words rushed to my lips all at once, crashing into each other. "I wasn't trying to—"

"I know why you did it," he said, waving his hand to stop me. "Well, I didn't at first, but your brother came back dripping with the deep darkness. I know my father's rules, so it wasn't hard to figure out."

"You can't tell Neven," I said, glancing over my shoulder to make sure he was still occupied with the Yōkai.

Tsukuyomi frowned. "You think it would upset him?"

"I know it would."

Tsukuyomi gazed past my shoulder at Neven. "I don't understand Reapers. My sister wouldn't even kill a mayfly for me if my life depended on it. Neven should be grateful." Something in his expression had curdled, withering past disapproval into something fouler. I didn't know how to respond, so I turned back to the horizon.

"I can't believe you watched me," I said.

"You make it sound so indecent."

"Is it not?"

His face flushed pink. "It's not as if I watch people undress or anything like that. You only walked around and murdered people."

I laughed, shaking my head. "I would argue that that's a fairly intimate act."

Tsukuyomi said nothing. It was hard to tell if he was still blushing or just getting sunburned. I looked up at the sun, its rays warm but not unbearable. Was Amaterasu really punishing him?

They had both asked about each other, so clearly they both thought about one another to some degree. But it made little sense to me why Tsukuyomi hoped for the approval of someone like Amaterasu who had nothing but a rigid sense of duty, sharp edges, and echoes of pain that hadn't grown quieter after thousands of years. At the thought, Ambrose's face appeared in my mind, his eyes so dim despite their vibrant colors. I supposed we were all drawn to sharp things, against all logic.

I turned to Neven, who was leaning over the railing at the edge of the path, once again turning his face to the sky and smiling while the Yōkai balanced on the ledge. I couldn't help but smile too, though the feeling vanished as I remembered once again why he craved sunlight so much.

"Come on," I said loudly, making them both turn around. "We have to find Ikki before sunset."

If not for Obon, it might have been easy to follow the pull of Death to the nearest cemetery, but as we headed into town, the spirits of the dead began to lead us in different directions.

"It's this way," I said, pointing toward a road that ran along-side a canal of mossy rocks.

"No, the pull is stronger this way," Neven said, pointing toward a street of merchants selling fruits. But then the wind shifted and the smell of Death wafted in the opposite direction. Both Neven and I turned around with it, shoulders drooping as we came to the same realization—it was impossible to trace the scent of Death during Obon.

We were blocking the flow of the crowd, humans parting to stare at us as we lingered. The four of us must have looked quite odd together—two foreigners and two Japanese in muddy kimonos, like we'd just wandered into town from an unsanctioned swamp burial.

"Allow me," Tsukuyomi said.

I frowned. "Allow you to what—"

"Excuse me," Tsukuyomi said, towering over a human pulling a cart of boxes. The human withered under Tsuku-yomi's imposing presence. "Can you tell me where the cemetery is?"

"There are several," the human said, gaze twitching to me

and Neven like we might punch him in the stomach and steal his money. "Which one are you looking for?"

"The one where Ikki is buried."

"Humans wouldn't know that," Tamamo No Mae said, crossing her arms. "We should just find the closest cemetery and I'll smell all the graves. It will be faster that way."

"Humans?" the man echoed, taking a tentative step back.

I sighed and resisted the urge to smack both Tsukuyomi and the Yōkai as the human slowly backed away from us. Tamamo No Mae blushed, grabbing my arm and hiding behind me while Tsukuyomi loudly asked the man what was wrong. Another human crashed into Neven, stumbling and spilling a basket of sweet potatoes across the street. Neven apologized in English as the potatoes rolled under the feet of passing humans, sending them falling to the ground. My face burned. Even in full British attire, I'd never attracted so much attention.

"Excuse us," I said, grabbing both Neven's and Tsukuyomi's sleeves and hauling them down a side street toward the coast, the Yōkai still clinging to my clothes. I didn't let them go until the crowd began to clear, the sea breeze washing away the tangled scents of Death as we reached the shore.

"Have I done something wrong?" Tsukuyomi asked.

"You loomed over a human like you wanted to eat him," Neven said, glaring.

Tsukuyomi blinked. "But I didn't want to eat him."

"Your presence is overpowering for humans," I said, massaging my forehead. "And, Tamamo No Mae, you can't call humans 'humans' to their faces."

"But they *are* humans," she said, pouting.

"And her name is Mikuzume," Neven said, shifting his glare from Tsukuyomi to me.

"It's okay. I have many names," the Yōkai said, still looking toward the street we'd just escaped from. "Do you think that man has any more of those sweet potatoes?"

I bit back a scream of frustration. This would have been easier by myself. Perhaps I could distract the others and run off to find Ikki. But I couldn't leave Neven in case the Reapers found him, and Neven wouldn't abandon the Yōkai, and Tsukuyomi surely wouldn't tolerate being left alone, so it seemed that the four of us had to stay together.

I sat down in the sand to think as the Yōkai started skipping stones across the water, sweet potatoes forgotten. Neven hovered by me and Tsukuyomi for only a moment before joining her.

"We could split up," Tsukuyomi said, standing beside me rigidly. "Me and you, your brother and the Yōkai."

"I suppose that's the only combination you would accept?" I said, raising an eyebrow.

"It's my duty to protect you," he said.

I sighed. "Finding Ikki would go a long way toward protecting me from the Reapers."

"Not if you're dead before their ship even docks."

"Do you think I'm incapable?" I said, scowling up at him.

"I think you have a weakness they can exploit," he said, glancing unsubtly at Neven.

"Everyone has a weakness."

"Yours is a six-foot-one flesh target that just tripped over a potato."

"Be careful," I said, narrowing my eyes. "Neven is a part of me. You'd do well to remember that."

Tsukuyomi blinked like I'd spoken another language, then turned without a word to look out across the shore where Neven watched the Yōkai skipping stones.

"I can throw it all the way to the volcano!" the Yōkai said, grinning. Then she reeled back and hurled a flat stone into the air.

But instead of skipping across the water, it clunked against a great invisible wall and splashed back into the sea.

"Hey!" a voice called from somewhere in the empty waters.

I rose to my feet, but there was nothing but clear summer sky above us and flat sea before us. The voice had come from across the water.

Tamamo No Mae darted away, hiding behind me and peering over my shoulder. The heat waves that rolled off the water had the faint smell of Death, a bitterness that itched under my nose.

"Who's there?" I called, one hand on my clock. Neven and Tsukuyomi stepped in front of me and the Yōkai, two needlessly chivalrous fools, hands on their weapons.

A pale mist began to glow along the dark waters, swirling high into the air. As it drew closer, the outline of a wooden ship tore through the fog, translucent and glowing pale green, as if halfway in this world and the next. It looked as if the hand of God had outlined its shape in watery ink but never colored it in, leaving a skeleton of a ship in pale colors that bled with sunlight. Its giant black sail shuddered from the weak summer breeze as it rolled closer.

Humans milled around the street behind us, but none of them took notice, or perhaps they just couldn't see. Some spirits took different forms to different eyes, depending on what they wanted.

"We should go," Neven said, nearly stepping on my toes as he backed up.

I pressed a hand to his shoulder blade to stop him as the ship sailed closer, cutting through the waters without rippling the surface, as if sliding along a plane of flat ice.

"These Yōkai won't hurt us," I said.

"Yōkai?" Tamamo No Mae said, perking up and leaning around me to get a better view.

The ship came to a gentle stop, its broad side parallel to the shore before us, giving us a better look at the whispered planks and hazy sails, the whole image like a trick of light. Then out came a crew of ghostly silhouettes—skeletons wrapped in white kimonos that rippled against their bones as the wind blew them back, revealing the lines of their rib cages and joints on their spindly arms. They sounded like old machinery as they walked, their bones scraping together, yellowed teeth chattering.

These were funayūrei, ghosts of shipwrecked soldiers trapped forever at sea. They came out during Obon, but also on full moons and new moons and stormy nights, filling sailors' boats with water one ladle at a time until the ocean dragged them all the way down, and death by death their crew became larger.

"The Goddess has come out for Obon!" one of them cheered.

The other crew let out vague cries of approval and lifted bottles of what might have been beer, or whatever spirits liked to indulge in during festivals.

It wasn't the first time I'd run into funayūrei since taking Izanami's place. I'd seen them while out collecting souls, their ghostly sea shanties echoing across still waters on full moon nights. Unlike my Shinigami, many Yōkai respected me solely because I left them alone, not terrorizing them as Izanami had done. It wasn't that I was benevolent—I just knew Izanami would have hated it, and I desperately wanted to be unlike her. Besides, I had more important things to do. For as much as I'd needed souls in the last decade, it was much easier to wrestle them from humans than Yōkai.

"Come celebrate with us!" one of them said, leaning precariously over the ship's railing and holding out a clear bottle. "There's only a few hours left!"

"That's why I'm here, actually," I said, calling across the water. "I need to find the grave of Ikki of Kagoshima. Do you know where that is?"

The Yōkai turned to each other, murmuring among themselves.

"We've met a lot of people over the years, Your Highness," one of them said. "Names don't really stick like they used to."

"He would have been popular among Yōkai, and wielded a godly sword," Tsukuyomi said. "Surely that rings a bell?"

"Oh!" one of the funayūrei said, throwing his arms up. "They're looking for the human who fed all the ghost cats! Okesa neko gave him some of her treasures from Nagoya."

The others nodded, making sounds of agreement.

"I remember him," one said. "He's a good man. Good at shogi."

"Too good, in my opinion," said another. "He's all too happy to take my money."

"Because you're a terrible player. You can't even read."

Tamamo No Mae peeked around my arm.

"Kitsune?" one of the sailors said. Then he shouted at her in a dialect I didn't understand. She shot him a cold look and replied evenly in the same dialect. He spit some of his beer in the water and turned away, heading back belowdecks.

"He's mad that I threw rocks at his boat," she said, shoulders slumped, not looking at anyone in particular as she spoke.

Tsukuyomi shook his head and said something to her in the same dialect, making her jump and curl her lips back like she was trying to hiss in her human form. They crossed their arms and stared each other down.

"We don't have time for bickering," I said, glancing to the sun, which was nearing its highest point in the sky. Both of them scowled, turning back to me.

"Tell me where Ikki is," I said to the funayūrei.

One of the skeletons began to speak, but another elbowed him in the ribs. "What will you give us?" he said.

I sighed. Was I doomed to walk around Japan incurring debts with everyone? I opened my mouth to threaten them, but realized that seemed an awful lot like something Izanami would have done.

"What do you want?" I asked instead. "More souls? Kagoshima can spare a few." The Yōkai were already promised a thousand souls a day as part of their agreement with Izanami, and I hadn't been keen to change that rule and start a Yōkai rebellion. I could bully some other Yōkai into giving up their share without too much trouble.

But the funayūrei let out a chorus of displeased sounds, shaking their heads.

"No, no, not here!" one of them said. "Kagoshima is our home. What about in Iki?"

"No. The population there is small enough as it is."

The skeletons murmured among themselves. I turned to Tsukuyomi for ideas, but his gaze was focused on the pale moon overhead. It seemed that he and the funayūrei had something in common.

"The moon dictates when you can sail, doesn't it?" I said.

"Of course!" one of the funayūrei said. "Our souls are bound by moonlight."

I turned to Tsukuyomi, who had already tensed up beside me.

"Ren," he said, his expression rigid, "I don't like making deals with Yōkai."

"And I won't like it when Ikki's soul slips away in a few hours," I said, smiling sweetly so the Yōkai in the distance wouldn't suspect anything, even if my tone was venomous. "If you really want to protect me, prove it."

He closed his eyes, letting out a thin breath.

"I can give you an extra night of full moonlight to sail," he said, his voice echoing across the water. "On the autumnal equinox, the moon is supposed to begin to darken, but I can illuminate it one night more."

"Two nights!" one of the sailors called.

"One," Tsukuyomi said, his eyes narrowed. "If you alter the moon too much, it affects the tides."

The funayūrei turned and whispered among themselves. Tsukuyomi stood with his arms crossed, looking thoroughly godlike as the sea breeze rippled his white kimono, like he alone could pull the tides and keep the world turning.

"Deal!" one of the sailors said at last, raising a glass bottle as the rest of them cheered.

"How do they know he'll keep his promise?" Neven whispered to Tamamo No Mae.

"Because I have honor," Tsukuyomi said, frowning.

"Because it's very bad luck to break a promise to a Yōkai,"

Tamamo No Mae said. "Sooner or later the tides would find him and pull him under."

The ship rocked back and forth as the funayūrei continued toasting, falling against the rails.

"Tell me where Ikki is!" I said, before their celebrations could grow too loud.

"He's in Korimoto cemetery!" one of them called, right before another drunken sailor pushed him overboard into the clear waters that inhaled him without so much as a splash.

I didn't bother calling out my thanks, knowing they wouldn't hear it over their cheers.

"You shouldn't make a habit of trusting Yōkai," Tsukuyomi said as we hurried back toward the main road. "They only look after their own interests."

"Unlike you and your siblings, who help Ren out of the goodness of your hearts?" Neven said.

Tsukuyomi pressed his lips together and didn't argue further.

After asking for directions to Korimoto cemetery without causing another spectacle, we wound our way uphill once more, this time on the city's eastern side, up mossy stairs carved into a small hill where the air grew cooler, far from the crowded throng of the market. The higher we climbed, the clearer the volcano across the water became, as if it was rising out of the ocean to greet us. The sounds of humans on the main roads below became a distant murmur, the scent of Death once again growing stronger, dragging us up the stairs like it had been expecting us.

At last, we entered the cemetery.

The graves had been freshly washed and weeded for Obon, decorated with bright flowers in small vases—crisp orange hozuki, white chrysanthemums, lotuses and carnations and bamboo grass.

Unlike the wide graves and angel statues of Highgate Cemetery where I had grown up, most graves in Japan were solemn pillars stacked on stair-like platforms, names carved vertically into the stone. The whole cemetery had been decorated with red and white paper lanterns to guide the dead.

A hot breeze whipped my hair around, the wind like fingers combing through the strands and shivering across my face. The spirits knew we were here.

A hand gripped my arm. I turned, expecting the Yōkai again, only to see Neven huddling close to me as the spirits caressed his neck, ghostly fingers running down his ribs.

"Leave him be," I said, waving a hand in their direction. Instantly, the winds picked up and spiraled off into the sky, shaking the canopy of leaves above us.

Neven's grip loosened, but he didn't let go.

"Thank you," he said, the words stiff. His hand fell away from my arm as he took a step back, eyes fixed on the ground.

"The spirits won't hurt you," I said.

"I know," Neven said, staring at the dirt road. "They're just unsettling."

"Nothing will hurt you." I shouldn't have said it, because we both knew that promises like that were so very hard to keep.

He winced, like it physically pained him to look at me. "Ren," he said, sighing.

But I didn't want to hear what he had to say next, so I turned around, only to nearly trip over a fox.

I caught myself on a grave, but the fox bit the hem of my kimono and started to drag me.

"Tamamo No Mae?" I asked. The fox squeaked in response. Neven followed behind me as I waved for Tsukuyomi to come.

The fox stopped at an unmarked grave, then with a shudder of glittering light, transformed back into a human.

"Don't do that in public!" I said, shielding her with my body as I looked around the cemetery to make sure no one had seen. Luckily, most people were down in the city celebrating or in their homes preparing meals. A few humans lingered near the entrance of the cemetery, but they seemed to be leaving. Death repelled most humans.

"I found him!" she said, ignoring me and pointing to the unmarked grave in front of us.

"Are you sure?" I said, exchanging a glance with Neven, who looked just as perplexed.

"I can smell him," she said, tapping her nose. "People touched by gods have a certain smell."

"His bones smell?" Tsukuyomi said, grimacing.

"No, his soul," Tamamo No Mae said, frowning as if it should have been obvious. She turned to me with a wide grin and edged closer, eyes bright, like she expected me to pat her on the head.

"Well done," I said, feeling like the words had been forcibly squeezed from my throat. The Yōkai beamed, latching onto my side.

The sun had begun to sink low on the horizon. Soon, the sky would darken and the bonfires would begin. I lit the lanterns above Ikki's grave, then placed my hands down on the cool stone platform. I had never tried summoning one of the dead before, but if humans could guide their souls during Obon with nothing more than paper lanterns, surely the Goddess of Death could do it.

"Ikki," I said, the language of Death making the trees around the graveyard tremble, *"I am Death, and you answer to me."*

The sky darkened, the sun plunging into the horizon and a bitter red staining the sky. The dirt beneath my feet grew cold, the warmth of summer chased away by the chill of Death.

"Come to me now."

All around us, paper lanterns flickered, the ones beside Ikki's grave glowing the brightest of all.

Then abruptly, the wind stilled and the lanterns extinguished themselves, casting the cemetery in darkness. Both Neven and Tamamo No Mae grabbed my sleeves. I turned to Tsukuyomi, who frowned at the grave, unmoving. Where was Ikki?

From behind us, a voice broke through the fragile stillness of the cemetery, old and crackled like a tea-stained treasure map.

"I've never met a god who was younger than me."

CHAPTER 13

A translucent silhouette of a man stood before me, his face hidden under a wide-brimmed hat, his body shielded with a needle-sharp straw coat. He held some tool that looked like a rake over his left shoulder, its three long teeth hanging rusty and jagged. He looked like he'd been ripped from an old photograph, the colors of his clothes time-weathered. The cemetery grew colder around us, the sky silent.

Death had begun to swirl around the cemetery, its bitter tang washing away the smell of incense. Both Neven and Tamamo No Mae shivered behind me, while Tsukuyomi stood next to me and frowned at the specter.

"So this is the new Izanami," he said. His voice sounded faraway, like he was speaking to us from the other side of a door. "The Goddess of Death can't even pronounce my name right."

An insult burned at my lips but I somehow held it back, reminding myself that we needed Ikki's cooperation. I knew my Japanese was accented, but few people were rude enough to correct a goddess. He'd clearly understood me well enough to accept my summons.

"I'm not the new Izanami," I said. "I'm Ren."

"Yes, perhaps that was too generous a comparison," he said. "Izanami created Japan, but all you've done is destroy it."

His words stung, but I shoved the hurt down, glancing at the darkening sky. We had less than an hour, if even that. Emotions could be felt anytime, but I could only get information from Ikki now.

"I'm all that stands between Japan and a fleet of Reapers," I said.

"Then we're doomed," Ikki said. "You are a child, and a foreigner. When Japan collapses underneath you, that will be your legacy for all eternity."

The lanterns in the cemetery flickered once more, my shadows slowly seeping across the ground as I glared back at him. *He's right*, I thought. But what else could I do but keep trying when it was my responsibility to save Japan?

"I need Kusanagi No Tsurugi."

Ikki scoffed. "You're hundreds of years too late," he said. "I gave it to my son before my death, and he gave it to his son. It is a family heirloom, not something easily parted with."

I sighed. Part of me had expected this, but secretly I'd hoped that he'd been buried with it. Was I doomed to keep chasing humans across Japan?

"And where is it now?"

Ikki crossed his arms. "My sword is forged from the light that began the universe. Why should I give it to a little girl who can't even speak Japanese properly?"

"Because she's your goddess," Tsukuyomi said. He loomed over Ikki the way he'd terrified the human in the street, his eyes a swirling carousel of stars and darkness. "In life, you may do as you wish, but in Death, you answer to her."

"If I don't, what will she do? Kill me?"

"There are worse things than death," I said. "If you don't believe me, the Reapers will prove it when they come here."

Neven shifted behind me, knowing well just what cruelties High Reapers were capable of.

But Ikki only rolled his eyes. "You couldn't even win a game of shogi, much less defeat a Reaper."

He's a good man. Good at shogi, one of the sailors had said. I had played shogi with Chiyo a few years ago. In the ten years without Neven, I'd needed something to pass the time, and reading Japanese for hours on end made my eyes cross. Chiyo had taught me the basics, but considering that she'd lost every single match, I'd assumed there was some unspoken rule not to beat a goddess. I'd challenged other servants, but all of them had lost as well, so I'd grown bored and given up.

It was a strategy game with a similar setup to Western chess. But chess was a battle of wits, the faster and dirtier the better, as long as you won. In Japan, shogi was a game long protected by the shogunate, a fine arts performance given to honor the shoguns, akin to poetry. It was a thread tied to Japan's beginnings, even as more and more of the West filtered across the sea and washed up on our shores. The basic premise was the same—the first to capture the other person's king won.

"Do you want to bet?" I asked.

Ikki hesitated. "What?"

"I bet I can beat you at shogi," I said.

"Shogi is a man's game," he said, crossing his arms.

"You don't think you can beat a woman?"

Ikki bristled. "I could beat you blindfolded."

"Then show me," I said. "But if you're wrong, tell me where your grandson went with your sword."

Ikki smirked. "Now that's rather unfair," he said. "You've put my honor on the line. I should be spending the last hours of Obon with my family."

"And I should be sitting on my throne being spoon-fed souls by my servants. But the Reapers are coming, so here we are."

Ikki sighed. "If I win, you need to give me what I want."

"And that is?"

Ikki smiled, revealing a crooked row of yellow teeth, his eyes still covered under the brim of his hat. "I don't want to tell you."

I crossed my arms. "That's not how deals work. I can't agree to something if I don't know what it is."

"If you're confident that you won't lose, then it won't matter what I ask for."

"Of course it matters!"

Ikki shrugged, then began turning away. "Suit yourself. I'm not the one who woke a dead man because I needed his help."

"Wait!"

Ikki paused, looking over his shoulder. I couldn't let him leave just yet. I wasn't certain that I'd be able to bring him back again so close to the end of Obon.

"Are you actually considering this?" Neven said.

"All options should at least be considered," Tsukuyomi said.

Neven glared, turning back to me. "Can you not bribe him like you did the Yōkai?" he whispered.

"I am a thousand years dead," Ikki said, scowling. "I do not eat or drink or keep the company of women. What I want is to play shogi."

I had suspected as much, and that was why I hadn't bothered with a counteroffer, but of course Neven couldn't have known. He didn't understand the dead as I did.

The longer they remained in Yomi, the less they wanted anything at all. Their souls wore out and stretched until holes appeared, like paper that grew too damp. They did not have dreams or desires the way the living did, nor did they feel the agony of yearning that they used to. They found ways to pass time in comfort, simple and quiet afterlives that lost their hard edges as the years wore on, river rocks smoothed over in the current.

"I don't trust him," the Yōkai whispered.

I didn't either, but that hardly mattered. I took one more look at the sinking sun, then turned back to Ikki.

"You can't have any of our souls," I said.

Ikki scoffed. "What would I want with those? I'm not like your Shinigami."

"So you have no intention of killing us?"

"Again, for what purpose?" Ikki said, scowling. "To drag your corpses behind me like wind socks? Now, will you play or not?"

"Ren," Neven said, "I don't think—"

"Fine," I said, just to stop Neven from making me doubt my decision. It was either this or torture the answer out of him in the hour left before sunset, and something told me Ikki wouldn't spill his secrets quickly.

Ikki sat cross-legged on the ground and gestured for me to follow suit. As soon as I sat down, he waved his hand over the earth between us and the grid of a shogi board carved itself into the dirt. He emptied a cloth bag on either side of the board, the koma clattering to the ground. Unlike the polished wood pieces I'd used with Chiyo, this set contained different shades of off-white and sickly yellow, like milk that had gone sour. I picked up one of the cleaner pieces and ran my thumb across the words carved into it.

"What are these?" I said.

"Ko-ma," he said, drawing out the word as if I didn't already know it.

"You know that's not what I mean," I said, picking up one of the yellow pieces. This one bent like rubber, its name carved in a messy slant across its warped surface. "You act like you're a meijin, yet you don't even have a real shogi set?"

"This set is the most valuable one you will ever see," he said, not looking up as he arranged the pieces on his side of the board. "It brings me good luck." He picked up a silver general, twirling it between his fingers. That piece looked like it had shattered and been glued back together.

Tamamo No Mae leaned forward to examine the pieces, her face twisted as if she'd smelled something rotten.

"What are these?" I asked. "I won't stand for trickery before the game's even started."

Ikki let out a dry laugh, like dead grass bristling in a sharp wind.

"It's not a trick," he said.

He finally looked up, raising the brim of his hat. His eyes were a vacant white, no pupils at all, but pale glowing spheres of moonlight. He extended a hand to me, tutting with impatience when I didn't immediately respond. Slowly, I set my hand in his papery palm.

"Fingers make the best koma," he whispered, caressing my skin with his scratchy fingertips. I tensed and tried to pull away, but he held tight. "Cartilage makes a decent piece, but it's hard to carve, especially ears with all their curves. Noses work decently, if you can pry them from the bone."

Behind me, Neven and Tsukuyomi had gone very still. The Yōkai clutched my sleeve, shivering against me.

"Teeth make quite sturdy pieces, if you can get enough of them," Ikki said. "But of course, those are the hardest to remove. Fingers pop off quite easily with a good knife, but teeth need to be yanked out."

"This is what you want from me?" I said, my mouth dry. "A new shogi set?"

Ikki grinned. "This is the currency of the dead, Your Highness. You're the one who wanted to play."

I tensed, grinding my teeth, my jaw aching from the force. The Yōkai let out a distressed sound, while Neven and Tsukuyomi shared an uneasy glance. Ikki pulled out a knife speckled with dirt and rust and staked it into the ground. "I'll be quick," he said. "I've had practice."

I closed my eyes, taking a steadying breath. Any body parts the ghost hacked off me would grow back in time, but that didn't mean I wanted my nose sawed off my face with a rusty knife. I didn't have time to lie around like a starfish regrowing body parts when Ivy was coming in three days.

"Let me play for her," Tsukuyomi said. I frowned and turned around. He was wringing his hands, refusing to meet my eyes as he looked at Ikki.

I slammed another piece on the board. "I told you not to get in my way," I said.

"Ren, I'm good at shogi," he whispered, his eyes pleading. I didn't doubt that he was. He'd probably filed away a thousand strategies in his annoying, encyclopedic brain. "Let me help you."

"It's not a bad idea," Neven said.

I turned to him, scowling. *Suddenly he was siding with Tsukuyomi?* Neven's expression was pinched as he stared at my fingers, pale blue eyes flickering back up to my face. I almost preferred it when they were beating each other up in my lake rather than collectively fretting over me.

But Ikki solved the problem for me.

"She's the one who wants information," Ikki said. "She can earn it herself or not at all."

I turned to Tsukuyomi, shaking my head. This was my game to finish, not his. Neven's shoulders drooped and the Yōkai huddled closer to him.

As we finished arranging the koma, Tamamo No Mae sat down and leaned against my side, clutching my arm as she stared wide-eyed at the pieces. Neven sat beside her and Tsukuyomi knelt on my left. Their intense stares did little to ease my nerves.

"You can do it, Ren!" the Yōkai said, squeezing my arm tighter. Then she leaned close to my ear and whispered, in crisp, perfect English, "He underestimates you."

"No cheating!" Ikki said.

Tamamo No Mae whimpered and grabbed my sleeve, turning away from the ghost. I didn't know if I could win, but with everyone watching me, I had to at least try. I reached for a piece, but Ikki slapped my hand away.

"We haven't decided who goes first," he said, swiping five of his pawns off the board and shaking them between his cupped hands. "Ignorant girl. You challenge me to a game and you don't even know how to play."

I said nothing, my face hot. Chiyo had always let me go first, so I'd assumed it hadn't mattered. In hindsight, me being her goddess might have had something to do with it.

Ikki dropped the pawns to the board and watched them spin around and settle, some landing on the sides with red words and some on the sides with black words.

"Black starts," Ikki said, snatching the pieces away before I could properly see them. He slid his pawn forward and looked to me expectantly. "Well?" he said.

I sat up straighter, looking down at the severed parts in the dirt that made up my koma pieces, like a tiny graveyard of those who had challenged Ikki and lost.

I picked up a pawn and began to play.

Ikki and I took turns moving our pawns forward as everyone else's gaze nervously traveled between us. Tsukuyomi's rigid silence felt like cold judgment while Neven's wide-eyed stare made me feel like a circus monkey. The Yōkai curled up against my arm and watched wordlessly.

Ikki slapped his pieces down without hesitation. In a normal game, the pieces hit the wooden board with a satisfying thwack, but this game was eerily silent, pieces sinking into the dirt and rolling onto their sides because of their warped shapes. Shogi was supposed to sound like a conversation, but this game was only a whisper.

I tried to think back to the games I'd played with Chiyo. She'd always insisted that I choose each move with exquisite care, while I'd merely tossed the pieces down in whatever aggressive attack I could think of, working out a strategy as I went. Most of the time, it had worked.

I reached for my rook and Ikki scoffed, crossing his arms, making chills break out across my skin. I dared to glance up at him, his lips curled into an infuriating smile. Was he pleased that I'd fallen into his trap, or was he bluffing?

I slid my piece forward and captured his gold piece, snatching it off the board. Ikki only shook his head, instantly capturing my pawn.

I tried to map out my next moves, but I was too aware of the sun sinking lower in the sky. I could only see a thousand ways every move could go wrong, a million different methods Ikki could use to capture every piece. There were too many possibilities and not enough time to think them over. Even if I froze the tiny cemetery so I'd have more time to think, I couldn't stop time all the way into the sky to prevent the sun from falling toward the horizon.

"You have lovely fingers," Ikki said. "So long and thin. Such clean nails."

I moved another pawn forward just to stop him from staring at me, but he only sighed.

"You need to know the next three steps," he said. "Before you make a move, you need to know how I will respond to that move. I know how you will respond, and that is why I will win."

I swallowed. That was never how I'd played with Chiyo. My plan had always shifted as the pieces on the board changed. There was never a great overarching strategy, just a quick response to sudden attacks.

"You don't know how I'll respond," I said.

Ikki shook his head, capturing another one of my pieces.

"I have known a thousand girls like you," he said. "You are not as special as you like to think."

Apparently, Ikki didn't know me as well as he assumed, because I didn't think I was special at all. He was so convinced he knew my next moves, but how did he determine them? Who, exactly, did he think I was?

Ignorant girl, he'd said. *You don't even know how to play.*

The board had grown sparse between us, more than half of my pieces now in Ikki's discard pile. Even to Neven, who didn't know how to play, one glance at the board was enough to know that I was losing. Ikki knew it too. That was all he saw when he looked at me. A foreign girl. Ignorant. A loser.

Maybe it was time to prove him right.

I grabbed a pawn from my captured pieces and began to place it in the same column as another one of my pawns. Before it could touch the board, Tsukuyomi coughed and the Yōkai squirmed beside me, pinching my arm. I yanked the piece back as if burned, shooting a panicked glance at Tsukuyomi.

"I can't do that?" I asked.

He shook his head, looking pained. Across the board, Ikki grinned. If he hadn't thought me incompetent before, now he surely did.

I set the pawn down and picked up a rook, dropping it to the right of Ikki's king. He sighed and immediately captured the piece.

"Somehow, I thought this would be entertaining," he said. "Your nose will do nicely. It's very tall."

Now there was only one empty space between his king and my last pawn. I tried to smooth out my expression, praying he didn't know what I was planning. But Ikki wasn't even watching his own king. He was watching mine.

I had one captured gold piece left, and the sun had almost reached the horizon. I picked up my gold piece and slapped it down between his king and my pawn.

Ikki had already begun reaching for his next piece, but his hand froze, his eyes turning the color of stone.

Backed against the last row of the board, there was nowhere his king could run without being captured. It wasn't a complicated move, but it had worked because he hadn't thought I was capable of it. He thought he knew me, but all he had seen was a foreigner when he should have seen a goddess.

He clenched his fist around the piece in his hand, crushing it to dust. I leaned across the board and grabbed his collar, yanking him toward me.

"Where is your sword?" I said.

"You're a dirty hustler," he said, struggling against my grip.

He was already growing more translucent in my hands, his soul being drawn back to Yomi. In the distance, I smelled the crisp fires of the festival beginning to burn. I only had moments before the night would eat him away.

"Tell me!" I said, shaking him even as he felt like silk slipping through my fingers.

"I gave it to my great-grandson," he said, the language of Death wrenching the words from his throat. "In Yakushima."

I froze.

Yakushima. The land of blue fires and green forests across the water. The place my mother had lived.

A gust of cool wind rushed through the cemetery, extinguishing the lanterns. Ikki's shirt turned to air in my hands, his spirit whisked away into the sky like shreds of paper. The wind wiped away all traces of the shogi board, leaving only smooth earth beneath my palms. For a long moment, no one spoke, staring into the space where Ikki had existed only moments ago. Now there was nothing but an empty path and a bleeding horizon.

"Yakushima is not far," Tsukuyomi said softly. "This is actually quite convenient."

"Yes, that's one word for it," I said, standing up.

The Yōkai threaded her fingers through mine, swinging our hands as she pulled us toward the cemetery gates. "I knew you would win, Ren," she said.

Yes, it certainly seemed like she knew. She'd thought Ikki was underestimating me, but it wasn't as if she'd seen me play shogi before.

"How did you know?" I said, drawing to a stop.

The Yōkai blinked. "You're you, Ren. You can do anything."

I hesitated. Perhaps she truly saw me as an infallible goddess, and her compliment had only bothered me because I was so unused to flattery. But I didn't like people who were too certain about the future. Either they were fools, or they knew something you didn't.

"Ren," Neven said.

I turned instantly at the sound of worry in his voice. He pointed past the cemetery gates at the city downhill. The smell of fire had suddenly grown stronger, smoke blurring the pale starlight overhead.

These were not the traditional bonfires and sounds of celebration at the end of Obon. The fire had spread to the rooftops, swallowing an entire street, and the screams were of terror, not excitement.

Kagoshima was burning.

CHAPTER 14

The fire had devoured all the stalls on the main road. It seared through all the paper lanterns and the strings that held them above the street, covering the road in a canopy of flames. Smoke churned high into the night air, blacking out the last of the sunset and painting the sky in choking darkness.

The humans shoved past us as we descended the hill, some of them carrying buckets of water from the nearby shore, but many falling over coughing and rubbing their eyes from the stinging haze of smoke.

At the end of the street, the towering pile of firewood for the departing bonfires had spilled into nearby stalls. They shuddered with flames, the wooden skeletons of their frames cracking inward as they turned to ashes.

"There should be people standing guard to make sure this

doesn't happen," Tsukuyomi said, holding his sleeve up to shield his face from the smoke.

"Well, it's happened," Neven said. "Are we going to stand here and watch the whole city burn down?"

Tsukuyomi has a point, I thought, though I wouldn't say it in front of Neven. The humans had been holding this festival for centuries. Surely they knew better, or at the very least, would have had a few buckets of water on hand to stop the fire before it reached such proportions.

The dirt beneath my feet squished and pooled as I stepped across it, like it had recently rained. The air was damp with an impending storm. Fire should not have spread so quickly on such a wet day.

For a moment, the winds shifted and the smoke parted, revealing one gasping breath of clear sky overhead. Without the smoke that stung my eyes and coated my throat, I sensed Death above us, splitting the sky with a thousand hairline cracks, ready to fracture and bury us all in star shards.

Neven yanked my sleeve and I tore my gaze away from the sky.

"Stop gawking. We have to help them," he said, dragging me closer to the chaos.

"Right," I said, glancing over my shoulder at the Yōkai pulling Tsukuyomi after us.

"How, exactly, are we going to help?" Tsukuyomi said, snatching his sleeve away from the Yōkai. We stopped in the middle of the street, smoke swirling around us, humans fleeing in every direction. "Last I checked, none of us controlled water."

"Can't you control fire?" Neven said, fingers twisting in my sleeve, as if Tsukuyomi's protests were my fault.

"We control *light*," said Tsukuyomi, squinting, or possibly glaring. It might have been from the smoke stinging his eyes, or maybe he was just tired of Neven's questions. "It's not the same thing. Fire is just a vehicle for light. We could make the fire very dim, but the flames themselves don't answer to us."

Neven sighed. "We have two gods with us and neither of them can put out a fire?"

Hiro could, I thought, glancing out to the sea. Hiro could have made a giant wave from the nearby ocean fall over the town like a soft blanket, soothing all the flames instantly. I remembered for the thousandth time that somehow felt like the first, that Hiro was gone.

"Let's just stop it from spreading farther," I said.

I reached for my clock but hesitated as ashes spun down from the sky. I would probably need two hands to put out any fires. Hiro's ring swung back and forth on its chain around my neck, reflecting the shifting light of the flames. Before I could overthink it, I pulled the chain over my head and slipped the ring onto my finger. With its pure silver and gold, it worked just as well as a clock.

A time freeze inhaled the street. The crackling of fire and collapsing wood fell silent, the flames twisted but motionless, like watercolor strokes of light painted onto the black sky. The ring was heavier than I remembered, the metal warm as it drank up the heat from the fires. *This is just for convenience*, I thought. *It doesn't mean anything.*

I grabbed Tsukuyomi and Neven, who touched the Yōkai, jolting her to sudden awareness.

Neven didn't waste a moment once he took in the time freeze, already accustomed to being ripped on and off the timeline. "We need to get water," he said.

Tsukuyomi looked a bit dazed from the time change. I took his arm and led him a few stumbling steps down the path until he was steady on his feet. We carefully slipped through the crowd, contorting ourselves to dodge the humans' hands and feet. Neven and I wove easily down the street, but Tsukuyomi and the Yōkai started to fall behind, carefully angling themselves around all the bodies.

Some of the humans had already found large buckets and were starting to haul the ocean water up from the shore. I grabbed one that two men had been carrying together, carefully prying it from their hands without touching their skin, and sloshed it over the closest flame. The fire didn't hiss or smoke as it was extinguished, but merely blinked out of existence. The other physical effects would come when time restarted.

I looked down the street at the frozen walls of fire on either side. Even with our inhuman strength, this was going to take a long time, especially if we had to contort ourselves to get through crowds of humans. I didn't want Kagoshima to burn, but how much of my lifespan was I willing to sacrifice for humans? One hour? Two?

As Death herself, I'd ended lives every day for a decade. Many of my people had died by fire, and many more would die the same way. To me, these natural deaths were tragic but necessary, just as I myself was necessary to keep the world in balance. But with Neven so determined to quench any human suffering in his path, what kind of monster would I be to refuse? He wanted so badly to save these humans, but he had no idea just how many humans had already died for him in the years he'd been missing.

The other three had already emptied the buckets of water

from nearby humans and were heading toward the sea. I turned to follow them, but as the crowd thinned, something silver gleamed at the end of the street. A brief twinkle of light, like a fallen star that had whispered my name.

"Neven," I said.

He ground to a stop half a block away.

"What?" he called, eyes narrowed with impatience, sweat dripping down his face.

I pointed to the silver sparkle in the distance. His gaze followed the path of my finger, squinting as he pushed his glasses up his nose. When he saw it, he dropped his buckets. We both moved toward it, ducking around the humans.

"What is it?" the Yōkai called. But Neven and I ignored her as we slipped through the crowd, racing closer.

Neven reached the human moments before I did, bending down to get a closer look. He reached into the pocket of the man's coat and pulled out a silver and gold clock, tethered by a glistening silver chain.

I yanked back his hood, revealing white blond hair and violet eyes. I pulled down his companion's hood for good measure and found the same. Both young Reapers, hardly even Neven's age. Their expressions were blank and lost, not callous as I'd expected. They wore kimonos like the humans but hadn't thought to conceal the chains to their clocks.

Neven's gaze flickered up to mine, his expression tense. "I know them," he said. "They were in my class."

"So they're Low Reapers?"

Neven nodded. "I don't think it's a coincidence that they're here at the same time as us."

Tsukuyomi and Tamamo No Mae finally caught up, pausing several feet from the Reapers.

"What are they doing here?" the Yōkai asked, taking a step back.

I shook my head. "I don't know, but I think we've found our fire starters." After all, fires didn't spring up within moments without a sound. Not after recent rain. But the limits of time meant nothing to Reapers. They could dry out wood and let fire simmer for hours before anyone in the streets realized.

"What do you plan on doing with them?" Tsukuyomi said.

Neven and I shared a look. Without a word, we grabbed them under the arms and began to drag them off the street, their limbs frozen stiff.

"Where are you taking them?" Tsukuyomi said, watching with wide eyes. The Yōkai shifted into her fox form and scampered after us.

"Away," Neven and I said at the same time.

"They're too dangerous to keep near humans," Neven said. "Now, if something goes wrong, the humans won't get caught in the cross fire."

"And if nothing goes wrong, the humans don't need to see what I'll do with them," I said.

Neven grimaced at my words but didn't protest as we dragged the Reapers farther away from the crowd. The coat on Neven's Reaper snagged on something, making Neven stumble. He gave a hard tug to dislodge it, but Tsukuyomi leaned forward to help him.

I reached out a hand to stop him. "No, don't—"

But as Tsukuyomi leaned forward, his bare hand brushed the Reaper's forearm where the sleeve was rolled back.

The Reaper jolted, twisting out of Neven's grasp and slamming into the ground. He looked around wildly, his eyes spinning purple as he took in the four of us blinking down at him and the frozen crowd of humans around us. I dropped the other Reaper to free my hands to subdue him, but he was already reaching for his clock.

A time turn slammed down on us like all the weight of the sky had collapsed.

When someone else turned time on me, I was never conscious of the stopped time itself, only the disorienting aftermath. This time, I was no longer standing by the shore but tossed at the edge of the water, a Reaper's hands around my throat.

My eyes rolled to the right, where Neven was splashing in the water, face held down by the other Reaper. Where had Tsukuyomi and Tamamo No Mae gone? Above me there was only smoky darkness.

I curled my hand into a fist and punched the Reaper in the face.

As my hand crashed into his cheekbone, I cranked time to a stop once again. But the more one layered time turns, the more fragile time became. The world had tilted off-balance, stars sliding across the sky as if the blackness had turned to wet paint.

I hadn't been thinking clearly, because the touch of my skin when I'd shattered the Reaper's face had carried him into the time freeze with me, leaving us once more on even ground. We fell onto the wet sand and I stumbled away, my throat still feeling like it had been pinched shut. I reached for another time turn and—

I was underwater, crushed from the weight of yet another time freeze. Someone was pulling my right arm and someone else was grabbing my throat and my bones were vibrating with timesickness, my skin screaming as if trying to flay itself.

I gasped in a breath of cold air and Tsukuyomi was pulling me out of the water and looking down at me with eyes full of stars, a flash of light that must have been Neven's clock in the background, then someone yanked my hair back and the world turned upside down, a Reaper's fierce green eyes staring down at me, his trembling hand yanking at my scalp.

My ring burned on my left hand, but I didn't think another time turn would help. The whole world felt like it was about to shatter to pieces, or maybe just my body, blood screaming through my veins, bones jolting as if trying to break free from the cage of my skin, the sky rumbling as if ready to be cracked in half by thunder.

This was why Reapers weren't meant to fight with time—too many changes burned holes in the fabric of the universe, made paradoxes that could snap the timeline in two. Time grew thinner and more brittle the more it was manipulated.

But with my hazy vision, I saw that the other Reaper had Neven by the throat, thumbs digging into his flesh. My body burned as if I'd swallowed hot coals.

So what if the whole universe ends? I thought. Without Neven, there was no world worth saving.

I clenched my hand into a fist and dragged yet another time freeze over us.

Like a glass filled with boiling water, the whole world cracked in half.

With a great shattering sound overhead, the pressure in my skull released, like my head had been cleaved open and brain matter spilled across the dirt. I was on my knees, panting. In the distance, the fires of Kagoshima blazed on, all of the time turns released. My ring burned against my finger and my clock smoked, warning me not to try turning time again.

In the wet dirt before me, Neven was rising to his feet, a hand massaging his throat.

"The Reapers," I said, stumbling to my feet, "where—"

"I've got them, Ren."

I turned around.

Tsukuyomi stood with his arms crossed, the two Reapers frozen on the ground in front of him. They knelt perfectly still in a bright circle of moonlight cast down from the crescent moon that had finally risen over the volcano in the distance. Though they breathed shallowly and their panicked gazes darted around, they didn't move at all.

"Tsukuyomi?" I whispered.

"They won't escape my moonlight," he said, smiling and brushing dirt from his collar. "Don't worry, Ren."

Tamamo No Mae leaped forward in her fox form, grabbing one of their clocks in her mouth and tugging until the chain ripped free from their clothing. She spit the clock at Neven's feet, then went back for the other one.

"What should we do with them?" Neven said.

As if that was even a question.

I stepped forward and my shadows unfolded like dark wings, reaching out to tie pretty bows around the Reaper's throats, tighter and tighter.

"Why are you here?" I said. "Why did you set fire to Kagoshima?"

I relaxed the shadows just enough to let one of them gasp out a few words.

"Ankou said to smoke you out like a bug," one of them said, "and if we killed any humans while doing it, that was even better."

"Shut up, Xander!" the other Reaper said. I squeezed his throat tighter to stop him from discouraging the other.

"How did she even know that I was here?" I asked.

"Reapers have eyes everywhere."

I grimaced. Ever since I was a child, that same saying had haunted me. Our teachers reminded us in classes that no sin would go unpunished, not even the secrets we kept in our hearts. I'd always suspected it had less to do with eyes and more to do with our sensitive hearing and echoing catacombs, where even whispers could be heard if you pressed your ear to the stone walls. It was the reason I'd never had friends—anyone who met with me, even in secret, was instantly mocked by our classmates, as if they'd somehow seen it with their own eyes. Reapers were like spiders and all the world was their web. A vibration on a single strand could catch their attention.

"Whose eyes?" I demanded. I knew enough of the High Reapers that I would probably know their name. That would at least tell me their weaknesses, how to avoid them, or at the very least, whose face I should be looking for.

The gagged Reaper cried out against my shadows, shaking his head, eyes pleading. The other Reaper looked away.

"Tell me who saw us!" I said in Death, loud enough that the humans might have heard, but I didn't care.

When they didn't answer, I sighed and took out my knife.

"As much as I would love to do this for hours, I'm on a bit of a tight schedule here."

"Ren?" Neven said, stepping forward. "What are you doing? They're unarmed now."

"Did you hear what they said? There's a network of Reapers in Japan reporting on where we're going. We can't leave any loose ends."

"What are they going to do without clocks?" Neven said. "They're basically humans now."

I turned to Neven, wishing I were kinder, more patient. "Neven. I cannot afford to underestimate the Reapers," I said slowly. *Your life depends on it*, I thought. But I didn't say it, because I was fairly sure that Neven still hated me and wouldn't appreciate me trying to protect him now.

"They're my classmates, Ren," Neven said. "You know they don't have any choice but to follow Ankou's orders."

"There is always a choice!" I said, stepping forward so suddenly that Neven flinched back as my shadows began to twist around us, caging us in. They could have chosen not to come after me. They could have chosen to do their jobs in England instead of becoming soldiers for their xenophobic god, but they were too scared. I was the only one who didn't have a choice. I couldn't simply choose to *not* be a Shinigami so they wouldn't hate me.

Neven crossed his arms. "You can't kill every Reaper you come across."

"Can't?" I said. "I didn't realize I needed your permission."

"They're our people. You know there aren't enough Reapers as it is."

"*I have no people!*" I said. "The closest thing I have is Japan, and they want to take that from me!"

"You're just as bad as Ivy if you slaughter every Reaper you come across!"

I hesitated. "I don't want to be as bad as Ivy," I said.

Then I turned around and slit the Reapers' throats.

Blood gushed down their necks and soaked their clothes,

watering the soil. They coughed and gagged, eyes wide with fear.

"I want to be worse," I said. The sudden thrum of agreement from Izanami wrenched through me like a forest fire tearing across a tree line. Her voice rose in my ears, and when I opened my mouth to speak, her sharp words rushed out in Death:

"I have to be worse if I want to beat her. Why don't you understand that?" But of course Neven would never understand. He hadn't seen the dying faces of all the humans I'd slaughtered just to bring him home. He didn't know that I would eat thousands of hearts from living, screaming humans all over again if it meant that he would be safe. I would never get what I wanted by doing things that were easy. And if the cost of it was my soul—every part of me that Neven had loved—then so be it. Being a good person meant nothing if my brother was dead.

Besides, what kindness did I owe the Reapers? When I was a child, they'd painted *bastard* on my door in pig's blood and cut off my braids in class. When I was old enough to fight back, they'd gutted me on wrought-iron fences and crammed me into sewer drains and threatened to do even worse to Neven. This was a natural consequence for their cruelty.

They deserve to suffer, Izanami said, her words burning at my lips as if begging me to voice them, but I clenched my jaw tight.

"You haven't changed at all," Neven said, his words a bitter whisper.

I turned around, the knife suddenly a thousand pounds in my hand.

"Neven—"

"No," he said, backing up. He grabbed the Yōkai's hand

and headed toward the village. She cast me a sad look over her shoulder but let him tug her away.

Tsukuyomi watched me, standing half in the moonlight and half in the shadows. Izanami's rage cooled down to whispering embers, her voice suddenly far away.

"Don't say anything," I said.

He frowned. "What is it that you think I'm going to say?"

I shook my head. "I just want him to be safe," I whispered. I hadn't intended to say it out loud, but it felt like everyone in the world despised me except for Tsukuyomi. He looked at me for a moment like I was a math equation he couldn't solve, then he took a breath and the frown smoothed off his face.

"He will be, one day," Tsukuyomi said.

"I don't like lies, even if they're well-intentioned."

"I have never once lied to you," Tsukuyomi said. "I believe that Neven will be fine, because he has the protection of a goddess. That is my sincere belief."

I said nothing, staring at the burning town. Tsukuyomi's faith in me was naive. He hadn't seen me fail the way Neven and the Yōkai had. Soon, he would.

"Keep watch for anyone following us," I said. "They'll be close by."

"They will?" Tsukuyomi said.

I nodded. "Reapers don't see very well from a distance. Whoever it is won't be far behind us."

I flinched as the sky cracked once more. Had we not escaped the time turns?

But then a hot rain fell down over Kagoshima, turning the fires to smoke. With all the lanterns now nothing but wet cinders, a quiet darkness fell over the city. The only light came from far away on the horizon, where a ghostly ship of funayūrei bobbed in the distance, watching the charred remains of their city crumble to ashes.

CHAPTER 15

We rested under a blanket of darkness beneath the redwood trees in the Shimazu clan's garden. It was the largest area in Kagoshima without humans—acres of perfectly curved rivers and carefully sculpted trees and polished stone walkways. Beneath my blanket of darkness, no guards or groundskeepers would see us until morning. At first, we'd searched for a hotel, but after finding that two of them had burned down, we decided not to spend more time wandering through crowded areas where Reapers might still be lurking. Besides, nightfall had washed away the scorching temperatures of the afternoon, leaving the city pleasantly cool. I climbed one of the garden's tallest trees and sat on a high branch, arms crossed as I stared out across the shore.

Neven had tried to settle as far away from me as possible, but Tamamo No Mae had shifted into her fox form and curled up at the base of the tree, forcing Neven to grumble and shuffle closer. Tsukuyomi had taken up the other side of the tree, telling me to wake him up to keep watch when I grew too tired.

I looked across the water in the direction of Yakushima, twirling Hiro's ring on the chain around my neck. When I'd thought my mother was alive, I'd wanted so badly to see the place where she had collected souls, the place that could have been my home. But now it felt like a dream ripped away from me, a cruel taste of what would never be mine. I half hoped that we'd arrive at a small and ugly island of dead trees and filthy water, just so I wouldn't feel like I'd lost anything by growing up in London. But Hiro said Yakushima was beautiful, and while he'd lied about many things, he had no reason to lie about this.

As much as I didn't want to, it seemed that we had to go there—Tsukuyomi had said human towns kept archives of family records that we could use to trace Ikki's lineage. Now that Obon was over and I couldn't call on souls at will, that seemed to be our only option.

I leaned back against the branches, closing my eyes. The deep night and spattering of stars above the volcano only reminded me that another day had passed without finding the sword. Somewhere out at sea beyond the islands, Ivy was drawing closer.

As a child, she reveled in holding me down and pulling my teeth out with pliers to see how fast they grew back. She liked the sound my knuckles made when my fingers popped out of their sockets and the color of my blood on new snow. But bones always realigned and skin stitched itself back up. The worst part about Ivy was never what she had already done, but wondering what she might do one day.

One night in London, I'd been waiting for Neven after his classes, standing in a dark alcove of the catacombs so the other Reapers would pass by me as if I didn't exist. When the entire classroom had emptied but Neven still wasn't there, I peered into his empty lecture hall, panic festering in my stomach.

"Lost something?"

Ivy stood behind me, arms crossed, her shadow creeping up the stone wall like mold. I hadn't heard her approach because she always abused time jumps, preferring to appear out of thin air and terrify everyone.

"Where is he?" I said, clutching my book to my abdomen, protecting my organs.

Without a word, Ivy turned and headed down the catacombs. I glanced around, in case any of her friends were hiding in the shadows, then hurried after her. She led me out to the lobby, through The Door, into the wet cemetery grounds where the thick evening mist clogged my throat. We walked farther and farther back where the graves were older, the weather-cracked headstones overgrown with moss, tilting in every direction in the uneven ground. Here, the scent of Death was fainter, the bones older, quieter.

The mist parted with a sigh, revealing a patch of freshly dug earth, piled high before a slate headstone, the word *SCAR-BOROUGH* scratched crookedly into it.

At first, I didn't understand.

Then, I smelled fresh blood in the soil. I sank to my knees, my fingers digging into the dirt that stained my hands deep red, filling in the cracks in my palms.

Far below the layers of rain-soaked dirt and rocks, I heard

nails raking across wood and quick, shallow breaths. My gaze shifted up to the name on the headstone, then back to Ivy.

"What did you do to him?" I whispered, suddenly unable to stop shivering.

But Ivy only smiled. "I would hurry, if I were you," she said. Then she turned away and vanished into the fog.

I reached for my clock, but it wasn't there—one of Ivy's friends must have snatched it through the mist. I cast my books to the side and clawed through the dirt with my bare hands, my nails splitting as I jammed them into rocks and roots, gasping down breaths of the cemetery fog that felt like it was choking me.

I could heal from Ivy's tricks well enough, but Neven wasn't even a century old yet, so a High Reaper like Ivy could do a lot of damage to him. Did she even care if she killed him? The scent of blood was so strong, growing sharper the deeper I dug—had she hacked him to pieces and thrown him in a box? There was so much blood pooled beneath the dirt, great pools of it in the soupy soil. My fingers bled as the night grew colder and the church grims started howling in the distance. Let them come for me, it didn't matter. I dug faster and faster because the scratching had stopped, and so had the breathing. Sweat poured down my face, and the hole grew so deep that I had to jump down inside of it to keep digging.

Finally, my fingers raked across a hard wooden surface, splinters jamming under my nails. I cleared more of the dirt. This wasn't just a box, but a coffin.

"Neven!" I called, banging my fist against it. No one answered. I felt for the edge and hooked my fingers under it, yanking hard until the lid popped open, rusted nails flying everywhere. The scent of blood and Death forced a sour retch up my throat.

The coffin was filled with dead rabbits, bellies ripped open and guts spilling out.

Then a foot collided with the back of my head. I fell forward, my face slamming into the bottom of the casket, over the soft rabbit corpses. As I rolled over, I barely caught a glimpse of Ivy's crooked smile before the lid slammed shut, sealing away the night sky.

"Good night, Scarborough," she said, dirt falling over the lid of the coffin like heavy rain.

I opened my eyes to the Shimazu garden as the branches shuddered around me. A pale hand grabbed the branch below me and Tsukuyomi pulled himself up.

"Judging by your brother, I'm assuming that Reapers need to sleep," he said, settling onto a nearby branch.

"Yes. What of it?"

"Do you intend to keep watch all night?"

I looked out at the town, the last lingering wisps of smoke like a screen of silk over the rooftops. I needed to rest, but waking up would mean another sunrise, another day closer to Ivy coming. Tomorrow morning would mark the last two days before she arrived, and I still had no way of stopping her. Just two Reapers had burned Kagoshima—a whole fleet could raze the entire country. I pictured all the rooftops I could see on the horizon collapsing, the dirt roads turning dark with blood, and a ringing silence once everything that used to be Japan was gone forever. How was I supposed to sleep knowing that in only a few days, Death would dock on our shores?

I looked away. "You haven't slept either."

"I don't need to sleep when I can see the moon," he said,

turning his face toward it as if basking in its light. "I'm like a plant that soaks up moonlight instead of sunlight."

I sighed. "You could have said that when I offered to take first watch."

"I intended to. But when I tried, you said, if I recall correctly, 'shut up and go the hell to sleep.'"

I winced. I hadn't exactly been in the best of moods by the time we'd left the city center.

"Will you at least sleep now?" he asked.

I looked down the trunk of the tree to where Neven and the Yōkai were fast asleep on the ground. *You haven't changed at all*, Neven had said. But he was wrong. I'd changed so much, just not the way he'd wanted. Sourness churned in my stomach, and I didn't know if it was shame or just anger that Neven still didn't understand, but either way, the tree branches seemed like a quiet oasis compared to joining Neven on the ground.

"I'll stay here," I said.

"I can keep the darkness over us," Tsukuyomi said. "The three of you will be safe, I promise."

"That's not the problem," I said.

"Then what is?"

I closed my eyes as my fingernails scraped into the bark. Absolutely everything was a problem. Two young Reapers had nearly bested me and churned the timeline through a meat grinder. We were so lucky the time turns had canceled out instead of killing us all. If Ivy was now Ankou, she'd be infinitely more powerful than her Reapers. She'd probably find a way to scrape my soul out through my pores for one thousand years. And worst of all, Neven would be so relieved when I was gone.

I almost told Tsukuyomi everything. His eyes were so clear and impartial that it would have been as easy as tossing a coin into a wishing well with a whispered prayer, lifting a weight off my chest but expecting nothing in return.

But I remembered sitting in a dark cave with Hiro off the shores of Takaoka and telling him how I was made of Death. He'd comforted me and told me exactly what I'd wanted to hear, and in the end, it had destroyed both of us.

Before I could answer Tsukuyomi, I tasted Death on my tongue.

A sudden wave of names flashed across my eyes in red, so fast that I could hardly read them, wiping away my vision and stealing my breath. I grabbed the branch with fingers I could hardly feel, tilting precariously to the side.

This was more than the usual influx of souls brought in by my Shinigami on any given night. The soreness in my limbs melted away, exhaustion sapped from my bones. As the names faded, my night vision grew clearer, every leaf on the trees around us suddenly knife-sharp, every blade of grass in crisp detail, every crater on the moon clear as day.

"Ren?" Tsukuyomi said.

I realized he'd been calling my name. He'd climbed onto the same branch as me, suddenly very close, one hand gripping my arm so I wouldn't fall to the ground. "What happened?"

I swallowed, backing up against the trunk to steady myself. I could see the entire galaxy of stars in Tsukuyomi's eyes, the smooth planes of his face, his lips chapped from the scorching midday sun. "Death," I said, too overwhelmed with the sudden sharpness of the world to form eloquent sentences. "Many souls have crossed over… I feel stronger, which means many humans have died at once."

"Here?" Tsukuyomi said, looking out across the town. "From the fires?"

I closed my eyes and inhaled deeply, but smelled nothing but the flora of the Shimazu garden and the distant sea, no waves of Death wafting up the mountain. I shook my head. "The fires only killed a few humans," I said. "Nothing that would explain this."

"Is it an earthquake somewhere? A tsunami?"

"I don't know," I said. I could admit that I'd been somewhat distracted during Chiyo's weekly briefings as of late, but surely I would have remembered an incoming wave of this many souls. Everyone's names were recorded in the Death Day book long before their lives ended, so sudden deaths shouldn't be a surprise. Chiyo always seemed to sense when I was ignoring her, so surely she would have spoken up if I'd been daydreaming when she tried to tell me about a massive natural disaster.

"Well, whatever it is, I'm sure it will be in the newspapers tomorrow," Tsukuyomi said. "Perhaps this is a good thing, if it's made you stronger."

"Perhaps," I said. The extra strength could hardly be bad, but not knowing where the souls had come from was unsettling. I was the only one who was supposed to tamper with Death in Japan. No one else had the right. "At the very least, I definitely don't need to sleep now."

"Wonderful," Tsukuyomi said, smiling, "now you can bask in the beautiful moonlight with me."

"Are you complimenting yourself?" I said, raising an eyebrow.

"It is an objective observation," he said. "Have you ever met anyone who thought moonlight was ugly?"

"So you think the whole world thinks you're beautiful? That explains a lot."

"I..." Tsukuyomi sputtered, his face red. "I'm a god," he said. "It's not about physical appearance. Gods are just inherently captivating."

"Oh? Does that include me?"

Tsukuyomi somehow turned an even deeper shade of red. I hadn't meant to embarrass him—I truly wondered if we saw each other in the same way, if he looked at me and saw something too perfect to be real—though it seemed he had taken my question a different way.

But it would be a lie to say I didn't enjoy seeing him so unbalanced.

"No!" he said, like the word had been squeezed out of him. "I—I mean—"

"No?" I said, crossing my arms.

"I mean, no, I wasn't thinking about you, specifically, but that doesn't necessarily mean you couldn't be included in that generalization, I mean, you certainly could, I just, it's not me who—"

"Would you two be quiet?" Neven said, pounding his fist against the tree.

"Yes, of course!" Tsukuyomi said far too quickly, clambering back to his own branch and resolutely turning away from me to face the moon.

I held back a laugh, not wanting to fluster Tsukuyomi further. If I teased him anymore, he might toss himself out of the tree to escape. So instead, I settled back against the trunk and peered through the branches at the crisp white moonlight that was, unfortunately, quite beautiful.

★ ★ ★

At dawn, we set off for Yakushima, and Death came with us.

I sensed it in the sharp salt of the ocean, the low hum of the volcano in the distance, the pheasants flying fast and far away. Our shadows seemed to stick to the dirt roads like molasses, tugging us backward rather than following behind us. A creature of Death was nearby.

Neven and I had stopped time and inspected our surroundings, but found nothing out of the ordinary. We had no choice but to keep moving forward and stick to more populated areas, hoping that whatever it was would be too afraid to attack in broad daylight with so many humans around.

The humans in the streets spoke of a strange plague in the north, one that had ravaged Aomori overnight, turning healthy humans to piles of bones, papery skin, and sunken eyes. No one had ever heard of such a disease. Either Chiyo had neglected to inform me of it, or some other force had evaded the Death Day book and taken souls anyway. I would have to discuss it more with Chiyo when I returned to Yomi, but at the moment, the Reapers were a more pressing problem. Besides, it was hard to be too distressed by an event that gave me perfect vision and endless stamina.

As we arrived in Yakushima, drawn up through the shadows onto the shore, all thoughts of the plague vanished.

Beyond the rocky coast, endless mountains rolled into the horizon, covered in green. Yakushima was a living, breathing creature. My Reaper's hearing caught the sound of birds in the forest, the whispering leaves of thousand-year-old trees, rivers flowing downhill through mossy rocks, cicadas crying and dewdrops bursting.

I had come from a land of darkness and Death, yet my

mother had come from a place of so much life. Having grown up in cold catacombs and then moving straight to Yomi's perpetual darkness, I'd never thought of life as anything beautiful or rich. It was a temporary flash of pretty lights, an opponent to the cold eternity of Death that I was born from, a language I would never speak. But Yakushima felt like being born again, this time as a creature of sunlight instead of shadows. Would I have become Death if I'd grown up in a place like this?

"It's beautiful!" the Yōkai said, grabbing my hand and running down the street. I let her pull me along the shore to a rocky ledge where water sparkled below us, like the sea was full of diamonds. I wondered if these bright, shimmering waters were anything like what Tsukuyomi had said Amaterasu created.

"Let's go swimming!" she said, kicking off her shoes.

"What? No," I said, grabbing her wrist before she could dive off the cliff into shallow waters. "We need to find Ikki's great-grandson first."

"And then we can go swimming?"

I sighed and nodded rather than argue further. She crushed me in a hug and I lifted my arms up, unsure where to put my hands as I looked to Neven for help. Mercifully, he pried her off me.

The Yōkai pouted but let Neven drag her away, shifting into her fox form. She snatched some yakitori away from a street vendor, gnawing carefully around the stick as she darted under our feet. Tsukuyomi asked for directions without scaring anybody and brought us to an office on the outskirts of town. Its walls were painted a dingy yellow color, the windows dark and boarded with wooden planks.

"Maybe they're closed for lunch?" Tamamo No Mae said, once again in her human form, her mouth full of stolen sweet potatoes.

"Or maybe government funding has run dry," Tsukuyomi said, peering through the cracks in the boards.

"This is the right place, isn't it?" Neven asked.

"According to the sign, yes," Tsukuyomi said. He knocked twice on the door and then tried the handle, but it was locked.

"Move," I said, sliding past Tsukuyomi and threading my shadows under the door, unlocking it from the inside.

I stepped into an office full of dust and towers of papers, some bound in old tomes and scrolls, others floating to the ground as the sudden rush of ocean air from the open door disturbed them. Sunlight fell in stripes across the disarray, filtered through the wooden planks. I waved my hand and lit the overhead chandelier, casting warm light over the papers.

Everyone stepped inside, taking in the mountains of clutter. Neven instantly started sneezing at all the dust, while the Yōkai's eyes tracked a spider scurrying across the wall with thinly veiled hunger. Tsukuyomi knelt down without hesitation and started examining the papers.

"These are family records," he said. "Though they seem rather...unorganized."

"To put it lightly," Neven said. "It doesn't seem like anyone's been here in years."

I grimaced as a scroll rolled off an overflowing table, unfurling across the floor.

"So we just start reading?" the Yōkai said, picking up a sheet of paper and folding it into a paper crane.

"Yes, carefully," Tsukuyomi said. "Ikki himself may not

have his own file, but his name should be in the records of his descendants born in Yakushima."

Neven shifted from foot to foot and I remembered that he likely hadn't learned to read Japanese in a century of total darkness.

"Here," I said, grabbing an ink brush from one of the desks and dipping it in a black inkwell. I took Neven's arm and scrawled a few different characters that Ikki could have used for his name on the back of Neven's hand. "Just look for one of those."

Neven nodded and walked away without a word of thanks, moving to the other side of the room with the Yōkai, who tried to subtly snatch a spider from the wall and stuff it in her mouth. Tsukuyomi watched us from the other side of the room, his expression eerily blank, then turned and began unrolling scrolls.

I picked up a scroll, scanning for any useful information. It had grown a bit easier to read handwritten Japanese in the last decade, since I'd spent a lot of time deciphering Chiyo's notes, but it still made my eyes ache after too long. I set aside the scrolls and moved to a pile of printed texts, but page after page showed nothing but lists of tax payments. I pushed the pile aside and hunted for anything that resembled a family registry, but instead I found property deeds, school records, marriage certificates, loan letters, even a hastily bound set of elegantly painted but sickeningly sweet love poems. I cast them to the floor, massaging the back of my neck.

Something shifted in the stacks behind me.

I rose to my feet, expecting one of the others, but Neven and the Yōkai were on the opposite side of the room, while Tsukuyomi was still by the windows.

"Ren?" Neven said, peering around a tall stack. "What is it?"

Tsukuyomi had paused in his reading, appearing behind me.

"Ren, what—"

"Shh!" I held a finger to my lips. Once again, paper scratched across the floor, though none of us had moved. Someone was here with us.

But who could it be? Reapers couldn't make themselves invisible, and I would have heard a human breathing the moment we stepped inside. I scanned every corner of the room, trying to figure out what I'd missed. There had to be something I wasn't seeing.

A stack of birth certificates tilted and collapsed, bursting across the floor in a great paper tsunami. The documents fluttered around the room like a swarm of birds, spinning in tight circles. I held my hands up to shield my face, trying to see through the whirlwind. The others took cover under tables, the Yōkai whimpering in her fox form beneath Neven.

The flurry of papers began to spiral into a hurricane, heavy scrolls sucked into its coil. Stacks of books toppled over with a thundering crash, sliding toward the center of the room until the twister inhaled them too. Pots of ink crashed to the floor and burst into shards, the ink oozing across the floorboards like black blood.

With a low rumble, like the earth was threatening to collapse beneath our feet, the hurricane began to settle. The papers hovered in midair, crowding tighter and tighter until they formed the shape of a creature.

A paper dragon loomed over us, its eyes glistening black circles of wet ink, its teeth shreds of torn parchment hanging over its lip. A scroll unfurled, forming the twisting length of its neck, with a majestic cape of red and gold pleated papers running down its back. A sharp paper tongue swiped out of its mouth, droplets of black ink drooling from its lip and splattering across the floor.

"Kyōrinrin!" Tamamo No Mae said, rushing forward with her arms outstretched.

The dragon hissed at her, his hot breath casting stray papers into a flurry around us. Tamamo No Mae shrieked into her fox form, cowering behind me.

"What is that?" Neven whispered, clutching a scroll in front of him.

"A spirit of knowledge," I said, edging closer. "A Yōkai."

I'd studied all of my kingdom's Yōkai in the past decade, but I'd never met a kyōrinrin. It was said that abandoned scrolls left unstudied for many years could sometimes transform into these dragons of wisdom.

This was far more fortunate than finding a human or a Reaper. Perhaps it could actually help us.

"Fascinating," Tsukuyomi said, stepping forward and tilting his head as he examined the Yōkai. "I've never seen one before. I always keep my scrolls very organized, so none had a chance to manifest."

The Yōkai regarded him calmly, like it was studying Tsukuyomi just as hard as it was being studied.

"Is it dangerous?" Neven whispered.

"It's made of paper," I said, nodding toward the twelve candles suspended on the chandelier overhead. It wouldn't exactly be hard to subdue an origami dragon.

"I wouldn't be so certain that it won't hurt us," Tsukuyomi

said. "The Chinese have a method of execution called ling-chi, or 'death by one thousand cuts.'"

Indeed, the Yōkai's papers had edges that rivaled the sharpness of Izanami's katana. I pictured running my fingers across them and could almost feel the way my skin would split open. The dragon watched me with a jagged grin, probably aware of my thoughts. There was little that a kyōrinrin didn't know.

"If it's a spirit of knowledge, would it know about Ikki's great-grandson?" Tamamo No Mae asked, backing away from the kyōrinrin as it arched its neck down to smell her, teeth bared. One of its long whiskers brushed my shoulder, tearing my sleeve.

"One can hope," I said, stepping slightly out of the dragon's range. "Yōkai, we require your help."

The kyōrinrin fixed its gaze on me, paper nostrils flaring. It responded, "Then his Augustness Izanagi announced to the peaches: 'As you have helped me, so must you help all the living.'" Its words sounded like a storybook, a voice that could recount ancient tales and epic journeys, a deep and important timbre that shook the floorboards. But what did any of that mean?

I frowned, looking to Tsukuyomi. He blinked, staring at the wall ahead as if digging through the palace of his memories for information that would explain the Yōkai's reaction.

"Peaches?" Neven said, scratching his head.

"The poet Basho used the pen name 'Tosei,' meaning 'green peach,'" said the kyōrinrin. "This was an homage to Chinese poet Li Bai, meaning 'white plum flower.'"

Was this a Yōkai, or an encyclopedia? I drummed my fingers across the counter, for once wishing that Tsukuyomi would swoop in and start explaining everything, but he kept blinking at the wall. "Tsukuyomi," I said at last, "do you—"

The dragon turned to Tsukuyomi. "The name of the Deity that was next born as he washed his right August eye was Tsukuyomi, Possessor of the Moon and Night."

Tsukuyomi finally tore his gaze from the wall, narrowing his eyes at the kyōrinrin. "That was a quote from the Kojiki," he said.

"The Kojiki, also known as the Furukotofumi, is Japan's record of ancient matters, such as—"

"All right, enough," I said, holding up a hand. "Can you do nothing but quote?"

"There is nothing you can see that is not a flower," the Yōkai said, baring its teeth in a mocking grin. "There is nothing you can think that is not the moon."

"I suppose that's a yes," Tsukuyomi said, crossing his arms.

I resisted the urge to slam my face into the nearest table. Of course, none of this could be easy. We'd found a Yōkai of infinite knowledge, but he could analyze none of it, only parrot it back to us.

"All right," I sighed, rubbing my forehead. "Just tell me where the sword of Ikki of Kagoshima is."

The dragon swayed, tilting its head to one side, but said nothing.

I scowled. "Now you have nothing to say?"

"'There is nothing more to do, so slay me now,' he said. So Tsuburu pierced the Prince with his sword—"

"Stop!" I said, holding up a hand. Darkness sparked in my fingertips but I clenched my fist until it retreated.

"Perhaps that answer isn't written anywhere," Tsukuyomi said, leaning back against a wall and rubbing his forehead as if trying to coax the answer out of his skull. "The Yōkai only seems to repeat words that have already been recorded, not create original sentences."

Neven nodded in agreement. "So we'll need to word our questions more carefully." He turned to the dragon. "Who is the great-grandson of Ikki of Kagoshima?"

The Yōkai blinked at Neven, saying nothing.

Tamamo No Mae hopped up on the counter, sitting cross-legged in front of the dragon and edging closer. "Maybe that's too specific," she said.

"Fine," Tsukuyomi said. "Tell me anything you know about anyone named Ikki who lived in Kagoshima before the Common Era."

The dragon's ominous silence chilled my blood. Its gaze rolled slowly over the four of us, then back to me.

"There is no one named Ikki, is there?" I whispered, feeling like the floor had turned to quicksand, like I was trapped and sinking fast. "That wasn't his real name."

A crooked grin warped the kyōrinrin's jaw, its tongue lashing across its teeth, licking up a strand of inky saliva.

Maybe Amaterasu hadn't known Ikki's true name, or maybe she couldn't be bothered to lay out a clear path for me, but I'd been a fool to not ask more questions. Now Ikki was gone, and there was no way to get more information from him.

Neven slumped against a table in defeat. Tsukuyomi's eyes moved very quickly around the room as if parsing through a book that only he could see, his face pinched with concentration.

"Is Ikki short for something else?" I said, while Tamamo No Mae unwittingly distracted the kyōrinrin with more of her origami.

Tsukuyomi blinked hard, as if he'd just remembered where he was. "Maybe Ikko, Ikuo, Ikurō," he said, half to himself. He shook his head. "There are many surnames as well. There could be thousands of people to parse through. Did Amaterasu say anything about his real name?"

I looked to Neven for help, but he only looked ill, probably having realized just how badly we'd miscalculated.

"She barely said anything about him," Neven said after a moment.

Tsukuyomi huffed out a breath and started to pace, which did nothing to ease the sinking feeling that I'd deeply and irrevocably ruined everything.

Had Ikki himself given us any clues? I tried to replay our conversation. I'd been so focused on his bone koma at the time.

"Stop pacing!" Neven said, taking off his glasses and rubbing his eyes.

"I'm thinking," Tsukuyomi said, not even looking up.

"You're making it harder for *me* to think," Neven said, grabbing Tsukuyomi's arm.

He jerked away as if burned. "I am the god of the moon. My gravity keeps the tides churning on Earth, which in turn keeps all sea life alive, and also prevents countless earthquakes and volcanic eruptions. So please, if you would be so generous, allow me the indulgence of *walking back and forth across this tiny square of floor while I think of how to save Japan!*"

Neven threw his hands up, looking to the sky as if asking the gods for help. Except two gods were already here, and neither of us could do anything.

"Why is it that every god I've met is completely absurd? First there was your mother, the rotting corpse," he said, jabbing his finger at Tsukuyomi, "then you and Hiro, who either want to kiss my sister or kill her but can't make up your damn minds. And don't even get me started on Amaterasu. Aren't gods supposed to, oh I don't know, *make our lives easier?*"

"Having sunlight certainly makes your life easier," Tsukuyomi said, crossing his arms and mercifully ignoring Neven's comment about wanting to kiss me. "You can thank Amaterasu for that."

Neven glowered. "It's her fault we're in this mess. She's supposedly all-seeing, yet can't manage to find a godly sword or learn a human's real name."

"She should know his real name," Tsukuyomi said, shoulders slumping. "It's not like her to lie about something like this."

Neven replied, but a sudden haze of blackness overtook my vision and washed his words away. The names of the dead flashed across my vision, kanji burned in red light onto my eyelids.

I wondered, for the first time, exactly how Amaterasu learned the names of humans. Did she simply know them the way humans knew how to breathe? Or was she like me, who saw their names when I closed my eyes? Surely that left little room for ambiguity. Unless…

The Goddess of Death can't even pronounce my name right, Ikki had said. I'd thought he meant I was too foreign to pronounce Japanese correctly…but maybe Ikki wasn't his name at all.

"How did Amaterasu know his name?" I said as my vision cleared, silencing Neven and Tsukuyomi's argument.

"She knows all the humans, Ren," Tsukuyomi said slowly.

I shook my head. "Yes, but *how*? Did she speak to him? Did she read it from a list?"

"She can see anyone's name when she closes her eyes," Tsukuyomi said. "All the gods can."

I grabbed Neven's arm, yanking up his sleeve.

"Ren?" he said. "What are you—"

"So Amaterasu only saw Ikki's name written down?" I said to Tsukuyomi.

He nodded. "Yes, but—"

I pointed to Neven's arm, dragging him closer to Tsukuyomi so he could see. One of the things I hated most about learning Japanese was that kanji could be pronounced differently in different contexts. "All three of these can be read as Ikki," I said, "but also as—"

"Kazuki," Tsukuyomi said, sighing. "Perhaps that's why the funayūrei didn't remember him at first." He turned to the kyōrinrin, eyes narrowed. "And perhaps that's why our pedantic friend over here is so suspiciously silent."

"How would a kyōrinrin even know that?" Neven said, rolling his sleeve down.

"Because they know everything," Tsukuyomi said. "It's just a matter of how much they deign to share. Isn't that right, Yōkai?"

"Don't answer that," I said as the dragon opened his mouth. "Just tell us who the last descendant of Kazuki of Yakushima is."

"Iwasaki Seiko, born in Yakushima in 1891," the kyōrinrin said. The wet ink of its eyes gleamed as it focused on me, its papers tearing as its devilish grin stretched its jaw. It had known the answer all along.

"*What?*" Tsukuyomi said, face pale.

"What?" Neven said. "Do you know him?"

"Her," Tsukuyomi said, glaring. "How do you not know her? That's the empress consort."

"Pardon me, but they didn't have newspapers in the deep darkness," Neven said.

Tsukuyomi said something sharp in return, but I could only hear Amaterasu's ominous words.

Things touched by gods do not tend to have quiet lives, she had said. The sword had been given to the royal family at the beginning of the world, and, like a magnet, it had found its way back.

"Isn't this good?" Tamamo No Mae said, hopping down from the counter. "We know who has the sword now!"

"Don't you understand?" Tsukuyomi said. "She's in the imperial family. The sword was probably part of her dowry."

"So the sword belongs to the emperor," Neven said, eyes wide. "We have to ask the emperor for his sword?"

I laughed, the sound coming out meaner than I'd intended, but Tsukuyomi's distress was contagious and a dangerous numbness ate across my skin.

"The emperor is not going to simply hand us a gift from the gods," I said. "We have to rob the royal family."

CHAPTER 16

Neven shrank back like he'd been slapped, but Tamamo No Mae looked all too delighted. "This will be the third palace I've visited this week!" she said.

"*You* won't be going anywhere near the palace," Tsukuyomi said. "You nearly killed the emperor in a past life."

"I didn't realize you were in charge," Neven said, glaring.

"I didn't realize you completely lacked common sense," Tsukuyomi said. "Well, that's not true. I did realize, but it felt impolite to point it out at that moment."

I sighed. "Tsukuyomi—"

"And the god Tsukuyomi killed the goddess Ukemochi with his bare hands," the kyōrinrin said. "He sank his thumbs into her eye sockets and pushed down until they bled."

The room fell silent. I looked to Tsukuyomi, too aware of

how accusing my gaze must have felt, but unable to stop my-self. That wasn't how Tsukuyomi had described his encounter with Ukemochi to me.

"What?" Tsukuyomi said, turning around slowly to face the kyōrinrin. All the stars in his eyes had dimmed. "That is not what happened."

But the kyōrinrin ignored him, its endless neck twisting in dizzying spirals before coming to a stop inches from Tsu-kuyomi's face, its inky black drool falling in sticky droplets at Tsukuyomi's feet.

"She screamed and begged for mercy," the kyōrinrin said, "but he laughed as he drank the blood from her eyes and crushed her bones to fine powder."

"That's a lie!" Tsukuyomi said, clenching his fists. The shock had washed away from his expression, his eyes suddenly murderous. His skin began to glow brighter, like the surface of the moon on clear nights, the sudden brightness stinging my eyes. "Why are you saying this?"

I looked between the kyōrinrin and Tsukuyomi, unsure what to think. All legends were told from a certain point of view. There was no absolute truth to any story, no single ver-sion of events. Surely I could trust Tsukuyomi more than a Yōkai I'd just met, but the dragon's words still made coldness ripple across my skin.

"He kept laughing as her tears flooded the rivers of Niigata and wet the soil of the land," the kyōrinrin said. "Her screams became thunder that echoed high in the mountains, a tor-tured cry that echoed across the canyons on stormy nights."

"Stop!" Tsukuyomi said, unsheathing his sword. Before I could stop him, he slashed his blade through the kyōrinrin's winding neck.

With the crisp sound of tearing paper, the Yōkai burst into a thousand sheets, metal scrolls slamming to the ground, paper falling like jagged snowflakes. Ink pooled at our feet, flooding the floor with swampy black. I doubted the Yōkai could have been killed so easily, but it seemed to have gone dormant once more.

Tamamo No Mae slipped her hand into mine, staring wide-eyed at the last of the falling papers. Tsukuyomi panted, slamming his sword back into its sheath.

"Do you plan to explain any of that?" Neven said, arms crossed.

Tsukuyomi closed his eyes, letting out a long breath. "The kyōrinrin was lying," he said, his voice low.

"So it lied about you but nothing else?" Neven said.

Tsukuyomi massaged his forehead. "Your pet fox was busy whispering to it while the rest of us were actually helping," he said. "Why don't you ask her what she said?"

"I was showing it my paper cranes!" the Yōkai said, her grip on my hand tightening.

"And she's not a pet," Neven said, stepping forward.

Tsukuyomi moved forward in response, but I grabbed his wrist and pulled him back, not wanting a repeat of the lake incident. As much as I disliked the idea of Tsukuyomi glee-fully drinking blood hundreds of years ago, it wasn't an urgent problem. We only had two days before Ivy would arrive, and we still had nothing to show for all our searching.

"We have what we need," I said, squeezing Tsukuyomi's wrist in one hand and the Yōkai's palm in the other. "Let's go."

As we returned to the streets, the scent of Death fell over us like a sudden deluge of hot rain. The few humans lingering outside hurried indoors, as if they too could feel the earth shuddering beneath our feet like something was trying to crawl its way out. The flowers grayed and curled into the dirt, the clouds dispersing into a hazy mist across the sky.

"Where is it coming from?" Neven asked as the door slammed shut behind us.

I scanned the area, but saw no sign of blond hair, no silver clocks that caught the light. The streets were near deserted, save for a small tent where a yakitori seller was packing up.

"We should go back to the mainland," I said. "We have what we came here for. Let's find somewhere with soft ground so I can take us to Tokyo."

"I agree," Tsukuyomi said. "We should travel through the shadows, just to be safe."

I started walking toward the shore where we'd arrived, Tsukuyomi by my side, but Neven's footsteps didn't follow.

"What is it?" I said, glancing over my shoulder, not doing a very good job of hiding my impatience.

"Where is Mikuzume?" he said quietly.

I spun around, scanning the street. Only a moment ago, she'd been holding my hand. It was as if she'd evaporated into the thick summer air, swallowed by the heat waves. I looked at Neven, whose face had gone paper white. We both knew what this meant.

For Reapers, who saw a million facets in every moment, nothing was truly sudden. Nothing happened in the blink of an eye. That was, unless someone was playing with the timeline.

"Have you lost something?" a man's voice said in English.

Three Reapers stood in the middle of the deserted street, where a moment ago there had been nothing but dirt and footprints. The Reaper in the center, a head taller than the others, held Tamamo No Mae by her wrists. She struggled, but the Reaper restraining her drew a knife and pressed it to her back, forcing her to go still.

Here? I thought. *They're going to threaten us in broad daylight with humans so close?* This street was mostly quiet and residential, not like the dense crowds at the town center, but humans might notice the sound of fighting behind their thin paper doors and come out to investigate. Perhaps the Reapers thought it would somehow give them an advantage, or perhaps they simply didn't care. But it wasn't like Reapers to be so sloppy.

Before I could think of how to respond, both of my wrists snapped. I whirled around but didn't even have a chance to feel pain before I saw another Reaper wrenching Neven's arms behind his back, yanking his shoulders out of their sockets and cutting his clock from his clothes as he fell to his knees. Another Reaper threw Tsukuyomi to the ground, jamming their knee into his spine.

I rushed toward Neven, but something yanked me back by my throat. Someone had grabbed my pendant, choking me backward until the chain snapped and I fell to the ground. I flopped facedown in the dirt, unable to catch myself on broken wrists. I didn't even realize the Reaper had taken my ring until he spoke.

"This must be it," he said.

I rolled over just as the Reaper held Hiro's ring up to the pale sun. The silver chain lay discarded on the ground by his feet.

I rose to my knees and tried to snatch it back, but my bones were still clicking back together and my fingers wouldn't respond. Instead, I jammed my shoulder into the Reaper who yanked me back by my hair, still holding up my ring in his right hand. Hiro's ring, that no one else had touched since he'd given it to me.

"He said she was turning time without a clock," the Reaper behind me called to the others.

Who said? Was this the "eyes" the other Reapers had been talking about?

The Reaper pocketed my ring and it felt like my whole chest had caved inward. So long ago, Hiro had knelt in front of me and slipped that ring on my finger and told me I was beautiful, and no matter how much had gone terribly wrong after that, I'd always wanted to keep that moment safe and secret. I could no longer taste that kind of hope, but for that small moment, it had been so real. I never wanted to forget how that felt, even if I could never feel it again.

"Let's forgo all the time turns now," the Reaper holding Tamamo No Mae said, his burning blue eyes focused on me. "You nearly gave the Timekeepers an aneurism."

"Is that supposed to deter me?" I said, cracking my left wrist back into place.

"No, *this* is supposed to deter you," the Reaper said, poking the Yōkai's back with his knife, making her squirm. "Try layering time turns again and we'll spear her through."

The Yōkai's eyes went wide. She whimpered and twisted to get away, but the Reaper held her tightly. Despite all the trouble the Yōkai had caused, I didn't exactly want to see her dismembered by Reapers. Not to mention that Neven would murder me for letting it happen.

Her eyes met mine, and for one single moment, her expression changed. I'd almost missed it, but in one thin sliver of a moment, so fast that it almost didn't exist at all, the fear dropped off her face. She was no longer a whimpering rabbit with its foot caught in a trap but the true Tamamo No Mae, the one who had lived thousands of years and seen chaos and death and creatures far more fearsome than Reapers.

Then she wrenched her head to the side and tried again to squirm from the Reaper's grip, her eyes filling with tears. My pulse began to slow back to normal, my blood cooling down to its regular corpse coldness. Even without our clocks, this situation wasn't completely out of our control.

"Do you have any idea who that is?" I asked.

"Someone of importance to you," the Reaper said.

I bit back a laugh. They really had no idea. Yōkai like Tamamo No Mae could only be killed in specific, unique ways. I knew exactly how to kill her because I'd nearly done it once—she had to be shot through with arrows and then beheaded. Nothing else would permanently end her. But the Reapers carried no arrows or swords. They couldn't kill her, no matter how hard they tried.

"Not really," I said, shrugging.

"Keep bluffing and we'll paint the streets with her blood," one of the Reapers said. "Come with us quietly. You'll be a present for Ankou when she arrives."

I shrugged. "All right."

The Reapers shared confused looks. "You'll come with us?"

"No," I said. "Kill her."

The Yōkai whimpered, and I almost felt bad, even if it was a charade. But not as terrible as I felt when Neven glared at me. He must have known I was up to something, or surely he would have intervened, but clearly he wasn't pleased.

"You're sure that's what you want?"

"Positive," I said. "Kill her, please."

"You think I won't do it?" the Reaper said, his grip tightening on the Yōkai, making her wince.

"I think you'll certainly try."

The Reaper scoffed. "They always said you were a monster. Now I see they were right."

I clenched my jaw and forced my expression not to change, refusing to show them that anything they said mattered. I cataloged my options as fast as possible. The sun was weak in the cloudy white sky, so my shadows had grown thin and pale. Perhaps I could subdue a few of the Reapers, but probably not all of them before one reached for their clock.

My eyes shifted over to the fire at the nearby yakitori merchant's grill. Once upon a time, a lifetime ago, I had escaped Ivy and her friends not with darkness but with light.

I turned back to the Reapers. "You may want to close your eyes," I said. "All of you."

Neven, who likely understood where this was going, immediately closed his eyes. The Reapers only scoffed, while Tsukuyomi and Tamamo No Mae shot me confused looks.

"Escaping us will not be that easy," the Reaper holding Tamamo No Mae said.

"Believe me, you want to close your eyes," I said, shooting a brief, desperate look to Tamamo No Mae, who frowned but finally closed her eyes. Tsukuyomi pressed his lips together in a firm line but quickly did the same.

"I don't know what kind of witchcraft you're attempting," the Reaper said, "but we don't answer to you."

I finally turned back to the Reaper, narrowing my eyes. "You will when you're dead."

Then a surge of light burst from the fires, swallowing the street in blazing white.

I closed my eyes and threw an arm out to shield my face, but the light still seared shapes into my vision. Warmth wafted off the fire, flames scorching my left side and charring my sleeve until it fell off like dead skin. The Reapers screamed over the roar of fire, still wailing even after I released my pull on light and the heat disappeared, leaving my skin raw and blistered.

I let the light die down and blinked until my vision cleared. All the Reapers had fallen to the ground, hands clapped over their eyes, blood seeping between their fingers. It wouldn't take long for their eyes to heal, but for a few precious moments, we had the advantage.

Neven and Tsukuyomi stumbled to their feet and rubbed their eyes, their clothing a bit scorched, but otherwise they seemed unharmed. In front of me, Tamamo No Mae had shifted into her fox form and sunk her teeth into the Reaper's bare arm, snarling as blood ran down his skin. It was almost comical, the way a High Reaper was rolling around and crying out like a human, felled by a wild animal. But why didn't he use his clock?

The Yōkai snarled and bit deeper, sharp claws digging into his arm. The Reaper tried with all his might to force her off, still ignoring his clock. A Reaper wouldn't simply forget about his clock while under attack... Unless he knew for a fact that it wouldn't help.

"Grab them!" I shouted over my shoulder to Neven and Tsukuyomi, who were still blinking stars from their eyes. The Reapers that had held us before the blast were still on their knees, trying to crawl or stumble away while rubbing their eyes. "If they're touching our skin, they can't escape us with a time turn."

I didn't wait to see if Neven and Tsukuyomi listened. Instead, I grabbed a Reaper by the throat and crushed him into the dirt with one hand while I searched his pockets with the other. He gasped and clawed at me until his fingernails scraped blood to the surface, but I ignored the sting as I sliced open every pocket. At last, my clock fell to the dirt, my ring rolling in a tight circle beside it. I pocketed both my clock and the Reaper's, then slipped my ring back on my finger and punched him in the face.

The metal crunched against his nose and a burst of blood soaked my shirt. I rose to my feet, my skin itching where the scratches were beginning to heal. I needed to make sure Neven was all right.

I turned just in time to see a Reaper jam his knife into Neven's hand, pinning him to the dirt.

Nothing will hurt you, I'd said. What a beautiful lie that had been.

Neven was trying to dislodge the knife from his hand, but he couldn't let go of the Reaper's wrist with his other hand, or a time turn would be the end of him. Blood rushed across the dirt road, pooling at my feet. At last, my shadows ripped free from the ground, swirling in ribbons around my arms despite the afternoon light.

The darkness congealed overhead, swallowing the sun. The sky dimmed to gray and then black and then the deepest, loneliest hollows of night as my shadows drank up every color in the world. I was drenched in a cape of night, my shadows spilling off me like sludge, like I'd drowned in darkness and clawed my way out of my own grave. I felt it spilling down my face, burning my eyes. My footsteps caused quakes in the earth as I crossed the distance between me and my brother.

Both Neven and the Reaper looked up as my shadow eclipsed them. Their eyes widened, and they both drew back as if repelled. Inside, I was endless planes of night, so I couldn't even imagine how I looked on the outside.

My shadows lashed out like snakes, shooting down the Reaper's throat. He tried to bite through them, but it was no use. They slithered down his throat and wrapped ribbons around his tiny, cold heart, then cleaved his chest open from the inside, ribs opening with a spray of blood.

The ground trembled below me, the smooth dirt roads fracturing into shards as the Earth pulled itself apart. My shadows presented me the Reaper's heart and I took it in both hands, blood rushing down my arms. The Reaper could only stare wide-eyed with his last breaths as I loomed over him, his heart in my hands. I wished that I could appreciate his pathetic gurgles as he realized that his soul would belong to me forever. But this didn't feel like victory at all. He had hurt my brother only a few feet away from me. I was a goddess, and yet I hadn't been able to stop it.

I took a bite of his heart, blood bursting from the muscles and running hot and sticky down my neck. His soul felt like acid tearing its way down my throat, but I swallowed it anyway and cast his heart to the ground. But the soul didn't make me feel better, or stronger, or even a little bit satisfied that I had won. Instead, it sizzled on my lips and churned deep in my stomach. I stomped on his heart and it burst across the road, splattering across my skirt, but still it wasn't enough. I was supposed to feel like a goddess when I won, but instead I was just a wild animal ravaging a dead thing. My skin had peeled away once more, my trembling hands nothing but bloodstained bones, Izanami's voice that wanted *more more more* thundering through my head, her hunger gaping wider, an empty chasm unfurling inside me and maybe I could devour the whole world, maybe that would be enough to save Neven next time.

"Ren?"

At the sound of my name, my shadows withered and paled, light cutting through them once more. I didn't know if it was Neven or Tsukuyomi who had called for me, but the voice sounded so hesitant, like they weren't sure if I was really there at all.

I turned around.

Neven and Tamamo No Mae stood beside each other, Tsukuyomi kneeling before me, all three of them staring at me like I wasn't Ren but someone wearing her skin as a cape. My hair stuck to the blood on my neck and my feet sloshed in red puddles around me and my eyes burned from the sharp scent of Death in the air. Suddenly I felt filthy, the iron scent all over my clothes nauseating. I dropped my gaze to Neven's hand, which had already started to scar over, then to his eyes, wide and horrified.

Other sounds began to filter in—the cries of humans and clattering of wood. I turned around.

My earthquake had ravaged the street, tearing the roads to puzzle pieces, toppling buildings into piles of planks, squishing humans like grapes inside. The street smelled of potent, acrid Death. My shadows overhead released the sky completely, casting the chaos in stark sunlight—the blood pooling in the streets, the shattered roofs and overturned carts.

This was my mother's home.

What would she think if she could see me now? It was just like Ikki said. I trampled into Japan and destroyed everything in my path.

I turned away from the others and started to run.

"Ren!" Neven called.

But I clenched my fist around my ring and stopped time, giving myself a head start. To them, it would look like I'd simply vanished into the summer air, like I'd reached for the horizon and the afternoon had swallowed me whole, leaving behind nothing at all.

CHAPTER 17

I kicked up a cloud of sand and sat on the shore. The air smelled sour from blood and Death, the sky still dripping darkness on the white canvas of a clear summer afternoon, blurring the sky to a murky gray.

I'd flattened my mother's hometown, and for what? I hadn't even prevented Neven from getting hurt. If I couldn't protect one person, how could I protect an entire country?

I sank my hands into the sand and let out an inhuman sound, somewhere between a scream of frustration and a sob, wishing I could tear the Earth to shreds. My hands began to shake and I curled further into myself. I wished that I could at least cry, because then I would know that I wasn't the monster Neven thought I was. But I couldn't manage even a single tear. Instead, all of my bones trembled like it was the dead of winter and I was a rickety wooden house shaking apart.

The worst part was that I'd asked for this.

I'd agreed to marry Hiro because I'd wanted the world to bow at my feet, for everyone who'd ever called me a foreigner to smash their face into the dirt and cower beneath me. I hadn't known then that power wasn't just being better than everyone else. It was trying to keep the world turning all by yourself, and a palace of a thousand rooms but no one inside them, and spilling the blood of everyone who mattered just to keep your kingdom breathing. I'd inherited a kingdom I couldn't protect, and Ivy would take it all. Would she leave once she killed me? She'd probably turn Yomi into an English colony out of spite. I didn't think anything could be worse than dying, but dying in vain seemed the most terrible fate of all.

Light began to flicker on the horizon. I looked up as a ribbon of blue fire glimmered along the water, snaking up and down in wide arcs. It wound its way closer to me and I rubbed my eyes to make sure it was real. I'd been awake for two days, so perhaps the influx of souls last night couldn't make up for the lack of sleep.

The shape spiraled closer, not touching the water, as if it was only an illusion of light. Then piece by piece, it began to crystallize into the shape of a creature—sharp claws appeared along the ribbon, crooked legs extending. At last, white teeth appeared, hanging down like a prickly row of stalactites. Sapphire eyes formed above the mouth, made of the dizzy shades of half colors that you saw when you closed your eyes, like the creature was made of dreams. The sharp lines of its face and curves of its scales settled, and at last the light took the shape of a fanged dragon hovering above the water.

Blue fires dance across the sea just beyond the beaches. That was what Hiro had said when he first told me about Yakushima. This was a ryūtō, a fire dragon made by tricks of light. It was nothing but beautiful illusions cast in cold fire, the echoes of the dragons that had once swum in the deep waters. This Yōkai wouldn't hurt me.

"Your Highness."

The ryūtō drifted closer until its front claws sank into the sand before me, carving deep scars into the shore. Its voice sounded like wind chimes, more music than speech, while its eyes up close were made of one thousand glittering prisms. It knelt down as if bowing, and silver fish spilled from its mouth onto the sand.

"I bring you these fish as an offering," it said. "Please, may I have your blessing?"

I blinked, startled by the request. On occasion, I'd given my blessing in Yomi, often during the weddings of Shinigami. Chiyo had always made them formal affairs, with many prayers in Japanese so ancient I could hardly understand them, a spray of dead flower petals, offerings of gold and jade that I threw into the vault when everyone finally left.

The dying fish flopped on the sand before me, making me feel ill.

"Put them back," I said. "I have no need for them."

The ryūtō scooped them back into its mouth and vanished beneath the surface of the water, reappearing moments later.

"I'm sorry, Your Highness," it said, "it is all I have to offer you."

"I don't need your offering," I said, "and I don't know why you would want my blessing."

The dragon blinked, tilting its head to the side. "Your Highness?"

"I am Death," I said. "Unless that is what you seek, why do you come to me?"

"Death is also creation," the dragon said. "The two cannot be separated."

"Your village is destroyed because of my carelessness," I said, digging my hands into the sand. I'd come here to be alone, not to be reminded of everything I wasn't. "Soon, everything else will be ruined too."

The dragon watched me carefully, its long whiskers gently waving as if bobbing in the sea.

"It is not destroyed," it said. "The buildings have fallen, but my village is alive."

"Humans are dead," I said, dropping my gaze down to the sand.

"Creatures are not destroyed just because they are dead," the dragon said. "Surely you of all people know that, Your Highness."

"Will you maintain your optimism when the Reapers plunder Japan?" I said in Death.

The ryūtō bristled, a shiver rippling down its spine and tail, scales glimmering from the light reflected on the waters. I paled, instantly regretting the effect the language of Death had on the Yōkai. Could I do nothing but terrify everyone around me?

I shifted onto my knees. "Come here," I said gently.

With unhesitant trust that only made me feel worse, the

dragon moved closer, bowing its head. I placed my palm across its nose, which felt like cool pearls beneath my hand.

"As the keeper of night and the end of all things, I give you my word that the shadows will walk beside you, and that you will never be alone in darkness."

The dragon shivered, light flashing across each individual scale as it caught the sunlight on its back. Those were the words Chiyo taught me, though I didn't know if they had any power or were just a kind sentiment. The Yōkai seemed to appreciate them all the same, preening in afternoon sun.

"You say the Reapers are coming here?" it said at last, settling back down to the sand.

I nodded. "Soon, their god will come to challenge me."

The dragon blinked slowly, making a low humming sound. "It wouldn't be the first time that another god has tried to take Yomi," it said. "The Mongol gods came long ago, and they were defeated. The Reapers will be defeated too."

"How were they defeated?" I asked, leaning closer. Perhaps there was another way to drive away the Reapers, something Izanami had done before.

"Susano'o washed away the ships in a great storm."

My shoulders slumped. Of course, the only way to protect an island nation was by sea, and that meant Susano'o. But at least he had been willing to wash away foreign ships in the past. That meant he would likely hold up his end of our bargain, if I delivered on my end.

But that was looking less and less likely by the day. How ridiculous it was that everything depended on an old piece of metal. Why couldn't Susano'o have just asked me to marry him and be his sea prisoner?

I tipped my head back, looking at the gray sky. "The Reapers are going to disembowel me."

The ryūtō hummed. "The Reapers are fearsome indeed," it said, "but there is greater danger on the horizon."

I frowned. "What could be greater than the fleet of time turners about to invade my shores with the sole purpose of killing me?"

The dragon bowed its head, nostrils flaring. "Your Highness, I know who you walk with."

I blinked. "Yes?"

"I am an old spirit," the ryūtō said. "I know the hearts of many creatures. That is why I know that the Reapers are not the ones you should fear the most."

My skin went cold. A dark, rotten feeling bloomed in my chest.

"Who, exactly, am I supposed to fear the most?" I said.

"Ren?"

I turned around. Tsukuyomi stood on the shore, his shoes in one hand, the wind on the beach blowing back his blood-stained white kimono. In the approaching dusk, with the backdrop of a sky slowly turning red, he looked like a fallen angel who had crawled his way up from hell.

I turned back to the ryūtō, but it had vanished. *The Reapers are not the ones you should fear the most*, it had said. I was only traveling with three people, so it wasn't hard to figure out who the dragon had been implying. I could never fear Neven—even if he somehow ended up betraying me, he could go right ahead and carve my heart out and feed it to Ivy, because I didn't want to exist in a world where my brother would turn on me.

That left Tsukuyomi and Tamamo No Mae, two ancient

creatures who had done terrible things long before I was born. But neither of them felt evil the way Ivy did, and if either of them wanted me dead, then they'd missed lots of opportunities to easily end me.

What did a ryūtō know of them, anyway? He said he knew the hearts of ancient creatures, but I knew their hearts here and now.

"Everyone is looking for you," Tsukuyomi said.

"I know, I know," I said, turning back to the sea. "I'm your only way to Tokyo. I wasn't going to abandon you here."

Tsukuyomi let out a sharp laugh, sitting beside me. "We weren't looking for you because we needed transportation, Ren."

"Then why?" I said, scowling at him. "To reprimand me?"

"Reprimand? Ren, we're all alive because of you."

"And some humans aren't," I said, pressing a hand to my eyes.

"Ren." Tsukuyomi took my wrist, gently pulling my hand away. "You've taken human lives before."

"That was for Neven. This was because I'm careless."

"No, this was because the Reapers backed us into a corner."

I shook my head. "I don't need meaningless consolation."

"Yes, I know. You prefer stewing in the hellfire of your own anger."

I hugged my knees, feeling like a small child being scolded. Why should he care if I clung to my anger? It didn't matter if it made me feel rotten inside, or made everyone hate me. At least they would be alive.

"Does that make me a true god now?" I said, kicking a line in the sand with my foot. "Every god I've ever known has ruined everything with their temper, including you."

I'd wanted the words to hurt, but somehow I hadn't anticipated the way Tsukuyomi's shoulders slumped, his gaze dropping to the sand.

"You're not wrong," he said. "In the legends of all the deities in Japan, emotions do tend to lead to ruin. Susano'o's longing for our mother, my shame at losing my power, Hiro's vengeance... All of us, except for Amaterasu, I suppose. She has no attachments, and that is why she's the most powerful goddess."

"I can see why she's the favorite sibling," I said, resting my chin on my knees.

Tsukuyomi's lips pinched together. He started to speak, then shook his head like he wanted to erase the thought from his mind.

"What is it?" I asked.

He sighed. "For a long time, I believed she was perfect," he said. "But then I saw you and Neven, and I knew she could never love me the way you love him."

I turned to face Tsukuyomi, unable to stop myself. The stars in his eyes looked dimmer, somehow much farther away than before. "All I'm saying is that there are many kinds of gods, Ren," he said. "None of us are entirely good."

I stayed perfectly still, unable to look away from Tsukuyomi. In truth, I hadn't stopped to think that Tsukuyomi was the kind of person who cared about something like love. I knew he wanted his family's approval and respect, but those things were very different from love. I traced his gaze up at the sky, where he always seemed to be staring at something I couldn't see. It occurred to me for the first time that maybe he wasn't looking at his home on the moon, but at the sun.

"Then what makes us gods?" I said.

Tsukuyomi frowned. "What do you mean?"

"What makes us so special if we're just as flawed as humans?"

Tsukuyomi blinked, his eyes flat. Then he laughed, shaking his head. "I don't know," he said. "Maybe we're not special at all."

Maybe *I* wasn't, but Tsukuyomi certainly was. Humans stared when they walked past him. He was fireworks and great white waterfalls and the sky unfolding at the top of a mountain. I was just Ren.

"If we're not special, then we'll never keep the Reapers out of Japan," I said.

He shook his head. "That's not quite what I meant. We know where the sword is now. We just—"

"—just have to meddle in Japan's politics and possibly involve the emperor in what's supposed to be the business of gods, then trust that your capricious brother will keep his word."

Tsukuyomi clenched his jaw but made a hum of agreement. "Even without Susano'o, we'll find a way to stop the Reapers."

"Ivy would dismember me."

"I wouldn't let her," he said, his words oddly sharp.

I stared back at him for a long moment, the promise in his eyes stripping away everything I'd wanted to say. He must have realized he'd startled me, because he blushed and his gaze softened.

"I told you I'd protect you," he said, softer this time.

Tsukuyomi wasn't breathing anymore, just sitting perfectly still apart from the slowly spinning stars in his eyes, looking at me like I was the first breath of light on the horizon after a long, dark night. He was closer to me than before, though I had no memory of him leaning in, like I was a planet drawn into his orbit. My skin grew warm despite the ocean breeze and damp sand beneath my feet. I felt like the next breath of the sea would carry me away, and nothing was tethering me to Earth but the look in his eyes.

I knew that look. But I couldn't afford to play such a dangerous game.

"Don't," I said.

He blinked, drawing back slightly. "Don't what?"

I swallowed, searching for something that would make him turn away, but it was hard to think with his starry eyes so close to me.

"We made a deal," I said at last. "That's all this is. A deal."

The words came out stiff the way lies often did, and I was sure Tsukuyomi knew it, but what else could I have said?

At my words, the stars in Tsukuyomi's eyes froze in their slow circles, like an entire universe had held its breath. He looked away, shoulders falling. I wasn't supposed to care about the sad slope of his lips, or the way his fingers clenched in the white sand, or the stiff curtain of propriety once more falling over him, smoothing out his features until he looked more like a painting than a person. It wasn't supposed to matter, because I was smarter than I was ten years ago. I wouldn't sell my soul to darkness for a false promise of power, and I certainly wouldn't fall for the same face twice. Hiro didn't matter to me anymore, so why did a cold ache spread through my chest, like ice had woven through my ribs and cracked them one by one?

Because he's not Hiro, I thought.

"If that's what you want," Tsukuyomi said, sounding faraway even though he was right next to me.

It wasn't what I wanted, but as a goddess, what I wanted hardly mattered at all. But Tsukuyomi was a god too, and somehow that didn't stop him.

I shouldn't have risked falling the same way twice. I should have looked away, or stood up and left, or stopped time to gather my thoughts before I did something foolish.

Instead, I set my hand on top of Tsukuyomi's.

He tensed beneath my touch, then his hand relaxed, releasing his death grip on the sand.

I didn't know what to say, so I turned back to the shore, letting my hair hang over my face so he couldn't see my expression. His hand was so warm beneath mine. I knew it was a mistake, but for the first time in a very long time, I felt the embers of irrational hope beginning to stir, like maybe the world wasn't doomed and ruined, maybe something awaited me at the end of my journey besides a cruel and slow death. It was dangerous to hope for happy endings, but maybe I was still a fool.

The next wave of the tide rushed up underneath us, spreading a stinging coldness down my legs. We both flinched, pulling our hands back.

"We should find Neven and the Yōkai," I said.

Tsukuyomi nodded, slowly rising to his feet. "We may need a change of clothes before we attempt to infiltrate the royal palace," he said, inspecting his bloodstained sleeve with distaste.

"*You* certainly do," I said. "White is the single most impractical color you could have worn."

Tsukuyomi scowled, though the twinkling stars in his eyes told me he wasn't really angry. "I am the moon. Which is, as you may have noticed, white."

"And I am Death, but somehow I don't combust if I put on a colorful kimono."

"White is easy to clean with bleach."

I shook my head. "Don't lie. You just enjoy your celestial aura so much that you dress impractically."

"It's not an aura," Tsukuyomi said, his face red. "I am celestial, regardless of my clothing. Even with no clothes at all, I am celestial."

I raised an eyebrow. Tsukuyomi's face turned an even deeper shade of red and he turned around.

"Don't," he said.

"I didn't say anything."

"Just—come on," he said, holding out a hand to help me up. I didn't hesitate this time, allowing him to pull me to my feet. Along the shore, the bright sun burned across the waters, the white summer day slowly darkening with the promise of dusk.

CHAPTER 18

On my own, Tokyo was an inconvenient destination. For one thing, the city was all wood and stone, not enough soft earth that I could travel through by shadow. Too many humans walked the streets at all times of day and night, so appearing suddenly almost guaranteed that I'd accidentally scare a nearby human out of their mind. Besides, I so rarely visited Tokyo that I didn't know its dark alleys or dead ends or any central location that I could appear without attracting undue attention.

With four people, it was an impossible task. I imagined the four of us tumbling out of the shadow of a streetlight, all the humans around us screaming and fleeing. It was much safer to bring us just outside of Tokyo and then travel into the city by foot.

I took us to a village just outside of the city, beside a flat plane of green water and trees just beyond the city's border. We could find a hotel nearby, then catch a bus into Tokyo in the morning, once we'd figured out a plan to infiltrate the palace.

Now that humans were involved, the entire quest suddenly felt wrong, like I was straying too far from a path and venturing out into dark woods. I'd always thought that creatures of Death should only cross paths with humans at the end of their days. We weren't given such great power to bother humans, or trick them, much less steal from their head of state. All I'd ever wanted was a quiet house in Yomi for me and Neven to mind our own business, and now I had to rob the emperor just to stay alive. I only hoped I wouldn't flatten the imperial palace the way I'd done to my mother's hometown.

My feet dragged in the mud as we trudged through the trees. Moonlight filtered between the branches, glowing a ghostly white. The Yōkai held my hand, Neven on her right and Tsukuyomi on my left, the silence between us almost physically heavy, like the canopy of trees was slowly shrinking down, caging us in.

Tsukuyomi and I had met Neven and the Yōkai at the outskirts of Yakushima after leaving the shore. Both of them had stared at me from a distance, like I might burst into tears at any moment. Now Neven watched me uneasily whenever I turned away, as if I couldn't sense him staring, while the Yōkai decided the best remedy was to hold my hand and whine that she wanted to be carried on my back. I tolerated the handholding but firmly drew the line at piggyback rides.

As the trees began to thin, city lights glowing in the distance, Tamamo No Mae squeezed my hand.

"Ren?" she whispered.

I closed my eyes, wondering if she would simply stop speaking if I didn't answer. My bones felt impossibly heavy, there was sand in my clothes, I reeked of blood, and I hadn't slept in almost two days.

"Ren?" she said again, louder this time.

"What."

She glanced uneasily around us. "I don't mean to alarm you," she said, "but we're being followed."

I closed my eyes, coming to a stop. Could I not have even one night of peace?

"How do you know?" I asked. "I don't hear anything."

"I can smell them," the Yōkai said.

I sighed, squeezing the Yōkai's hand so hard it probably hurt. I wished that, just once, someone else could solve my problems for me. I would gladly hand over my sword and throne to anyone who would handle the Reaper trailing us and let me sleep.

I sank down to the grass, ignoring the others' questions as the wet dirt formed to the shape of my legs. I tried to conjure some sort of plan, but my mind was frayed and torn and all I could think about was the taste of hearts on my tongue and the coldness of the earth seeping into my bones.

I breathed in, and suddenly felt as though my chest had unfolded, my lungs drinking in all the air in the world, every warm summer day and starless night, the smell of wet grass and touch of moonbeams. My fingers sank into the earth as a thousand names burned across my vision—more souls were dying, probably of the mysterious plague. The ache in my bones melted away, and once again my vision grew sharper, my heartbeat slowing. Then, even the wet earth and my clothes drenched in blood and ocean couldn't make me cold anymore.

"Ren?"

The Yōkai's timid voice cut through, the names fading from my vision.

I yanked time to a stop, rising to my feet and tapping the others to bring them into the tiny circle of frozen night.

"This ends now," I said. "The Reapers always know our next step. We need to get ahead of them."

The others nodded in solemn agreement.

"How can you get ahead of someone who controls time?" Tamamo No Mae asked quietly.

"They're not the only ones who can control it," Neven said, gripping his clock.

"Fighting with time doesn't work," I said, wincing at the memory of our last attempt at layering time turns. "We need to set a trap. We'll force them to come out when we're ready for them, when they think they have the advantage."

Neven raised an eyebrow. "There's not much we can do to surprise Reapers. They know all of our tricks."

"Do they know all of mine?" Tsukuyomi said.

I turned to him. As the moonlight cut through the branches, it reflected off his skin, like he was the only star in a cold, dead universe.

"You have more tricks?" I said.

"Moonlight can do many things," he said, nodding. "You said that Reapers don't see well from a distance, right? I think we can use that to our advantage."

From high up in the trees, I watched myself sleeping in a clearing on the forest floor, curled up among the leaves.

Everything we see is just a trick of light, Tsukuyomi had said. Then he'd turned around and carved me out of moonlight with a single stroke of his hand.

From a distance, I looked far too real. He'd painted me in vivid detail, down to the creased folds in my kimono, the lopsided bow on my obi and the strands of my long hair that got caught in it. When had Tsukuyomi managed to catalog all those details in his mind? My face felt warm and I was suddenly grateful for the darkness that hid my expression.

The only problem was that up close, within a few feet, the angle of the moonlight through the trees changed, and the light cut through me like I was halfway in another dimension, made of only air.

Tamamo No Mae hid in her fox form among some bushes on the ground, probably the best disguised out of the four of us. Neven hid in the branches of a tree on the other side of the clearing, while Tsukuyomi pretended to sleep a short distance away from "me" but still bathed in moonlight. Anyone who stepped foot into his moonlight would be under his control.

For an hour, we waited in silence for the Reapers to arrive. Holding my breath for that long wasn't a problem, but the bark dug into my back and tiny ants crawled up my skirt. I began to worry that Tsukuyomi might actually fall asleep if we had to wait for too long.

Soft footsteps crunched through the dying grass. I froze, taking exquisite care not to breathe, not to shift my weight onto my other leg, or adjust my grip on the bark, or even shake my hair away from my face, because a Reaper would hear every single sound.

A hooded figure in a black cloak entered the clearing, hesitating just at the barrier of the circle of moonlight. Tsukuyomi had stopped breathing, so I was sure he'd noticed it too. But he couldn't act until the Reaper was in the moonlight.

The broad shoulders told me it was likely a male Reaper, but he was turned away from me so I couldn't make out his face. The moment he stepped inside the circle, he would be our prisoner.

He stood unmoving for far too long at the clearing's edge, watching me and breathing slowly.

Had he realized that it wasn't me sleeping in the grass? I considered deepening the shadows to obscure his vision, but I didn't know if that would ruin Tsukuyomi's illusion. The longer he stood there, the sweatier my palms grew against the tree. I would need to adjust my grip soon, or risk falling down to the forest floor.

Tamamo No Mae growled from inside the bushes. The Reaper turned to her, but before he could react, she barked and lunged forward, snapping her jaws. The Reaper took a startled step back into the circle of moonlight.

He hit the ground and didn't rise again, unable to move as the unfiltered moonlight bound his limbs like invisible chains. The illusion of me vanished and Tsukuyomi rose to his feet.

I clambered down the tree, bark scraping my palms. Neven had climbed down faster than me and reached the clearing first, but came to a sudden stop, his face washed of all color.

My feet hit the ground and I ran to the other three, who had all stopped moving. The Reaper was kneeling on all fours, facing Neven. I circled around to stand beside them, and suddenly understood why Neven's face had gone so ashen.

"Ambrose?"

My shadows locked around my father's hands and feet, slamming him backward against a tree and binding his arms around the trunk. He hung his head, staring down at the ground and letting the shadows conceal his expression.

I know who you walk with, the ryūtō had said. Had this been what it meant?

Once, I had dreamed of seeing Ambrose one more time just so I could shatter his nose with my fist, to show him just one fraction of the pain he'd caused me in the century of being my landlord when he should have been my father. I used to have great speeches planned, monologues of scathing condemnation that I muttered to myself at night on the off chance that we ever crossed paths again.

But then time weathered the edges of my anger, unfolding it like an origami crane whose paper was too worn to hold its shape any longer. When I thought of Ambrose, I thought of empty gray skies and whispers of rain not quite ready to fall and a thousand things that could have turned out differently.

Neven stood before him, eyes a shocking shade of violet. His hands shook just like when he was a child awaiting punishment for his poor grades.

"Are you the one who's been following us?" I asked.

Ambrose said nothing, not even moving, his gaze still fixed on the ground.

My shadows tightened a few degrees around his wrists, threatening to cut off circulation, snap the bones through. The very least he could do, after everything, was look me in the eyes.

"How did you even find us?" I said. "We travel by shadows."

Ambrose sighed. "I was assigned to Naoshima upon my arrival here. Your Shinigami there were quite…forthcoming about your plans."

I closed my eyes, barely suppressing the urge to tear my own hair out. The Shinigami couple who'd asked for a transfer several nights ago were stationed in Naoshima. My Shinigami talked among themselves, and with so many people coming in and out of my palace each day, it wasn't surprising that word of my journey to the sun palace had made it back to them.

"You always talk about where you're going next," Ambrose continued, his voice dry and cracked. "It's not hard to catch up with you when time is no obstacle."

I cursed. I'd discussed our plans mostly in English, simply because it felt unnatural to speak to Neven any other way, even if his Japanese had improved. But I should have thought about who might overhear us.

Ambrose lifted his head, turning his gaze toward Neven.

"You've grown up," he said. It was the same even-keeled tone that I remembered from my childhood. Not quite a compliment, just a detached observation. Neven responded with a small, uncomfortable smile before looking away. I couldn't stop my shadows from wrapping tighter around Ambrose's limbs.

How dare he look Neven in the eyes, but not me? Sure, Neven had grown taller, but I had become a goddess.

"And you have nothing to say to me?" I said.

At last, Ambrose looked up. In my memory, his eyes had always been gray and vacant. Now they were sharp blue, like the morning sky. He seemed so much older than I remembered, the corners of his eyes wrinkled and folded.

"Wren," he said, the word sighed out like it had drained all his energy. "I'm sure you know why I'm here."

I wished I could cleave the Earth in half and saw down every tree in the godforsaken forest, because even now, Ambrose was so damned cold. I wished he could be cruel instead, anything but that infuriating calmness, like he couldn't be bothered to feel anything at all.

Maybe he would feel something if his life was on the line. Like all the humans in their very last moments, he would come untethered, squirming and crying like a beetle on its back.

I pulled my knife from my sleeve and pressed the tip to his throat.

Neven grabbed my arm, but he wasn't strong enough to stop me.

"Ren," he said, tearing at my sleeve. "Ren, please."

My shadows wrapped around Neven's waist and pulled him away from me. The fox circled quickly around Neven's feet while Tsukuyomi crossed his arms and watched with a sour expression. I kept my gaze fixed on Ambrose.

"You do understand that we can't let you go," I said.

The colors in his eyes stilled, like a rushing river suddenly iced over.

For the first time in my life, Ambrose looked genuinely surprised. As a child, I'd wanted so badly to carve emotions onto his face, even if they were hate or sorrow. Just like every other creature, low or high, Death was what he feared most of all.

"I never meant for things to turn out this way," he said.

"Stop," I said, clenching my teeth. The knife pricked his skin, a single pearl of blood running down his throat. "Don't lie to me just because you're scared."

"I'm not lying," he said. "I want you to understand what really happened when I brought you to England. Once I'm dead, you'll never know the truth."

"I was there. I know what happened and I know how you treated me. That's the only truth that matters."

"You were a child," he said, desperation tearing at his voice as more blood trickled down his neck. "There was so much I couldn't explain to you when you were younger."

"You think explaining changes anything?" I said. The ground began to rumble, like a great dragon beneath our feet was slowly waking. How dare he think that words alone could erase the past? Besides, I had never been some naive brat who couldn't handle the truth, the harshness of reality. Whatever he had to say, he should have said it much sooner.

"Please," he said. "I'm your father."

"I have no father!" I said in Death, my voice peeling the leaves from the branches, stripping the grass of all its color and making the lake shudder in the distance. "You renounced me, Ambrose!"

"I didn't want to!"

I froze. The wind settled down, the branches falling still, like the whole world had turned to glass, a breath away from shattering. Ambrose's eyes were wide and blue and earnest.

"What?" I whispered, lowering my knife.

Ambrose let out a breath, hanging his head.

"When Izanami killed your mother, I didn't know what she would do to you," he said. "I took you back to England with me to be safe, but High Councilor Cromwell wanted to kill you. He said it was shameful for a High Reaper to have an impure child. So I told him that I would formally renounce you, that we'd keep you off any official records, keep you out of everyone's way, like you didn't even exist."

I scoffed. *So he was trying to blame Cromwell for his cruelty?* "I'm sure it wasn't hard to convince you."

Ambrose shook his head. "I had to convince *him*," he said. "If I hadn't, you would have been killed."

"All that tells me is that you were always a coward," I said. "You think that just because you didn't bow to Cromwell while he killed your only child, that makes you brave? You think that absolves you of anything? Cromwell didn't make you treat me like an unwanted pet, even in private."

"The High Council has eyes everywhere," Ambrose said, sighing. "You know this."

I shook my head, even though I knew he was right. It was hard to keep secrets from High Reapers when your voice echoed endlessly along the stone walls of the catacombs, when they could hear even a bead of sweat rolling down your face.

"I needed to be sure that the High Council never found out you mattered to me. The only reason they let you stay was because they thought you were nothing but a houseguest. They didn't want you to interfere with Council business, or distract me. As long as you were no one, they were willing to look away."

"And that was fine with you?" I said, my voice cracking. "That I was no one?"

Ambrose hung his head. "I did what I had to do to keep you alive."

I let out a sharp laugh. "You've sent other Reapers to kill me."

"I don't have a choice anymore!" he said, tears pooling in his eyes, tracing the wrinkles in his face. "Ankou is forcing my hand, and disobeying her won't save you. They would just send someone else in my place. But I led them astray as best I could. I never told them where you slept."

"Or maybe you were just never smart enough to know where we slept," Tsukuyomi said, crossing his arms.

Ambrose shot him only a fleeting glance before turning back to me.

"I am not a good man, or a good Reaper," he said, his voice low. I realized that Ambrose had never before looked me in the eyes when he spoke. He would always stare past me like I was a dirty window. But now he looked at me like there was nothing and no one else in the world. Though his skin had paled and cracked, his eyes were blue lightning and angry star fire instead of the weak gray and whispers of blue that I'd always known. "All my children have left me because that is what I deserved. I understand that now."

"Father," Neven said, struggling against my shadows. But for once, Ambrose ignored him, looking only at me.

"I don't expect forgiveness," Ambrose said, "but I need you to know that everything I was, and everything I did, was because I love you."

His words felt like mountains crumbling, the whole world trembling apart, scorched forests and parched riverbeds and the death of a thousand things all at once. I wanted to clap my hands over my ears and scream until I couldn't hear his words echoing in my mind anymore. Out of all the things he'd ever said to me, this was the cruelest of all because it could never be true.

I thought of every time my father had turned away from me, had left me alone to cry in my room, had pretended that I didn't have a birthday, had told the other Reapers that Neven was his only child. All of that had been a lie?

I closed my eyes, wishing my shadows would drag me straight to the center of the Earth where I would blister and burn and die. For centuries, I'd wished that Ambrose would say those words to me. But now he came too late, after I'd already become cruel and ruined, after he'd planted seeds of hate in me and let them bloom into thorny flowers.

Ambrose didn't know what love was. To him, love was a weapon, a tool to set himself free. How dare he use love to save himself when he had no idea what it truly was. Love meant that I would burn the whole world to make Neven smile. It meant that I would carve my heart out just to see Hiro one last time. I'd had limbs severed and organs crushed and bones shattered and none of it had ever hurt as much as love.

Maybe Ambrose thought he understood love in whatever way his tiny, cold heart was capable of. But however much he'd loved me, he'd feared Ankou more.

"You didn't come here out of love," I said at last. It hurt so much to look in his eyes, but I was no stranger to pain. "You came here because you want to be absolved. You want to be Ivy's dog and not feel bad about it."

He shook his head. "Please, believe me, Ren, I wouldn't—"

"It doesn't matter if I believe you," I said. "It's too late." I raised my knife to his throat again.

"Ren, I love you," he said again. I closed my eyes because it stung even more to hear the words a second time.

"Stop saying that when you don't even know what it means!" I said, my shadows digging clawed fingers into his scalp and wrenching his head back, baring his throat to my blade. Loving someone meant giving every part of yourself to protect them. That was what I'd done for Neven, and what Neven had done for me. But Ambrose's love stopped when it inconvenienced him.

"Ren, don't!" Neven said. Tsukuyomi was restraining him, but Neven elbowed him in the ribs and struggled to break free, his tears reflecting Tsukuyomi's perfect moonlight. "He's our father!"

"He's *your* father," I said.

"I won't tell the other Reapers your plans," he said. "I promise."

The loudest sound in the world was Ambrose's thundering heartbeat. Drool pooled in my mouth—a Shinigami reflex—the sudden sharpness of my teeth slicing open my bottom lip. I wiped the blood away with a hand that was now only bones, Izanami's hum of approval rushing through me, like my blood had turned to fire.

"I know you won't," she said, her words like burning copper on my lips. *"Corpses don't talk."*

Ambrose's eyes clouded over, as if he finally realized he wasn't going to win. He stared back at me with strange determination, like he wanted to look Death in the eyes when it swallowed him whole.

For all of my childhood, I would've given anything for the chance to shatter that mask, crack him open like an egg, force him to suffer exactly as much as I had. He was lucky that I'd never been trained as a High Reaper, that I didn't know how to torture him with time. Otherwise, I would have made him die a thousand times in excruciating slow motion. The darkness crescendoed until I could hardly see through it at all, except for Ambrose's stark blue eyes.

But he no longer looked like a High Reaper at all. Not the fierce marble statue that sat rigid in High Council meetings. He looked sad and old, a lost soul who'd wandered into his own death.

"Okay," he whispered. "I understand, Ren."

But suddenly I could no longer move, my grip on the blade shaking. He was supposed to cry and plead with more beautiful lies and pray to Ankou for his salvation, not kneel down and accept his punishment like he actually thought he deserved it. My shadows began to pale and gray, growing translucent in the moonlight. The roaring in my ears died down and I could hear Neven sobbing and begging beside me, no longer fighting Tsukuyomi but collapsed onto his knees, bowing into the dirt. I'd promised him I would never hurt him again. I turned to Ambrose, my rage suddenly stale, like a phantom pain I could no longer reach.

I whirled back and jammed my knife into the tree above Ambrose's head.

The bark cracked and splintered, and it wasn't what I'd wanted but at least *something* was breaking. I wanted the whole universe to split open and swallow us all, but for now this would have to do.

Neven fell silent, looking up at me with wet eyes as I stepped back. Ambrose blinked, his jaw falling open.

"Ren," he whispered.

I turned away so I wouldn't have to see his face. Neven rose to his feet, but I stormed off into the woods, the darkness dragging behind me like a wet blanket.

I should have killed Ambrose. Ivy would have done it if she were in my place, and that was why she was stronger than I would ever be. But Ivy didn't love Neven, or anyone at all.

"Ren!"

I walked faster, even as Tsukuyomi's moonlight cleaved through the curtains of darkness.

He grabbed my wrist. "Ren."

I yanked my arm away. "Were the clouds of darkness behind me not a clear enough indication that I want to be alone?" I said. "Let me be clearer—leave me alone."

"There could be other Reapers around here."

"Wouldn't that be wonderful?" I said, shoving aside branches that whipped back into Tsukuyomi's face. "What a fantastic day this has already been."

"Slow down," Tsukuyomi said. "We're getting too far from your brother and the Yōkai."

He was right. I came to a stop near the edge of the forest, the lake beyond the trees shimmering in the moonlight.

"I should have killed him," I said, sinking to my knees. "I know that letting him live puts all of us at risk. We can't trust someone who fears Ivy more than me."

Tsukuyomi sighed, sitting down beside me. "I don't think it's quite that simple."

"How is it not?" I said.

"Because he's your father. Or Neven's father, at the very least."

I choked down a sound of frustration. "*You're* sentimental about killing family?"

Tsukuyomi's face darkened. "You're being cruel."

"I *am* cruel."

"You're not," he said. "That's why you're angry."

I whirled around, grabbing Tsukuyomi by the throat and slamming him against a tree. The trunk shuddered from the impact, branches trembling overhead, but Tsukuyomi didn't resist. He grabbed my wrist to hold me back from crushing him, but didn't try to push me away. How dare he try to tell me what I was?

"Ukemochi is not dead, Ren," he said, his words strained and whispered against the force of my hand.

I shook my head, trying to press down harder, but Tsukuyomi's hand held firm. "You killed her."

"And yet, she's everywhere," he said, his fingers clamping down on my wrist so hard that my bones creaked and my grip loosened. "She is every grain of rice, every sweet potato and radish and bamboo shoot in Japan. She is in Amaterasu's eyes every time our paths cross during the solar eclipse and she looks at me like I'm a stranger. She's in my father's voice when he tells me I'm a disappointment. She's here, now, in the way you act like I'm a monster because of what I did to her. Killing someone is not the same as erasing them, Ren."

My fingers felt numb on Tsukuyomi's throat, his words sending warm vibrations through my palm.

I shook my head. "I just want—"

"I know," Tsukuyomi said. "I know how you think it will feel, but you're wrong."

He gave my wrist a gentle tug, easily pulling it from his throat. He didn't let go, his thumb rubbing over the veins as the bruises melted back into my skin. The darkness ached beneath my bones, crying to break free but left with nowhere to go.

His eyes were too patient. Someone who had watched me take a bite out of a pulsing heart wasn't supposed to see me as anything but a monster, and yet he held me like I had paper skin and bird bones that would tear apart at his touch. I reached out and held his face with one hand because somehow I felt that he would tether me here, stop me from ripping the whole world to shreds.

"Ren?" he whispered.

My thumb traced the edge of his lips, and they parted with a faltering breath.

"Ren," he said again, the word warm on my face.

It would have been so easy to close the distance between us. Nothing about him even looked like Hiro to me anymore. Now that I knew Tsukuyomi, I wondered how I ever confused him with Hiro when their souls were so distinct. I could begin again with Tsukuyomi, and let his touch burn away Hiro's memory for good.

But then Tsukuyomi leaned in closer and my chest seized up, my breath trapped in my throat. Once we crossed this bridge, we could no longer pretend that all of this was merely transactional. Just like the path to the sun palace, I would be holding Tsukuyomi's hand and letting him pull me into empty sky, trusting his word that we wouldn't fall. It was easy enough to daydream about happy endings, but now that I was actually chasing one, it felt like nothing more than a fantasy, wafer-thin beneath my feet.

Maybe Hiro was gone, but he was still a gaping wound that only seemed to scream wider and wider as the years passed. I had given him everything, and for that I'd found myself alone in the dark, kneeling on a shrine painted with blood. I could no longer imagine what a life with Tsukuyomi—or anyone—would even look like, or how I could ever let myself believe that it was real this time. I'd hated Hiro for taking my brother away, but I hadn't realized until I held Tsukuyomi just how much Hiro had ruined *me* as well.

I turned away just as Tsukuyomi drew closer, his lips brushing my cheek. He pulled back, still holding tight to my wrist.

"Tell me what you're thinking," he whispered. "I don't understand."

But Tsukuyomi would never understand. He didn't know what it was like to feel as cold and hollow as the corpses you reaped, to never even know if you had a heart at all until you met someone who proved it to you, to love them and drink their beautiful promises and burn the world down just to keep them, then find out that you never even knew their name.

Tsukuyomi's gaze dropped to my hands, and I realized I was twisting Hiro's ring.

"It's because of him?" he asked.

When I said nothing, he tilted his head to the side. He would have had every right to be frustrated, but instead he just looked perplexed.

"I don't know what the right words to say in this situation would be," he said at last, his posture wilting as if this disappointed him. "If I could remove my face and wear a different one, I would, if that pleased you."

I let out a dry laugh. "Don't remove anything for me, please. And your resemblance isn't really the problem."

"Then what is it you want me to do?"

I don't know, I thought, but those words were so painfully unhelpful that it seemed a waste of breath to say them out loud.

Tsukuyomi sighed, perhaps sensing that I had no intention of answering. He tucked my hair behind my ear, pulling a leaf from the tangled strands.

"I'm not owed an answer," he said, his gentle fingers brushing dirt from my face, "but you know our time together is not infinite."

I closed my eyes, leaning into his touch. "I know."

His fingers froze. "You know?"

"Ivy is coming in two days," I said, opening my eyes.

He blinked, all the stars in his eyes halting in their orbit. "Oh," he said. "Yes."

"What did you think I meant?"

Tsukuyomi went still. I would have pressed him further if not for the sudden sound of footsteps on the grass. He moved in front of me, but I drew my knives anyway.

Tamamo No Mae stepped out from behind a tree, her face shadowed.

"Neven wants to speak with you," she said, her tone flat and cold as a single note on a piano. She shot Tsukuyomi a stony glance, then turned and walked away.

I tucked my knives in my sleeves, already dreading seeing Ambrose again. Tsukuyomi walked a careful distance beside me as we headed back to the others.

Neven stood beside Ambrose in the clearing, his arms crossed. Ambrose had two black eyes that were rapidly fading, his teeth realigning themselves with a series of clicks. I dropped my gaze to Neven's bloodied knuckles, which he quickly hid under his sleeves.

"We need to decide what to do with him," Neven said, showing me Ambrose's clock. "He's unarmed."

"We can hang him from the trees by his arms like a puppet?" Tamamo No Mae said, clapping like the idea excited her.

Neven turned to me, but I didn't know what to say. This wasn't a decision I wanted to make right now. I wanted Ambrose to simply blink out of existence.

"My shadows can hold him here overnight," I said. "Then we can get some rope and leave him until someone finds him or he hops back to Tokyo with his ankles bound."

Ambrose grimaced but said nothing.

I turned away, waving for the others to follow. Tsukuyomi tried to catch up to me, but Neven beat him to it, tugging me by my sleeve.

I steeled myself for a confrontation, but Neven pulled me close and linked arms. It was just like when we'd first come to Yokohama ten years ago, leaning on each other as we confronted all the monsters of a new and strange land. That time felt so faraway, that version of Ren so young. To think that back then I had thought Yōkai to be the most fearsome beasts of all.

Neven stared straight ahead at the forest, not saying a word as he tugged me closer. I curled my fingers into his sleeve and tried not to think about how his gentleness came from thinking I had been merciful to Ambrose, that I was someone who could be cast off and scorned but would forgive instead of biting back. Neven must have thought I was trying to be a good person, but really I was just weak. It was far too late for someone like me to ever be good.

I clung to his sleeve and let him believe the lie, just for to-night, as we headed deeper into the forest and farther from Ambrose, where the whispered winds through the trees would carry our words away and the night's shadows would hide our footprints.

CHAPTER 19

I woke to hands on my back.

Before I'd even opened my eyes, I seized my attacker by the throat and pinned him to the floor. My servants knew better than to touch me. I jammed my knee into the attacker's sternum as the room's shadows slid back and forth from the haze of sleep.

"Ren, stop!"

I blinked away sleep, taking in Neven below me, the small hotel room around us, the futons scattered across the floor. I released Neven, who sat up and coughed.

"Sorry," I said as he rubbed his throat, waving away my apology. "What's wrong?"

His eyes darkened, his expression grave. "Father is gone."

I stormed out of the room, struggling to wrap a tie around

my waist to hold my kimono closed as Tsukuyomi and Tamamo No Mae's voices echoed from the front yard. The other hotel guests eyed us nervously as we hurried half-dressed down the hallways.

If Ambrose was gone, did that mean the Reapers were going to descend on us at any moment? The Ambrose I knew would go crawling back to Ivy. But if any of his words had been sincere, if even a small part of him cared for me, maybe he had simply run away in case I changed my mind and killed him. He could be across the sea by now, saving his own skin from both me and Ivy. I didn't know what to believe, other than the fact that he was a coward who neither deserved forgiveness nor understood what it meant.

"Stop pretending!" the Yōkai shouted from outside. I'd never heard her raise her voice. The sharp sound startled a flock of birds from a nearby tree. They fluttered past the open window in a rush of wings and feathers.

"I'm not the one who's pretending!" Tsukuyomi shouted back. The raw power of a god's anger vibrated through the ground of the hotel, branches trembling and grass withering to a faded yellow.

"What happened?" I said, throwing open the door.

Both Tsukuyomi and the Yōkai whirled around, their faces red and furious.

"She released your father," Tsukuyomi said, pointing at the Yōkai. "I went to check on him and found her standing in the forest, your father long gone."

"I didn't let him go!" Tamamo No Mae said, furious tears burning down her face. "He was already gone when I got there! Someone else must have freed him."

"Don't cry and pretend you're innocent, Yōkai," Tsuku-yomi said. "Everyone knows you're not really a child."

"Hey!" Neven said, coming to Tamamo No Mae's side and setting a hand on her shoulder while glaring at Tsukuyomi. "Mikuzume doesn't lie."

Tsukuyomi huffed out a breath and turned to me. "I wouldn't lie to you either, Ren," he said. "I've always told you the truth since we first met, even when you didn't like it. You know that."

Then everyone was staring at me, waiting for my response, even though my brain felt like it had been doused in cold water. My father couldn't have escaped on his own, that was certain.

"Maybe another Reaper found him?" I asked.

Tsukuyomi shook his head, his eyes murderous. "Then why was she just standing there instead of running back to tell us?"

"I *was* running back, you liar!" she said. "You're the one who can cut through Ren's shadows with moonlight!"

"Oh please," Tsukuyomi said, rolling his eyes. "I'm here on my father's orders. Handing his kingdom over to foreigners wouldn't exactly make him proud."

"Your family is full of liars," Neven said, crossing his arms.

Tsukuyomi's eyes burned as he faced Neven. "I never even met Hiro!" he said.

The two of them kept bickering while I closed my eyes and contemplated ripping my hair out. The idea that either of them could betray me made me feel like my chest was caving in, ribs puncturing my lungs. Was this what it meant to be a goddess—that I could never trust anyone but Neven? Tsukuyomi certainly had a bad reputation among other gods, but he was earnest, if nothing else.

I'd thought that Hiro had been sincere too. I knew I wasn't the same naive and lovestruck girl who had washed up on the shores of Yomi a decade ago and given everything to a man who promised power, but would I even know if Tsukuyomi was using me? I was truly a fool if Hiro came back in another body just to ruin me all over again and I *let him*.

But Tamamo No Mae wasn't innocent either. In past lives, she had killed kings and corrupted kingdoms. Yōkai did not think and feel like Reapers or Shinigami. They were base creatures with simple goals, whether they wanted to spook schoolchildren or eat human flesh or cause utter chaos. No matter how much Tamamo No Mae looked like a sweet little girl, that was not her true face. But her wits had saved us many times, and it was true that if she'd hoped to kill me, there certainly were easier ways than whatever she might be attempting.

I wished I could build walls around Yomi a thousand feet high and seal my palace forever, so no one could worm their way inside.

Tsukuyomi raised his voice, the grass shuddering away from his thunderous words. "You can't hold me responsible for my brother's mistakes!"

Neven clenched his jaw and let out a breath through his teeth, then wheeled around and turned his rage to me. "Are you really going to do this again, Ren?"

My breath caught in my throat. I didn't know how to answer Neven without upsetting him. I obviously should have trusted Neven's instincts when it came to Hiro, but that didn't mean he was always right, did it? Or was I just dooming us all over again?

Tsukuyomi stepped in front of me, shielding me from

Neven's glare. "Ren can make her own choices without you holding Hiro over her."

Neven scoffed, then strode forward and seized Tsukuyomi by the collar. "Do you have any idea what he did to me and Mikuzume?"

Tsukuyomi gripped Neven's wrist, bones creaking warningly. "She already killed him for it!" he said. "What more do you expect her to do for you?"

Neven froze, the color draining from his face. His fingers went limp and his arm fell to his side as Tsukuyomi released him. His pale gaze shifted from Tsukuyomi to me.

"You killed him?" he said.

Everyone turned to me again. I couldn't read Neven's expression, the colors in his irises so dim that his eyes almost seemed pure white.

"Where did you think he'd gone?" I said, looking down and kicking at the dirt. I didn't want to discuss this in front of Tsukuyomi and the Yōkai. "You think he just handed me his kingdom and walked away?"

Neven shook his head. "You just said he was gone. I thought maybe you'd fought."

"We did," I said. "Once."

"But you were going to marry him," Neven said, frowning.

I let out a sharp laugh. "How could I marry someone who did that to you?" I said, glaring at Neven because *how could he still not understand that*?

Neven's expression softened, and I looked away because I didn't deserve whatever kind thought was crossing his mind. "You never told me," he whispered.

"Because it's not enough," I said, my words too sharp. "It will never be enough, and it changes nothing."

A secret part of me hoped that Neven would say I was wrong, that it changed everything, but he only pressed his lips together and stared at the ground. It didn't matter that I'd eventually chosen him over Hiro, because I'd done it too late.

I sighed, turning my gaze to the sky, so I wouldn't have to see the others staring at me like some sad, wounded animal. Their pity repulsed me.

Another wave of fresh souls washed over me, sharpening the sunlight that pierced through the leaves overhead, every branch so crisp and stark like it was tattooed onto the sky. If it had been nighttime, surely I would have been able to see every star in exquisite detail.

"Ren?" Tsukuyomi said, touching my arm like I was made of thin glass.

I leveled my gaze at his starry eyes, then at the Yōkai's teary face, then at Neven, staring off into the distance.

"Neven and I will go on alone," I said.

"What?" both Tsukuyomi and the Yōkai said at once. Neven looked up in surprise.

"Neven and I will go to the palace and get the sword before Ambrose can warn the other Reapers," I said. "You two will stay behind."

"Ren," Tsukuyomi said, frowning, "I'm supposed to protect you."

"If you're telling me that the Yōkai is a threat, then stay here and protect me from her," I said.

He watched me for a long moment, like he heard my words but couldn't make sense of them. Then he straightened his shoulders, his expression perfectly blank.

"Yes, I understand," he said. Just like when I'd first met him, his voice sounded cold and empty. I'd probably upset him, but it was better than making Neven feel like I'd betrayed him again.

"You think he might be telling the truth?" Tamamo No Mae said, her voice cracking.

"This is not personal, so save your tears," I said, my tone making the Yōkai flinch away. "Ivy is coming tomorrow." My heart seized—*tomorrow.* "I need to get Susano'o's sword today and I don't have time for an inquisition."

The Yōkai's lip wobbled, but she nodded and slumped her shoulders.

"We'll meet back here tonight. I don't want to see either of you interfering. Try not to kill each other before we return."

I turned to Neven, who was still staring wide-eyed at me. I offered him my hand. "Are you ready?"

He nodded, casting an apologetic glance to Tamamo No Mae before taking my hand. I closed my fist around my ring and stopped the world around us, leaving Tsukuyomi and the Yōkai as frozen statues behind us. They would have a hard time following this way.

We walked through the forest, squinting through the harsh sunlight. We didn't speak for several minutes, Neven's face unreasonable.

"You don't honestly think it's Mikuzume, do you?" he said at last, his words soft.

I sighed. "I don't know what to think, Neven."

"I would have been dead within days if not for her," Neven said. "I wish you would understand that, Ren. I've spent nearly a century with her. You've known Tsukuyomi for less than a week. Do you really trust—"

"There is only one person I trust with my life," I said, "and it's not either of them."

To this, Neven had no reply.

I held on tight to time until we reached the edge of the forest and boarded a nearly empty streetcar, watching as the trees gave way to canals and brick buildings. The forest grew smaller behind us, the endless line of pine trees hardly stirring in the wind, as if guarding a dark secret deep within. I checked my clock and nearly choked when I saw the time— we'd been up so late waiting for Ambrose last night that somehow I'd let myself sleep into the late morning. No wonder Tsukuyomi and the Yōkai had grown restless and wandered off. This was the last full day before Ivy's arrival, and I'd already cut it in half.

We drove deeper into the city, where the overhead electric lines for streetcars carved black diamonds across the sky. Even from inside the stuffy vehicle, I sensed Death bleeding through the city, far stronger than when I'd come a week ago. The windows fogged up from its sour heat, the tires of the streetcar sinking into the spongy, rotting earth. Fewer humans than usual walked the streets, the ones who remained scurrying quickly like they wanted to be absolutely anywhere else. The brightness of the late-morning sky began to dim, gray clouds like curtains pulled over the sun, as if Tokyo knew Death was coming.

I tugged Neven's arm and motioned for him to get off once I could see the imperial palace in the distance. The nearby signs said we'd arrived in Marunouchi, a business district that I'd visited on occasion to eat the hearts of embezzling businessmen, of which there seemed to be an endless supply. Eventually, I had to tell Chiyo to stop sending me there so the humans wouldn't see a pattern.

Even before I'd first set foot there, it had always seemed

like a soulless place—nothing but tall brick office buildings with sparse windows facing away from the sun and humans in Western suits who were so busy that they couldn't even spare the time to look at you. I probably could have paraded down the street drenched in blood and no one would have said a word, which made it a perfect place to regroup.

Or so I'd thought. The humans in the streets had waxy gray complexions, stumbling past us like the Earth was tilted off its axis. Some of them leaned on each other, tripping down stairs and spilling into the streets, coughing up milky white liquid. Men were sleeping on the sidewalks, curled up against buildings, which wasn't entirely unusual for a high-powered business district, if not for the blood trickling from their ears and eyes, papery skin withered from dehydration.

This must have been the plague that the humans had whispered about. Only yesterday, the humans said it had torn through Aomori. How had it already ravaged Tokyo, halfway across the country? Was it something in the water supply?

Neven knelt down by the nearest collapsed human.

"Don't touch him," I said. Reapers couldn't catch human diseases, but somehow the idea of Neven being close to such an unexpected plague unsettled me.

"He's already dead," Neven said, frowning. Another hot breeze bathed us in the scent of Death and vomit, making Neven cough. "Ren, I've never seen anything like this before," he said, his eyes watering from the scent.

"I have," I said. Neven hadn't been old enough to collect during the last big cholera outbreak back in London, so he wouldn't have seen such rampant sickness before. But I remembered when all Reapers had to work around the clock to harvest souls from bodies so shrunken and shadowed that they begged for death. Surely my Shinigami weren't pleased, but if I didn't handle Ivy first, then they would have to complain to my corpse.

Neven covered his nose as the next breeze rolled by, so I tugged his sleeve and pulled him away.

"I'll ask Chiyo about this when we go back to Yomi," I said, because in truth there wasn't much else I could do. I pointed to the palace beyond the office buildings, shuddering in the heat waves. "That's where we have to go."

Neven squinted, pushing his glasses farther up his nose. "How do we get in?"

From here, there wasn't an obvious answer. The palace's outer buildings were clean white with nothing that could be used as a foothold blemishing their sheen. The tiled gray roofs curved up at the edges, far too high to reach from the ground. The whole structure perched on tall stone platforms far above the dim waters, a moat beneath them dug as deep as an abyss, but with only a shallow pool of black water left after the summer drought. A row of ginkgo trees shielded the rest of the interior buildings from view.

"There must be an entrance somewhere," I said. "We can freeze our way past the guards."

"And once we're inside? I don't suppose you have a map?"

I shook my head. "It looks massive," I said, nodding to the moat that wrapped around the palace grounds far into the distance. "Larger than some of the city districts here. It will take ages to search."

"Well, we do have time at our disposal," Neven said, twirling the chain of his clock around one finger.

I looked away to hide my gray expression. Neven had already used up far more of his lifespan on time turns than he ever should have. I didn't want him shaving any more minutes off the end of his life.

"I think we'd be better off interrogating some guards, rather than rifling through such a massive space in stopped time," I said.

Neven nodded, turning back to the palace and narrowing his eyes as if he could see the weaknesses in the fortress through sheer determination.

Somewhere beyond that row of trees is Susano'o's sword, I thought. It felt so impossibly close that part of me wanted to throw myself into the moat and tear through any human who got between me and the sword. But now was not the time to be careless.

"Let's check the perimeter for weak points and see if the humans know anything," I said. "We want to be in and out as fast as possible." As easy as it would have been to tear down a section of wall and ransack the entire palace in stopped time until we found the sword, we needed to be discreet. Humans were good at blaming other humans for things they didn't understand, and the last thing I wanted was for Japan to start another war with China because they thought someone had attacked their emperor.

I cast one more glance at my clock, grimacing at the hour, then tucked it away. "Come on," I said, waving for Neven to follow me, "we have a palace to rob."

In the time it took us to walk the perimeter of the castle and speak to the humans, darkness fell heavy over Tokyo, like the whole city sat at the bottom of a well with the sky capped off overhead. My well-fed shadows rolled across the town like molten lava, lapping up all of the remaining light.

The humans had barely been helpful at all—some claimed they had seen the sword at ceremonies and parades, and it was a relief to hear that we were in the right place, but no one could agree on where it was kept. The palace held tours on occasion, but some humans said the regalia was displayed in the east wing, others said the west wing, while others said they hadn't seen it at all.

Not wanting to scale a wall or swim through a murky moat, it seemed the only way in was the main entrance. We passed right beneath the palace guards' feet, across the damp underbelly of the stone bridge leading across the moat. I extinguished the lanterns with a wave of my hand, draping darkness over us as we crept past the guards, approaching the great iron gates that led to the palace interior. My shadows slithered under the gates and unlocked them from the inside, letting us slip into the palace grounds.

We stepped into an endless garden, a maze of smoothed sand paths and shallow lakes where lotuses lay perfectly still despite the night breeze, like their petals were made of glass. The tulips had closed for the evening, the ponds had been cleared of algae, and strands of lanterns cast gentle light on the path. It was the kind of clean perfection that didn't seem possible, almost like we had stepped into a painting. In the background, more stark white buildings loomed above the tree line, a world away.

I waved out these lanterns as well, darkness crashing over the beautiful garden like a sudden typhoon, swallowing all the perfect pathways and drowning the meticulously weeded gardens in pure night.

At the sound of footsteps, Neven grabbed a low hanging branch and clambered up onto a sloped roof, offering me a hand and pulling me after him. Guards hurried below us, murmuring in confusion about the lights. We could stop time if they noticed us, but for now it didn't seem worth the effort, or the minutes that would be scraped off the ends of our lives.

"I'm sorry," I whispered once the guards had dispersed, "I know you don't like total darkness."

Neven scoffed. "This isn't total darkness," he said. "You've never seen what that looks like."

"I live in Yomi."

"Yomi is not total darkness either," Neven said, frowning. "In total darkness, you can't even remember what light looks like. If you were there, you would know."

An apology caught in my throat, but those two words felt so pathetic compared to centuries of darkness.

"I wish I'd been there," I said at last. "I would've…" But my words died at Neven's sharp look.

"It's easy to promise things that will never happen," he said. They were my own words, some of the last I'd said to him before Hiro's servants took him away. I dropped my gaze to the tiled roof and said nothing at all. I didn't think Neven wanted a response from me as much as he hoped the shame I felt would deepen and spread.

"There were monsters," Neven said.

I looked up. "What?"

"When I first came back to Yomi, you asked me what happened in the deep darkness," he said. "There were thousands of monsters, but I could never see any of them."

I swallowed, my mouth suddenly dry. "Neven—"

"They bit me," he said, "they tore off my arms and legs whenever they got the chance. And even though my limbs always grew back, that just meant there was more for the monsters to eat."

I clenched my fists, my stomach sick. I didn't want to hear this, but if Neven had lived through it, the least I could do was listen.

"I waited for you," Neven said, his voice cracking. "For so many years, all I could think was *Ren is going to save me.* But in the end, you never did. I found my own way out. And when I finally made it back to Yomi, you weren't even there. You were out with Tsukuyomi."

He grimaced when he said Tsukuyomi's name, like it was a curse. I could feel Neven's furious gaze on me, but I couldn't bear to look at him, because even now I was a coward. I closed my eyes, but then I could only picture Neven in the deep darkness with monsters ripping off his arms. I pressed my palms to my face like I could crush the image out of my mind. I wanted to carve my own eyes out, but the image was probably seared into my brain.

Neven waited for my response, and for once, I had no idea what to say to him. There were no words in the world that could erase everything I'd done. But Neven thought I'd abandoned him for Tsukuyomi, and I needed him to know that he was wrong.

"Forty thousand one hundred and eighty-three souls," I said at last.

Neven stopped breathing. "What?" he whispered.

"That's how many souls I ate, trying to get you back," I said. I dropped my hands from my face, turning to Neven. His eyes were wide and confused and I wanted more than anything to pull the darkness over me and hide, but I forced myself to hold his gaze. "Every day, I ate extra souls to grow

strong enough to bring you back. They were the worst criminals Chiyo could find, so it wasn't supposed to matter, but
they cried and screamed and begged for their lives, so much
worse than any human in England ever did. I think they knew
it wasn't their Death Day yet."

Neven had gone very pale, and I didn't know if my words
were helping or making everything worse, but my stomach clenched and wrung them up my throat like bile and I
couldn't hold them back.

"They called me a monster, and they were right. I was everything you said that I was. Worse than Izanami, worse than
any Yōkai we've ever met."

Neven shook his head. "Ren—"

"But my only regret is that I didn't take more."

Neven went still, his next words dying on his lips, his skin
sickly white.

"I would have eaten ten thousand more souls if it meant I
could have found you even one day sooner," I said. The words
scraped up my throat like glass, my eyes burning. "Even one
minute sooner. I would have taken the whole world for you.
But I didn't do enough, and I'm sorry, Neven. You deserve
so many things that I can never give you, because I'm not
enough."

Neven slammed into me, his arms wrapping around my
shoulders and holding me tight. He would have knocked us
both off the roof if I hadn't thrown back a hand for balance.
His arms crushed me, hands grabbing fistfuls of my kimono
like he was afraid I would dissolve into the darkness. His
heartbeat was the same slow, quiet cadence as mine, his skin
the same corpse cold temperature.

I had expected Neven's forgiveness to feel like the whole

Earth adjusting its tilt, like every problem in the world had suddenly been fixed. But as I pressed my hands to his back and his cold tears tracked down my neck, I felt more like I'd taken my first breath after drowning, because everything still hurt and nothing had changed, but somehow I was alive again.

"I didn't want you to ruin yourself for me," Neven whispered, "I just didn't want you to forget me."

"Forget you?" I said, my hands clawing into Neven's clothes, as if anchoring him to me. "Neven, I thought of nothing else but you every day for the last ten years."

He let out a teary laugh, his hands combing through my hair. "I thought of you every day for the last century."

He probably hadn't meant for his words to hurt, but they wrung more tears from my eyes and I pressed my face into his shoulder.

"It's okay, Ren," he whispered. "I found my way back."

Because I was too late, I thought. Because I was too terrible to deserve Neven and yet not terrible enough to do what it took to keep him safe. I said nothing, all of my words having dried up, and just held Neven so tightly that the seams on his kimono started to stretch and tear.

"Okay, okay, I can't walk around here without clothes on," Neven said, laughing quietly. He pulled back, mopping my tears with his sleeve like he was my older brother and not the other way around. He took off his glasses and scrubbed his own face, taking a deep breath. "Let's find this sword, shall we? All our problems are going to be over soon."

I didn't believe him, and I knew he could tell from the look on my face, but I nodded anyway. There was no time to cry with Ivy's ship due tomorrow.

"Come on," he said, tugging my wrist until we both slid

to the lip of the roof. He hopped down first, then waved for me to jump and caught me easily before I hit the ground. "I'll take the east wing and you take the west."

I shook my head. "We'll stay together."

He sighed. "Ren, you said it yourself, this place is the size of a whole city district. Staying together isn't efficient."

"But the Reapers—"

"—aren't going to find us here," Neven said. "Father was their informant, and we took his clock. There's no way he's made it back to them already, traveling on human time."

I shifted from foot to foot, not wanting to sound childish but desperately not wanting Neven to go.

He set a hand on my shoulder. "This is probably the safest we've been since I came back to Yomi," he said. I knew he was right, so I nodded even though my throat felt closed up. Goddesses didn't get upset over things like this. Ivy certainly wouldn't.

"Let's stop time and meet here in…fifteen minutes?" Neven said.

I winced. There was yet another reason to stay together. "You shouldn't use your clock unless it's an emergency," I said. "You've already—"

"Already made myself look your age, which is so incredibly old?" he said, smirking.

I punched him in the arm. "I'm serious."

"I lost a century or two, not a millennium," Neven said. "We're basically the same age. And I would rather shorten my lifespan by an hour now than by eighteen hundred years if Ivy kills us all tomorrow."

"Fine," I said, even though none of it was fine at all, but I knew I would start crying again if we kept bickering. Neven must have noticed my pale expression because he smiled and squeezed my hand. Then he turned to leave, the sight of his back making me feel like I was never going to see him again.

"If anything goes wrong—"

"I'll call for you," he said, shooting me a soft smile. Then he dashed off into the darkness that swallowed him whole, like a lake of spilled ink.

The palace was expansive, full of locked doors and echoing floors polished so thoroughly that they looked like sheets of ice. Just like in my palace, every paper door told the story of Japan in brilliant hues—waterfalls and mountain ranges and golden skies. But here, the paintings had no blood or pulse or soul the way mine did, nothing more than colors splashed across paper, an exquisitely decorated corpse. The palace didn't breathe like mine.

In stopped time, I strolled past imperial guards in their black-and-gold coats and Western hats like I was walking through a museum. I slid open doors to several studies, a dining room with an impossibly long table, and more sitting rooms than seemed practical, but nothing in this wing looked important enough to store an ancient sword.

I'd already started to sweat, hearing an invisible clock ticking alongside my heartbeat the way it always did when I froze time for too long. If the sword wasn't someplace obvious, I would need to punish the answer out of someone.

I grabbed a guard by the throat, holding him up against a wall. His eyes bulged as he was ripped from his own timeline and into mine. I hadn't left him enough breath to scream, but he kicked and flailed until my shadows pinned his limbs against the wall.

"Where is Kusanagi No Tsurugi?" I said, releasing his neck just enough to let him gasp out a few words.

"In the west wing!" he said, his eyes flickering around as if looking for escape routes.

I rolled my eyes. "You're lying. Do I really look like someone you should lie to?"

My shadows tickled across his face like spiders, pulling up his lips to examine his teeth, tugging at his eyelids.

He shuddered, trying to turn his head away.

"They don't tell many of the guards," he said, squirming away from my touch. "It's supposed to be a family secret."

Family? I thought. Then that was who I had to ask for directions.

"There, that wasn't so hard," I said. Then I tore the decorative silk cord from the shoulder of his uniform, ignoring his protests. My shadows turned him around for me as I bound his hands, then dragged him to a nearby storage room and tossed him to the floor. He tried to rise to his feet, but I slammed the door in his face and twisted the handle, warping the metal to lock the door.

"Let me out!" the guard called.

"You'll be fine," I said. The other guards would hear him once the time freeze ended, and by then I would be long gone.

It wasn't hard to find the imperial suite once I was on the second floor, because it had the most guards stationed outside of it. I extinguished the lanterns lining the walls and cast the hallway in darkness, then grabbed the shadows on the ground and melted into them, sliding under the door to the suite.

I entered a room lit by a stone fireplace, where a young woman sat frozen on a futon, facing away from me as she brushed her long hair. This had to be the empress, for no one else would warrant such security. A great stretch of reed mats separated us, the room large and empty and glowing unnaturally. My palace had the same sheen, where each speck of dust and fingerprint was instantly polished away by servants. A decorative katana was mounted on the wall over the futon, but it was too curved and shiny to be Susano'o's.

I took a few moments to paw through the drawers and peek under the futon, on the off chance the sword was kept in here. But the guard had said the sword was a family secret, so the fastest way to find it would be to ask the royal family.

I took a deep breath, then touched the back of the woman's neck with my bare hand, pulling her into the time freeze.

She jolted at the contact, reaching back to rub her neck, but I had already withdrawn my hand, and she would feel nothing but the ghost of my touch. For a moment, she kept brushing her hair, then her arm froze again as if time had stopped once more. I knew I hadn't made a single sound to alert her to my presence yet, but she let out a weary sigh, setting down her hairbrush.

"What do you want?" she said.

CHAPTER 20

There were fast ways to force people to spill their secrets, and there were clean ways, but few methods could be both at once. Maybe a younger Ren would have had the stomach to torture answers out of the empress, but my path was already paved with corpses and I desperately didn't want to return to Neven covered in human blood. I prayed the human would cooperate through fear alone.

"I know you're there," the woman said, turning around.

I held my breath. She had a face like Amaterasu, stunning in its smooth innocence, glowing like new sunlight on a winter landscape. The woman looked at me like she was invincible, like she knew that time seemed to slow around her, the edges of the world blurring away so I could focus on nothing but her stark brown eyes. It was easy to see why an emperor would want to marry her.

"If it's money you want, name your price and I'll write a check," she said, leaning over to a bedside table and pulling out a checkbook. "My husband might even pay you if you tell him how you broke in here. He's always trying to improve security."

"I don't want money," I said. "And you're awfully calm." *Too calm*, I thought. People were only calm in the face of danger if they didn't think it was dangerous at all.

The empress rolled her eyes. "I'm only the empress consort. My husband would still keep the throne even if I'm dead, so killing me wouldn't accomplish much." She narrowed her eyes, drinking in my appearance, my black clothes tinged a sickening burgundy color from blood, my stained white socks, my tangled hair.

"You could always be here to murder me for sport," she said. "Not everyone kills for a reason."

I grimaced. I was a god, and a human mistook me for a serial killer.

"Or perhaps you're here to kidnap me for political leverage? A Russian interested in the Liaodong Peninsula?"

"I am Japanese, not Russian," I said, clenching my jaw.

"Pardon me," the empress said, not looking particularly apologetic. "You have an accent. At any rate, I regret to inform you that I'm quite expendable. Money is no object to this family, but they'll draw the line at making political sacrifices for me."

"I don't need any of that," I said. "I need Kusanagi No Tsurugi."

The empress blinked, tilting her head. "Why would you want old garbage like that?"

That "garbage" is all that stands between you and colonization, I thought. But there was no point in dragging humans into this.

"It doesn't matter if you understand," I said. "All that matters is that I need it."

The empress gave me a long look, as if she could read every word of my story through my face. At last, she turned away, reaching for her hairbrush.

But her hand slid past the brush and slipped under her pillow instead. Before I could speak, she spun around and tossed three spinning shuriken at my face.

The blades whirled as they cut through the air, like three prickly silver stars orbiting at eye level. I ducked as they flashed across the room, not particularly wanting to yank them from my eyes, even if they would heal. Two of them stuck to the wall behind me, but one bounced back. Human weapons did not move fast enough to threaten Reapers, so it was easy enough to snatch the shuriken from the air by pinching it along its flat sides. I examined the four slanted blades, deathly sharp.

"How cute," I said, tossing the shuriken onto her bed, where it stabbed into her pillow, "but that's not what I asked for."

Rather than getting angry, the empress's eyes gleamed, a hungry smile curling her lips.

"Where did you train?" she asked, crawling across her sprawling futon until she was right in front of me. "No one has ever done that before."

"I'm not here to tell you my life's story."

The empress frowned, crossing her arms. "The only reason you're here and not being dragged away by my guards is because I find you interesting, but that could change at any moment."

I raised an eyebrow. "You think I can't handle your guards?"

"I think you know that only I can tell you where Kusanagi No Tsurugi is, and I'll only do that if I'm feeling generous."

"I can make people talk," I said, tightening my grip on the katana.

The empress waved her hand, dismissing my words. "Then why didn't you just kill all my guards and barge in here threatening me rather than making requests and skulking in the corner? You don't intend to hurt me."

I tried not to change my expression. I didn't exactly want to hurt her, mostly because of the political implications, but it was better if she thought I was ruthless.

"That could change at any moment," I said.

The empress laughed. "Everyone else talks to me like they think I'll have them beheaded, you know."

"Won't you?"

She gave a noncommittal hum, crawling off the bed and prying her shuriken from the wall. I drew my sword, pointing it at her back. She stilled, shooting a dark glare over her shoulder.

"Don't try that again," I said.

She shot me a challenging look. "You're giving orders to the empress?"

I am a goddess, and I will order you around as I please, I thought. But it was perhaps better to let her think I was human. I didn't need humans misinterpreting godly interference in their politics.

"Your title is worth nothing to me," I said. "You're not special just because you're royalty."

"How progressive of you," she said, raising an eyebrow. "Clearly, you're not descended from samurai. That would also explain why you're holding your blade wrong."

She gestured like she expected me to hand her my katana. I shot her a sharp look and she rolled her eyes again.

"Fine. It's not like I don't have my own."

Then she turned to the display rack behind her, taking down a katana with a green handle that looked more ceremonial than sharp enough to draw blood.

"You're holding it like a baseball bat," she said. "The handle should fall diagonally across your palm."

She demonstrated, turning to the side to show me her hand position.

"Why would you help me?" I asked.

"You already said you're not here to kill me," she said, shrugging.

"And you believe me?"

"You somehow snuck through the gates, across two miles of courtyard, and infiltrated the most highly guarded wing of the imperial palace. Now you've stood here and listened to me belittle you for two minutes. If you wanted to kill me, I would already be dead."

She stepped forward, sword still raised. I held my katana up to stop her, trying to mirror her hands.

She hummed in approval, lowering her blade. "Better," she said.

"Now, Empress," I said, "take me to the sword."

"Why thank you for using my title, even though it means so little to you," she said, her words sour. She lunged forward and swiped her sword at my head, but I ducked easily. She smiled, as if she'd expected this. "You have quick reflexes, but you clearly don't know what you're doing."

"I don't have time to play games with you."

"It's not a game," she said.

Then she struck again, this time at my center. I easily blocked her, but the tip of her sword cut a line through my sleeve as I pushed her blade to the side.

"I'm not from a noble family, you know," she said. "I wasn't raised on pearls and gold for breakfast like half the women in this palace. Do you even know how a farmer's daughter became the empress?"

"With a pretty face?"

She laughed, readying her next blow. "There are millions of pretty faces in Japan that don't belong to peasants. Try again."

She swiped at my ankles, a move that likely would have disarmed a human, but I stepped back easily.

"You cut the old empress to pieces?" I said. "Is that what you're trying to say?"

She shook her head. "That part came later."

I hesitated, and that was enough for her to swing at my face. I ducked, swiping back in retaliation, but she leaned away from my strike without flinching.

"Make your point before I lose my patience," I said.

The empress laughed. I struck her, hoping that disarming her would convince her to end this charade, but she blocked the blow, our blades scratching against each other. But no matter how skilled she was with a sword, I was a goddess and she was a human. I leaned into my sword, making her arms tremble and forcing her down to her knees.

She must have known I was too strong, for she didn't even

try to push back. Instead, she pulled her sword closer to her body and tilted it diagonally, the sudden lack of resistance sending my blade sliding to the side. Then she grabbed a pillow from her bed and hurled it at my face.

I slashed it in half, a burst of feathers raining down over us. The empress jumped from the bed, crashing through the deluge with her blade raised over her head. I planted a kick against her sternum, sending her flying back onto her bed.

She lay stunned, staring up at the ceiling, the breath knocked out of her.

"I recited poems," she whispered.

"What?"

"I recited ancient poems at competitions," she said, rising to her elbows, "until a minister was willing to sponsor me as a court lady. Then I learned to play the koto so beautifully that the emperor would request me personally to play songs that lulled him to sleep."

I lowered my blade slightly. It seemed she was done fighting.

"And that's how the emperor fell in love with you?" I said. "The end?" I added, hopefully.

Her face darkened. She sat up, grabbing her katana. "No. He fell in love with another court lady. But I took care of her."

"Took care of her?"

"Don't be naive," she said. Then she struck so sharply that my blade tumbled from my hands.

Humans weren't supposed to be strong enough to disarm me, but she'd struck so dangerously close to my fingers that I'd let go instinctively.

Before she could strike again, I kicked her in the stomach, sending her back across the room, sword clattering to the floor.

She didn't move, her head hanging low, one hand clutching her abdomen. For a moment I thought I'd killed her and my mind spun with all the political fallout I'd have to handle, but then she coughed and looked up.

"So yes, you're right," she said. "Marrying into the royal family doesn't make me special. I wanted this more than anyone else, so I made myself the best and slayed anyone who got in my way. You should respect my title because I paid for it in blood."

She grabbed her katana, sheathing it and setting it down beside her on the bed. Her life here must have been dull for her to so eagerly engage an intruder. Why would she choose this life of pampered boredom, giving up everything to live in a gilded cage?

But I supposed I had done the same thing. When you came from dirt, you clawed your way up with anything you could grab, not realizing you were trading one hell for another until you were already there.

"Come," she said, rising to her feet. "I'll show you where we keep the swords."

The empress hesitated in the doorway at the sight of her time-frozen guards, so I quickly released my hold on time to avoid a lengthy explanation—she thought I was just a human, after all. The guards jolted at our sudden appearance, but the empress dismissed them and led me to the end of the hallway, through a set of tall green doors.

The room glittered with display cases full of great jewels—

jade bracelets and golden earrings, intricately embroidered silk, polished samurai armor.

"Where is Kusanagi No Tsurugi?" I said.

The empress gestured toward the far end of the room. There, in the last cabinet, was a weathered sword the color of slate. Despite the warped blade and obvious chips, it gleamed like it had been forged from pure light, the same shape of the coral Susano'o had shown me.

Finally, the sword was mine.

The Reapers had tried everything they possibly could, even throwing my own father in my face, but still, they hadn't been able to stop me. I pictured Ivy's ship overturning in the middle of the sea, all her cruel Reapers choking on the stormy salt water and clinging to rotting driftwood. A sense of peace rushed over me like a cold wave.

I pried open the sliding glass doors, my hands suddenly sweaty. I reached out with trembling hands, cradling the sword, feeling as though I was falling even as I stood still.

But the moment I picked it up, I knew something was wrong.

This sword was far too light.

I ran my finger across the blade and it didn't so much as dent my flesh, unlike the godlike sharpness I'd expected. This wasn't the weight or cut of metal, and it certainly wasn't a weapon forged by a god. I snapped the blade in half with only a fraction of my strength, wooden splinters falling across the floor.

"This isn't the real sword," I whispered.

"Of course it isn't," the empress said. Her words from her bedroom echoed in my head. *Why would you want old garbage like that?* "It's a replica, obviously."

"Where is the real sword?" I said, whirling around. "I need it!"

She shrugged, like it wasn't a matter of life and death for all of Japan.

"No one knows," she said. "It was lost hundreds of years ago in the battle of Dan-no-ura. The Taira clan disposed of the sword rather than let the Minamoto clan steal it from them. But all the people want is a symbol, so it doesn't matter if it's real or not."

"Of course it matters!" I said. I let out a scream of frustration and hurled the broken pieces of the fake sword against the wall.

What was I meant to do now? After this whole journey, I'd reached a dead end. Was I supposed to scour all of Japan for a sword I'd never seen? It was hopeless, with Ivy and her Reapers arriving on my shores tomorrow. I pressed a hand to the glass, sinking down to my knees. I had never cried in front of a human before, but this seemed like a great time to start.

"What does same ancient sword matter to you?" the empress said, her voice a bit more guarded now, perhaps not wanting to be the next target of my rage.

I sighed. "I need it to defeat someone."

After a breath of silence, she laughed.

I whirled around and glared at her, but she only kept laughing.

"That's rich," she said.

I ground my teeth together. "What is?"

"You don't even know how to use a sword properly."

I strongly considered punching all of her teeth in, but luckily she spoke first.

"I don't mean that you can't fight," she said. "You can. But whatever skills you used to break in here had nothing to do with a sword. Whoever this person is, you were never going to use a katana to kill them, even if you found it here."

"It wasn't for *me* to use," I said.

The empress scoffed. "Then why bother?" For the first time since I'd barged into her room, she looked genuinely irritated. "So someone else could fight your battle for you? What kind of victory would that be?"

Then she turned and stormed off toward the hall.

"I don't like cowards," she said. "Feel free to come back and visit if you win whatever you're planning. I'll even let you use the front door next time."

She slammed the door behind her, leaving me in darkness.

I climbed out the window, landing softly in the shadowed courtyard and kneeling on the ground. I needed to call Neven over so we could both escape, but that would mean telling him that I'd failed, that despite being able to twist and warp the timeline as I wished, I'd run out of time. Part of me would have preferred to throw myself into the palace moat and drown in tepid water rather than tell everyone that this whole journey had amounted to nothing at all.

"Hey!" a man's voice called.

I sighed. Could I not even have the luxury of wallowing in self-pity for a single minute? The footsteps of two men, probably the palace guards, ran toward me.

"Don't move!" one of them shouted.

I took a steadying breath, slowly rising to my feet so I could break their arms. Then a sound like a clap of thunder pealed through the courtyard, echoing across the still waters and the stone gates.

I stumbled back, my chest warm. The air smelled like charcoal, crisp and burnt. I turned to the guards, who both had rifles aimed at me.

I looked down at my kimono. The black fabric had grown darker, a strange heat welling up between my ribs, like I was filling up with fire.

"You shot me?" I said, my voice sounding faraway to my own ears. I pulled my hand away, holding it up to the moonlight. Yes, that was definitely blood.

"I told you not to move!" the guard said. "Get down on the ground!"

I let out a sharp laugh. I hadn't known that the imperial guards would be armed. I knew that it was near impossible for civilians to acquire firearms, and I didn't much concern myself with military business. I was supposed to stay out of politics, after all. Strange how that had changed.

I winced as the bullet slipped out from between my ribs, my skin sewing itself back up. I was too breathless for any kind of retaliation. "I was on my way out," I said, reaching for my clock.

But before I could so much as move a finger, another shot rang out, fire exploding in my left hand. *How are bullets this fast?* I thought. I'd hardly even seen firearms in England, much less had them pointed at me, and hadn't known human attacks to be anything but clunky and slow. But now it felt like I no longer had a hand at all, nothing but swirling agony at the end of my wrist. I could have cried with relief when I saw that everything was still there, just shattered and coated in blood. I ran my fingers across the numb, unresponsive limb, searching through all the blood to make sure Hiro's ring hadn't been blown clean off.

What kind of a Reaper had such a slow response time? If I hadn't indulged in such a pathetic, humanlike display of disappointment, then surely I wouldn't have let the first bullet hit me and would be on my way. As my arm hung limp, my knife tumbled out of my sleeve, falling to the grass.

"She's armed!" one of the guards said. Then another shot clipped my right ear, the air around me burning.

"I said get down!"

"I don't bow to you, human!" I said, the words of Death scorching through the grass, even as I fell to my knees anyway because my ears were ringing and the courtyard seemed to tilt back and forth. But now my clock was in my kimono and my hand with Hiro's ring had gone numb, the pull of time not responding to me. This was why I didn't deserve to be a god. This was why Japan would fall.

One guard was reloading his rifle, while the other one was taking aim. My shadows stretched out to stop him, but darkness could not outrun bullets. The shot thundered through the night air.

I braced for pain, my broken hand twitching as it repaired itself, but none came. The guards stood silent and unmoving, moonlight casting their faces a shade of paper white, their eyes darting around.

The bullet hung suspended in front of my face. I reached out to touch it and it fell to the ground, rolling in the grass.

Then Tsukuyomi hopped over the palace walls and into the courtyard.

He wore a cape of moonlight, his kimono a billowing banner of crystal snow behind him, his steps scorching white light into the dirt. The haunting glow of his skin drank up the weak lantern light, making the whole world look pale and gray in comparison. He rushed across the lawn toward me and my breath caught in my throat, feeling like the Earth had changed its orbit, like every comet in the sky was rushing toward me at once, like the universe was mine.

When focused on my quest, it was so easy to forget what Tsukuyomi truly was. But here, in the frozen courtyard, he was the guardian of the night sky who collected secret dreams and whispered prayers, beautiful not just by human measurements but in the breathtaking way of frosted lakes and swaying silver grass. He was someone meant to last forever.

He knelt in front of me, then took my bloody hand and examined it.

"I had it under control," I said, though my voice sounded dizzy.

"Clearly," Tsukuyomi said. He helped me to my feet, his hands startlingly warm.

"I told you to stay away," I said, but there was no heat behind my words, not a true complaint, and we both knew it.

"I did, at first," Tsukuyomi said, gesturing for me to climb the wall before him. "But supervising the Yōkai was...grating. I decided I could watch her just as easily from the moon, while watching you as well. When I saw you down here covered in blood, I couldn't just do nothing."

My wounded hand slipped as I came over the side of the wall, muscles still weak and fingers unresponsive. I hit the wet grass with a thump, but before I could even rise onto my elbows, Tsukuyomi had pulled me into his arms.

"Are you all right?" he said. "Did they hurt you anywhere else?"

His eyes had never looked so bright. His heartbeat pounded in my ears, so loudly I could hardly hear his words at all.

Soon, I would have to face Ivy, and there was a chance I would never see him again. I didn't know if he had released my father, but I'd sent him away and he'd come back for me anyway. I wanted to push him away, to never let myself be carved open again, but more than that, I didn't want Hiro's memory to keep destroying me. He had taken so much from me already. I wouldn't let him take Tsukuyomi too.

"Ren?" he said, his hand cupping my face.

"I'm fine," I said, my fingers tracing the back of his hand, holding it in place.

"Okay," Tsukuyomi said, not looking fully convinced. "Shall I go back and inform Neven that you're finished?"

He started to put me down, but I clung to his shirt to stop him. "He'll have heard the gunshots," I said belatedly. "He's coming, I'm sure."

Tsukuyomi blinked, kneeling back down. "So then, what do you—"

I grabbed his collar and pulled him down into a kiss.

He didn't move for a moment, eyes wide-open, arms rigid on my back. But before I could pull away, he melted against me, one hand falling to my hair and the other to my waist.

He held me like a flower that the wind might tear apart, his lips sweet and gentle. I kissed him and saw a thousand galaxies full of bright stars and the cool quietness of a bone-white moon in all its bright shapes. My murmuring shadows fell silent, and there was nothing but Tsukuyomi and the stars and a peace I had never known since becoming a goddess.

He fell on top of me, and then we were both lying in the wet earth of the palace's outer gate. I had never felt so warm, even with the cold ground on my back, soaking into my clothes. But above me, Tsukuyomi was a heavy blanket, his heart pressed closed to mine. I could feel every beat deep in my bones.

Loving Hiro had been like holding on tight to a shooting star as it rocketed across the sky. But Tsukuyomi felt like a sunrise unfolding over a dark and silent morning, the thousands of locked doors to empty rooms in my palace suddenly thrown open, and for once I didn't need to be destroyed to know that I was real. All I needed was this one moment when I was someone worth coming back for, someone worth saving.

I pulled away at the sound of footsteps. His hands lingered on my sleeve, even as I put distance between us. As the footsteps grew louder, I remembered what we'd come here for and pressed my eyes closed with a sigh.

Neven appeared on top of the wall, straddling it for a moment before hopping down.

"Sorry, I got trapped in a closet hiding from some guards," he said. "Have you…"

He trailed off, gaze falling on Tsukuyomi, who was very clearly no longer in the forest where he was supposed to be.

"Why are you here?" Neven said, crossing his arms. "Where's Mikuzume?"

"She's still in the forest," Tsukuyomi said. "Believe me, she was happy to see me go."

"Shame that you won't offer us the same courtesy."

"Neven," I said, rubbing my forehead, "not now, please."

Neven grudgingly looked away from Tsukuyomi, scanning our surroundings as if the mythical sword would suddenly appear, hidden in the tall blades of grass. When he saw nothing, he turned to me expectantly.

I could do nothing but shake my head and try to hide the disappointment on my face, even though Neven probably sensed it. I'd always tried so hard to be someone he could rely on. Someone who had a plan even when the world was collapsing in on itself. Now I was just a failure.

"What should we do now?" he asked, rather than press me for details.

I forced a smile onto my face even though I felt like I was sliding off the edge of the Earth, fingers sinking into mud just to hang on one moment longer.

"We have other options," I said. "We can still rely on my Shinigami, and I have some other contacts among the gods that I can call on."

Neven sighed with relief, but Tsukuyomi only stared at me, his fierce gaze unwavering. He knew I was lying. But how could I tell Neven that no one in the world would help us, that the four of us were all that stood between Japan and Ankou's army? Everything terrible in Neven's life was supposed to be in the past.

"Let's collect Tamamo No Mae and go back to Yomi," I said, rising to my feet. "I need some time to arrange everything."

I stood up and pretended that my knees weren't shaking, that I was a real goddess who had no weakness and feared no enemy and had nothing to lose but pride. Neven smiled at my beautiful lies, and I would have given anything to keep that look on his face for the rest of my life.

That might be possible, Izanami's voice said, her words burning through my bones, *because your life is ending much sooner than you'd planned.*

CHAPTER 21

Upon our return to Yomi, the shadows pooled around our ankles, staining our socks black, gnawing at the wood of our sandals as if the night sensed my hopelessness.

I feigned tiredness and retreated to my room, ignoring Tsukuyomi's concerned expression. Then I sat in front of my mirror and extinguished all the lights.

Even when I slept, I almost always left a candle burning in Yomi. The darkness was a pulsing tide that could creep up on you while you slept, dragging you into the brine and filling up your lungs. But tonight I wanted to be taken away.

I pressed my hand to the mirror, waiting for my eyes to adjust to the night. Slowly, like a dream descending over me, the hazy outlines of my furniture reappeared in the darkness, the shape of the door frame and the window that overlooked the courtyard. The pale lines shifted, like memories I couldn't quite grasp.

In the mirror, my own face began to take shape.

My hair, now down to my waist, glowing like spider silk in the dark. My eyes that tapered off in the corners, the harsh lines of my jaw, my thin lips pressed too tightly together.

As I watched, the flesh peeled off my reflection and hit the floor like rotten meat, revealing yellowed bones and empty vacuums where there should have been eyes. A skeletal hand reached out and mirrored my own where it pressed to the mirror.

"Hello, Ren of Yakushima," said Izanami.

A decade ago, I had screamed and shattered the mirror at the sound of Izanami's voice. But now I knew that gods were only legends, and legends never truly died.

"Tell me what to do," I said.

Izanami laughed, the sound like glass shards scraping together. *"You and I are the same,"* she said. *"I have no answers that you don't already know."*

But I knew that wasn't true. Even if Izanami and I were connected, she was a different facet of me, someone dark and cruel and unapologetic. That was who I needed to be now.

"How would you stop the Reapers?" I asked.

"Reapers wouldn't come here for me," she said.

I pounded my fist against the mirror, regretting the sound that echoed through the room. I couldn't wake Neven.

"You know what I mean," I whispered.

Izanami stared back at me, her hollow eyes hypnotic, pulling me closer and closer to the mirror.

"I would kill them," she said at last.

"Of course, but how?"

She scoffed. *"You are a Death God. Do not insult me with that question."*

"But I don't think I—"

"It doesn't matter what you think you can do," Izanami said, her words venomous. *"What matters is what you are."*

"And what is that?" I said, my voice too loud.

But before Izanami could answer, my door began to slide open.

I lit every candle in my room with a wave of my hand, jumping to my feet. Izanami's face vanished in the sharp light.

Tsukuyomi stumbled back, shielding his eyes from the sudden brightness.

"Ow, Ren!"

I swallowed, my heartbeat pounding all the way up to my ears. "Why were you sneaking into my room?"

Tsukuyomi blushed, rubbing the back of his neck. He looked much younger in his sleeping clothes than he did in his regal white kimono.

"I was wondering if you were awake," he said to the floor. "I didn't mean to scare you. I would have left if I'd seen you sleeping."

"My servants could have killed you on sight just for opening my door."

"Chiyo was the one who told me where your room was," Tsukuyomi said, shrugging.

Damn her. It was impossible to hide anything from Chiyo.

"She just wants me to marry so I don't die heirless and leave her serving a bunch of Reapers," I said, rolling my eyes and sinking down into my blankets. Tsukuyomi's eyes went wide.

"Calm down, that wasn't a proposal," I said, patting the space beside me on my futon.

Tsukuyomi sat down carefully, like my bed was made of thin ice that might shatter with his weight.

"I want to be clear," he said, staring resolutely at his feet, "I did not come here for indecent purposes."

"That's a shame," I said, ignoring the way Tsukuyomi blushed even redder than before. "Why have you come, then?"

"I was waiting until your brother fell asleep so I could speak to you," he said. "You lied to him."

"I am aware," I said, turning away.

"We do still have options," he said. "You know I can bind the Reapers in moonlight."

I shook my head. "They're not going to come at night. They know Shinigami can control light and darkness, so they're not going to give us an advantage."

Tsukuyomi sighed. His eyes looked shadowed, like he was slowly turning into the dark side of the moon instead of his normal brightness.

"You're tired," I said.

He yawned, but waved a hand as if to dismiss the thought. "There's no moonlight down here, that's why. I'm fine, we should—"

"Lie down," I said, lifting a corner of the blankets.

He eyed me warily. "Ren, I told you, I'm not—"

"I'm not going to corrupt you. Just lie down."

He looked unconvinced but slid under the blankets all the same, exhaustion winning him over. I waved a hand and extinguished the candles, casting the room in darkness, then lay down beside him. He was flat on his back, so I put my head on his shoulder and rested an arm across his chest. With my ear pressed to him, I could hear every beat of his heart, the blood rushing through his veins, every breath that filled his lungs. His body was like an entire universe all by itself.

"You're freezing," he said, but made no move to pull away, instead wrapping a warm arm around my shoulders.

"I'm cold-blooded."

He hummed sleepily. "Like a turtle?"

"More like a snake."

"You're venomous?" he said, a small smile on his lips even as his eyes fell closed.

"There's only one way to find out."

"Don't bite me," he whined, his voice slurred with sleep. "Well, not right now, at least. We can discuss it later."

I laughed. "Go to sleep, Tsukuyomi," I said, deepening the darkness another few degrees.

"I shouldn't," he said, his words already melting together. "We need more time before..." He trailed off, his muscles growing limp.

"Don't worry about that," I said. I would handle it. Somehow.

"...before the solar eclipse," he whispered, his words quiet and faraway, like he hadn't meant to say them out loud. But then his heartbeat slowed and breathing evened, as he finally rested.

What did that have to do with anything? I thought.

I slid out from under his arm and sat up.

You can keep him safe down here, Izanami's whispered in the darkness. *Forever. You know what you have to do, Ren.*

I thought of my wedding ceremony, the priest trying to force sake past my lips, binding me to the underworld for eternity. Even one drop poured in Tsukuyomi's mouth while he slept would be enough. I could keep him and Neven and the Yōkai down here forever, where they'd be safe.

But Tsukuyomi belonged on the moon, and Neven feared the darkness. They would be alive, but it wouldn't be a life for them.

Soon, they'll have no life at all, Izanami said.

I clenched my jaw and rose to my feet, tiptoeing into the hallway. As soon as I slid the door shut behind me, I ignited every candle I could see, and Izanami's voice vanished from my mind, like I'd risen from a bad dream.

I walked away from the west wing, safely out of earshot from all the bedrooms, then slid to the floor, gripping my hair. Maybe if I pulled hard enough, I could force out some new ideas. Anything would be better than standing before Ivy with an army of four versus hundreds of Reapers.

I stood and started walking again, filled with a strange urge to keep going until the ends of the Earth. The hallway stretched longer and longer, the murals fading away to empty panels that would one day be filled with the rest of the world's legends. Soon, my own end would be painted onto the thin paper.

I kicked one of the panels, half expecting it to hurt or repel me, but the paper tore easily, now a yawning hole into the dark room behind it. I kicked another, the sound of tearing paper far too satisfying. Maybe if I destroyed the rest of the hallway, time would stop and the future would never come.

When there were no doors left to break, I trudged back the other way, glaring at the perfect paintings of deities, everything so epic and picturesque, not at all as dirty and ugly as life really was. I stopped in front of one depicting Susano'o meditating at the bottom of the sea, surrounded by shimmering fish and waters in every shade of blue. The murals didn't show the truth—that he had the power to save Japan from Reapers but instead chose to sit alone in dark waters because he wanted his sword back a thousand years too late.

Perhaps there was something else I could offer him. But Susano'o didn't seem to want anything but to spite his family, and I couldn't exactly give him that.

"These empty panels won't regenerate, you know," a voice said behind me. "You're just making more work for me tomorrow."

I turned to Chiyo, who stood at the end of the hallway in her sleeping clothes, the dim light making her look older than usual.

"Sorry," I said, staring down at my hands.

Chiyo sighed, crossing the hallway toward me. I expected her to start lecturing me but jolted when she knelt down beside me instead. I didn't think I'd ever seen Chiyo sit before.

"You haven't found the sword," she said.

"What gave it away?" I said dryly. "This is how I act when I'm happy."

Chiyo sighed. "You should rest. You've been traveling for days. Maybe it will help you think of something."

"I don't need rest," I said. "Not with this plague."

Chiyo frowned. "What plague?"

"Is it not in your ledgers?"

She shook her head slowly. "I will check again," she said, though I doubted she would have missed something so important. "In the meantime, perhaps you can research in the royal libraries? Maybe they'll have information about the sword."

"Even if there was, there's no time to find it," I said. "Ivy is coming tomorrow, and the sword was lost hundreds of years ago."

"Lost?" Chiyo said, raising an eyebrow. "How does one simply lose the sword of a god?"

"All the empress said was that it was lost at the battle of Dan-no-ura," I said, shrugging. "It's probably buried somewhere."

Chiyo shook her head. "It wouldn't have been buried."

"How would you know?" I said, perhaps too harshly, but I didn't want to argue about a sword I'd never find.

"Because I was alive during the Genpei War," she said. "The battle of Dan-no-ura took place at sea."

My next words caught in my throat, my breath stolen away. When the empress said the sword had been disposed of, I'd pictured Taira troops tossing it into a great hole and rolling a boulder on top of it, or melting it over a hot fire, or casting it off a cliff into an abyss. But how did one dispose of something at sea? They had probably thrown it overboard, hoping it would be lost to the depths of the ocean.

But the sea was not a secret hiding place. Like everything else, it belonged to the gods.

"Thank you, Chiyo!" I said, rising to my feet and running down the hallway. I had business in Izumo.

I stood barefoot on the shore, the moon looming overhead, dimmed by a layer of clouds. Without Tsukuyomi and the shimenawa connecting us, I felt too light, afraid the waters would carry me away. But the time for fear had come and gone. Soon, the sun would rise, and the Reapers would come.

I took a deep breath and dived under the water.

The brine felt like it was flaying my skin, the coldness

splintering my bones. I forced myself to swim deeper, even as the waves tried to pull me back to the surface and the fish nibbled on me like I was a decaying corpse. I waved them away, stretching out my shadows to grab hold of coral and seaweed, dragging me deeper and deeper.

My bare feet sank into the ocean floor, the sand jagged and cold.

"Come out, Susano'o!" I called in Death. Sea creatures stared in silence all around me. Fish three times my size blinked dead yellow eyes at me, hovering just beyond the coral clearing, lips hanging open as if hungry.

The waters began to stir, sands rising up in spirals, stinging my eyes that already felt raw from salt water and ready to pop out of my skull from the pressure of the deep sea.

Susano'o appeared in a cloud of sand, the ocean floor rising beneath him like a sparkling white carpet. He crossed his arms as the sand settled, not seeming all that bothered at being awoken, but I knew better than to trust appearances.

"You're alone this time," Susano'o said. "Have you killed Tsukuyomi too?"

I glared, my shadows itching to choke that annoying glimmer from his eyes.

"It's all the same to me," he said, perhaps misreading my silence. "My brothers should know better than to sleep with Death. They deserve whatever end comes for them."

"I didn't kill Tsukuyomi," I said.

Susano'o stilled, raising an eyebrow. "He doesn't know you're here, then."

I didn't bother to answer. He had already figured it out.

"That means you're doing something he wouldn't approve of," he said, a dangerous smile curling one side of his mouth.

"Yes, he might object to me killing you," I said. "Or maybe he would thank me when I told him why."

"Don't make me laugh, Reaper," Susano'o said, waving his hand as if swatting me away. "I can see that you're not carrying my sword, which can only mean you've failed and come begging me for charity."

"I didn't find your sword," I said, my jaw clenched.

"How shocking," Susano'o said, crossing his arms and leaning back against a coral bed.

"I was never going to find it," I said, taking a step closer, "because you already have it."

Susano'o's expression didn't change. "Oh?" he said. "Is this what Reapers do when they fail? Blame everything but their own incompetence?"

"Kusanagi No Tsurugi was tossed into the sea hundreds of years ago," I said, ignoring his taunts. "Are you really so weak that you don't know when a godly weapon is dropped into your own waters? Even I can sense when every single human in my domain dies. Are you really less powerful than me?"

All at once, the sands lost their shimmer, the crowd of hungry sea creatures slowly backing away into the dark waters. Susano'o locked his gaze on me, eyes hollow black.

He pounded a fist into the white coral formation behind him, the sound like the whole world cracking in two, rippling through the waters and forcing me backward. The coral shattered apart, and from the ruins Susano'o drew the shape of Kusanagi No Tsurugi that he had showed me last week.

He ran his left hand across the surface and the coral fell away like dead skin, revealing polished metal. He held the blade up to the weak and distant sunlight far above us, and even through the dark waters, it gleamed with the light of a thousand beginnings, sharp enough to slice the ocean to pieces.

I thought of Neven's hand with a Reaper's knife through it, the bullets between my ribs, and a village turned to ashes, all for nothing.

"We could have died on your pointless errand!" I said, drawing Izanami's katana and pointing it between his eyes.

Susano'o didn't even flinch or move his sword to defend himself. "If only I had been so lucky," he said, his lip curled with bitterness.

"I could have been preparing for Ivy!" I said, my hand trembling, shadows pooling at my feet, scorching the white sands black. "I might have stood a chance if I hadn't—"

"In case I haven't made this abundantly clear, Reaper, *I don't like you*," Susano'o said, jamming his sword into the sand, sending quakes through the water. "All I wanted was to shut you up and send you far away. If I inflicted you on my sorry excuse for a sister and you died along the way, all the better."

I swung the katana down. The ocean's weight made it impossibly heavy, but I was strong enough to crush diamonds with my bare hands.

Susano'o raised his sword, catching mine in its curved edge and knocking it away from his face without so much as flinching.

"Don't try to fight me down here, Reaper," he said. "You'll lose."

With my clock, I probably could have at least injured him, but what was the point anymore? I didn't need a dead ocean god, I needed a living one who knew how to sink Ivy's ships.

"I held up my end of the deal," I said. "I found your sword."

Susano'o let out a sharp laugh. "We never had a deal. I only make deals with gods."

I clenched my teeth, wracking my mind for something, anything I could say to persuade him. I thought of his solemn silhouette on the panels of my palace, scowling at the bottom of a cold and lonely sea.

I lowered my sword.

"I can give you something else," I said. "Something better than a sword."

He raised an eyebrow. "I regret to inform you, Reaper, I am not like my brothers. I do not want your body."

"I am not offering you my body," I said, scowling.

"Then what do you think you could possibly offer me?"

"A place in Yomi."

He froze, his dark expression unchanged as the ocean swayed around us.

"You are banished from the kingdom of the living, but your father has no control over my domain," I said. "You may go there if I allow it."

"Why would I ever want to go to Yomi?" Susano'o said, the water growing darker and denser around us, like a heavy syrup. "I was born of Yomi's darkness, and look where it led me."

"You think that the darkness ruined you," I said, "but me and so many others live in the same darkness and aren't undone because of it. I am made of Yomi's darkness, yet I don't go around scorching fields of rice for fun."

"And what would *you* know?" Susano'o said, his words a sharp hiss that made me flinch away. All the creatures in the ocean seemed to turn toward us, white eyes staring at me, seaweed pointing accusingly in my direction. "You think you understand darkness, little girl? I terrified the sun goddess so fiercely that she fled into a cave for hundreds of years, leaving the world dark and cold and dead. I flayed her favorite horses and laid them at her feet. I shit on the palace floors of great gods. You may live in Yomi, but you haven't even begun to learn what darkness truly is."

"But I know who you are," I said.

"Do not presume to know me like you know my brothers."

"I know that you were cast out for crying for your mother," I said. His eyes narrowed, but his rage halted, like a candle extinguished.

"I know that you've been alone down here for thousands of years," I said. "I know that you were punished like a criminal before you did anything wrong."

The water grew warmer, bubbling and boiling around us.

"You understand nothing," Susano'o said, his voice eerily flat.

Maybe he was right, but all I could see when I looked at Susano'o was Hiro, cast out of the land where he belonged for ridiculous reasons, growing sharper each day in his loneliness. But Hiro had traveled all across Japan and at least made friends. Susano'o had been left down in these deep waters with no one but sea creatures to keep him company.

"I understand that you're not poisoned by darkness," I said. "I understand that you cared for your mother, so you're capable of caring for other people as well. I—"

Before I could speak another word, water rushed in my mouth, pouring down my throat. The salt scraped my insides, filling up my stomach and lungs. I sank to the ocean floor, feeling like my whole chest was made of lead, my katana falling to the sand beside me.

Susano'o towered over me. "You, of all people, are appealing to my morality?" he said. "The girl who killed my brother and brought monsters to Japan, drawn to you like flies to rotting meat? You offer yourself to me as proof that the darkness does not ruin, yet you have ruined everything around you."

I thrashed in the sand, trying to force the water out of my lungs, but its pressure only crushed me harder into the sand.

"You think I want a place in Yomi, the land that corrupted and ravaged my mother's body? It was my mother's kingdom, and even *she* didn't want it. But thank you for deigning to welcome me to a place that you stole from my family."

More water forced its way into my lungs until I felt like my rib cage was going to explode. I gave up trying to cough it out and swiped my shadows at Susano'o, grabbing him by the ankles and yanking him down. Once he was close enough, I yanked a knife from my sleeve and jammed it into his leg, the only part of him I could reach.

He let out a cry, and all at once the water rushed out of me. I suddenly felt too light, like I would float all the way back to the surface. Susano'o yanked the knife out, lunging toward me.

But the water slowed his movements, and I easily dodged, forcing his arms behind his back and driving his face into the sand, my knee crushing down on his spine.

"Yomi is my kingdom," I said, feeling his spine crack under my weight. He hissed and struggled but couldn't break free. "You don't own it just because your mother did. I paid for it in blood. And I offered you something that no one has ever offered me. A home."

Susano'o's movements grew weaker, until he lay still in the sand. "I know your intentions," he said at last, "but Yomi could never be my home. I am the storms and the seas. Yomi has neither."

Susano'o had become almost as pale as the sand beneath him. I loosened my grip on his arms, and when he didn't immediately rise up to strangle me, I removed my knee from his back.

"You are one of the strangest creatures I've ever met," he said, making no move to rise. "Still, I cannot help you."

"You *can*," I said, grinding my heels into the sand.

"The Reapers are not my problem," he said. "If you truly believe you are a god, then handle them yourself."

"How?" I asked. "Everyone says that, but I'm outnumbered. That's always been the problem."

Susano'o sat up, his face white and shimmering from the sand.

"Have heard of hitobashira?"

I shook my head.

"They are pillars of protection made from human sacrifices."

I froze. I had already taken so many human lives just to bring Neven back. To save humans, I had to sacrifice them?

"How would dead humans possibly keep out a Death God?"

"Hitobashira can change the current of rivers and stop mountains from crumbling. Enough human souls could surely conjure up the energy to keep out enemies. A couple hundred would probably suffice. Women's corpses are said to be even more auspicious than men's."

I closed my eyes. I had to kill several hundred humans and bury them on the shore?

"I'm trying to save humans, not sacrifice them."

Susano'o scowled. "You expect to receive miracles without giving up anything in return? You say you care so much for the fate of Japan, yet you can't even decide how much it's worth to you."

"How can you just—"

But Susano'o was done talking to me. He turned, giving me one last glance, his face young and pale, all its sharpness washed away by the current. He stretched out his arms and the white sands breathed him in, enveloping him like a blanket, pulling him deep into the ground.

Killing them all would be so easy.

I sat on a half wall by Izumo station, the churning sea at my back and the city spread out before me, streets lit up by yellow streetlamps. Children tossed a ball in the overgrown grass of an empty lot. A woman sold takoyaki under red lanterns. Men walked home from work, carrying briefcases and wearing suits like Westerners.

I took my knife from my sleeve, holding it up to the stars, examining the sharpness of the blade. Who cared if the humans saw? If they complained, I could just cut their tongues out. Well, maybe my knife was a bit too dull for that, but I would find a way. I lowered my knife and tried to count how many lives I needed.

My shadows could tear the foundations of the nearest house apart, crushing the family inside like grapes under the rubble. That would be at least five.

I could latch on to the ankles of the children playing in the park and drag them out to sea, holding them down until all the air left their lungs. That would be eleven.

I could even grab the throats of everyone in this street and choke the life out of their eyes, pinching their windpipes shut until their flimsy spines snapped. That would be thirty, maybe thirty-five dead. Not enough.

When I had lost Neven, I hadn't thought twice about tearing out human hearts to bring him back. Even when I'd felt like a wild animal with raw flesh caught in my teeth, like all the blood inside of me was stolen and no part of Ren was left, I'd kept going because I'd thought it was the only way.

But in the end, it had all been for nothing. Neven had saved himself, and I knew exactly how many souls I had taken in vain.

A few hundred more shouldn't have mattered among the thousands I'd stolen, but now I couldn't even hold my knife straight in my hand without feeling a bone-deep tremble and sweat loosening the hilt beneath my palm because all of this was my fault. A true goddess would have had an army of loyal Shinigami at her side and the respect of both the sun and ocean gods. But they all had abandoned me because they thought I deserved to die, and maybe they were right.

Do it for Neven, I thought. I told him I would do anything to keep him safe. But I could still hear him saying *I don't want you to ruin yourself for me*, as if it wasn't already too late. If it meant Neven would be safe, I should have been willing to swallow all the darkness of Yomi, become every nightmare in the world, every sudden sound in the dark forest and ominous churning of black waters far out at sea because my life had never been my own anyway—it had never mattered enough.

I thought of Tsukuyomi and the way he looked at me like I was the last green leaf on a tree ravaged by winter's breath, the way he held me and expected nothing in return, no promises of power or eternal kingdoms, just moments that unfolded one by one like pages in an endless story.

I jammed my knife into the wall, splintering the wood. Humans around me jumped and hurried away, whispering to each other. The children playing in the park were heading back home, summoned by a woman's voice calling their names out into the dark.

I couldn't do it. And maybe that made me weak and selfish for not going to the ends of the Earth to protect Neven. But so much of me had decayed over the last ten years that there was hardly anything left. The humans had long overpaid for my failures, and I couldn't justify saving myself with their blood. Not if it meant hiding from my reflection, afraid of what nightmare would stare back at me.

I felt Izanami's rage simmering beneath my skin and looked down at my hands, expecting bones and tangled veins, but all I saw was pale skin and dirty fingernails.

You're going to die, Izanami said, though her voice sounded faraway, as if calling up from the bottom of a well.

Death comes for us all, eventually, I thought. This time, Izanami had no response.

I yanked myself back to Yomi through the shadows, crashing hard into the courtyard of my palace.

I took a deep breath once I was finally outside in the cool bath of darkness. For once, the nothingness was soothing. I walked through the garden, out to the stone veranda where I'd nearly married Hiro, and sat on the steps. The blood had of course been cleaned, but sometimes I could still see it staining the floor, even in total darkness. I could still hear him crying for me while I refused to look at him. I'd entered this veranda for the first time thinking I was going to have everything I ever wanted, and I'd left it with nothing at all.

That was what I imagined death felt like. Not burning

hellfire but a thousand miles of lonely darkness, the blood of everyone you'd ever loved on your hands.

That was what I would have again soon. Nothing.

I might stand a chance at fending off Ivy because I was a god and could turn time just like her, but everyone else would surely die. Then, even if I somehow slaughtered Ivy and all of her friends, I would still be alone in the dark. I'd only suffered through the last decade of loneliness because of the hope of finding Neven. But if he was gone, then an eternity alone was worse than any hell that awaited me after death.

I couldn't let Neven face Ivy with me.

I thought of Tsukuyomi, probably still asleep in my room. The idea of him bleeding out like Hiro was unbearable. And poor Tamamo No Mae. Even with her fierceness, she still looked like that small child Neven had carried across the fields in the early morning. I couldn't ask her to die either.

In the end, it would make no difference whether it was four of us against a fleet of High Reapers or only me. Either way, we would be hopelessly outnumbered. Ivy was my responsibility, and Yomi was mine to protect. I would not run away like a coward, but I couldn't ask anyone to come with me.

I turned at the sound of footsteps in the distance.

Tamamo No Mae approached me, her expression solemn. Without a word, she sat beside me on the steps, leaning against my shoulder.

"Are we all going to die?" she said. I shouldn't have been surprised by the question. The Yōkai had always been smarter than she let on.

"No," I said. "I'll take care of it."

She lifted her head, looking at me strangely. "I've died before, you know."

Right, I thought. This wasn't the Yōkai's first life, after all.

"You're lucky you'll come back," I said, staring up at the sky.

"I am," she said, hugging my arm. I could feel her staring at me, but couldn't bring myself to look. Her eyes were too big and earnest.

"You're worried," she said softly.

"I'm not," I said. "I told you, I will take care of it."

"Just you?" she said. "Not us?"

At last, I turned to face her. She shrugged. "I told you, I can see what's in your heart."

I shook my head. "It doesn't matter what I want. I can't control other people."

"No," she said, "but maybe I can help. Maybe I can convince Neven to stay behind."

"I don't think you can talk him out of this one, Mikuzume."

"I'm a Yōkai," she said, shrugging. "I can be very persuasive."

I narrowed my eyes. "Do not enchant my brother."

Her expression didn't change. "Even if it saves his life?"

My anger fizzled away. It would be far from the worst thing I'd condoned. "I... All right."

The Yōkai nodded. "But I want to go with you."

"No," I said. "Ivy is here because of me. She's my responsibility. There's no need for anyone else to get hurt."

"Even if I die, I'll be reincarnated." Tamamo No Mae's eyes were wide and wet. I still couldn't see anything but the little girl I'd first met in the village, the one who I'd almost killed.

"You're not scared of dying?" I asked, raising an eyebrow.

She looked away. "If I die, at least I won't be alone," she said. "And you won't either."

I closed my eyes, my chest aching. "Right," I said, wiping my eyes with my sleeve.

Tamamo No Mae squeezed my arm, then stood up. "I'll go talk to Neven," she said. I nodded, and she ran off. That only left one person.

When I came to the throne room, Tsukuyomi was bent over a map, a brush in each hand.

He looked brighter after resting, his hair slightly askew from sleep, the outer layer of his kimono thrown over his pajamas.

"Ren," he said, still staring at his maps, "I think I've found the most likely points of entry for Ivy's ships."

I swallowed. "Tsukuyomi."

"This time of year, passenger ships only arrive in several ports. Out of those that have an origin point in Western Europe within the last year, it's most likely that she'll dock in Yokohama."

"Tsukuyomi."

"That's also where several other passenger ships that had transfers leading back to England have arrived this month, so it would make sense if—"

"Tsukuyomi," I said, "you need to go home."

He finally looked up from his map, but only to shoot me a cursory glance.

"Don't be ridiculous," he said. "As I was saying—"

"I don't want you here anymore."

At last, Tsukuyomi paused. He frowned at me like he was trying to crack a code.

"I understand that you're anxious about this confrontation, Ren, but, as I've explained to you before, I'm here to protect you."

"Well, you've failed," I said.

He winced. "The situation with Susano'o's sword is hardly my fault."

I took a deep breath. "The only reason I kept you here so long was because you reminded me of Hiro," I said.

Tsukuyomi froze. His stoic expression cracked for only a moment, and in that moment I wanted to fall to my knees and tell him it was a lie, but he shook his head and smoothed his features. "I assumed as much upon my arrival," he said, "but surely that's not how you see me now."

"You're right," I said. "I don't."

Tsukuyomi smiled. "Then—"

"—because Hiro was better than you."

The smile dropped off his face. All the air seemed to drain from the room.

"What?" he said softly.

I forced myself to stare straight at him. This was how I always spoke to humans when taking their souls. I could betray no emotion, no conscience, nothing but the merciless hand of Death and all of her darkness. I pictured Tsukuyomi dead on the shores of Yokohama, Ivy's scythe tearing his throat open, his blood filling the ocean. I thought of his starry eyes gone dark forever. That was the only way I could keep talking.

"Hiro was strong," I said. "You are a coward who hides behind his propriety."

Tsukuyomi shook his head. "Ren, why are you—"

"You can't compare to him. I've realized that now."

Tsukuyomi had gone very still. I would have thought he

was time-frozen if not for the audible beating of his heart. "You don't mean that," he said.

"I do."

"Ren, please—"

"I hate when people beg!" I said. And that, at least, was true. *Please, just go*, I thought. "Save your dignity and leave."

Tsukuyomi didn't move, and for a few terrible moments I thought I might have to force him out. But then he set his brushes down gently on the table and rose to his feet.

"As you wish," he whispered.

My throat dried up and I fought back the tears pooling in my eyes, not realizing how much I'd wanted him to keep arguing with me, keep fighting for me. But I had been cruel, and that was too much to ask.

I thought he would storm away and that would be the last I ever heard of him, but his footsteps stopped at the door.

This is the part where he tells me I'm a monster, I thought. *Please, make it hurt. I deserve it.*

"You know, at first, I didn't think you could really be a goddess," he said. "You cried and loved like a human. But now I see that I was wrong. You're just as stubborn and stupid as the rest of us, and your mistakes won't just ruin your own life. They'll ruin the world."

Then he turned around and vanished into the dark hallway.

This is what love is, I thought as I sank to my knees. This was the truth that Ambrose would never understand—that love only became real when it was no longer easy. Like Death and time and darkness, it demanded payment, and I would give everything I had left.

CHAPTER 22

I sat on the shores of Yokohama, Tamamo No Mae by my side and my katana in my lap. Above us, the afternoon sun and pale ghost of the moon watched from opposite sides of the sky in mocking silence. Perhaps they both wanted front row seats to my death, long overdue.

Ten years ago, I had arrived on these shores to start a new life. Back then, everything looked so new and strange and beautiful. I remembered when I said goodbye to London as I fled from Ivy, and now I was saying goodbye to Japan, to everything.

But I hadn't said goodbye to Neven.

It was the right thing to do, but I still had to press my eyes closed and slow my breathing when I thought of him. It had been hard enough to pretend to be cold and unfeeling when sending Tsukuyomi away. There was no way I could say good-bye to Neven forever and not fall to my knees in tears. If he saw me that way, he'd know that something was wrong, and then there would be no chance of keeping him in Yomi, enchantment or not.

I tried to remember the last thing I said to him, but yesterday felt gray and hazy. I hoped it was something kind and important, but I doubted it. Neven and I had rarely indulged in sappy human expressions of love. In lives that stretched out across millennia, words often rang hollow. We knew what was true and real without saying it. At least, I hoped Neven did, and that he would forgive me one day.

I prayed Tsukuyomi was right about Ivy arriving in Yokohama. But even if she didn't come here, the Reapers had eyes everywhere, and I was no longer hiding. She would come for me soon.

For what felt like hours, we sat on the sand, the Yōkai leaning on my shoulder, but not a single ship came to shore.

Maybe Ivy's ship sprang a leak and she's at the bottom of the sea, I thought. But I wasn't lucky enough for anything like that. My destiny and Ivy's were intertwined. She would come here—of that I was certain.

The afternoon sun sank low in the sky, and the Yōkai started pacing. I could hear her heartbeat battering her rib cage, the fox inside her trying to scratch its way out.

"I'm going to check the other side, make sure no ships have come in that way," she said.

I knew no ships had come. I would have heard the waters parting and the wood clunking against the dock, but Tamamo No Mae looked raw with anticipation, ready to claw her own skin off so her fox could run free, so I nodded and waved her off.

The moon had risen to the center of the sky, looming larger than before. With all of the new souls I'd gained from the plague, I could see its vast empty oceans of darkness, its bright dusty surface lit up on the side that faced the sun. I wondered if Tsukuyomi was there, looking down on me. But even if he was, he wouldn't care what happened. I'd made sure of that.

"I'm sorry," I whispered to the moon, knowing he would never hear me.

I clasped my hands together in some mockery of prayer, pressing them to my forehead. Who was a wayward god supposed to pray to? There was no one on heaven or Earth who could help me now. The cold metal of Hiro's ring burned against my finger. I unfolded my hands and laid them in my lap, staring at the ring that looked like it belonged to some magnificent princess, someone beautiful and wealthy and happy. It didn't match my cracked hands, fingernails cut raggedly with blood and dirt under the tips.

I took the ring off and turned it over, remembered Hiro slipping it on my finger, back when I'd been so sure that I had conquered every bad thing in the world.

I held it up to the moon, a perfect circle of silver and gold wrapped around all the snow-white silence. I had given up everything else that mattered, and somehow, accidentally, I had left Hiro for last.

Then, before I could change my mind, I threw my ring into the black waters.

Something in my chest ached when the metal hit the surface far away. With a quiet splash, everything I had left of Hiro was gone.

I closed my eyes and saw him smiling, leading me into snowy mountain passes and rocky islands and dark rivers that led to new worlds. But that Hiro was gone, just like the Ren I had been was gone too. Maybe somewhere, in another world, there was a girl named Ren who lived happily ever after with her first love. But that would never be me.

I jumped as the waters parted at my feet. A woman began to crawl onto the shore—no, not a woman, a sea turtle. A Honengame.

"Maho?" I whispered. We were far from Takaoka, where I'd first met her, but I supposed Yōkai were not bound by the Earth the way humans were.

The Honengame made a deep rumbling sound, staring at me sternly and blowing away strands of seaweed caked to her round face. She swirled something in her mouth, then spit a piece of silver and gold at my feet. Hiro's ring.

"Foolish girl," she said. "You could sell that ring and feed a family for a year."

"I'm sorry," I said, somehow irrationally afraid of the Yōkai's judgment. Maho had been kind to me, and I had re-paid her by murdering someone she cared for. "I'm sorry, I know Hiro was your friend, I—"

"Yōkai have no friends," she said. "We are not sentimental like humans."

I doubt that, I thought, remembering Tamamo No Mae on the other end of the shore. But if Maho wasn't angry about Hiro, I wasn't about to argue.

"You can keep it," I said, nudging the ring back with my foot. "I don't... It doesn't feel like mine anymore."

"Ah, yes, I'll wear it on my long, lovely fingers," Maho said, rolling her eyes and slapping her fin in the sand. But she listened all the same, crawling over to the ring on the shore and taking it in her mouth, pocketing it in her cheek.

"I've been searching for you," she said, turning back to me. "I've had visions of darkness for months now. The Southern water Yōkai speak of a great danger from the West."

"The Reapers are coming," I said, resting my chin on my knees. "Thank you for the warning, Maho, but I know. There's not much I can do."

Maho's expression soured, and I felt that I'd somehow failed her again.

But this Yōkai could see the future. Maybe she knew when the Reapers would come, or how they planned to attack.

"Do you know what's going to happen next?" I asked.

"Of course," Maho said, her expression still pinched. When she didn't elaborate, my heart began to beat faster.

"Can I kill Ivy?" I said. "Please, Maho, I need to know."

But the Honengame only stared back at me, her eyes cold, pale like bleached coral. "You're asking the wrong questions."

I shook my head. "Please, can I touch your shell? Can you show me?"

She made a grunting sound that I took as affirmation and quickly pressed my palm to her smooth shell.

Darkness slammed down on all sides of me. I let out a shuddering breath, but my voice didn't make a sound. As if the whole world had been scrubbed away, there was nothing but an empty vacuum of silence, a hollowness that went on forever.

I ripped my hand away.

"What was that?" I said, blinking away the black spots in my vision. Then a horrible thought crossed my mind. "Is that death, Maho? Is that what it will be like when I die?"

"It is the future," Maho said.

"Can you be less cryptic?" I said, my fingers gripping the wet sand. "Don't you understand that if the Reapers take Japan, they'll hurt you too?"

"I understand," Maho said, her eyes narrowing. "That is why I'm here. But the more I reveal of the future, the more unpredictable it becomes."

I wanted to scream for her to drop all her pretenses and just tell me the Reapers' every move, all their tricks and deceits, every single step they would take. But an angry Yōkai would never give me what I wanted. I couldn't expect her to win this battle for me. She could have just as easily watched me die from far out at sea.

I sighed, plucking a strand of seaweed from her hair.

"Thank you for coming all this way for me," I said, dropping my gaze to the sand. "I don't deserve it, but thank you anyway."

She raised an eyebrow. "I did not come for you," she said. "I came for Japan."

I couldn't help but smile. Only Maho could be so blunt. "Thank you anyway."

She huffed, craning her neck to look up at the sky. "It's a full moon tonight," she said. I waited for her to continue, because Maho didn't make small talk. All of her words had a purpose.

But she never got the chance to continue. She turned as footsteps crossed the shore, but I didn't bother moving. It was only Tamamo No Mae.

"Ren!"

I froze, my whole body suddenly cold. No. *No no no*, it wasn't supposed to be like this. I closed my eyes, hoping the voice would go away, that it was just another torturous hallucination, residual energy of Death worming through my brain. The Honengame must have sensed my fear, for she disappeared beneath the water.

"Ren!" Neven called again, kneeling down in the sand beside me, panting hard. Neven was supposed to be safe in Yomi, far from the bloodbath that was about to ensue. Everything I'd thrown away was meaningless if Neven wasn't safe.

"What are you doing here?" I said.

Neven frowned, then shoved my shoulder, sending me spilling back into the sand. I sat up, holding my arm up in case he struck again, but he'd sat down with his arms crossed.

"You were really going to fight the Reapers alone?" he said. "How stupid can you be?"

I shook my head. "You have to go back, Neven, it's not safe. Please, I'll take you back to Yomi, just wait for me there." I reached for his wrist to drag him down through the shadows, but he slapped my hands away.

"Ren, stop! I'm not going to sit underground while you fight Ivy alone."

I turned toward the horizon. Ivy's ship could arrive at any minute. Neven needed to leave.

"Please, Neven," I said, grabbing his shirt. "Please, just go before it's too late."

Neven let out a tense breath, then grabbed my shoulders.

"I spent a hundred years without you," he said, the words of Death like a flash of lightning down my spine. *"Don't send me away again, Ren. Don't you dare."*

I shook my head, slumping in his grip. "I want you to live," I whispered.

He scoffed. "Stop that."

"Stop what?"

"Stop acting like I'd let you go anywhere alone."

I sank deeper into his hold, my face pressed to his shoulder.

"Wherever we go, we go together," Neven said. "I don't care if we're walking straight into Death's arms. You're not going alone."

I closed my eyes, nodding. There was no way he would go back to Yomi now. Like always, Neven was everything I didn't deserve. And maybe I was a monster for keeping him here with me, but I still felt so much stronger when he was by my side.

"How did you even get here?" I said.

Neven tensed, looking around. "Where's Mikuzume?" he said. "She tied me up and left me in a closet."

I sighed. That wasn't exactly how I'd hoped she would "convince" Neven to stay back.

"I yelled until Chiyo let me out and told me where you'd gone," he said. "I had to track down one of your Shinigami and threaten them with my clock until they brought me up here through the shrine in the cemetery. Then I ran across town, just to find you trying to single-handedly demolish a fleet of High Reapers."

I winced. "Not single-handedly," I said. "Mikuzume is with me. She'll be back soon."

As if summoned, her voice cut across the shore.

"Ren!"

Both of us turned to see her sprinting across the beach toward us. She hesitated when she locked eyes with Neven, stumbling slightly, but whatever she'd come to tell me was apparently too important to wait.

"Look!" she said, pointing across the water.

I squinted, the glare of the sun casting bright shapes on the horizon. A dark silhouette cleaved through the prickly tinsel of the sea, a towering mast that cut the sky in half. A ghostly cloud of gray steam rose behind it, the faraway sound of a steam engine churning like a jagged and rumbling heartbeat.

CHAPTER 23

The ship drew closer on the horizon, passing through the curtain of heat waves as if breaking from the world of dreams into vivid reality. Its sails thrashed in the changing winds, but the steam engines pulled the vessel forward unhindered. Its growling engine became the only sound I could hear, slowly gnawing and gnashing its way across the ocean.

I found myself walking closer until the water lapped over my feet, soaking through my socks. I was eerily calm now that I could see Ivy approaching. There was no time left to imagine the worst, for it had finally arrived. Neven and Mikuzume stood on either side of me in silence.

The ocean thrashed harder as if unsettled by the incoming threat. I thought of Susano'o in the dark sea below, how easy this all would have been if he had simply raised a finger

to tip their ship over, dragging them down to his cold white
sands and sharp coral.

What kind of victory would that be? the empress had said.

I laughed, turning my face up to the sky. Of course, she
was right. Nothing could ever be so simple for me. No one
had ever handed me victory, and they never would. The only
reason I had lived so long was because of everything I'd taken
for myself. I had stolen an ancient throne, a palace of a thousand servants, an endless underworld and all the darkness in
the night, but all of it was only mine because I'd grabbed it
and refused to let go.

A green pheasant glided across the sky, blocking the sun for
a moment before it sailed far away. An idea struck me as another wave of cold water rushed over my feet. My gaze shifted
between the burning sun and the dark ship on the horizon.

The Reapers hadn't come at night because they didn't want
to give a Shinigami an upper hand in darkness. But darkness
was not determined by the sun or the moon or the tilt of the
Earth. I was the night, the end of all things, and the darkness
answered to me alone. If I wanted to win, I needed to strip
Ivy of every advantage.

I took a deep breath, turned my face to the sunlight, and
shattered the sky.

It was too early for sunset, but the sky cracked open and
darkness began to spill inside, like outer space was bleeding
into the atmosphere. Shadows spread across the ground, so
thick that they devoured the sand beneath my feet, the houses
in the town, the streets and ocean. They crept up walls and
across roofs, swallowing buildings whole. Up above, not a
single star glimmered, just an endless expanse of black in all
directions, like Yomi had risen to the land of the living. The

only light left was a pale circle of moon very faraway, a tiny white coin in a sea of darkness.

My shadows had never felt so endless, stretched so far without growing weaker. I felt like a house with all the windows thrown open, air rushing through me. I was every last breath and whispered good-night, the end of a thousand days, the calls of night herons over sodden forests and the silence of the cicadas. The humans fled into their houses, murmuring prayers, pleas to the gods to save them from the sudden eclipse.

"Ren," Neven whispered. Both he and the Yōkai had latched onto my sleeves, though I could hardly even feel them. "Ren, what have you done?" Neven said, his voice sounding so distant even as his fingers bit into my arm.

I wanted to apologize, but the whole night was blowing through me like I was made of silk and the words couldn't reach my lips.

So instead, I turned my shadows toward the sea. Long tendrils of darkness shot out across the waters and hooked their claws into the bow of the steamship, lancing through the metal. I took a deep breath and began to push.

My bones throbbed and creaked, muscles tensed as my shadows strained against the force of the engine. I felt like an ancient tree, roots clinging desperately to the ground as a hurricane spiraled all around me. My shadows tore the sails to shreds and reached for the propeller, but its blades sliced through the darkness. I tried to tilt the ship to one side and spill the bodies into the sea, but it was like trying to push the moon out of orbit.

Still, the ship was slowing, now trudging through the tar of my shadows instead of clear waters. I fell to my knees, forcing it back out to sea with all of my strength.

I don't need Susano'o at all, I thought. This was my problem to solve.

But no matter how hard I tried, the ship kept moving forward.

My arms trembled, fingers sunk into the sand to hold me still, while my joints felt like they would burst from the strain.

The ship surged forward, and my shadows snapped like elastics pulled too hard, falling limp across the water. I gasped, barely able to feel my arms.

I wasn't strong enough.

I hung my head, unsure if I could even stand, but Neven grabbed my arm and lifted me up, the three of us backing away as the ship began to dock.

A system of pulleys and chains lowered a wobbly set of stairs on the side of the ship, and the Reapers began to disembark.

They wore the clothes of British humans instead of their silver cloaks, but their white blonde hair was unmistakable, their eyes glowing shades of blue-green in the heavy darkness. The scent of Death and fresh blood wafted down from the ship—I didn't doubt that they'd disposed of the human crew once they'd no longer been of use.

More and more of them filtered out of the ship, at least fifty standing on the shore, yet none of them moved toward us. I vaguely recognized some of their faces from my classes and Council meetings, but in the darkness they all looked like pale echoes of my old life, memories that had grown brittle. Strangely, Ambrose wasn't among their ranks. I'd assumed he'd slithered straight back to Ivy once he'd escaped, but perhaps he'd set off somewhere faraway, too much of a coward to fight. Still, there was no sign of Ivy.

Then, at the top of the staircase, a Reaper in a silver cloak appeared.

Ivy had been menacing as a High Reaper, but as a Death Goddess, her presence made the sky tremble and the tide retreat back out to sea as if cowering away. She descended the staircase, her silver cloak and blond hair the brightest light in all the darkness, like a star slowly sinking to Earth. She held Ankou's scythe with one hand, the sharp lip glinting as it caught the shimmer of Ivy's cloak.

She crossed the dock, brushing past the other Reapers who waited patiently for her command. Maybe I should have stopped her then and there, but my arms felt like stone, and after all these years, I wanted to hear what she had to say. Besides, I knew she wasn't going to kill me on sight. She would make me wish for death first. I wouldn't be surprised if she'd told the other Reapers not to touch me so that she could dismember me herself.

The scent of Death increased tenfold as she stepped onto the sand, crossing the shore to meet me. Were two Death Gods even meant to meet, or would the universe collapse on top of us? Far away in the town, I could hear leaves withering and falling to the street, grass drying up, birds crashing down from the sky. The air smelled of sour blood and wounds that had festered for too long.

As she drew closer, I realized that her eyes didn't reflect light the way the other Reapers' did. While their eyes were blue and green and purple, her eyes were a faint blue, the skin around them scratched with white marks that stretched down to her nose and cheeks like strange spider silk. I drew Izanami's katana as she approached, stepping away from Neven and the Yōkai.

"I wasn't expecting a welcome party," Ivy said, sinking the end of her scythe into the sand. With shadows filling in the hollows of her face, she looked as skeletal as the first legendary Ankou, nothing but bones and a scythe sharp enough to tear the timeline in half. I hadn't heard her voice in so long, but instantly it reminded me of a thousand dark whispers in my ear as I grew up in London, promises of spilled blood and splintering bones.

"Three people hardly make a party," I said. My hand was so sweaty against Izanami's katana that I worried I might drop it. Surely Ivy could hear my hammering heartbeat.

"Yes, I'm not sure why you even bothered," Ivy said. "I can't say I'm shocked that no one wanted to help you."

"You are my problem, not anyone else's," I said. "This is my land."

Ivy blinked, her eyes wide. Then she laughed—a cold, wicked sound, like ice shattering. "Oh no," she said. "You actually think you're my equal now, don't you?"

I gripped the katana tighter. "I am—"

"I know what you are, Wren," Ivy said, waving a hand at me dismissively. I could have talked over her, but I still found myself obeying. "You somehow convinced these people that you're not a street rat. I've no idea how. It's really a testament to just how stupid they are in the east."

I clenched my teeth. "You've gone to a lot of effort to kill a street rat."

"Oh, but you're special, Wren," Ivy said. "You gave me a present the last time we saw each other." She gestured to her eyes, the fine red lines and white scars.

"When did I…" I trailed off, remembering a streetlight that had burst like a supernova. Three Reapers crying in the snow, hands clapped over bleeding eyes. Ivy in the High Council's chambers with bandages over her face that I'd thought were merely melodramatic.

But Ivy's eyes should have healed by now. I was only a Low Reaper back then, so any damage I managed to inflict on a High Reaper should have healed within hours, if not minutes. But Ivy's face still wore the echoes of a thousand tiny shards of glass.

"I just wanted to return the favor," Ivy said, "but I'm generous, so I think I'll just carve your eyes out completely. That sounds fair, doesn't it?"

"Go ahead and try," Neven said behind me. I held out a hand to stop him, shaking my head because I still didn't understand.

"You came after me because I gave you a scar?" I said.

The venomous smile melted off Ivy's face. Her expression went slack and dead, her grip on the scythe tightening and wood creaking in her hands. I'd never felt so much like I was staring at the face of Death, even when I'd seen Izanami's rotting skull. But true Death was not decaying flesh and yellowed bones and maggots. It was a dark and hungry ending, a thousand miles across a lonely chasm of night, ruined dreams and broken hopes. It was the look in Ivy's eyes now.

"I came after you because you dared to touch the face of a goddess," she said. Even though she didn't speak in the language of Death, her words felt like they were scraping my skin away.

"You weren't a goddess then," I said. "Neither of us were."

"*I am Ankou, and I always have been!*" Ivy said, Death rippling the water around her feet, sending shock waves out into the dark sea. The sky overhead made a crunching sound, as if the night was about to shatter and heaven would crash down on us. Ivy's hand trembled around her scythe, her knuckles bone white.

The Ivy I had known in England had never looked so untethered, as if the Death inside her was an electric current frying her from the inside out. The old Ivy had looked like nothing in the world mattered to her, but this one looked like she would dig her way down to Yomi with her bare hands if I didn't tell her how to get there.

I actually upset her, I realized. As a child, I hadn't thought anything could bother Ivy, that everything she did to me was out of boredom and sheer cruelty. But one didn't simply bring an army across an ocean out of boredom. This was personal.

Was Ivy really so vain that she'd seek revenge for a scar? She'd done much more violent things to me as a child, things that should have left a thousand scars—I'd been shoved in front of motor cars and stabbed through on fences and crushed into coffins. Yet, every mark she'd left on me had slowly faded into my skin, like it had never existed. I'd never contemplated it too deeply, but in truth, it didn't make much sense. Once Ivy had become a High Reaper, she should have been able to carve me up like a Christmas ham because she was the more powerful one and that was how it worked among Reapers. We had an unbreakable hierarchy, and Ivy had always been on top.

"I gave you a scar," I whispered, slowly realizing exactly what that meant. "Even when I was nothing but a Low Reaper, I was stronger than you."

The look in Ivy's eyes—one that could have melted glass—told me I was right. It wasn't the scars that Ivy hated, it was the knowledge that I had been more powerful than her.

She'd killed her entire family just to become Ankou, and yet, every day, when she looked in the mirror, she was reminded that I had beat her.

That meant that long before I'd become a goddess, I was stronger than Ivy. Maybe it was because I was a Shinigami, or maybe because I'd had to work twice as hard as every other Reaper in my classes just to earn the right to sit beside them, or maybe Ivy just wasn't as special as she thought she was. But before I had my own palace and servants and the entire night sky at my command, I'd still won. All this time, I'd agonized over beating Ivy, not realized I already had.

I laughed, tears stinging my eyes. "You shouldn't have come here," I said. "You should have learned your lesson the first time."

"And you should have stayed where you belonged," Ivy said. "On the ground, with my boot on your face."

She tightened her grip on her scythe, and I knew the time for talking was over.

We glared at each other as complete opposites—Ivy standing in the shallow sea as a beacon of starlight, her silver cloak glittering and scythe towering over her, while I stood on the shore, the epicenter of darkness in my black kimono, Izanami's katana in my right hand reflecting Ivy's light.

Now it was all down to who could turn time the fastest.

We reached for our clocks at the same time. It had been ages since I'd been so hyperaware of the thousand moments between every second. But here, with Ivy, I had to think like a High Reaper.

There was the moment we both began to move, upper arms pulling back so we could grab our clocks. Ivy's eyes flashed white and blue lightning.

Then there was the moment her fingers unfurled, sliding across the glittering silver of her cloak. Behind her, the sea hummed as if waking from a deep sleep.

We both reached for our clocks at the same time. All that mattered now was whose fingertips would brush theirs first. Whoever could yank time to a halt first would be the one in control, and that power was difficult to wrestle back once it was gone. A pang of regret for throwing away Hiro's ring rushed through me, but I crushed the thought—I didn't want to beat Ivy with Hiro's help.

In the very last moment between moments, I tore my gaze from Ivy and looked to the moon.

I had never beaten Ivy at time turning, not even once. She only lost to me all those years ago because even then, I'd carried the entire night sky inside of me, the light of every star, the nothingness that began the world and would one day take it back.

So, as my left hand reached for my clock, I let my eyes fall closed, welcoming the darkness as my shadows extinguished the moon.

Corpse-cold skin brushed against my face.

I opened my eyes to nothingness, but Shinigami didn't need light to see. Without the moonlight, the world was nothing but hazy shapes and dreamy outlines that only a Shinigami's eyes could parse.

Ivy must have reached her clock first. I could tell because I'd lost time, the images before me disjointed from when I'd closed my eyes.

Now Ivy stood in front of me in the darkness, her scythe striking out at empty air where she could only guess I was standing, her hand brushing my face on the down swing, dragging me into her time freeze. Even in the haze of my night vision, I could see that Ivy's eyes weren't focused on me, squinting through the darkness as she took another swing.

I ducked under it easily, slashing a line across her stomach with my katana. She winced and stepped back, dropping her clock but holding on tight to her scythe. The empress had been right. I didn't know how to wield a sword.

I tossed the katana to the sand and pulled my knives from my sleeves. Maybe it wasn't a very godly, majestic way to kill someone, but blood was blood, no matter how it spilled. Now lighter on my feet without the weight of the katana, I jammed my right knife between Ivy's ribs. She gasped and forced me back with the arc of her scythe swinging down toward my face. I leaped away as the scythe carved into the sand, spinning to plant a kick to Ivy's sternum, sending her into the water.

In the distance, the Reapers screamed, splashing through the sea.

I ducked away from Ivy, putting distance between us so I could make sure Neven was all right.

He and Tamamo No Mae moved like machinery, dancing around the Reapers who fumbled through the darkness. Neven yanked a Reaper's arms behind him and planted a foot on his back, forcing the Reaper facedown into the water. Tamamo No Mae dived down like an archangel crashing to Earth, barely making a sound as she gracefully hit the water and snapped the Reaper's neck with a quick twist.

Could a Yōkai and a Low Reaper kill High Reapers? I didn't know if it would be permanent, but the ones that they subdued were taking their time reviving.

I know how to fight now, Ren, Neven had said. Of course, both of them did. Neven was no longer a child who needed me to stand between him and danger. He and the Yōkai had fought for their lives for centuries in these exact conditions—total darkness.

Some of the Reapers flickered in and out of the timeline, appearing and reappearing in different places along the shore as they tried to retaliate. But in the darkness, they often grabbed their fellow Reapers, or managed to stumble into Neven before the Yōkai snapped their spines in half.

But the darkness wouldn't deter someone like Ivy for long.

One moment there was nothing but wet sand and night before me, then Ivy was crashing into me, her scythe carving into my forearm as we both hit the ground, a sleeve of blood running down to my fingertips, my knives tumbling away. She'd pinned my arm with her body, so I grabbed her by the hair and wrenched her head to the side, forcing her off me. I reached for my knife, but the whoosh of a blade cut through the air and I leaned back just as her scythe carved a shallow line across my face.

I seized the handle, yanking Ivy forward until she lost her footing, falling into the sand. Blood trickled down into my eyes and mouth as I planted my foot on Ivy's throat and leaned all my weight onto it, forcing her deeper into the wet sand and grabbing my knife where it was staked into the ground. She reached out, probably to shatter my ankle, so I kicked her under the chin, feeling teeth dislodge as her head snapped back. She spit blood into the sand, barely dodging as my blade scraped across her collarbone, splitting skin and flesh like a soft pear and scoring across exposed bone.

She let out a scream that made the darkness quiver, echoing like wretched thunder across the city. Her hand twitched and fingers fumbled for her clock.

I reached for mine, but the moment my fingers brushed across the taut chain, I knew it was too late. I could tell just by the pull of the chain that my clock was no longer in my kimono but somewhere on the ground behind me. Ivy was already almost touching hers, and this time, Ivy knew exactly where I was in the darkness. She would not make the same mistake twice. Once she stopped time, I would be completely helpless.

So instead of diving for my clock, or bringing down my blade, I dropped my knives and threw myself on top of Ivy.

My hands wrapped around her throat, nails digging into skin as my weight threw us to the side, halfway into the frigid waters.

Time changes flashed below us, the waves halting and then splashing against us again, alternating between frozen and furious like they couldn't make up their minds. Ivy yanked my hair and elbowed my ribs but I wouldn't let go, because as long as I was touching her, I would be carried with her through all of her time turns.

With a feral cry, she stilled, lying limp in the water.

"Fine," she whispered, her voice dangerously calm. "You want to be close to me, Wren? So be it."

Then she reached out and pressed her hand to my forehead.

CHAPTER 24

High Reapers knew all of Ankou's secrets. In their cold hands, the rigid and unrelenting timeline turned soft as honey, dripping through their fingers, bleeding onto their feet. They could stretch the darkest days of your life out across centuries, suspend you forever in that one breathless moment of terror when the shadows shifted in your bedroom at night and you wondered if you were truly as alone as you thought. Some said it was important to preserve all of Ankou's knowledge so his art would never be forgotten. But High Reapers were practical, never keeping anything that didn't serve them. The one and only reason they still studied Ankou's secrets was so they could shatter the minds of Low Reapers.

Ivy's touch sent ice through my face, like her scythe had stabbed straight through my skull to skewer my brain. The shore flashed away and left a plane of deafening whiteness in its wake, like the sun had scorched the whole Earth away.

Then Ivy's hands were inside my soul, rummaging around, pulling and stretching and digging. My bones itched like they were full of insects, my blood searing hot as it rushed through my veins, trying to flush out the wrongness that had crawled inside me.

The invisible hands sank their nails into a single memory and peeled it from the timeline like dead skin—it was one of the thousands of nights I'd lain alone in my bed in Yomi after I lost Neven, unable to sleep without the sound of someone else's heartbeat in the room. My eyes had drifted shut, heaviness gradually weighing my bones down, like I was slowly being buried in sand, my mind in the distant place of not-quite-sleep, nothing but darkness around me.

I waited for Ivy's next move. Soon, her fingers would plunge into my eyes, or she'd rip my nails out or snap my ribs one by one and play the pain out across a thousand years. But time unfurled on and on in the darkness, uninterrupted. My limbs felt heavy and dead, my lungs frozen, throat sharp and dry. I couldn't roll over in bed or stretch my arms or take a single breath. I could only lie there like a corpse deep beneath cold and airless earth.

I realized, with a sinking feeling, that this was Ivy's plan.

Reapers could scrape a single moment across centuries, uncoil a single word over millennia, draw out a breath for a thousand lifetimes. Ivy had pinned me down in the moment between waking and sleep, when the world felt faraway and I could see nothing but darkness and the vapors of fading dreams, my limbs numb and unresponsive from almost-sleep. Was this what it felt like to be buried alive?

I wasn't someone who could lie idle for long periods of time—I was hardly ever safe enough to let my guard down, so a few minutes of forced stillness were enough to make me want to claw my way out of my own skin. I told myself that this was just sleep, that I could afford to let the darkness soak through my mind and fill up my mouth and lungs because what choice did I have?

But even as my mind quieted, my lungs began to ache. Reapers didn't need to breathe, but my throat clenched as if begging for air anyway. I had never before appreciated the ability to turn to one side or pull a strand of hair from my face, but with my body now rigid glass, I could think of little else but trying to move. The impulse ate away all my other thoughts.

Days unfolded, and all I could think about was the relief of stretching my arms above my head or pointing my toes, but I lay still as death. Days turned into weeks and time unraveled like a sweater into an endless length of thread, on and on and on into the darkness. I felt years slipping away but couldn't hold them back. They were an endless rush of water I tried to cup in my hands, spilling through my fingers, overflowing onto the ground. *This is your retribution*, I thought. *Think of all the bodies that are in the ground now because of you.* It was so easy to say death was natural and necessary when it was someone else's body in a box.

As the years spun by, I began to rot.

Maybe it was Ivy's doing, or a trick of my mind to lend some sensation to my numbed bones, but I felt my organs festering and turning to gelatin, falling victim to the slow trickle of time. My eyes turned to a white soup that spilled down my face, my skin blooming open as bacteria gnawed holes through it, my bones growing soft and spongy. The creatures of the night fed on me, but still I couldn't move. I tried to cling to thoughts of my life to keep me afloat, but everything felt like a whispered memory too faraway to grasp.

Maybe this wasn't time turning at all. Maybe Ivy had just dug into my brain and scraped around until I bled out into my skull and died. Maybe this was my afterlife, the hell that I deserved for all the souls I'd eaten, all the humans I'd scorned on their deathbeds. The great nothingness that I had always feared was finally here. I had always prayed that my hell would be roasting over infernal flames and lashes at the hands of demons and walking barefoot across miles of hot needles and searing coal, because my worst fear was never death or suffering—it was being nothing at all.

When my body decayed, my mind soon followed, my thoughts melting together into sludge until all that was left were the rotten parts, the carrion that even starved wolves wouldn't touch.

Tsukuyomi walking away from me in the moment he stopped loving me, Hiro dying in my arms with his searing blood spilling down my wedding dress, Neven reaching for me while the shadows consumed him, my father's eyes full of sour disappointment, then my cheek in the snow and Ivy's boot on my face, because everything started and ended with Ivy Cromwell.

The moments tied together in an endless loop that spun and spun and spun like I was tossed into a hurricane, lost in airless space and so very far from the ground. For one hundred years, I watched myself destroy everyone who had ever loved me. I thought that after the hundredth time, I would grow numb to the sting, that their faces would become unfamiliar, that I would start to forget that I was the sad and spiteful girl in the memories, like I was watching some tragic film of someone else's life.

But just like snuffed-out candles left wisps of smoke, all the love I had lost endured even in the absence of light. I wanted it to keep hurting, because that meant it had been real. Only when it stopped hurting would I know that I was truly dead.

When Neven called for me for the thousandth time and I could do nothing but watch the shadows drag him away, I felt myself start to fracture, tiny hairline cracks rippling across my soul like ice over a pond. Each memory deepened the cracks until I felt like porcelain dropped on tiled floors, pieces of me cast out across the universe, and I could no longer see Neven's face or hear his words but I *felt* him, the pain now faceless but still there, drowning me, dragging me down and down and down and—

I gasped in wet air.

Sensations slammed back into me, the salt water scorching cold against my skin, each grain of sand excruciating beneath me after an eternity of numbness.

I am on a beach, I thought, my mind still foggy and faraway. There was endless dark and splashing waves that I distantly registered as Yokohama. Then white blond hair blew in the wind above me, and everything came back like a shock of lightning.

Ivy was above me but no longer looking at me, eyes focused behind her. I scrambled back in the water, my body no longer feeling like mine but something borrowed, a hermit crab's shell. I trembled so hard I could hardly move, but still managed to crawl a few meters from Ivy.

But why had she stopped right when she was finally unraveling me? I rubbed my eyes and rose to my feet while Ivy kicked and thrashed in the water.

"What the hell are you?" Ivy said, stomping a foot down on something hard, that echoed a thousand times across the water.

A turtle's shell.

Ivy fell into the sea, revealing a human's head and fanged teeth sunk into Ivy's ankle, painting it with blood.

Maho.

The Honengame yanked Ivy out farther into the sea, snarling as Ivy kicked and thrashed.

A Reaper charged through the darkness, sword held high, aiming for Maho's face.

"Maho, look out!" I said.

But the Honengame didn't need my warning. She released Ivy and dived into the waters just as the Reaper swung down, nearly severing Ivy's foot.

Ivy kicked the Reaper in the face and stood up. Her hair looked darker when soaked and matted. Covered in sand and seaweed, her dress clinging to her, she looked more like a swamp monster than a High Reaper. The glow around her no longer seemed ethereal but ghostly.

"Is that the best you could do?" she said. "A turtle woman?"

I glanced around for my katana, but it was lying far away on the shore.

Across the water, the Reapers slain by Neven and the Yōkai rose again, dripping with blood. Neven was panting for breath, and even the Yōkai's movements seemed slower. They couldn't continue this fight indefinitely against creatures that neither of them could kill.

Then Ivy was in front of me, and my limbs were still

too numb to stop her. She grabbed a handful of my hair and yanked me to the side, forcing my face into wet sand. I reached for the darkness to pull her away, but my shadows were stretched too thin across the sky and already growing thinner, as if the years trapped in time had sapped away my strength.

"I'm going to force this backward country to its knees," Ivy said, her hair dripping onto my face. "I'm going to have you and your brother skinned and made into leather bags. So tell me, Wren, how does it feel to know that you're dying for absolutely nothing?"

I was glad that we were both drenched so she couldn't see my tears. After centuries of stillness, any resolve I had left had been devoured. My arms shook just trying to keep the dome of darkness above us. Ivy leaned closer, and fear that I hadn't felt since I was a child made me flinch away. The movement caused the night to rupture overhead, moonlight suddenly crashing over Yokohama.

The abrupt contrast between the moon's pale glow and Yomi's total darkness made my eyes water. On the shore, Neven and the Yōkai spun toward me, panicked that their only advantage was gone.

"Ren, what are you doing?" Neven said, dodging a Reaper's sword.

I can't help it! I wanted to scream. But what was the point? It didn't matter why, only that I'd failed.

Ivy reached for my throat, laughing when I flinched again. I crawled away, even though I knew there was no outrunning her, but I couldn't stop thinking of the endless darkness she'd trapped me in. She crossed her arms and smirked as I dragged myself across the sand.

"Don't you know when to give in?" she said. "I thought you Orientals believed in honor, yet you're crawling on the ground like a bloodworm."

I managed to pull myself to a patch of seagrass before I lost the will to move forward, the sounds of Neven and the Yōkai's fight growing too distant. Ivy sighed, picking up her scythe.

"When I tell the Reapers the story of how I conquered Japan," she said, "I'll be sure to tell them that in the end, you were a coward."

She took a single step forward.

Both of us heard the sound before we saw it cutting through the darkness—a sharp whistle, then a *thwack* at Ivy's feet. She stepped back, then crouched down to pull a ghostly white arrow from the sand. It quivered in her palm, then dissolved into the night.

Ivy stared at her empty hand for a long moment. Her face slowly sank into a frown, and she narrowed her eyes at me as if I was singularly responsible. But I had no idea what was happening either.

Behind Ivy, white arrows arced onto the shore like hundreds of falling stars, planting themselves into the Reapers' backs, spearing them straight through their spines. The Reapers spilled forward into the bloody water, struggling to stand before another flurry of arrows pinned them down again. Neven and Tamamo No Mae had ducked for cover, but it seemed that the arrows weren't aimed at them.

Ivy turned away from me, her fists clenched. She scanned the empty shoreline for the source of the arrows, but there was nothing but still water and endless black sky. With a frustrated huff, she closed her eyes. A Reaper's best sense was her hearing, so our teachers had always encouraged us to block out any visuals when our eyes couldn't be trusted and focus on the soundscape around us.

I didn't dare close my eyes with Ivy so close to me, but I tried to ignore the sounds of splashing waves and Reapers groaning to figure out what was going on.

Far out on the still water, the ocean lapped against a hard surface that I couldn't see. Wood creaked as if the ocean had turned to a hardwood floor, and low voices murmured in a dialect I couldn't understand.

A translucent shape outlined in hazy blue began to take form above the water. The rounded bottom half of a ship appeared, three massive sails billowing in the wind.

A crew of skeletons wrapped in white kimonos stood at the ship's starboard side. They drew their bows in unison, releasing another sharp burst of arrows that skewered the struggling Reapers. The funayūrei cheered as the Reapers fell, hurling glass bottles over the edge, showering the shore in shards of glass and shouting *That's for Kagoshima!* as they readied another round of arrows.

Maho must have called for them, I thought, swallowing back tears as I realized that she hadn't left me to die.

I didn't know how much damage funayūrei could do to High Reapers—the arrows didn't seem to keep them down for long, dissolving as soon as they'd pierced through the Reapers and reappearing back in the Yōkai's hands before the Reapers could fully recover. With another round of arrows, Neven and Tamamo No Mae rushed back into the water, taking the opportunity to snap their necks.

"*Kill them!*" Ivy said, eyes like blue fire. The language of Death blasted the water away, forcing the tide to retreat. "*Get up and destroy them!*"

Time came in flashes as the Reapers tried to bend the time-line, revealing only fractured images as they climbed aboard the ghostly ship. Some of the Reapers managed to twist the Yōkai's skulls off their necks and cast their bones into the sea, but the funayūrei rose again almost instantly. They simply brushed off their clothes, straightened their heads back on their necks, and charged onto their ship to throw the Reapers off.

I couldn't help but laugh as the funayūrei tossed a flailing Reaper overboard. Yōkai could only be killed in very specific ways, and simply snapping their necks wouldn't do it. The Reapers had no idea what they were facing. Most importantly, they clearly didn't know that if you upset a Yōkai, you'd better make sure it was dead. Yōkai weren't known for their forgiveness.

Ivy charged forward as if she planned to climb onto the ship herself, but a sudden blaze of blue seared through the sea, making her flinch as it wrapped the boat in ribbons of light. A roar thundered across the waters, vibrating deep in my bones, making the whole world tremble.

In a dizzy trick of light, a thousand scales glimmered above the waters, rippling like a banner. It circled around the boat, its shape growing clearer as if phasing out of the spirit world and into ours. The next time it rounded the boat, a dragon's maw opened wide, sending a cascade of fire across the waters.

The funayūrei cheered as the ryūtō circled once more. This time, the fires cast their light on a figure clinging to the dragon's nape, a black cloak rippling behind him, hair the color of moonbeams.

Surely Ivy had already killed me and this was some illusion conjured by my dying brain. Surely I wasn't really seeing

Ambrose on the back of a Yōkai. He was a coward who was probably hiding away in a cave while he planned his escape to some discreet Eastern European country. My eyes had to be playing a trick on me—my Reaper vision was poor anyway.

The ryūtō dipped closer to the water and the thin moonlight spilled sharply over the Reaper's face, and then there was no denying it any longer. Ambrose reached out a hand for the funayūrei, helping them clamber onto the dragon's back, where they used their high perch to take better aim at the Reapers. The ryūtō dived halfway into the waters, scooped up a mouthful of Reapers and bit down hard, blood rolling down his scaled throat. It spit out severed body parts into the ocean, arms and legs splashing in the deep sea.

I rose to my knees, my throat tight with something that wasn't exactly sadness, but made me want to cry all the same.

When I first came to Japan, I had forged my path to power by slaughtering the Yōkai who got in my way and scorning anyone who dared to interfere. Now the Yōkai were fighting on my side, and so was my father. Maybe they weren't doing it for me. Maybe the only thing we had in common was hatred for the Reapers who had taken so much from us. But for the first time in my entire life, it wasn't just me and Neven against the entire world.

I might not have to die here, I thought. It was such a dangerous thing to hope for, but it was enough to help me stand on shaking legs and lift the katana from the sand. Not Izanami's katana anymore—mine.

Most of the Reapers were lying at the bottom of the ocean in pieces, and even when they regenerated, they'd be far out at sea. Neven and Tamamo No Mae's work was easy now that most of the Reapers were gone, and they finished slicing up those that remained for the ryūtō to scoop up.

Ivy was still standing in shock on the shore, watching as her army of the most skilled Reapers in England turned to dragon food.

I raised my katana with the loose grip that the empress had taught me, stumbling toward Ivy. The Yōkai had taken care of the High Reapers for me, but I was the only one strong enough to kill a god. I would show them that I deserved their loyalty, that I was the true Goddess of Yomi.

Ivy didn't even move as I lifted the blade above my head and struck down.

The blade sank into the sand.

I fell forward with its weight, feeling woozy from the sudden drop in adrenaline. Ivy had vanished, my sword carving through empty air.

I spun, frantically trying to comb through the night for Ivy. In the distance, the remaining Reapers fled back to their ship to take shelter from the ryūtō, their numbers too depleted to keep fighting. Had Ivy given up and gone back to her ship too?

Footsteps crunched in the sand behind me. I whirled around.

Neven stood behind me, a scythe curled around his throat, hands holding the blade back as it scratched a thin line across his neck. Ivy held him against her, one hand on her clock.

Neven's eyes met mine, the panicked colors in his irises paling. He knew as well as I did that if Ivy killed him, there was no coming back. Behind him, Ivy's gaze burned, her hands trembling where she gripped the scythe's handle, sweat and sand stuck to her face. Tamamo No Mae rushed across the beach toward us, but I held out a hand to stop her. If Ivy felt threatened and turned time, there was no way we could save Neven. I looked toward the water for Ambrose, but he sat still and silent on the ryūtō's back as it bobbed above the waves. Why wouldn't he come help us now? He'd fought against the Reapers but wouldn't stand up to Ivy herself?

"Unchain your clock and throw it on the ground," Ivy said, her voice low.

Without hesitation, I unclipped the chain from my clothes and lifted my clock from the kimono, slowly setting it on the sand.

"Ivy," I said, "please—"

"Here's what's going to happen, half-breed," she said, her words booming across the empty shore. "You will lie on the ground, with your face under my shoe, and I will cut a line from your head straight down to your toes, until your organs spill out and your body is in two halves, just like you. Or, you can watch me cut your brother into a thousand pieces and leave his soul in the void."

I swallowed, my mind racing for a solution. I had been backed into corners before, by Ivy or Yōkai or even Izanami, but there had always been a way out if I thought hard enough. But this time, my mind couldn't grasp on to any plan, no matter how unrealistic it was, because all I could see was the scythe around Neven's neck and the clock in Ivy's hand. If I made any sudden movement, anything that surprised Ivy in the slightest, she would stop time and kill Neven.

I couldn't let her do that.

After everything I had put Neven through just so I could

belong, this was one risk I couldn't take. I took a deep breath and looked up at the sky, then leveled my gaze with Ivy.

"Let him go," I said, "and I'll do whatever you want."

"Ren," Neven whispered, "no, you—"

Ivy yanked the scythe closer to his throat, silencing him.

"Promise me in Death," she said.

I swallowed. There was no way to lie in the language of Death. No careful wording would get me out of this.

"If you let my brother go unharmed," I said, *"I—"*

"Ren, stop!" Neven said. Instead of looking sad or panicked like I'd expected, his eyes burned with anger. "You said we'd go together!"

"I lied," I said. It wouldn't be the first time. "I'm sorry, Neven."

Ivy grinned just as the clouds parted and the moonlight illuminated her face, beautiful and deadly, perfect and eternal. She was the kind of god who was meant to live forever. Not like me, who would burn out fast and bright.

I hoped that one day Neven would forgive me for being selfish and dying first. I wasn't trying to be a martyr. I just couldn't imagine a world without Neven and I wasn't brave enough to try.

"I promise," I whispered, my voice trembling, for the language of Death had never felt so heavy on my lips. *I promise, Neven,* I thought, *that whatever comes after this life, wherever I end up, I'll tear the world apart to find you again. Death will never stop me.*

"I think that's enough, Ren."

I held my breath, afraid to turn around in case I had imagined his voice. But I had never been good at fighting my impulses.

Tsukuyomi stood on the shore, backlit by the pearly arc of the full moon. His pale skin and white robes glowed brighter than summer daylight, illuminating the sea of blood and bones behind him. He'd said that the moon had no light of its own, but I no longer believed that was true. Looking at him was like watching the universe begin again from the cold nothingness of space.

His eyes met mine and my breath caught in my chest. Then I remembered how I'd sent him away and my heart dropped.

I turned back to Ivy, but she had gone deathly still where she stood in the moonlight, her eyes darting around.

"What have you done to me?" she said, her face turning red as she fought with all her godly strength against Tsukuyomi's moonlight. But Tsukuyomi didn't dignify her with an answer, breezing past me and prying Ivy's scythe from her stiff fingers. Neven wasted no time stumbling out of the moonlight and grabbing onto my arm, the Yōkai scrambling to his other side.

"Why did you come here?" I whispered.

Tsukuyomi didn't answer at first, and I dared to meet his gaze once more. The sight of such a stern look—like when I'd first met him—made my chest clench, but a soft smile curved one side of his mouth.

"You have a strange way of saying 'thank you,'" he said.

Ivy let out a furious sound, but I ignored her.

"I'm sorry," I said. "Tsukuyomi—"

"I know," he said, nodding toward the full moon. "I heard you the first time."

Then he turned to Ivy, bending down to examine her. He hummed, walking a slow circle around her while she seethed.

"Interesting," he said in English. "I didn't expect Ankou to look like a drowned rat."

"Get away from me before I spear you with your own ribs," Ivy said.

Tsukuyomi ignored her and unclipped her clock from her clothes, tossing it to Neven. "There, that should make you a bit less confident," he said. He turned to me, taking a step away from Ivy and gesturing toward her. "I believe you've been waiting for this, Ren."

I picked up my katana, rising to my feet. Tsukuyomi set a warm hand on my back, and I let out a stiff breath because finally, this nightmare was going to end.

As the tension left my body, my grip on the darkness overhead weakened another degree, the ring of daylight yawning wider. A haze of clouds rolled over the moon, and suddenly Ivy was no longer cast in glaring moonlight, but in cool shade.

She collapsed forward, fingers grappling for her scythe that had fallen in the sand. Tsukuyomi rushed toward her, but her gaze had already snapped to Neven—her key to controlling me, to hurting me. She lunged as Neven took a startled step back.

But this time, she wouldn't reach him. I had already let her put her hands on my brother once, and it would never happen again.

I crashed into Ivy, trying to pin her to the ground, but instead of falling into the sand, we punched straight through the earth like it was a paper screen, down and down through tangled roots and jagged rocks and groundwater that tasted like blood, locusts and worms and bones. The darkness of Yomi gasped open, the lotus pond in my courtyard swallowing us in its inky waters.

Ivy scratched at my eyes and kneed me in the stomach, but I grabbed fistfuls of her hair and wouldn't let her go, wouldn't let her escape from me now that she was in Yomi. Who knew what she would do to the dead, to my Shinigami? I needed her even farther away, where she couldn't hurt anyone.

I wrapped my hands around Ivy's throat and pushed her harder into the silt of the pond, and that too unfolded below us like a door swinging open, dropping us into a starless sky.

We crunched into the ground. For a moment, I thought the sound was my whole body shattering on impact, but every part of the Earth crackled beneath me. As Death, I knew the touch of bones.

The air here somehow didn't satisfy my lungs at all, feeling tacky in my mouth. I stood up, my skin stinging as if pricked by thousands of insects. The ground rumbled below us, starving, insatiable.

The fall had tossed Ivy from my arms, and while I heard her shuffling and cursing near me, my Shinigami senses didn't grow any sharper as the seconds passed. The darkness had scraped the whole world away, leaving nothing but Death and echoes. My Shinigami eyes were useless here, because there was nothing to see.

In Yomi, the darkness often felt like a blanket draped over an evil world to cover up its crooked secrets. But this was not a place shrouded in darkness. This was not a place at all. It was an ending, something that might have been but never would be. If I were to burn a candle here, surely the landscape would look exactly the same, for light could not illuminate something that didn't exist.

"Where the hell did you take me?" Ivy said, her voice farther away than I'd expected.

Blood trickled down from my nose, slicking my lips, as if this world didn't want me to exist either.

"The deep darkness," I said.

This was the place my brother had suffered for centuries, the place that Izanagi had tried so hard to keep me away from, afraid that I would lose his precious kingdom. After ten years of pushing against his impenetrable wall, I had crashed straight through it.

"What the hell is the deep darkness?" Ivy said, her voice echoing back across the expanse, the rumbling growing louder.

I heard Neven's voice in my ear, as clear as Izanami's once was:

There are thousands of monsters, but I could never see any of them. They tore off my arms and legs whenever they got the chance. And even though my limbs always grew back, that just meant there was more for the monsters to eat.

A wave of hot air sighed across my shoulders, prickling the back of my neck. I turned around, but of course, there was nothing there. I straightened my shoulders and faced Ivy.

"This is where you're going to die," I said.

I wished that I could see the look in Ivy's eyes at that moment, but the hitch in her breath was satisfying enough. Ivy didn't know the legends of the deep darkness, but any living creature could sense that this place was cursed.

"The monsters here will eat you for hundreds of years," I said. "And when they're done with you, they will inherit your kingdom."

Ivy's breath shuddered. Heavy footsteps grew closer. A whooshing sound rushed overhead, like wings beating against the sky, and Ivy cried out. I heard crisp crunching and a sudden gush of blood falling like heavy rain over the carpet of bones, then took another step back, putting distance between us. The monsters would surely come for me when they were through with Ivy, but I could still sense the solid ground of my courtyard and knew I could pull myself back up if they got too close.

"I can end you quickly, if you prefer," I said, my bones humming as I drew my knife.

Ivy was cracking apart like kindling, the air growing humid with blood, her breaths coming out choked. I heard tendons tearing like snapping elastic bands, soft organs bursting and oozing hot acids over the ground, bones splintering, skin ripping like paper. And above it all, Ivy's jagged screams and frantic clawing across the earth. With a sharp pop, Ivy gasped and the sounds of her struggling came closer. The beast's hot breaths grew quiet as it crunched through pieces of Ivy, sucking on soft flesh and spitting out bones.

Ivy's hand grabbed hold of my ankle, soaking my sock through with burning blood. I didn't flinch, because I knew she was too weak to hurt me. She was drowning, reaching out for land.

"Please," she whispered.

I tightened my grip on my knife, kneeling down and pressing her onto her back, my blade resting over her exposed throat. She didn't fight me as she lay limp and shivering cold in the darkness.

For so long, I had wanted Ivy here, and finally, she was mine. The first monster I'd ever met, more terrifying than any Yōkai. The first time I'd heard the words *half-breed* they'd come from her lips. The first time I'd feared for Neven's life, it was because of her wicked smile.

I will inherit her kingdom when I kill her, I thought, the realization winding around my heart and clamping down tight, like flowered vines with prickled thorns. Both Reapers and Shinigami had looked down on me, and now I would rule them all. I could make all the Reapers pay, strip them of their titles, abolish the High Council and lock them in mausoleums until they turned to dust.

The thought was intoxicating, a sweet poison rushing through my blood. Izanami's voice screamed through my veins, *end her end her end her, feed us more, let our empire expand across the ocean.*

I thought of all the souls in England I could devour, all the names that would burn across my vision, how I would be strong enough to turn the tides and realign the planets all by myself, how I would never again have to go crawling to another god for help.

My skin burned away and my teeth tore into my lip and I breathed in the salty scent of gushing blood and waited for the feeling of exhilaration and ravenous power, like when Hiro had first asked me to be a god. But the only feeling I could conjure was nausea.

I had never wanted to be Death. I'd only ever wanted to be *someone*.

Even if that someone was a monster who ate hearts with her bare hands, I'd wanted a name to cling to, something to anchor me in the darkness.

But Ren Scarborough was already someone. Ren Scarborough had been stronger than Ivy, even when she had no idea who she was.

I sat up, pulling my blade from Ivy's throat.

"Promise me in Death that you'll leave this country without hurting anyone and that no Reaper will ever come back to Japan."

Ivy sucked in a broken breath. Behind her, the monster's chewing grew slower. Its stomach gurgled as it burped out the burning scent of flesh. It was still hungry.

"Promise me now, or I'll leave you here."

"I promise," she whimpered, like the words had been squeezed out of her.

I grabbed her by the collar just as the beast's footsteps thundered toward us. But we were already long gone, tearing up through the lotus pond that washed away the bitter taste of the darkness, crashing through layers of rocky earth.

Every grain of sand felt needle sharp under my palms, like my skin was fresh and new. Even the dim moonlight on the shore was agony to my eyes. Tamamo No Mae called out for me from a distance, then hands were pulling me to my feet.

"What happened?" Neven said.

I rubbed my eyes as they adjusted to the shore. Tsukuyomi was trying to hold down Ivy, who lay halfway in the water, frothy and red with blood. Her skirt had been torn at the knee and her legs looked pale and clean, like they'd only just grown back. Darkness sloughed off both of us, dyeing the salt water black.

"Let her go," I said, rubbing the deep darkness from my eyes.

Tsukuyomi looked bewildered, but released Ivy and took a step back. She stumbled to her feet and folded forward onto the ground.

"My clock," she said, clawing through the sand as if she could find it buried there.

"Give it to her," I said to Neven.

"But, Ren—"

"Do it."

Neven pursed his lips but pulled Ivy's clock from his clothes and tossed it in front of Ivy. She dived for it like a wild animal fighting for scraps, cradling it between her palms. She looked at me for a single moment, her eyes red from burst blood vessels, then turned and crawled across the sand. Before I could even blink, she'd dived into a time freeze and vanished into the night.

"Ren," Neven whispered. "You—"

"She's not going to bother us anymore," I said. "I made her promise."

Neven let out a sharp laugh, shaking his head. "I've known you longer than anyone, yet I never seem to know what you're going to do next."

Tsukuyomi still looked like he'd been slapped. "I've never known you to be merciful," he said.

"It was purely self-interest, believe me," I said, rinsing off the darkness from my hands in the ocean. "Being the Goddess of Death in one country is more than enough work."

Tsukuyomi smiled, but hid it quickly by gazing up toward the moon. On the sea, the funayūrei had set sail, the cheers echoing across the water.

The ryūtō hovered in lazy circles above the ocean, Ambrose staring back at us, his expression gray.

Then, from far out at sea, he spoke. A human would never have caught such pale, whispered words, but I heard them clearly.

"I'm sorry," he said.

Then the ryūtō spun into the air and chased after the

funayūrei, two bright blue stars fading farther and farther into the night.

My father had a great many things to atone for, so I couldn't be certain which ones he was apologizing for now. But this was a strange time to repent, after helping me for the first time in my whole life. Neven watched the empty horizon where Ambrose had disappeared, then after a long moment, closed his eyes and turned away.

"Come on, Mikuzume," he said, waving the Yōkai over from the edge of the shore.

But Tamamo No Mae was busy admiring Izanami's katana on the ground, staring in reverence at its immaculate sharpness.

"Careful," I said, holding out my hand for her to return it to me.

She didn't move for a long moment, watching the moonlight shimmer across the katana's polished surface. Then she turned to me, tightened her grip on the hilt, and drove the sword into my stomach.

CHAPTER 25

A heat bloomed across my abdomen, scalding hot and spreading fast. This blade—so sharp that it had killed Izanami herself—had sawed through me, and everything from my waist down had gone numb. My legs folded, my fingers grabbing at the sword to pull it out, but only slicing deep cuts into my palms because I couldn't stop shaking. There was so much blood, a river of it scorching down my legs and turning the sand red.

This was meant to be a slow, agonizing death. I always stabbed through the heart because I wanted to end lives swiftly, but Tamamo No Mae had aimed much lower, trying to bleed me out slowly.

Neven grabbed the Yōkai by the back of her kimono and hurled her into the ground so hard that her thin frame left a crater in the wet sand. She tried to sit up, but Neven pinned her wrists, her bones audibly cracking.

I fell to my hands, blood choking its way up my throat and spilling past my lips like a scalding faucet. Tsukuyomi crouched beside me, hands roaming frantically, as if afraid I would shatter apart at his touch. He was whispering something, but his words had no shape or meaning over my own frantic heartbeat, my gasping breaths as the muscles in my abdomen clenched and twitched around the foreign object.

"Why would you do that?" Neven said as he crushed the Yōkai into the ground, the language of Death blasting the waves back out to sea, whipping a furious salty breeze around us. "You *liked* Ren! You told me you wanted to help her! You s-said—"

The Yōkai rolled on top of Neven like he weighed nothing at all, sending both of them into the shadows and wrapping her thin hands around his throat.

I crawled forward, even as it drove the katana deeper and more blood gushed past my lips. Tsukuyomi tried to stop me and I waved a shuddering hand at him, streaking blood across his face and perfect white kimono.

"Of course I like Ren," the Yōkai said, her voice just as poetic as always, even with her robes painted in blood and one hand locked around my brother's throat. "And I've already helped her." She gestured to the red sea, the bobbing corpses of High Reapers, like it was her greatest achievement. "I even gave her a plague to make her stronger. Isn't that what all Death gods want?"

She turned to me, grinning like she expected praise.

Blood pooled in my mouth, dripping into the sand. *I truly am a fool,* I thought. Tamamo No Mae had sickened Emperor

Toba with a strange illness hundreds of years ago. She'd killed children all across Japan, stealing them from their beds in the dead of night. Time and space were no limits to her crushing power. Of course casting a plague over Japan would be easy for her.

"I even enchanted your cowardly little father to go fetch the ryūtō for you," she said. "Was that not helpful?"

My throat closed and the taste of blood burned at the back of my mouth, but I didn't know if it was due to the stab wound or the Yōkai's words. *Of course Ambrose didn't help me of his own accord*, I thought, my chest stinging at the realization far more than I expected. He'd done exactly what the Yōkai had asked and absolutely nothing more, then turned away and fled. Were any of his words true? Had he looked me in the eyes and told me he loved me, knowing it was a lie? It shouldn't have mattered. I didn't need love from someone like him. But the idea that he might have toyed with my emotions so easily was nauseating.

"Why?" Tsukuyomi whispered, the word as sharp as an arrow. "What's the purpose of helping Ren just to kill her?"

The smile dropped from the Yōkai's face. In the shadowed light of the moon, she suddenly looked centuries older.

"Who else could clean up the foreigners for me?" she said, nodding towards the Reapers' corpses in the sea. "I've subdued many kinds of creatures, but I don't interfere with those who can break the timeline. They're far too dangerous."

"You mean you're far too weak," Tsukuyomi said.

The Yōkai rolled her eyes. "I could enchant every Shinigami and human in this country to fight for me if I wanted to," she said, "but I didn't want another war. I've seen so many wars already, both of humans and creatures of Death.

I've seen dynasties fall and ancient gods perish at the hands of newer ones. At first, it's always thrilling. So many bleeding into the dirt for dreams they don't even truly understand, enough passion in their eyes to tilt the whole world off its axis. But none of them are ever brave enough to do what it takes to hold on to power. They always lose it eventually, and it's so painfully boring every single time."

Fox ears had appeared on her head, despite her human form. Her teeth elongated into fangs.

"Now the foreigners know not to threaten my kingdom," she said, "and my hands didn't even get that dirty."

I swallowed, more blood spilling down my neck. The blood loss was already numbing my hands and feet, the Yōkai's words paralyzing. So this was what she'd wanted all along. I'd known that she'd corrupted kings and toppled dynasties, and yet I'd believed that she was different in this lifetime. She hadn't been softened by Neven's kindness, as she'd said. She'd merely been biding her time, worming her way into all of our hearts. I thought of the thousands of times she'd whispered in my ear. Had she enchanted me like all those kings across Asia? But her deception wasn't the way I'd imagined it from her legend. There was no haze descending over my vision, no trance that rendered me half-dreaming, no sudden eclipse of evil that made me crave human flesh. It only felt like making a new friend.

"*Your* kingdom?" Tsukuyomi said, his eyes narrowed. "Yomi will never belong to a Yōkai."

"Oh?" Tamamo No Mae tilted her head, her eyes now a vivid yellow. Neven choked as she squeezed his throat harder. "Who should it belong to then? A foreigner?" She glared at me. "A rotting corpse? A fisherman who couldn't even hold on to the throne for a day? What, exactly, makes any of them better than me?"

"Mikuzume."

Neven's quiet word halted her rage. He had stopped struggling, lying limp on the sand. "Please let me up. I want to be with Ren."

She let out a sharp laugh. "Let you up so you can turn time on me? I'm not a fool, Neven."

"No, you're not," he whispered. "You knew how to survive in the deep darkness for centuries, even as a child. You let the monsters peel off your skin and rip out your nails and teeth just so they wouldn't hurt me again. You might not care about Ren, but I know you care about me. Please, let me up."

The Yōkai hesitated, her grip loosening around his throat before letting out a weary sigh.

"Oh, you poor thing," she said, shaking her head. "A couple centuries might seem long to you, but not to me. I was alive long before there was anyone to write about me. Physical pain is fleeting, Neven, and I've met plenty of boys much more interesting than you."

She pressed down harder on Neven's throat and he tossed his head back with a choked gasp. Tsukuyomi moved to help, but without his support I toppled forward, spearing myself further on the katana, more blood gushing past my teeth. He rushed to hold me up again, looking between me and Neven with panicked eyes.

Poor Tsukuyomi, I thought distantly. The Yōkai had tried so hard to convince me that he was the one who couldn't be trusted. I already knew in my heart that Tsukuyomi wasn't Hiro, that he wouldn't betray me like his brother did, but I'd wanted so badly not to be taken for a fool twice. Somehow it had happened anyway.

I pressed a trembling hand to Tsukuyomi's shoulder to force myself upright.

"Take the sword out," I said, my words weak.

He shook his head, eyes wide. "You'll just bleed out faster if—"

"Take it out," I croaked, Death searing like white fire up my throat. I coughed, spraying Tsukuyomi's kimono with blood.

"Don't—" Neven started to say, trying to tear the Yōkai's hands from his throat, but it was hard to resist the language of Death. Tsukuyomi was already gripping the handle of the katana, yanking it out with a wet squelch.

I gasped, falling forward. Tsukuyomi pressed his hands to the soaked fabric over the wound in my stomach. Neven was fighting Tamamo No Mae in earnest now, and Tsukuyomi was whispering about how everything would be fine.

I started to laugh.

Everyone froze, turning toward me. Neven and Tsukuyomi shared a panicked look, while the Yōkai's face slid into a frown.

"She's in shock," Tsukuyomi said, his face white. "Ren, just lie down on your side, I'll—"

"Oh, calm down," I said, wiping my mouth with my sleeve. My hands still shook, but I could already feel my blood replenishing itself, the wound finally beginning to knit itself closed now that the blade was no longer in the way. The pain grew distant, my breathing slowing back to normal. The world no longer spun like it was sliding off the edge of a precipice.

Tamamo No Mae grew very still.

"No," she said, the word so bitter it sounded like a curse.

She rose to her feet, fists clenched and trembling. "Izanami's katana is the sharpest, deadliest weapon in the world," she said. Her face warped with anger as she pointed an accusing finger at me, her fingernails now black claws. "It can kill a goddess! You said so yourself!"

"It's a piece of metal," I said. I picked up the katana, wiping it dry in the sand. "Its strength doesn't come from its material, but from the person who wields it."

Already, the cut was almost sealed, the pain a hazy memory.

"Do you understand, Yōkai? It's only powerful because *I* wield it."

"I skewered you like a fish!" she said. "I felt your spine crack!"

"You're just as bad as the Reapers," I said, rising to my feet. "You go to so much trouble to kill, but you haven't even bothered to learn how."

"What do you mean?" she said, taking another step back, her eyes fixed on the blade.

"I mean that Reapers can only be killed by more powerful beings," I said. "I am a goddess, and you are a Yōkai. Who do you think is the stronger one here?"

The Yōkai stood still before me, her eyes bright with fury. Even Ivy had never looked at me with such boiling hate, like she wanted to flay me and wear my skin as a pelt. How long had it been since Tamamo No Mae lost at one of her games? The legends said that she only left a place once she'd thoroughly ravaged the kingdom, bringing it to ruin and growing bored.

I raised the katana. "My turn, Yōkai."

With a feral hiss that was half human and half animal, she

shifted into her fox form. Neven lunged for her, but the fox easily darted away, sprinting into the darkness.

Neven started to run after her, but I grabbed his arm.

"Don't," I said. "She won't bother us anymore."

"How can you know that?" Neven said, trying to shake his arm free.

"Because she wins by tricking people," I said. "She can't trick us now."

Neven gazed out across the seagrass that the Yōkai had dived into, his jaw tight, the colors in his eyes melted together into a sickly green-tinged gray. He fell to his knees and hung his head, but before I could come closer, he stood up again, having picked up my katana's sheath from the sand.

"Please let that thing stay on the wall as a decoration from now on," he said, handing me the sheath with a dull expression. "And please don't go around casually mentioning that it can kill a goddess."

"You don't have to remind me," I said, sheathing the blade.

I turned to Tsukuyomi, who stood to the side, looking slightly lost and visibly uncomfortable with the blood splashed across his clothes. I glanced back at Neven, who stared at us for a moment before rolling his eyes.

"I'll go make sure the humans are all right," he said, walking up the shore toward the town.

When Neven was far enough away that he could at least pretend not to hear us, I turned back to Tsukuyomi. He smiled, but his eyes were dim. He took my hand and looked at me like I was the last star in the universe, and that was how I knew something was wrong.

"I think you're safe from the Reapers now," he said, like he was commenting on the weather and not a god who had tried to destroy Japan. But I knew what he was trying to say. The Reapers were the reason he had come to me in the first place, and now they were gone.

"There are many dangerous things in Japan," I said, dropping my gaze. "I don't think all the Yōkai care for me as much as the funayūrei and ryūtō. And my Shinigami could start an uprising at any moment, seeing as I've neglected them for almost a week."

Tsukuyomi smiled, though he looked pained. "Or Izanami could come back from the dead? Or the moon could crash to the Earth?"

"Yes," I said. "There are lots of dangers still."

Tsukuyomi let out a tired laugh, squeezing my hand.

"The moon doesn't belong on Earth, Ren."

I shook my head, gripping his hand tighter. "And where does a half Reaper half Shinigami belong, then? There is no single place in the universe carved out for you. You belong where you choose to belong."

"I know," he whispered, closing his eyes. "And I know that this is not the place for me."

"Then where?" I said. "Alone on the moon? Is that really what you want?" I couldn't hold back the bitterness that bled into my words. Tsukuyomi had begged to stand by my side, and now that I allowed him to, he was leaving?

"The solar eclipse is coming soon," he said, rather than answer.

He'd said the same thing as he was drifting off to sleep the night before, though I hadn't thought much of it at the time.

"What of it?" I asked.

He turned his gaze to the sky, as if searching for something in the darkness.

"I think this time, when the sun and moon cross paths again, I'll try to talk to her. I won't leave until she listens to me. I'll make her understand, somehow."

The anger drained away from me, leaving me cold and paper-light on the shore, like a gust of wind could send me spiraling into the sky. I thought back to all the times he'd looked at me and Neven like our bond was a puzzle he couldn't quite piece together, how he'd told me he didn't think Amaterasu loved him, how he'd known our time was short before I did.

"And that means you can't stay?" I said, my voice cracking.

"It means that I need to head to the sky as soon as possible, and that I may not return for a while. It will likely take some time to win her favor."

I shook my head, because I knew too well that "some time" for a god could mean years, decades. Tsukuyomi reached for me, but I took a step back.

"Why?" I said. After all that had happened, he was choosing Amaterasu over me? "She threw you down from the sky!"

But Tsukuyomi did not cower from the force of my anger. His eyes turned stony, and he wouldn't look away. "And that makes her unforgivable?" he whispered, staring at me like a challenge until I understood the words he didn't dare say out loud—*you threw your brother away too.*

"We are not the same."

"You're not," Tsukuyomi said. "She's been alone for far longer."

I wanted to snap back at him, but couldn't summon the anger.

"When did you decide this?" I asked, because my bones felt full of lead and I didn't know what else to say.

He stared at the sea as if thinking over his answer. "Did Neven ever tell you why he threw me in the pond the day we set off for Mount Tate?" he said, rather than answer my question.

I shook my head. That felt like a lifetime ago.

"His complaints about you had grown tiresome, so I asked him why he hadn't killed you if he hated you so much."

I winced. The memory of kneeling before Neven's blade still stung.

"He didn't answer me. I told him it would be safer for you if he stayed in Yomi and left your protection to me," Tsukuyomi said. "He told me he would rather eat glass than leave his sister alone with a monster. Then he threw me into the lotus pond."

I stared back at Tsukuyomi, unsure what to say. I was so sure that Neven had only recently forgiven me. Was it possible that he came with me to the human realm not for sunlight...but for me?

"When I was alone on the moon," Tsukuyomi said, "I thought that love was only for lower beings because it shattered so easily, that it could not belong to a god because it could not endure forever. But perhaps—for the first time in many, many years—I was wrong."

He turned his gaze once more to the sky. "Maybe I am a fool to hope that my sister will ever forgive me, much less love me. But I have to try, Ren."

I knew that look in his eyes too well. Maybe it would take a hundred years for his sister to forgive him, or a thousand, or all the time left in the universe, but no price was too heavy. I could hardly blame him for that.

"You can come with me," he said.

I smiled but couldn't meet his eyes. For the first time since arriving in Japan, I was finally able to give Neven a safe, quiet life like he deserved. I couldn't do that if I dragged him up into the stars to chase after a vengeful sun goddess, and I couldn't leave him behind in Yomi. It wasn't even a choice.

"Neven has suffered enough for the things that I want," I said.

Tsukuyomi nodded. He was no fool, and he'd probably known my answer before I spoke it.

"You can come back to visit," I said.

"Yes," he whispered, though as the word disappeared in the sound of waves breaking on the shore, it felt too small, too quiet. The air filled up with everything we both wanted to say but couldn't.

He stepped forward and took my hand. Planets spun in his eyes, stars arcing across the sky, supernovas dying in white-hot balls of fire.

Then he kissed me like I was going to turn into smoke and vapor at any moment, fingers knotting in my hair and pressing impossibly hard into my hip, leaving fingerprints on my bones. He kissed me like we were dying, and for that instant, we could both pretend that no one and nothing else mattered, that there was a world where people like us could be together.

I wished he hadn't done it. I was too painfully aware that our time together was ending. I couldn't help but catalog every moment between moments, the way he held his breath just before he kissed me, how he pulled back and pressed his forehead to mine, our lips just barely touching, his heartbeat loud in my ears. A tear rolled down my cheek and as he kissed it away, I wondered if I would ever feel so warm again.

I closed my eyes when he let go, because that was one

memory I didn't want to keep. He stepped away, and my body grew cold again. He lingered for a moment, and I wondered if he would say anything else. But then his slow footsteps carried him off across the shore, crunching across wet sand, until eventually I couldn't hear them at all.

When I opened my eyes, I was standing alone on an empty beach. My grasp on the shadows had waned in my distraction, and a blue afternoon was starting to bleed through the darkness overhead, like the night had been torn open. I could just barely make out the silhouette of the city's skyline, jagged buildings and roads cast in gray-blue light, humans wandering into the streets to see what had happened. Yokohama was breathing once more, and night was ending.

I turned my gaze skyward, to the moon that was once again a full and perfect circle, growing dimmer and dimmer as the darkness gave way to day, casting pale light across a small and broken world.

CHAPTER 26

"You are impossible," Chiyo said.

"Indeed." I didn't look up from my book, my feet hanging over the arm of the chair. I'd been hoping to finish Natsume Sōseki's new novel about life from the perspective of a cat, but it was hard to concentrate over Chiyo's complaining. I thought that half listening and agreeing with her might calm her down, but it seemed to have the opposite effect.

"I know when you're ignoring me!" Chiyo said, stomping her foot.

I sighed and hung my head over the other arm of the chair, peering at Chiyo upside down.

"That was rather the point," I said, smiling.

"To enrage me?"

"No," I said, sitting up and closing my book with a shrug. "I just hoped you'd grow bored and walk away."

Chiyo looked to the ceiling as if beseeching the help of the gods. Except I was her god, and I was the one she needed saving from.

"Do you truly think it was wise to demote all of your head Shinigami?" she said, her voice a low, warning growl.

"Oh, is that all you're upset about?"

That morning, I'd summoned all of my head Shinigami to the throne room. I'd stomped into the meeting wearing a blue kimono and a bare face, rather than the traditional juni-hitoe and pasty white makeup. They'd hardly recognized me at first, and when reality set in, their eyes had gone wide, as if my normal appearance was stranger than wearing twelve dresses at once.

"Thank you for coming," I'd said, bowing. "All of you are demoted. Any questions?"

They blinked at me in stunned silence.

"I beg your pardon?" one of them said. "Izanami appointed us head Shinigami."

"Yes," I said, "and she is, as you may have noticed, dead. Next question?"

Several Shinigami began to speak at once, but my shadows wrapped around their mouths, forcing their lips shut.

"Actually, I've changed my mind. I don't want to hear any of you speak. So allow me to answer questions that I expect you to ask." I cleared my throat. "Why? Because all of you are cowards who ignored your duties to not only me, but to your country, in order to save yourselves. You are unworthy of being my head Shinigami. I have already found your replacements among the newer ranks of Shinigami, who are,

I assure you, thrilled with their promotions. What will you do now? You all will go back to practicing in your respective regions, but you report to my new appointees. And if you have any objections, please remember that I defeated an entire fleet of Reapers and the British Goddess of Death in your absence. If I see any of your faces in my palace again, I will cut them off and hang them in my parlor, which is desperately in need of some wall art."

I released the shadows, snapping them back to me. "Any other questions?"

Chiyo seethed in front of me, snatching Natsume's book from my hands.

"They will turn against you," she said.

I shrugged. "They fear me more now that I've driven the Reapers out. Besides, my new Shinigami are hungrier than them. They want their titles more. They will work hard to keep them and devour anyone who tries to take that power away. And unlike those appointed by Izanami, these ones will actually be loyal to me for giving them a chance."

Chiyo wilted, massaging her forehead. "You underestimate them. I am here so you can discuss these things with me instead of making rash decisions on your own." She dared to open an eye, glaring at my strange posture, draped over the chair. "And what kind of goddess sits like that?"

I sighed. "How I miss the days when you feared me." My antics had finally driven Chiyo to a breaking point when I'd returned to the palace after defeating Ivy and offhandedly remarked that I'd let Tamamo No Mae get away. Chiyo had hurled a pile of laundry to the floor and berated me for my total lack of self-preservation, followed immediately by throwing herself to the ground and begging for my forgiveness. I only laughed and told her to stand up because I hated begging. Now that she knew she wouldn't be executed for speaking out of turn, she seemed to have no qualms saying everything that crossed her mind. I liked her better this way.

But she was wrong about the Yōkai.

Tamamo No Mae was not a warrior, but a con woman. She wasn't going to lead an army of Yōkai to my front door or shoot arrows at my guards or throw explosives into my courtyard. She claimed power by convincing others to love her and using that love as her shield. She must have known that taking over Yomi was a lost cause, for neither Neven nor I would ever trust her again.

I pulled my clock from my kimono to check the hour, then sat bolt upright. It was almost time.

"Your brother respects me, you know," Chiyo said.

I smirked, standing up and gently taking my book back. "Only to your face, Chiyo."

"I am already dead, and yet I feel like you are killing me all over again."

"Have a good evening, Chiyo!" I said, backing out of the room.

She sighed heavily, waving a weary hand. "Be careful."

I only stopped long enough to toss my book into my room, then hurried through the halls toward the courtyard. Much to Chiyo's dismay, I now kept the halls brightly lit. But now it wasn't to banish Izanami's face, but because Neven preferred it that way, and it was the least I could do for him. At times, I still caught a glimpse of her skeletal face in the mirror. I was Death, always and forever, and that kind of power came with ghosts.

For weeks after the Reapers left, Neven had stayed mostly

in his room in my palace, lit at all hours with an absurd and probably unsafe number of candles. I knew he missed the Yōkai, or rather, who he'd thought she was, but there were no words I could say that would help and I didn't like tossing out hollow platitudes. So, by the third week, I went up to Tokyo, plucked a stray cat from the street, then barged into Neven's room and deposited it on his lap.

"What is this?" he said, wrapping his arms around it immediately.

"A cat, obviously."

"Because?"

I paused. "Do you not like cats anymore?" Perhaps I'd made a mistake. Neven had liked cats over a decade ago, but centuries in darkness could certainly change a person.

He blinked. "You hate cats."

"That is why it's on your lap and not mine."

A small smile twitched at the corner of his lips. He petted the cat, who nuzzled into the touch. It was the first time he'd smiled in weeks, even if it had lasted only a moment.

I checked the time, then headed for the door, waving for Neven to follow me.

"Come on," I said.

"Why?" he said, even though he was already on his feet, trailing me into the hallway.

"Because it's almost time."

"For?"

"Omagatoki."

I'd brought him up to the land of the living just before dusk. In the several months that passed since that first time, it had slowly become our nightly routine, even as the seasons changed and the sun fell earlier and earlier.

Now Neven was already waiting for me in the courtyard, arms crossed.

"You're late," he said, grabbing my wrist and pulling me forward. Neven knew the courtyard by heart, even without a lantern. He only stopped when his feet sank into soft soil.

I took his hand and held on tight, dragging us up through earth and roots, water and silt, until we stood in the late-afternoon shadows of Izumo, the sun sinking low and pink across the sky. The humans shuffled into their homes at this hour, doors sliding shut as the world grew quiet to welcome the hour of dusk. The waters had gone still, and I wondered if that was Susano'o's doing, somewhere deep and cold below.

"Come on, we're going to miss it!" Neven said, dodging the last of the humans as he ran down the path into the city. I hurried after him, the two of us running toward the largest shrine in the town. It had a roof with support beams that looked like the ribs of a great white whale from underneath, heavy shimenawa hanging curled in the front.

Neven clambered up a banister on the side, grabbing onto the roof and hauling himself over the lip. My shadows curled into a rope that I twisted around my arm, letting it pull me up to the sloped roof, where Neven had already crawled to the top, straddling either side so he wouldn't slip.

From here, we could see all of Izumo. Every pine tree and torii gate, every wide sloped roof and footprint in the dirt roads. The world fell into hushed whispers as the daylight dissolved into Susano'o's waters, the sun gushing red across the landscape like spilled wine.

And one by one, the Yōkai emerged.

First, from behind the pear trees, came the gumyōchō—two-headed pheasants with feathers of pure gold and lavender—strutting out into the empty roads. They spread their wings in wide arcs and circled until they came to rest on telephone lines, so weightless that the wires didn't even sway. They opened their golden beaks and sang songs of nirvana, wordless melodies so breathtaking that they could only have come from some place holier than this.

At the sound of their voices, the other Yōkai started to appear.

Next was the kotobuki—a chimera of all twelve zodiac animals with a dragon's endless neck, a horse's glossy mane, and a tiger's striped belly—hopping forward on monkey's feet. It gobbled up some yakitori that the street vendors had dropped while packing up, licking the stick clean before prancing off for more food. From the tsubaki trees, a beautiful woman emerged, covered in winter roses, and far away on the shore, kōjin lurked in the rocky waters, covered in black scales and grinning with sharp teeth. For just this hour, the world belonged to the Yōkai, beautiful and strange and hungry as they were.

Neven smiled and leaned closer. I held on to the back of his shirt so he wouldn't topple off the roof, but he was too busy watching the Yōkai to notice. In the burning light of sunset, he looked healthier than in Yomi's dim passageways. He probably would have been happier living somewhere aboveground, but my kingdom would always be in darkness, and he would always be tethered to me, like the shimenawa that had tied me to Tsukuyomi. So this was our compromise.

Far away, a ship cut across the sea on the horizon, glowing before the setting sun. I wondered if Ambrose was somewhere in those vast waters, sailing farther and farther away. I was unwilling to leave any loose ends when it came to Reapers, so I'd told my Shinigami to search for him. Weeks ago, they'd reported seeing him boarding a ship bound for Russia. That meant he hadn't gone crawling back to Ivy, though he probably knew that she'd decapitate him after his stunt with the ryūtō.

He could have stayed. If not for me, then for Neven. He could have spent the rest of his life begging for our forgiveness like Tsukuyomi was doing with his sister. But, as always, it was easier for him to turn his back on us. I didn't know whether he had ever truly loved me, but it didn't matter. To him, love was only a word.

As I did every night, I turned my gaze to the moon. Tonight it was a waning crescent, no more than a thin sliver of white. The worst was when it was a new moon, invisible both day and night. I simply had to believe it was there, even when there was nothing to see.

Tsukuyomi's story had changed on the murals in my palace. A new panel had appeared, where the moon came down to Earth and dragged a girl dressed in black up to the land of the living, then stood between her and a churning sea of warships and silver cloaks. In the last panel, the moon was once again in the sky, reaching for the sun.

I didn't expect any more panels to appear for me or Tsukuyomi. I had read the myths of so many creatures, and I knew when a story was at its end. I only hoped that the tales they told of us would be kind and truthful, not twisted like the windows of Amaterasu's palace, or the words of the kyōrinrin. But in the end, that was out of my control. Legends didn't die the way living creatures did. They lived and breathed and shifted long after their characters were dust. When the humans one day told the Legend of Ren Scarborough, Ren of London, Yakushima, and Yomi, I hoped it went something like this:

Once, a little girl stole a kingdom and became a crooked queen.

She filled the canals with blood and burned the skyline red and each day she became a little more rotten, a little more alone.

She was the most powerful being in all the land, and yet not a single person loved her. They had all left her alone in her great empty palace that she knew would never truly belong to her, staring out into the darkness, waiting for years and years for someone she thought would never return.

She had tried to live in the land where she was raised, and then the land where she was born, and finally the land that she had stolen. But every time, the soil dried up, the stars dimmed, and the tides retreated as if to say, *This will never be yours. You are the queen of nowhere, and you deserve nothing.*

But one day, just when she began to wonder if she had a heart as dead as all the withered souls of her kingdom, the moon crashed down to Earth and offered her his hand. The brother she had forsaken clawed his way back from the heart of darkness, and suddenly her great palace was no longer cold and empty.

They held her hands and stood beside her when the stars of her stolen kingdom began falling in broken shards, burning her villages and crops, killing her people. Together, they held up the jagged pieces of the night sky.

But when the kingdom was once again quiet, she realized that still, it did not belong to her.

No land on Earth, or the moon, or the sun, could ever be

her true home. So instead, she built a home inside the hearts of those who loved her. This home had windows that looked out across Japan's rolling red skies at dusk, and the green forests of Yakushima, and the autumn trees of London, and all the shapes of the moon on a clear night.

That is where she lived, and that was where she would remain until the end of all things, when the darkness of space that had birthed the universe once again inhaled it, and nothing remained but silence, an infinity of clear and perfect night.

AUTHOR'S NOTE

It is said that Tamamo No Mae recited poetry for Emperor Toba at the age of seven, gaining his favor and earning a position in his court. When she was eighteen, her talents impressed the emperor so much that he made her his consort. It will probably not shock you to know that this did not end well for Emperor Toba. Does this story remind you of a suspiciously well-trained ninja empress, by any chance?

As much as I like to let readers come to their own conclusions, it is important to point out that the empress of Japan depicted in this story is not meant to be the Empress Shōken (the actual empress of Japan at the time this story takes place) but rather a fictional empress based on the legend of Tamamo No Mae. Does this mean the Yōkai was hedging her bets in case plan A failed? Has she really run as far away as Ren thinks? Perhaps we'll never know.

At the time I am writing this, in March of 2022, Sesshoseki, a volcanic rock said to be haunted by Tamamo No Mae's spirit, has split in half. Some have speculated that this means her spirit is once again free. If you've learned anything about Yōkai after reading this series, I hope it is that you underestimate them at your own peril.

ACKNOWLEDGMENTS

Sophomore books are notoriously hard to write, and *The Empress of Time* was no exception. The fact that this book exists at all is a miracle, and I genuinely believe I would never have finished it at all without the love and support of so many people.

I'm forever grateful to my agent, Mary C. Moore, for being the fiercest advocate for both me and Ren, and for making all of my dreams possible.

Thank you to my editor, Claire Stetzer. It's terrifying to have your project passed to someone else, not knowing if they truly like your work or if they're simply doing their job, but after meeting you, I knew you were here for both me and Ren until the very end. Thank you for loving my impulsively written giant centipede.

Thank you to Tashya for giving me and Ren a chance and starting this amazing journey.

Thank you to everyone at Inkyard Press. In my time here, I have never once doubted that me or my books were important to the team. Thank you for championing Ren through her journey, and me through mine.

Thank you as well to David Chart for your kind and insightful comments on this book and for teaching me so much about Japan.

I'm forever grateful for all my library coworkers who read *The Keeper of Night* (even if YA fantasy wasn't their preferred genre) and aggressively recommended it to every patron who walked through the YA section so that it hardly stayed on the shelves for long. Even those who didn't read it were so supportive of me and my dreams, which means the world to me.

Thank you to all my aunts, uncles, and cousins who read *The Keeper of Night*, and had bigger dreams for it than I ever dared to—I'll never take your support for granted.

Thank you so much to all the bloggers, BookTubers, Bookstagrammers, and BookTokers who have supported this duology. I know that you give so much of your time for free to the writing and book communities, and I hope you know how much authors appreciate you, not just for the publicity but for the moral support. Hearing some of you talk about how much my books meant to you is the only thing that kept me going some days.

Thank you to my writer friends for uplifting me and listening to me complain so that I don't have to be messy on Twitter, especially my agent sister Van Hoang. Thank you to Rebecca Kim Wells for being my mentor and maybe long-lost sister. Thank you to all my debut buddies in the class of 2021, especially the Monsters & Magic group for supporting and inspiring me. I hope I can grow into a woman as graceful and kind as all of you one day. Thank you to everyone in Mary's Squad for being the coolest, most supportive agent siblings ever.

Thank you to my friends who have no part in the writing community but are there to bring me back down to earth when book Twitter makes me want to eat my own hands. Thank you for telling all your coworkers about my book, for coming to my events, for asking questions in the hopes of better understanding the bizarre world of publishing, and for being there for me no matter how far away you are.

And of course, I couldn't ask for more supportive and loving parents. I'm so grateful that writing about Ambrose was a huge challenge for me as a writer—I will never know what it's like to have Ren's family, because I'm so lucky to have parents who have always loved me endlessly and rooted for my dreams.